Inn of the Open Door

A Chronicle of Philadelphia

By
David Phillips

HEARTBEATS OF COURAGE

Volume Four

Inn of the Open Door

A Chronicle of Philadelphia

By

David Phillips

Century One Chronicles
Toronto, Ontario, Canada

INN OF THE OPEN DOOR: A CHRONICLE OF PHILADELPHIA: HEARTBEATS OF COURAGE, BOOK 4

Published in the United States of America

Canadian Intellectual Property Office CIPO Registration Number: 1152519

ISBN
Paperbacks 978-1-9994752-6-0
E-Books 978-1-9994752-7-7

Century One Chronicles
PO Box 25013
255 Morningside Avenue
Toronto, Ontario, Canada M1E 0A7

Photo Credits
Front Cover and Back Cover: Dusan Arsenic
Maps of Philadelphia and Hierapolis: Dusan Arsenic
Map of Asia Minor: Anoosh Mubashar
Back Cover: Photo of the author by Sarah Grace Photography

For Dorothy and Jack, Jonathan, and David

For those who are insulted,
treated unjustly in courts,
suffer for the sake of
righteousness, and
suffer as they
bring comfort.

For believers experiencing persecution
for being a witness to their Lord,
whether through loss of family,
criticism, gossip, falsehoods,
beatings, loss of property,
imprisonment,
or death.

HEARTBEATS OF COURAGE

Book 1: Through the Fire: A Chronicle of Pergamum
AD 89–91

Book 2: Never Enough Gold: A Chronicle of Sardis
AD 91–92

Book 3: Purple Honors: A Chronicle of Thyatira
AD 92–93

Book 4: The Inn of the Open Door: A Chronicle of Philadelphia
AD 93-96

Book 5: Rich Me! A Chronicle of Laodicea
AD 96–97

Book 6: Fortress Shadows: A Chronicle of Smyrna
AD 97–111

Book 7: An Act of Grace: A Chronicle of Ephesus
AD 111

The Songs of Miriam: A Collection of Miriam's Songs

Prologue

The ancient city of Philadelphia, located about halfway between Pergamum and Laodicea, was founded as an outpost of Greek culture by kings who reigned in the Kingdom of Pergamum.

Throughout the years, and in every sector of the city, there was an emphasis on entertainment, drama, sports, and education.

Early democracy brought wealthy citizens together, and the entire population congregated at many places of worship. Countless gods and goddesses vied for the attention of all citizens. People gave sacrifices to their favorite deity.

Philadelphia was a city accustomed to occasional earth tremors following the Great Earthquake of AD 17. It was located on the road linking Laodicea and Smyrna, meaning hospitality and inns were important to merchants, travelers, soldiers, and entertainers.

A Jewish synagogue had been present for almost two hundred years when the message of Yeshua, the Jewish Messiah, Jesus Christ, came into this city. At the end of the first century, the daily life of early Christians in the face of the already ancient Greco-Roman civilization was made more difficult by interpersonal problems, financial struggles, and harassment from the authorities.

This novel continues the story of the first three books in the *Heartbeats of Courage* series. Anthony, a Roman soldier, and his wife, Miriam, a Jewish woman, arrive in Philadelphia.

Miriam was a member of the Ben Shelah family, immigrants to Asia Minor from Alexandria, Egypt. Her uncles lived in several other cities in the province: Pergamum, Thyatira, Sardis, Laodicea, and Smyrna.

These ancient cities, with Ephesus and Colossae, are known as the Seven Cities of the Revelation. Each year, millions of visitors tour these locations in southwestern Turkey.

Characters in *The Inn of the Open Door*

* Indicates a historical personage
Names in bold are the most important persons.

Emperor

Domitian, 43*, Emperor of the Roman Empire: AD 81–96

Kings, Governors

King Decebalus, 49*, King of Dacia (Romania/Moldova)
Marcus Atillius Postumus Bradua*, Governor of Asia, AD 94–95

Aristocratic Families

Aurelius Manilius Hermippus, 47, Mayor of Philadelphia
Giles, 42, Director of the Bank of the Philadelphia
Titus Flavius Zeuxis, 49*, Wealthy merchant from Hierapolis

The Roman Military

Felicior Priscus, 39, Commander of the Garrison of Philadelphia
Centurion Decimus, 29, Soldier in the Garrison of Philadelphia

Anthony Suros, 39, Legionary from Legion XXI, the Predators
Omerod, Bellinus, Soldiers serving in an elite squad

Servius Callistratus, 33, Commander of the Garrison of Soma

In Philadelphia

Damian, 35, Principal of Philadelphia Gymnasium, school
Calisto, 42, Head of the Department of Greek Literature
Timon, 19, Calisto's son and a recent graduate

Horace, 34, Steward of Giles and superintendent of works
Quintus, 38, Assistant to Horace and assistant superintendent
Cleon, 34, Amos's steward at the Inn of the Open Door
Menander, 27, A servant at the Inn of the Open Door
Ganymede, 35, Master carpenter, working on a restoration of the hot baths, father of nine children

In the Philadelphia Synagogue

Rabbi Haim, 38, Leader of the synagogue, a widower
Zacharias, 48, Widower, father of five sons, a goldsmith
Michael Ben Akkub, 62, Master potter, married to
Martha, his wife, 60
Isabel Bat Michael, 40, Daughter, married to **Obed Ben Shelah**

Daniel Ben Helkai, 39, Master carpenter,
Dorcas Bat Shammua, 38, Daniel's wife
Jesse Ben Daniel, 19, Married to **Ruth Bat Obed**
Mith Ben Daniel, 17, Engaged to **Sarah Bat Obed**

The Ben Shelah Family and Household

Eliab and Ahava Ben Shelah's children, all born in Alexandria, Egypt: Anna, Deborah, Amos, Antipas, Zibiah, Simon, Daniel, Joshua, Judah, Azubah, Samuel, Jonathan

Antipas Ben Shelah*, Martyred leader in Pergamum
Miriam Bat Johanan, 30, Anthony's wife
Chrysa Grace Suros, 2, Anthony and Miriam's adopted daughter
Amos Ben Shelah, 70, Owner of the Inn of the Open Door
Abigail Bat Edinnus, 73, Married to Amos, mother of seven children, six of whom died in Jerusalem
Obed, 40, Fourth son, married to
Isabel Bat Michael, 40
Ruth, 19, Obed's daughter, married to **Jesse**, 20
Asa, Ruth and Jesse's first son
Hakkatan, Ruth and Jesse's second son
Sarah, 17, Obed's daughter, betrothed to **Mith,** 17
Heber Ben Shelah, 40, Widower

In Pergamum

Lydia-Naq Milon, 56, High priestess of the Altar of Zeus

Diotrephes, 31, Lydia-Naq's son, Director of the Department of History in Sardis
Zoticos-Naq Milon, 45, Chief Librarian of Library of Pergamum
Trifane, 26, Birthmother of Chrysa Grace
Marcos Aelius Pompeius, 39, Lawyer in Pergamum
Marcella Aculiana, 40, Wife of Marcos
Florbella Aelius Pompeius, 12, Marcos's daughter

In Sasorta

Thelma, 20, Widow in Sasorta
Rastus, 36, a baker, and Selene, his wife

In Forty Trees

Penelope Longinus, 39 Widow and mother of **Evander**, 14, **Rhoda**, 11, **Hamon**, 9, **Sandra**, 7, and **Melody**, 1

Former slaves

Ateas, 24, and **Arpoxa**, 23, Former Scythian slaves
Saulius, 3, and Madis, 1, their children

Robbers and Highwaymen in "The Faithful"

(A rebel gang of army deserters being hunted by Anthony, Omerod, and Bellinus)

Mithrida, 38 (Flavius Memucan Parshandatha)
Sexta, 41 (Sesba Bartacus Sheshbazzar)
Craga, 34 (Claudius Carshena Datis)

Other rebels:
Taba, Maza, Harpa

ASIA MINOR IN THE 1st CENTURY - WITH KEY CITIES
(Current place names in Italics)
Byzantium (Istanbul)
Chalcedon
Nicomedia (Izmit)
Gallipolis
Sea of Marmara
Nicea
Prusa (Bursa)
Port Daskyleion
Troy
Bird Lake
Alexandria Troas
Dascylium
Inegol
Cotyaum
(Kutanya)
Assos
Adramyttium (Edremit)
Mytilene
Kisthene (Ayvalik)
Andeira Mines
Five Shepherds Village
Porsuk Canyon
PERGAMUM (Bergama)
Aizanoi
The Interior Roads to Antioch
Gambreion
40 Trees
Soma
THYATIRA (Akhisar)
Green Valley Inn
Karun
Aegean Sea
Kios
SARDIS
SMYRNA (Izmir)
PHILADELPHIA (Alasehir)
Hierapolis
EPHESUS (Selcuk)
Tripolis
Colossae
LAODICEA
MILETUS
Principal Road
(The Postal Road)
Secondary Roads

THE CITY OF PHILADELPHIA IN THE PROVINCE OF ASIA MINOR

1 Road to Sasorta and Sardis
2 Homes of Poor People
3 Valley Gate
4 Ruined Buildings, Hot Baths
5 Inn of the Open Door
6 Laodicea Gate
7 Road to Laodicea
8 Ruined Buildings/ Workshops
9 Central Agora, Market
10 Gymnasium, School
11 Military Garrison
12 Theater
13 Civic Buildings, City Hall
14 Upper Baths
15 Wall Around the City of Philadelphia
16 Jewish Sector in the Upper City
17 Synagogue
18 Amos and Abigail's Home and Farm
19 Theater Gate and Exit to Mount Tmolus
20 Shepherd's Trail
21 Shepherd's Hut
22 Mount Tmolus
23 Hospital
24 Cemetery

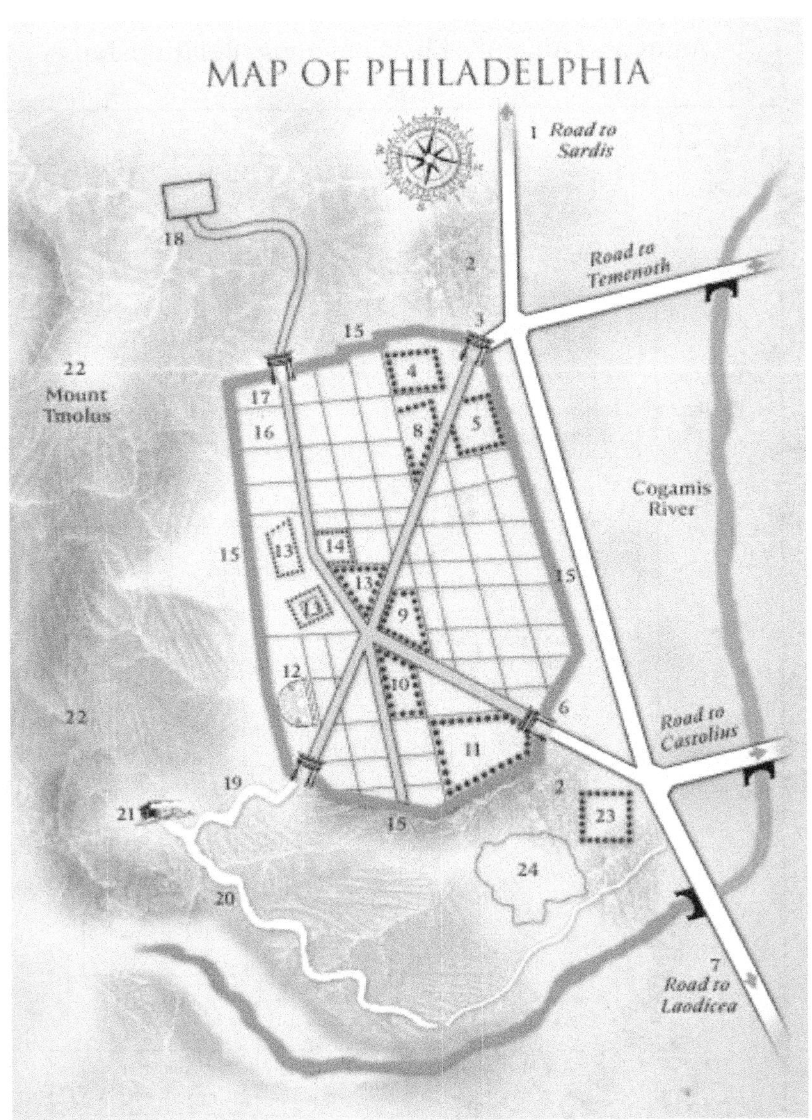
MAP OF PHILADELPHIA
1 Road to Sardis
Road to Temenoth
Cogamis River
Road to Castolius
7 Road to Laodicea
22 Mount Tmolus
22
18
2
3
15
4
5
8
17
16
13
14
9
10
12
6
11
19
21
20
23
24

Amos and Abigail's Chart of Family Relationships

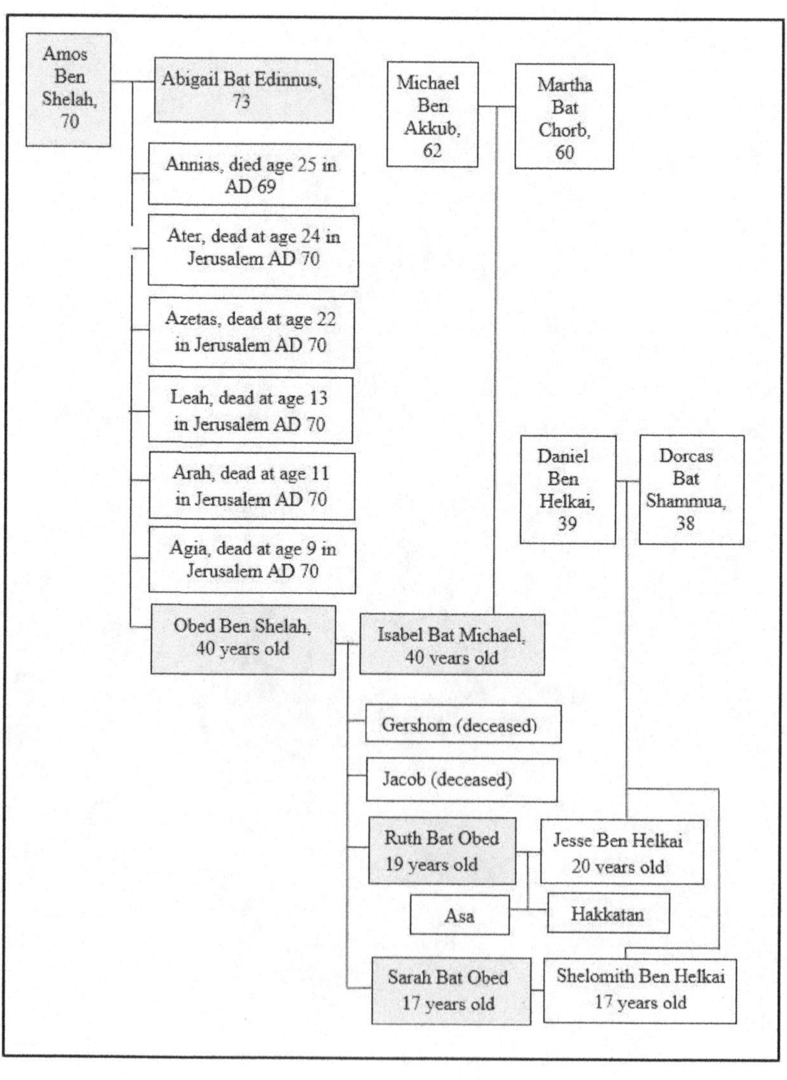

Inn of the Open Door

A Chronicle of Philadelphia

Part 1

June AD 93

Strangers and Enemies

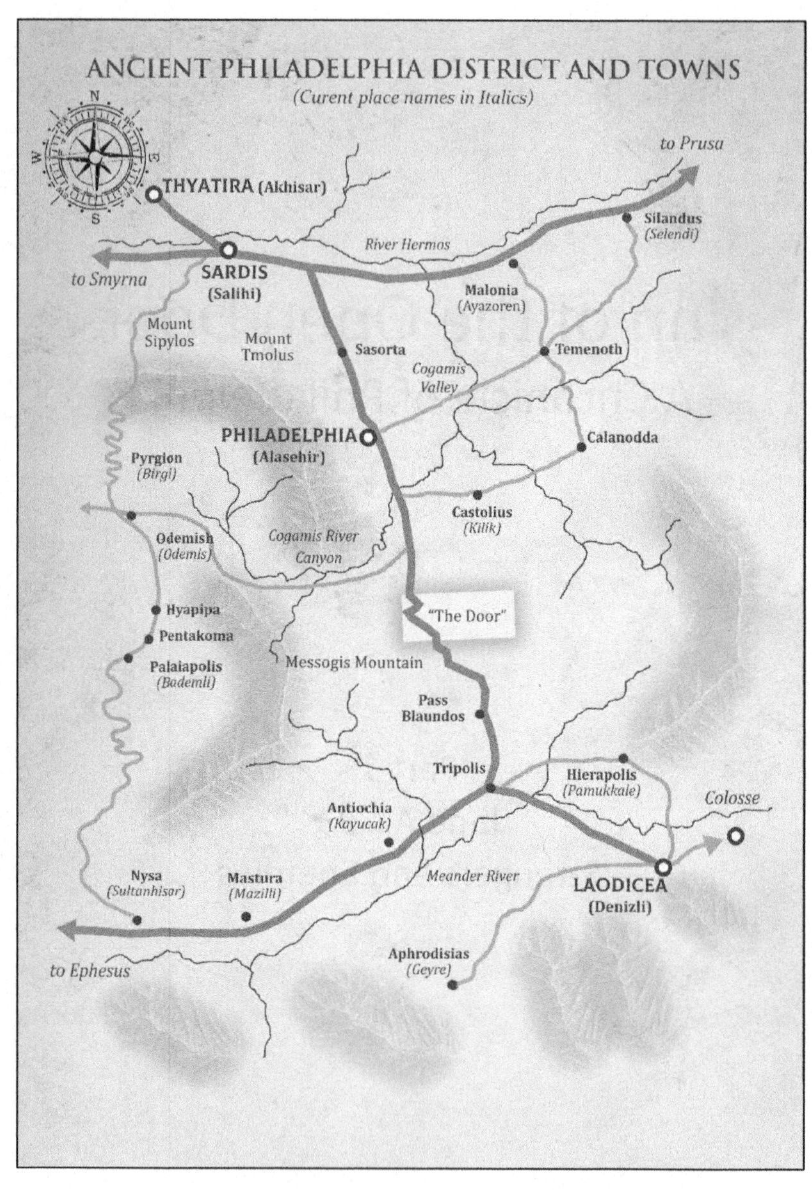
ANCIENT PHILADELPHIA DISTRICT AND TOWNS
(Curent place names in Italics)
N
S
E
W
to Prusa
THYATIRA (Akhisar)
Silandus
(Selendi)
River Hermos
to Smyrna
SARDIS
(Salihi)
Malonia
(Ayazoren)
Mount
Sipylos
Mount
Tmolus
Sasorta
Temenoth
Cogamis
Valley
PHILADELPHIA
(Alasehir)
Calanodda
Pyrgion
(Birgi)
Castolius
(Kilik)
Odemish
(Odemis)
Cogamis River
Canyon
Hyapipa
"The Door"
Pentakoma
Palaiapolis
(Bademli)
Messogis Mountain
Pass
Blaundos
Tripolis
Hierapolis
(Pamukkale)
Colosse
Antiochia
(Kayucak)
Nysa
(Sultanhisar)
Mastura
(Mazilli)
Meander River
LAODICEA
(Denizli)
to Ephesus
Aphrodisias
(Geyre)

Chapter 1
Disturbance at the Gates

TOWN OF SASORTA, THE PROVINCE OF ASIA MINOR

Thelma placed her foot firmly against the rough pavement, pushing back as hard as she could. Behind her, an angry, noisy mob kept shoving. They pressed toward stern-faced soldiers mounted on horses and on foot.

Thelma put her hand on a stout man's shoulder. He was trying to protect her. "Now I'm sorry that I brought you to this demonstration!" Rastus yelled.

It was hard to hear him, even with his mouth close to the young woman's ear. Rastus was the town's baker, and like everyone else in Sasorta, he had run out of wheat.

Ordinary people in the small town kept shouting. They demanded that the emergency storehouses be opened. Arriving here, they had been surprised by soldiers holding lances and swords. Between the crowd and the grain storehouses behind the civic buildings were a dozen soldiers sent from Philadelphia. They were ordered to keep protesters out.

Shoved from behind, Rastus stepped on Thelma's foot, but in the clamor, no one heard her sharp cry of pain.

"Sorry," he shouted, "I didn't mean to hurt you. I hoped they might give us access to the grain today. The situation is worse here in Sasorta than the town where you came from."

His voice was drowned out by constant commotion. Irate men kept elbowing toward the guards, who prevented access to the town's grain storage facility.

Thelma faced one of the soldiers guarding the storehouses. Sweat poured down his forehead. A bright, shiny helmet topped with red feathers came down to his eyebrows. He rode a black horse, and his knuckles were white as he gripped his sword. The stern look in his eyes suggested he hoped he would not have to use it on desperate men and chanting women. The soldier yelled at the mob demanding access to the grain bins. He kicked the horse's ribs with his heels, keeping it faced toward the incensed throng.

Fear showed in Thelma's eyes as she loosened her grip on Rastus's arm. She wanted him to hear her thoughts, but the shouting of the crowd was too raucous. *Why am I here? Can't Rastus see that the guards will keep everyone away from the storehouses? What can several dozen farmers do against a dozen armed soldiers?*

A man pushed Thelma forward, and she lost her balance, falling badly. Standing up, she bumped into a man holding a sharpened stick. Starving villagers, red in the face from yelling, waved farm tools and table knives.

A councilman barged past Thelma, shoving her backward and yelling at the soldiers. "I'm a businessman! Several of us make decisions here in Sasorta, and our children have nothing to eat! We demand that you open up the grain storehouse, at least the one closest to us."

The soldier with red feathers on his legionary's helmet snarled, "Keep back, councilman or a sword will slit your throat! No one gets into the emergency food storage area until the mayor of Philadelphia gives the order, and that will not come today!"

People turned around, hearing a horse rushing toward the soldiers. Thelma looked at the rider's face, stifled a scream, and grabbed at Rastus. The young man on the horse plowed through the crowd, and the mob parted to let him pass.

"Let us go to the grain bins!" the rider screamed. Clad in a workman's light brown tunic, his eyes bulging and one hand sweeping the air, he threatened the guards. "You're bluffing, and you won't keep us out!"

The young rider was no more than twenty years of age. His pale brown horse approached the line of guards, its nostrils quivering. As the steed reared up, unable to go on, the young man slid backward, falling heavily to the ground. Shouts and yelling resounded in the town square. The horse, off-balance, saw the point of a lance, tried to turn backward, and landed heavily on the young man's chest. The animal struggled to its feet, turned to one side, and trotted off, its ears twitching and tail swishing.

Thelma ran toward the young man.

"No! No! It can't be!"

Her long scream was a shrill cry for help. Few heard her above the uproar. She sobbed, begging anyone to help the limp figure lying on the polished marble pavement.

"Help him! He's injured."

Blood started to seep from his mouth, a sign of internal injuries. His chest had been crushed, and he was unconscious.

All around, men kept screaming, "We want food! We demand work! What are we going to take home to our families?"

However, they would not be satisfied today. Rome always had the victorious hand.

An hour passed before the crowd thinned out. Thelma, with tears streaming down her face, began to scream. Then she whimpered, crying mournfully as the man lying on the pavement stopped breathing. Her urgent cries for help were of no use.

"Rastus," she gasped, "look! My husband! He's dead!" She gazed at the lifeless body sprawled out on the ground. "Oh, my dear husband! Why did you do that?"

ENTRANCE TO PHILADELPHIA, PROVINCE OF ASIA MINOR

Miriam closed her eyes, flinching as the scene flashed again in her mind. An hour earlier, Anthony, her husband, and Grace, their daughter, had reached Sasorta. They heard wild cries from the raucous mob gathered in front of the civic buildings.

The screams still echoed in her mind. She had not seen the woman crying beside her crushed husband, but Anthony had stopped to see if he could help and told her about the accident when he got back onto the wagon.

Later, as they arrived in Philadelphia, they passed the homes of thousands of families. Impoverished families lived outside the city walls. Squalor was everywhere. Two- and three-story humble apartment buildings known as *insulae* were crowded together, leaving little breathing space. Children played near stinking, open sewers. Grace, who was two years old, cringed as she pointed to hungry dogs slinking along the walls.

As they entered the city, the Valley Gate guards examined the wagon. "We come from Thyatira," Anthony explained. "I'm an army soldier assigned to the Philadelphia Garrison. I'm moving my family from Thyatira. This document is the order for my transfer. It came from Commander Felicior Priscus. This is my wife, Miriam, and the little girl is our daughter. This wagon contains our clothing and a collection of scrolls. Our first stop in the city will be the garrison."

The guards were satisfied and let the wagon pass into the city after giving Anthony some brief instructions on getting to the garrison.

Inside the city walls, they found many buildings that had collapsed during earthquakes decades ago still lay in awkward, broken piles. The people remembered the scores of deaths that resulted and were reluctant to clear the land and rebuild. Miriam stared at one of the ruins. The buckled roof seemed ready to cave in, so not even vagrants dared to live in it. It had been elegant at one time. Robust and thick stone walls suggested a wealthy family had lived there, but now it was vacant and neglected.[1]

Hundreds of people were walking along the streets of Philadelphia. Sellers hawked their wares, hoping for a few more sales before the end of the day. Donkeys brayed, and merchants cursed their camels, telling them to move more quickly. The central avenue was crowded, full of animals, pedestrians, and four-wheeled carts. Farmers sold sparse supplies of vegetables and fruit. Shouts and raised voices continued until they clinched a favorable price. Then, shaking hands with their customers, they sealed a profitable deal.

Two merchants had just finished the long three-day walk from Laodicea and Hierapolis. They laughed, slapping each other on the shoulder as they sat drinking beer outside a tavern. Miriam watched their camels, which had lined up for fresh mountain water after a long walk over Mount Messogis Pass. Slaves owned by the merchants stood beside camels, guarding their cargo. Their animals knelt awkwardly, descending first to their front knees and then

---

[1] The earthquake of AD 17 struck Philadelphia and Sardis. It made a profound mark on the contemporary world, from the province of Asia Minor to Rome. Citizens of Philadelphia were afraid to re-enter their homes long afterward because of aftershocks. Many lived outside the city walls for years. Further destruction took place in later earthquakes. One was centered near Laodicea in AD 60. Rebuilding in Laodicea began almost immediately, but rebuilding in Philadelphia was slow to start.

throwing their weight toward the rear, onto their back legs and knees.

The merchants had passed through "The Door," a winding section of the road from Laodicea. The high mountain pass twisted and turned on its way down to the Cogamis Valley.

When they reached the garrison compound, Anthony presented his documents to the guard, who directed him toward Commander Felicior's office.

"Miriam, I will check in with Felicior and find out when he may want me to start work. Hopefully, I will be right back, and we can continue on to Uncle Amos's home."

THE MILITARY GARRISON IN PHILADELPHIA

The Philadelphia Garrison had a specific task: to keep the Southern Road open and secure for merchants, farmers, and random travelers. In the past, far too many robberies had taken place on the steep road connecting Philadelphia with Laodicea, Hierapolis, and other cities farther east.

Felicior was deep in thought, gazing out the window and admiring the plain to the east. The valley's bright green vegetation, which had sparkled three hours before, was now dulled. He had two hours before dusk. Like all officers in the army, Felicior was cleanshaven. Underneath thick, dark eyebrows, his attentive eyes took in every detail. His polished breastplate shone with two eagles in flight above two horses.

A square military table stood against the wall with three documents on it. The largest, a map held open with four lead weights, showed six small towns around Philadelphia.

A small scroll was an order from Emperor Domitian that was issued the previous summer:

Half of the province's vineyards are to be torn out and replaced by grain crops to increase the supply of food needs to Rome from Asia Minor.

The third was a scroll written only three days earlier by Commander Servius Callistratus. He had recently been reassigned from Soma to take control of the Sardis Garrison.

Felicior heard a knock at his office door and looked up.

"Suros, I'm glad to see you've arrived! I wasn't expecting you until tomorrow morning. The other two members of your team, Bellinus and Omerod, came in on Saturday." Felicior's sharp gaze held those he addressed. His low, raspy voice added to his overall image of authority. "I'm glad you came in a little early. We need all the help we can get."

Anthony Suros drew a breath and stifled a grimace; the centuries-old military office suffered from a stale smell. He rubbed the palms of his hands on his dark brown soldier's tunic.

Felicior held up the letter from Sardis. "Commander Servius is not satisfied with your previous mission, Suros." He stood erect behind his desk.

"Ah, yes, sir. Commander Servius told me several times that he was unhappy. He repeatedly asked why I didn't capture the four bandit leaders in Prosperity Village."

Why am I sweating? I'm glad to see Commander Felicior.

It was not the hot weather at the beginning of June that troubled Anthony. Instead, he did not want Commander Felicior to send him back to serve under Servius. He had not felt his stomach tightening up like this even when arresting sixteen bandits at Port Daskyleion last summer. Later, he captured another twenty rebels at Prosperity Village. *Felicior knows I captured those thirty-six criminals. And those arrests led to many others being taken in.*

A breeze blew, and the smell of food cooking in a nearby thermopolium brought a sharp pang of hunger. Anthony had not had time to eat anything since his family left Marmara City, where they had stayed last night.

Of all the commanding officers Anthony had known during his twenty years and six months in the army, he preferred Felicior. Perhaps the commander's appearance had something to do with it. Felicior had a thin, long face with high cheekbones, and he looked down his long nose when admonishing or commanding. Felicior exuded an aura of power and the ability to take control during challenging moments. Anthony appreciated such authority.

Anthony stood tall. "My wife, my daughter, and I arrived here just a few minutes ago. We left Thyatira yesterday morning and stayed in Marmara City last night. We were able to leave there very early, and fresh horses made for a quick trip. I would have been here earlier, but when I got to Sasorta, soldiers were putting an end to a riot. My wife and daughter are in a military wagon at the garrison gate. We were heading to her uncle's home just outside the city. His name is Amos Ben Shelah."

Felicior sat down at the table and looked up at Anthony. "You say that you witnessed unrest in Sasorta this afternoon? I need to talk to you about what you saw."

He then scowled, obviously making a decision. "I want you to stay inside the city walls tonight. Have one of the garrison guards drive your wife and child to the Ben Shelah home and unload the wagon for them. He can then bring the wagon back to the garrison for safekeeping. At the moment, we have too many things happening, and I may need you immediately. Come back to my office when the wagon has left."

Anthony returned to the wagon and motioned to one of the gate sentries. "Commander Felicior says that he wants a guard to drive this wagon with my family to Amos Ben Shelah's home, unload the wagon, and return it here to the garrison. This is Miriam, my wife, and she will give the driver directions to get there."

He turned to his wife. "Miriam, I am sorry I can't leave with you, but there are several disturbances. Felicior told me to plan on staying in the city tonight. I may come out to talk with Uncle Amos tomorrow if we get things calmed down. I'll have no way of warning you when I will be coming. You need to mention the possibility of Ateas and Arpoxa also coming to Philadelphia."

The gate guard was happy for an opportunity to get out of the garrison. After he explained to the remaining guard what was happening, he climbed onto the wagon, heading out toward the Ben Shelah home.

As Anthony returned to Felicior's office, he rubbed the long scar on his right cheek. It started above his right eye and disappeared at the edge of his jaw. He tended to rub the spot whenever he was anxious. Right now, he was concerned about the reception they were going to receive at Amos and Abigail's home. This Jewish couple had lost six of their seven children during the siege of Jerusalem. Amos and Abigail had never forgiven the army for their loss. Would they accept him or reject him because he was a member of the Roman army?

Felicior had been to Sasorta the previous day and wanted to understand how today's riot had played out.

Anthony explained, "We were coming through the town and had just reached the agora. You know how people gather every day, stopping and talking in the marketplace. I stopped at the relay station for fresh horses. People were rushing along the streets near the entrance gate to the civic buildings. Men were shaking their fists. Women shouted. Soldiers at the relay station said the riot started shortly before we got there. I saw a young woman kneeling and screaming, 'They've killed my husband!'

"When I later asked a soldier what happened, he said, 'Those men used to work the vineyards, but now that the fields are planted with wheat, many have no income. They want emergency food distributed. The young man tried to push past the guards, but his horse fell back, crushing him.' The young woman was apparently the man's wife; I was told they were married a few weeks ago."

Felicior shook his head. "I'm sorry to hear of a death. No doubt the army will get the full blame for it by the citizens."

He then pointed to the map. "The first riot took place two months ago. Sasorta is one of six small towns in Philadelphia's jurisdiction. Numerous smaller villages dot this valley as well.

"The problem really began fourteen years ago. When Mt. Vesuvius erupted, it destroyed vineyards around Pompeii. That prosperous area supplied most of Rome's wine needs—and most of Italia[2] for that matter. Since then, landowners in this province of Asia Minor found that they could make more money on wine and olive oil exports to Rome. So they began to plow under their grain crops. They planted grapevines and olive groves. That resulted in a reduction of available grain for sale in this area and for export to Rome. Prices started shooting up. Recently there was little grain to buy no matter how much money you had. Last year, the emperor decreed that half of the grape vineyards in the provinces had to be replaced with grain—a wise decision but made far too late.

"Ten months ago, the changeover was started in this area. But the grains planted last year will not be ready to harvest until later

---

[2] Until the time of Augustus Caesar, "Italia" referred to the lower portion of the Italian peninsula, but in *Pax Romana,* at the end of the 1st century BC, "Italia" expanded to include the region to the Alps.

this year. Little labor is required for those crops, so there is no work for farmhands now.

"The grain supply was low, to begin with, and is now down to what exists in the emergency storage. Many vineyard workers are out of jobs and out of money. Grain for their bread is not available for sale even if they have money. It's a mess!

"City Hall is run by men who seem to be deaf and dumb. They don't have the money, nor have they come up with a plan to save the region from starvation and riots. Until such a plan is devised, we must control these peasants and carry out the emperor's orders."

Felicior pursed his lips, thinking about the squad he had formed a year previously. Those six soldiers had served effectively. That was why he had sent an urgent letter to transfer Anthony and two other soldiers to Philadelphia from Sardis.[3]

"I need you three soldiers here to help control these riots like the one you saw in Sasorta. When Omerod and Bellinus arrived two days ago, I immediately assigned them to crowd control duties. But we also had a highway robbery that poses just as bad a problem as the riots.

"Once these problems are taken care of, I intend to send the three of you back to the Sardis Garrison. Perhaps I should let you see what Servius wrote about you."

He rubbed his chin as he looked at Servius's letter. "No. First, I will instruct you on handling the riots and keeping the highway free of insurrectionists and thugs. This map of the area shows the names of the towns and villages around Philadelphia."

THE TOWN OF SASORTA

Earlier that day, under a bright sun and a cloudless sky, agitated residents in Sasorta had demanded the release of food supplies. But now, after facing unbending soldiers and the accidental death of the young rider, people were returning to their homes.

Thelma's voice was weak from pleading. "My husband is dead," she wailed. "Crushed by his horse. Who will help me? I'm a widow! I have nothing! Oh, Zeus, help me!"

---

[3] The story of Anthony and five other soldiers pursuing bandits is found in *Purple Honors: A Chronicle of Thyatira.*

An hour later, crying and grieving, she stumbled between Rastus and his wife. His small cart, pulled by a speckled horse, carried a limp figure. Rastus did not speak a word. The cold fear wrapping itself around the three lonely people was not because the sun was disappearing behind the long Mount Tmolus range. None of the three had ever been in this cemetery, and they believed the spirits of the dead roamed this area.

Selene, whose womanly shape told everyone a baby was coming, hugged Thelma. "I'm so sorry," she said as she watched Rastus dig a shallow grave in the soft earth. It would soon hold the body of the brave but reckless young man who had challenged Rome's armor. He was covered with a cloth and gently laid to rest in the ground. Rastus piled the pale-brown dirt over the body, tears stinging his eyes.

They returned to the bakery. The building was also Rastus's and Selene's home, and on the way up to their tiny apartment on the second floor, Thelma, her eyes red from weeping, tripped. She almost fell, brushing against firewood hidden in a dark corner. She stumbled again at the top of the narrow, steep staircase. The young widow sat down, resting her weary head on the table.

"I'll make an early evening meal. We'll have soup bones boiled with some vegetables once again," said Selene. She patted the young woman's shoulder and then drew her husband aside.

"Poor dear," said Selene, whispering. "Thelma was so happy two weeks ago. She was married in town and came to the bakery the next day. I said, 'I haven't seen you before,' and she replied, 'No, I'm from Silandus.' We rarely have any customers from Silandus, that town across the valley. She came here to be married. Her husband came to find work."

"Rastus, on our way back from the cemetery, Thelma said, 'There is only one place I refuse to go—back to Silandus.' Imagine being twenty years old, with no job. Your parents are dead, your husband is crushed by a horse, and you refuse to go home! Only two weeks married, and now she's a widow!"

Rastus rolled his eyes. "She doesn't have anywhere to go. As I came back here to get the cart before going to the cemetery, her landlord growled at me, 'Thelma can come for her things, yes, but that woman will bring me bad luck. She must go away, right now.'"

"Well, she can stay with us tonight. It will be tight, but tomorrow, we will talk. Maybe we can convince her to return to her family."

Chapter 2
Miriam's Arrival

AMOS AND ABIGAIL'S HOME, ON THE FARM CLOSE TO PHILADELPHIA

The wagon carrying Miriam and Grace left the garrison compound, passed the city market area, turned onto the Avenue of the Temples, and then headed for the Mountain Gate.

Throngs were flocking into the Temple of Hera. An evening sacrifice was to be made, and Miriam saw one woman leading a goat toward the temple. The goat seemed to know what was happening and pulled back against the rope.

The woman called out to her friends, "I'm offering a sacrifice to get rid of the protesters at the gates. I'll also pray that Zeus will wake up and see the catastrophe in the Cogamis Valley! All these changes to our agriculture! It's terrible!"

Miriam noticed a marked difference here in the upper portion of the city. All the homes in this section had been rebuilt. In contrast, many homes, workshops, and other buildings in the lower part of the town were broken down and dilapidated. Up here, along the Avenue of the Temples, people walked with their heads up. A sense of dignity and pride held sway.

She looked at a large home as they rode past. Its freshly plastered walls were painted a light brown. And the women! They wore jewelry, and their hairstyles showed them to be comfortable in the summer. Hair was gathered at the back and then thrown high on their heads, freeing their necks from the sweltering heat and making life bearable.

She sniffed and thought, *No pigs here in the upper part of the city. I smell flowers—and look at these lovely tall trees. Why don't people restore the northwestern part of Philadelphia like they did here? That last earthquake in this area happened over thirty years ago! Why is this place still such a mess?*

The driver left the city through the Mountain Gate, and from there, Miriam saw the stone wall around Uncle Amos and Aunt

Abigail's house. The wagon bumped along Mountain Road until they were half a mile away and the whole farm could be clearly seen.

Wild bushes showed off every shade of green. On the far side of the farm, Miriam saw the orchard. Those trees would soon add to the harvest. Nearby, the open field was planted with oats, wheat, and barley. Birds chirped, flying from bush to bush. She waved to peasants who were clipping the excess flower clusters in a small vineyard. Too many clusters on a vine would cause small grapes. The grape harvest would begin after three months.

The wagon driver turned left onto the narrow lane leading up to Amos's farm, and the horses pulled slowly up the last one hundred paces due to the steeper incline.

Two-year-old Grace was talking and playing, jumping from Miriam's lap to the floor of the wagon and then climbing back into her mother's arms. Miriam kept her eyes on her daughter, and she giggled at Grace's comments about the bumpy ride. They arrived at the farmhouse at the top of a small hill.

Miriam held her breath as she looked down into the Cogamis Valley. The afternoon sun cast a golden hue on mountains twenty miles across the valley. Looking to the north, she had a thought. The road into Philadelphia, along which they had come an hour ago, was a thin white ribbon, hardly visible on the valley floor. She tried to locate Sasorta. There it was—a dark spot far away in a sea of green.

Their driver pointed to the south, "Going over those hills is Mount Messogis Pass. We call it 'The Door.' The road down from the hills to the valley floor has sharp turns. The Philadelphia Garrison keeps the road safe. It's where robberies took place and why Felicior called your husband here."

She closed her eyes for a second. *Anthony missed most of Grace's growing up last year while tracking down the criminals. Lord, please don't let him be away from home now as much as the previous twelve months! Humph! Philadelphia! Noise, confusion, and smells in the lower part! Old. Bedraggled. Buildings were destroyed in that earthquake so long ago! Can't someone repair them?*

Oh, dear God! I don't know what Aunt Abigail will do when she meets my husband! She lost six of her seven children in Jerusalem. What will she say when a Roman soldier comes to her house?

THE MILITARY GARRISON IN PHILADELPHIA

Felicior finished explaining what he knew of the robbery on the Southern Road. His plans included soldiers controlling the crowds in smaller towns under Philadelphia's jurisdiction.

Felicior looked at the letter on the table and pursed his lips, seemingly annoyed. "Commander Servius lodged a written complaint against you at the annual meeting of the Asiarchs last September. He implied that there were other concerns, so I know he was not satisfied with your leadership."

"Yes, sir. I know about that. Since then, our squad has dismantled that gang. Unfortunately, four leaders escaped at Prosperity Village. It made Servius furious, and he could not accept the fact that those deserters were physically out of our reach. When we raided the village, they were standing at the top of a high cliff behind Prosperity Village."

Felicior looked down his long nose. "What has he said to you about his other concerns?"

"One other complaint, and I suspect it is what he wrote in the report, is related to my farm in Philippi. I've been a soldier for more than twenty years. I joined Legion XXI, the Predators, in Upper Germania in the fourth year of Emperor Vespasian.[4]

"After I was injured, the army staff thought I would not recover enough for any work as a legionary. As a result, they awarded me a small farm in Philippi. Well, after a while, I did recover and requested the task of instructing scouts. Why Commander Servius is asking questions about the farm is a mystery. Everything was documented and officially approved by Rome."

Anthony moved his hand to rub his scar but controlled his movements. "He has several other complaints as well. I know Servius disapproved of several decisions I made."

A centurion barged into the military office, interrupting the conversation. "Commander Felicior! Rioters are at the city gates, and they are much bolder. Hordes are approaching the Valley Gate from the local farms. We need reinforcements!"

---

[4] Anthony joined Legion XXI, the Predators, on January 1, AD 73, the fourth year of Emperor Vespasian. Anthony recovered from his wound in Philippi on May 19, AD 86 and received his small land holding on October 1, AD 88, in the eighth year of Emperor Domitian.

Felicior walked around his desk and scowled. "That's all for today. Our discussion of other charges will have to wait. Decimus, this is legionary scout Anthony Suros. He will be leading a special squad for local road security. Suros, this is Centurion Decimus, in charge of city security. Go with him and control those people."

He addressed them both. "Don't use excessive force. Line up your horses across the entrance of the gate. No rioters may enter the city. Guard the broken-down portion of the city wall. Tell the rioters to return tomorrow morning at the third hour. We will form an orderly line for the distribution of grain. I will inform Mayor Aurelius immediately. The time has come to release some of the emergency supplies."

As they were leaving the office, Felicior gave more instructions. "Anthony, I don't have room in the barracks for you, so we will put you in the Inn of the Open Door. I'll make that arrangement now. Centurion, assign a horse to Suros."

Anthony saluted his commander and left the office. His meeting with his commanding officer had not gone as he wanted.

He bit his lip and briefly closed his eyes. *I will soon know where I stand with Felicior. Miriam and Grace will stay with Uncle Amos. Ateas and Arpoxa and their two boys are still in Thyatira, but they have no family or friends there. It's bad enough that they are both crippled. Lord, I don't want to see that little family becoming involved in the very complicated issues in Jonathan's household. If they try to live there, I'm concerned that some people will treat them poorly.*

Decimus led Anthony as they rushed directly to the stables from the commander's office. The guard at the stable told Anthony, "This will be your horse, a four-year-old gelding. His name is Brutus. When you leave the city, I'll give you another horse for exchanges at the checkpoints. Do not forget. Brutus is assigned to this stable."

Anthony turned back to look at the garrison. Located at the eastern end of Philadelphia, the military complex was constructed on a small hill. Below, the slope fell one hundred fifty feet to the level of the plain. On three sides, the steep, rocky approach provided natural protection from attack.

More than three hundred years earlier, the two rulers of the Kingdom of Pergamum required a unique site for their easternmost military garrison. They were brothers and supported each other through thick and thin. Since then, much had changed in the city, but their early decision was a wise one.

The garrison's watchmen had an unobstructed view northwest up the valley and east across the valley to the mountains on the far side. To the south were hills. If an approaching army invaded from that direction, it first had to travel eight miles over the open plain before attacking Philadelphia. Furthermore, any attack from the west was impossible. Steep, rocky, inhospitable mountain slopes protected the city.

Many small shops opened onto the long central Avenue of Philadelphia. Now, at the close of the day, women were busy seeking items for their evening meals.

Decimus and Anthony joined the other guards who had closed off the main entry into the city, keeping rioting men from entering. Outside Valley Gate, mounted soldiers faced angry and desperate farmers. Loud voices sounded out, and one man screamed, "We've been put out of our livelihood!"

"How do you expect us to feed our families?"

"We need grain for bread!" cried a third man holding a baby.

"Let us through to the storehouses!" a woman begged. She held a small child in her arms. "Some people live securely inside the walls, and their tables have food! Look at me! I have none!"

Another bellowed, "Giles the banker has food, but we haven't eaten for days!"

A short man walked up to Anthony, speaking politely, even with all the mayhem around him. "Excuse me, sirs," he said respectfully. "I'm not with these men who are rioting. Is the play on at the theater tonight? I came from far across the valley, from Clanodda. I hope to watch tonight's performance of *Electra*. You see, sirs, I love Sophocles' plays. I've seen most of his one hundred twenty plays. "These actors specialize in his tragedies. Sophocles—our greatest dramatist! Please let me through!"[5]

---

[5] Sophocles' dramatic plays (c. 495–406 BC) were performed by theater companies and were enjoyed by theatergoers. Of Sophocles' 123 plays, only seven survive. All his dramas may have been performed in Philadelphia, other cities of Asia Minor, and other Roman provinces. The seven existing plays of Sophocles heavily influenced Western civilization through literature, art, and psychology.

He begged the soldiers but was pushed back with the others, his meek voice lost in the pushing and shoving, swearing and cursing. Everyone knew where the grain was stored, and they demanded food for their families.

Decimus, a large man with a loud voice, felt pity for the hundreds of abject farmers. However, he had to keep the mob under control. "Tomorrow, at mid-morning, we will distribute grain from the emergency storage area. Go home now. Come back tomorrow, and line up properly when you come."

The guards at Valley Gate had doubled their numbers during the last half hour, and after Decimus instructed the mob to return the next day, the protest died down.

He grinned. "You came at the right time to help keep the peace, Anthony. Things are grim."

Anthony asked, "Are there many of these riots here? I saw some ugly scenes in Sasorta."

"Yes, many. The discontent started last year and has been getting steadily worse. People initially thought they would get grain given to them, but the rioting began when they learned that most of last year's meager harvest will be going to Rome. Prices went crazy, and supplies started drying up. You know the saying: 'What Rome wants, Rome gets.' As it is, there may not be enough emergency supplies to get us through the winter. Not everybody knows that yet. Most have vegetables that they have grown themselves, but those are starting to get scarce too."

AMOS AND ABIGAIL'S HOME

On the previous Sunday, Miriam's uncle Jonathan in Thyatira had sent Amos a note by pigeon informing him of Anthony and Miriam's imminent arrival. A servant was instructed to open the gate when they arrived, so Miriam and Grace were admitted. They left their sandals at the front door, and the servant washed the dust off their feet.

"Master Amos and Abigail are with the others of the family at the market, but they should be back soon," he said, serving them cool water.

Grace was no longer confined to the back of the wagon. She ran into the house, shrieking happily as she felt the cool floor, jumping up and down with joy. The child bent down to rub her hand on the smooth tiles after the long, hot ride in the bumpy wagon. In the large, open room, she saw a cat with three little kittens. Screaming with delight, she called, "Mommy, come and see the cats!"

The house servants helped the garrison guard unload the wagon, bringing in their possessions and the scrolls that had previously belonged to Miriam's grandfather, Antipas Ben Shelah. A servant stood at the front door, keeping it open while the wagon was unloaded.

Miriam slumped down onto a couch after the wagon left to return to the garrison. Her head seemed to be splitting open. Worse than the long, bumpy ride in the military wagon from Thyatira was the recollection of people screaming in Sasorta.

Soon squeaking wagon wheels in the courtyard told Miriam that Amos and Abigail had come. Amos, shorter than his wife, glowed with joy, his deep-set eyes sparkling.

Abigail carried even less weight than her husband. Was that a weary look on her aunt's face? Abigail appeared haggard.

Miriam rushed to the arriving wagon. Amos helped Abigail down, and two others were still in the wagon. She hugged and kissed the old man. "Uncle Amos! So glad to see you!"

Amos continued to hold her tightly. "Well, you look just the same as when I saw you last, when my father, Eliab, passed away in Pergamum! And now you have a little one! My, the years pass so quickly! Where have these past four years gone?"

"Aunt Abigail, I'm so sorry that we couldn't give you more warning about our arrival. Anthony has been assigned by Commander Felicior to..." She realized immediately, judging from the older woman's deep frowns, that she had made a mistake by mentioning the army.

"We heard you married a soldier." Abigail spoke much too slowly. "Simon sent us a letter from Sardis two years ago. He told us about you. But I never expected that *he* would come *here*!"

Miriam watched her aunt's eyes roll upward. The older woman's face was thin. Dark patches under her eyes suggested long nights with interrupted sleep. Abigail meant to keep her annoyance to herself, but Miriam made a note of her aunt's not-so-hidden feelings. *Talking with Aunt Abigail is going to be a challenge. I must be alert about what I say and how I say it.*

Next getting down from the wagon was a woman slightly older than Miriam. "Hello, Miriam! I'm Isabel, and this is my husband, Obed. He's the quiet one in the family. I guess I'm the one who does all the talking! I met him when our two families lived in Antioch. I was sixteen then. You were six years old."

Isabel gave Miriam a hug and then lifted Grace into her arms. Unlike her slim mother-in-law, Isabel enjoyed cooking and eating, and this showed in her plump curves.

Miriam responded, "I'm so happy to see you again, Isabel! This is my daughter, Grace. Can you say 'Hello' nicely to my cousins?"

Isabel and Obed reached out to pat Grace on the back of her head, but the child wanted to run around in the stone courtyard.

Isabel and Obed were both forty years old and the parents of two daughters. "Come meet our daughters, Ruth and Sarah. They are coming on the other wagon." The courtyard came to life as the second wagon entered the gate.

Isabel introduced them as they got down from the wagon. "Miriam, this is Ruth and her husband, Jesse." Miriam gave Ruth a hug. The young woman's figure showed she was expecting a baby. Jesse put down a firewood bundle to give his cousin a kiss on both cheeks.

"And here is the youngest in the household. Miriam, this is Sarah!" Isabel smiled.

Miriam greeted her too. "Obed and Isabel, Sarah, Ruth, and Jesse! I am so happy to meet you! My husband is Anthony, a legionary. He has to stay overnight at the garrison, but he'll come later."

The family members were taken aback. Details about Miriam's marriage had obviously not been mentioned to them.

"Welcome to our home," Abigail said a little too loudly. She turned to Miriam, speaking softly and with tears in her eyes. "My poor dear, I've wanted to hug you since I heard of the death of my dear brother-in-law, Antipas! So much death... Life includes too much death." Abigail wiped tears from her hollow cheeks. Perhaps the mention of Antipas brought back too many recollections.

Miriam warmly embraced her elderly aunt. She thought, *The agony of my grandfather's death and the loss of her six children binds us together...too many sad memories.*

Once inside, Amos invited her, "Come, I will show you my library." He took Miriam to his office, which was connected to the large central room. Amos possessed an extensive library, as did his four brothers: Simon in Sardis, Jonathan in Thyatira, Daniel in Laodicea, and Joshua in Smyrna.

Eliab, their father, had insisted that they learn to study at their home in Alexandria. Since childhood, they had all treasured scrolls, books, and learning.

Only Amos and Obed had access to the family's business papers and personal documents. Amos was proud of his precious scrolls, what he called "The New Writings." His eyes sparkled with child-like excitement when he saw the baggage stacked along the library wall.

"Miriam, are these scrolls from Antipas's library? Is this my brother's collection?"

He beamed as she nodded, and then Miriam ran after Grace, who was reaching to pick up a silver menorah. "No, Grace, you can't take that in your hands! Yes, Uncle Amos, Marcos, our family's lawyer, packed Grandpa's personal documents when we left Pergamum. Now, Grace! Don't pull the cat's tail!"

She picked her daughter up and held her tight. "These are not the business documents of our family business. I have Grandpa's personal records, the notes he wrote each day, and many copies of our sacred scrolls. That's why the wagon was so full. We don't have many possessions, but there are lots of scrolls from Grandpa Antipas's library! The Roman military brought those with us today. Just think! An army wagon brought Jewish treasures to your home!"

Chapter 3
Painful Memories

THE MILITARY GARRISON IN PHILADELPHIA

The following day, Anthony sat up, stretched his arms high above his head, and walked to the window. He had slept on a thin straw mattress on the room's hard floor. The Inn of the Open Door, built more than one hundred years earlier, was situated close to the Valley Gate, where the disturbance had taken place the previous evening.

When Amos had moved to Philadelphia, he had opened a shop to sell articles from the other Ben Shelah brothers. Four years ago, he had sold the shop and bought the inn. He felt fulfilled with farming and this new venture near the city's main entrance.

Opening squeaky wooden shutters, Anthony smelled the slightly putrid odor of rotting garbage drifting in from the inn's trash heap. Early morning light entered the dark, musty room. Close by, he could see a portion of the old city wall in ruins, having fallen outward decades before. Much of this section of the city was still a pile of rubble.[6]

He dressed and brushed back his black curly hair. *I hope I didn't disappoint Miriam. My first evening in Philadelphia and I had to stand guard at the Valley Gate! The valley looks peaceful right now, but the men who stood together yesterday shouted in fear.*

He walked outside through the Valley Gate and looked eastward to distant mountains. Clouds were changing color, turning from orange to yellow. Within an hour, the sun would quickly warm the land.

---

[6] Descriptions of the Inn of the Open Door are based upon four *caravansary* buildings in Turkey: those found in Kusadasi, Avanos, Sultan Hani (all restored), and Agzikarahani. Ancient inns reflect an age in which merchants, soldiers, and traders traveled by foot with caravans of animals composed of horses, camels, and donkeys. Inns offered safety and shelter, but not much comfort, for travelers and their animals.

Walking back to the inn, he smelled the strong odor of horses, donkeys, and camels wafting through the door as he entered the central courtyard. Amos's servants were carrying water to the animals at the back of the inn. Some men brought in feed. Others were scrubbing the floor.

Anthony went to the latrine area, where the inn had a small bath facility. Another soldier was already there, so they washed and took turns shaving each other's short black stubble. Both carried their own carefully knapped obsidian blades for shaving. Properly cared for, these blades could last a month before having to buy new ones. Some men preferred a thin iron blade, called a *novacila,* that required sharpening before each shave.

"That's a killer of a face, Anthony," said his companion. "How can I shave you without cutting the scar? What does a soldier have to do to get such a mark of approval?"

"It's a long story with a happy ending," said Anthony, smiling but unwilling to say more.

He left the inn and rode to the garrison. Felicior was already in his office. "You've arrived early, Suros," said Felicior. He instructed a guard to bring them breakfast. "Early arrival equals a good start to the day. What happened at the Valley Gate last night?"

"We held back the men demonstrating at the gate, sir. Only a few were let in after much arguing, men who had come to the city for the theater presentation. Most went back home after our announcement that emergency rations would be distributed at midmorning today."

Felicior was usually economical with words, but this morning he would give Anthony a lengthy warning.

"We were interrupted yesterday before we finished talking. For the moment, I will not get into all the complaints. Commander Servius Callistratus has a serious accusation against you. It has to do with how you declare the Sacred Oath. You must repeat, 'Caesar is lord and god,' yet you refuse. You leave off the two words 'and god.' For this, you could be severely disciplined."[7]

"Yes sir. I first explained these thoughts to you two years ago in Sardis. I believe the bylaws of the Senate: 'No emperor can claim that

---

[7] To the everyday stress of being a soldier, a Gentile follower of the Jewish Messiah would be faced with additional tensions. Conflicts arose because Roman law required the declaration, "Caesar is lord and god." Registered Jews were by law exempt from this requirement.

he is a god when he is alive. It is the task of the Senate to pronounce him to have been a god.' That can happen only after his death."

The officer took several seconds before speaking. Eventually he looked down his long nose and sat straight up.

"Suros, you are stubborn and intelligent. These qualities may lead to your downfall. I remember what you did when I gave you an impossible task. You were to capture the eagle standard from my instructor, Prosperus. I gave you the twenty smallest and weakest recruits, while he had the twenty toughest. Even against those odds, you captured the eagle.

"I don't know why you did it, but you would not permit Prosperus to be shamed. You let him get credit for discovering the cave where those bandits hid their loot. Consequently, he wasn't shamed for failure. So you do have some positive elements in your character, and that's why I am comfortable placing you under my command here."[8]

Now Felicior spoke more directly about the soldier's future. "You entered the legion in the Fourth Year of Vespasian and served sixteen years. As a reservist, you earned the right to marry, the right of *connubium*, under Roman law. I know your marriage was approved by the Asiarch of Pergamum,[9] so Servius cannot criticize you for being married. Your skills are what we need in scout instructors. You can retire well in four more years and go to your farm in Philippi. However, I reject this talk about 'agape love.' Selfless love? None of that is to be mentioned. You are near the end of your career. Don't spoil your future. Do not be known as an enemy of Rome!"

Breakfast was brought to the office by an auxiliary and placed on the table. Felicior broke off pieces of flatbread, and as he did so, he wondered how strict to be with this soldier.

Previously, he had been satisfied with Anthony, this soldier who had carried out complicated assignments. *Servius has seven concerns*

---

[8] This story is found in *Never Enough Gold: A Chronicle of Sardis*.

[9] A Roman soldier in the province of Asia Minor who served sixteen years as a legionary could then earn the right of *connubium*, the right to marry. Soldiers retiring after twenty-five years of active service were often granted a small property in an area where Rome was building colonies. Anthony had married Miriam after eighteen years of service.

about Suros, but only one is written as an accusation. They are all serious, especially the one about the Solemn Oath.

But I understand Suros's reluctance to give Domitian the title "god." My cousin, Senator Helvetius Priscus Junior, was recently executed for opposing the emperor. Helvetius openly stated, "Domitian may not use the Law of Majestas, the Law of Offenses Against the Empire, to reform the Senate."

And my cousin's father, Helvetius Priscus the Elder, also resisted Vespasian's authoritarian rule. Two men executed, a father and a son! They were my blood relatives! By two emperors, one a father and the other his son—Vespasian and Domitian.

I'm walking a fine line. I agree with Suros that even emperors should have limits upon their authority. But I cannot reveal it.

"So I have officially transferred you to this garrison. Soldiers assigned to the Philadelphia Garrison are busy keeping the peace here and in the six surrounding towns. Last year you led the soldiers I assigned to you: Omerod, Menandro, Bellinus, Capito, and Sextilius. Well, Sextilius has retired and gone back to Syracuse to manage his family's lands in Sicily. Capito and Menandro will not work with you here because Commander Servius needs their help in Sardis. So of the elite squad with six soldiers that I formed last year, only Omerod and Bellinus will work with you. I need more help...."

He stopped, as if remembering something, and then said, "Last year, you also had a Scythian civilian on your team. Did he come to Philadelphia with you?"

"That man was Ateas, sir. He has been in Prusa helping interrogate that last group of slaves the bandits brought in from Scythia. You authorized a fee and transportation for him to work with our team. He should be back in Thyatira this week."

"If you can convince him to do it, have him come here. I want him, and I can continue to pay a wage. He was a great help last year in shutting down that gang. Yes, we could arrange to have him stay at the inn—do simple tasks, clean tables, and do other simple chores.

"I'm thinking that he can talk to servants and slaves of merchants coming through the city. Let him be our ears and eyes. He will talk to Scythian slaves—something like a spy. I can authorize supplementing his pay from the inn owner enough to make him be a cheap help. We need as many people as possible to track down the perpetrators of that robbery on the Southern Road."

"Yes sir," said Anthony. "Ateas has a wife, and she is very crippled."

"If Ateas is willing to work for me under these circumstances, let me know. They must both come here as quickly as possible. I'll arrange for an auxiliary to bring them from Thyatira in that military wagon you came in.

"Now I have another assignment for you. On Saturday morning, I am sending you to Hierapolis to talk with Flavius Zeuxis. He is the richest merchant in this region and makes two trips to Italia each year. He's livid about what happened. One week ago, a robbery took place at the Door. Four bundles of his merchandise were stolen. Zeuxis was so upset about it that he abandoned his trip to Italia and returned to Hierapolis. I will have authorizations written for you by Friday. Take Omerod and Bellinus with you. You will all have a chance to see where the robbery happened."

"I understand, sir." Anthony saluted his commander with his right arm straight out and palm down, as he had done hundreds of times before.[10]

As he made his salute, Felicior added, "Now, this is for your ears only. Do not repeat this to anyone else. This rioting will not stop quickly in the City of Brotherly Love. I need guards at the gate for the afternoon and evening shifts. I'm giving you time off right now to go check on your family. Be back in two hours. When you return, I want you in the combat exercise arena for a couple hours. Tonight and for the next two evenings, you will stand guard at the Valley Gate until midnight. Friday night, you and your team get to sleep. No guard duty because you will get up early Saturday and leave for Hierapolis. For the time being, continue staying at the Inn of the Open Door. That is all."

As Anthony left the office, Felicior watched him.

Anthony, a skillful scout, notices details and thinks ahead. A remarkable soldier—yet a ridiculous belief in that "Messiah" put to death by crucifixion. What would I have done to him if two of my relatives had not been executed for opposing the emperor? I would have paid more attention to the accusations against him.

---

[10] The Roman salute of touching the heart area with a clenched fist was an early Hollywood invention. It was never used by Romans. Archeological evidence shows them using the style mentioned above.

AMOS AND ABIGAIL'S HOME

As Felicior and Anthony talked at the garrison, breakfast was being prepared in the Ben Shelah house. Grace awakened early, and Miriam brought her downstairs to not disturb the rest of the family still asleep. Moments later, Abigail awoke and was delighted to see the child exploring everything. A rare smile on her thin face said much about how she was facing the new day. Abigail held her hands together. *I can be friends with young Miriam.*

While Amos was working in his library, Miriam chatted with Abigail, recounting her last year in Pergamum with Antipas. Miriam's story momentarily dispelled Abigail's gloominess. The deep creases and dark shadows under the old woman's eyes undoubtedly came from years of grieving.

The older woman thought out loud: "Your grandfather, Antipas, was a thorn in the flesh to everyone in Pergamum. First he was ousted from the Jewish community of the covenant, and then the guardians of the Greek gods chased him! So sad how he died." Turning to Miriam, she asked, "Now, about Grace. I can't see any of you in her face. None at all! How did she come into your life?"

"Auntie, in the middle of grandfather's problems, a messenger came to our home and said that the next day a baby girl would be left at the edge of the city's trash heap. When I told Grandpa that I would be given a baby to care for, he almost collapsed. Sure enough, the next day I carried Grace home in my arms. Grandpa came to accept her and grew to love her."

"Who is her mother?"

"No idea. But our lawyer, Marcos, knows who she is."

"Marcos? The man who sends us our portion of Eliab's estate every six months? Is he involved? Perhaps Marcos is Grace's father." There was more than a glint of curiosity in the old woman's eye.

"No, definitely not! He told me that Grace's mother is a young woman who attends the House of Prayer at his home. Marcos said we have never met the mother."

"How did Marcos meet Grace's mother?"

"A few years ago, he had several properties in Kisthene, the summer holiday city on the coast. He sold them, and that summer, after the villas were sold, Marcos and his wife met a young woman and her mother. Those two women took care of his properties over the winter until the following spring, when the new owners moved in. It was during that time that Marcos talked with the younger of the women. She was expecting a baby. Marcos told her about Grandpa's village, and she decided to give her baby away. That young woman had never met me! I don't know who she is."[11]

Abigail frowned. "So who is the father? Maybe Anthony?" A deeper frown darkened her face. *How could Miriam marry a legionary! It makes absolutely no sense for a Jewish girl to marry one of those who destroyed our city. Soldiers have never come to my house except for that dreadful day, and now that I remember it, they were not Romans. They were Jews, my fellow citizens. Lord! Could you permit an enemy to enter my home?*

"No, Anthony is not her father! You'll see how different he is from Grace when he comes. The miracle of it was this: Grandpa let me keep Grace. A scrap of parchment came in the blanket she was wrapped in, and it said, 'Her name is Chrysa.' It also included her birth date. So we gave her the name Chrysa Grace Suros when she was officially adopted. Oh, I miss Grandpa so much. He was so kind and understanding."

"I know that Antipas was kind, but didn't he overdo it? He took in too many pagan slaves. And he didn't even know what they were like or what they believed!"

"Yes, Grandpa did buy slaves, one every year, down at the slave market. Then he gave each one their 'freedom papers.' He said, 'We Jews were slaves until God released us. We should do the same when we can.' He was kind to everyone, and he received lots of criticism for it. Six widows lived in his village: three Jews in one house and three non-Jews, younger women, in another. They didn't always get along well!" Miriam laughed. "When Anthony comes, ask him about Grandpa's village."

Grace ran to her mother and held her fingers out for Miriam to kiss. A kitten had scratched the little girl while Grace was playing with it.

Abigail got up from the table and went to the kitchen to talk to the servants preparing breakfast. Then she entered the library.

---

[11] Kisthene is a coastal town on the Aegean Sea, now known as Ayvalik. Since antiquity, it has been popular for summer vacations due to its favorable climate and beaches.

Amos had to schedule another payment to the bank. After a long transaction with its former owner, he had bought the Inn of the Open Door and he only owed two more installments.

"Miriam's husband is coming here and probably soon!" Abigail said in a low whisper.

The frown on Amos's face showed immediate displeasure. "Of course, we knew that would happen sooner or later. But we must show hospitality to my niece's husband, no matter how much we object to her marriage."

"But an enemy in my home!" The tremor in her voice betrayed her alarm. She could not describe the knot that had formed in her stomach. "A legionary! Amos, I've been listening to Miriam's story. She is about to tell me how they met and how they were married. Miriam is part of our family, but Anthony is a soldier! And guess what!" She kept her voice a whisper. "The mother of her little girl is a pagan!"

"What do you want me to do about it?" asked Amos, also in an earnest whisper.

"Amos, what if he kills us all? What if that's the reason he married into our family?"

Amos's shoulders slumped with dismay. "Abigail, he will not kill us or cause us harm. Miriam has already explained that he is a follower of the Messiah."

While Amos and Abigail talked in the library, Miriam walked around and examined the house. Amos ran their family farming business from their home while Obed managed the Inn of the Open Door, traveling there each day. She walked through the large open room and then took in the details in the kitchen, the toilets, the bedrooms, and the office.

Miriam studied the layout of the large room. Above the pillars, long white marble lintels supported light pine wood beams, and wooden ceiling slats rested on these. She traced the lines made by the red roof tiles where they joined, keeping out the rain. The light pine wood above and the white marble floor gave a sense of peacefulness to the room.

Facing the valley, four pillars formed a square space. In the original Greek home, this was a sacred area called the *peristyle*. Embedded in a wall between two windows was a narrow niche with a slight arch over the top. It was wide enough for a small statue and a basket of flowers. The Greek family would have brought daily oblations of oil or wine and flowers, which the goddess Hera demanded. Miniature figures of the goddess were gone. Now a silver Jewish menorah and two separate silver candle holders occupied the space. The two smaller Shabbat candles would be lit each Friday evening to mark the beginning of the Sabbath.

Abigail took a long time speaking with her husband, so Miriam walked into the kitchen. The windows in the kitchen faced north and east, with a panoramic view of the valley. Near the steps going up to the bedrooms were two toilet rooms: one for men and another for women. It was one of the few houses outside the city walls with such luxury. Water from a spring high up the mountain close by flowed continuously under the toilets, keeping them clean.

Amos and Abigail came out of his library and office to the small square table with the three couches set around it. They reclined, and Amos motioned for Miriam to join them. "Miriam, I missed your long conversation with Abigail. You know us businessmen, always working on payments for something or other. I overheard comments about Anthony."

Miriam saw concerned looks on their faces and decided to address the painful topic head-on. "I know that you are both sensitive about my husband. He is finishing his reservist duty. Please just listen to him. I am not asking you to accept him." She held out her hand toward her aunt. "Auntie, I know how you suffered the loss of my cousins. I was there in Jerusalem when they died, but I remember so little of those events."

"You must stay with us, Miriam," said Abigail. "Get to know our situation, and then you'll understand why I don't feel like my normal self. Enjoy being with my family. As you learn about us, you'll find out that there are strains on relationships, marriages, and weddings. I want to share them with you."

"Yes, tell me." Miriam knew from experience, not only in Sardis but in Thyatira too, that people held secrets close to their hearts. Individuals never invited Miriam instantly into a hidden room of their lives. She knew that today would only be an introduction to the tensions and concerns facing the household.

"Every day I mourn the loss of my children." Abigail avoided looking around the table. Her eyes became moist as she said, "Of the seven children Adonai gave us, only Obed is alive."

The old lady opened a small drawer under the table and pulled out a scroll made of fine parchment, a family treasure. On it were written the names of family members. It went back many generations. Out of respect for a famous ancestor, all the men took the same surname, "Shelah." On it were written the names of the Ben Shelah brothers and sisters born in Alexandria. The scroll was a prized document of the extended clan.

Abigail was too acquainted with death. She paused for a moment to wipe away tears that welled up while looking at the parchment. Her parents were noted, along with six children and two grandchildren. She had memorized all the dates, and she kept track of each birthday and funeral.

"Can you explain these names?" Miriam asked. She glanced at the names of unfamiliar people.

"Michael and Martha are a well-known Jewish couple in our congregation and in the city. Michael Ben Akkub is sixty-two and exceptionally strict. He expects everyone to obey the Torah and the tradition of the elders. Their daughter, Isabel, is married to our son, Obed.

"Obed and Isabel had two boys: Gershom and Jacob. Gershom died from a fever when he was only two. Jacob died too but much later. A horse kicked him in the chest when he was fourteen. They also gave us two granddaughters, Ruth, nineteen, and Sarah, seventeen."

"Oh, I'm so sorry, Aunt Abigail! You've lost six children and two grandsons! I'm so sorry for your loss!"

Abigail's eyes filled up with tears again. "There's a second couple in the congregation that is close to us, Daniel and Dorcas. Their older boy, Jesse, married Ruth, our granddaughter. She is expecting a baby in three months. I'm happy about this...so excited. Mith is Dorcas and Daniel's second son. That's short for Shelomith. He is betrothed to our second granddaughter, Sarah."

Miriam's finger went down the scroll. "With Jesse and Ruth married, one baby on the way, and Mith betrothed to Sarah, your three households are a clan!"

"Yes, we are three families constantly involved in one another's gossip!" Abigail smiled briefly and then swallowed hard before approaching the subject burning in her mind. "Now tell me more about Anthony."

"At first, Grandpa didn't like the idea of my being married to Anthony, but..."

"But nothing! He's a Gentile!"

Miriam laughed nervously. "You may accept him, or maybe you won't want to. Either way, I will respect you, Auntie. I know the Ben Shelah family was never linked to a non-Jew before."

The wrinkles on her aunt's forehead were a bit deeper. "I love children, and I want them around me. That's what I need right now. I'm happy that Grace is here. I only wish her mother was a Jew."

Miriam laughed confidently. "Anthony is a follower of Yeshua Messiah. After you meet him, you may find that I made the right decision in wanting to spend my life with him. And I won't tell you the reasons that my wonderful grandpa let me marry him unless you give me lots of time!"

They heard a voice calling from outside. Anthony had arrived from the garrison, and Miriam ran to the courtyard as he dismounted and kissed his cheek.

As they climbed the front steps, Amos avoided eye contact at the door. He spoke in a formal voice. "Welcome, Legionary Anthony Suros. I am Amos, and my wife, Abigail, is inside. Please come in."

Standing outside the front door, Anthony took off his sandals. He placed his sword, well-polished breastplate, and helmet on the floor beside them before entering the home. Without his soldier's belt, his light brown tunic hung limply.

Abigail, hearing him at the door, did a half-turn and then gasped, breathing deeply. She stayed on the couch, reclining, but her eyes were wide open, hinting at the fear she felt.

Anthony saw the older woman, whose back was slightly turned away from him. "I'm pleased to meet you, Uncle Amos and Aunt Abigail. I can only stay for a short while. Between marauders, swindlers, and rioting peasants, Commander Felicior at the garrison has his hands full. He won't let me stay long, but I had to come to introduce myself and to see that Miriam and Grace are well after our long ride."

Anthony's gaze, trained in seeing details, took in everything around the room. Abigail kept looking away from him. Amos's head was down as if he were examining the mosaics on the floor. Miriam, acting as a bridge, had one hand in his and the other stretched out toward her elderly aunt.

Nothing hinted at a welcome. The soldier breathed a short prayer. *Lord, I'm short of breath, and Miriam is tense! Amos wants to be friendly but is afraid to be. And Abigail is completely avoiding me. To think that I prayed two years ago for an opportunity to tell her what is in my heart! Show me the right time to speak with her! Will I ever have the words to confront her grief and sadness?*

He walked farther into the room across the black, white, and yellow tiles on the floor. Standing beside Miriam, he made no effort to sit down. "I have a message for you. Commander Felicior needs extra help because of the riots and the dangers of bandits on the road. He wants our friends Ateas and Arpoxa to come from Thyatira. They used to be slaves, but Antipas freed them. Both are followers of Yeshua Messiah."

"Ah ha!" injected Amos. "I was going to ask Miriam about that. The note Jonathan sent by pigeon two days ago telling of your coming to Philadelphia mentioned Ateas has returned from his last task.[12] Both Ateas and Arpoxa are willing to come here. There was no further explanation. So you're saying those people are coming to Philadelphia?"

"Yes, that was a question I left with Uncle Jonathan: Would Ateas and Arpoxa be willing to move to Philadelphia? Our team left Ateas in Prusa. He assisted with translating. His help in capturing criminals was invaluable. He's not a soldier. My commander said if they were willing to come to Philadelphia, he would send a military wagon to bring them. The commander wants Ateas to stay with me at the Inn of the Open Door. Would it be all right with you if his wife, Arpoxa, and her two small boys come to stay with you here? I need to tell you about Arpoxa...."

Before he could finish, Amos interrupted. "You're staying at *my inn*?"

---

[12] Ateas's contribution in capturing bandits is told in *Purple Honors: A Chronicle of Thyatira.*

"Yes, and several more soldiers are needed too. They will be coming from other cities to support the Philadelphia Garrison. Felicior told me that all of us will be staying there. I think that will be good for your business, Uncle Amos.... May I refer to you this way? That is all right? Thank you. Now, no one wants another robbery on the Southern Road. That's why I'm here. The military must capture those behind the recent caravan theft."

"Miriam," Anthony addressed her, sensing that he had raised concerns that could not be addressed now. "I am required to go to Hierapolis for several days."

Abigail let out a deep sigh. Hearing that he was leaving, she turned around. Without his armor, he could have been a farmworker from one of the Cogamis Valley's vineyards.

Amos addressed the Roman soldier. "Why the trip to Hierapolis?" he asked. "You've only just arrived in Philadelphia!"

Anthony moved toward the door, knowing that his welcome was over. "I'm sure you have traveled the road past Mount Messogis from Philadelphia to Laodicea. The danger lies close to the pass. Keeping that access road open to the interior is why the regiment from Italia was posted to the Philadelphia Garrison. However, recent riots required using some of those soldiers for crowd control, which meant fewer men for road patrols. A robbery took place halfway up the road, at the long double curve. Commander Felicior wants me to stay in Philadelphia until he knows the road is safe again. I'm working with a small team. We worked for Commander Felicior last year. These bandits are dangerous men, army deserters who turned against Rome's authority.

"So Saturday morning I go to Hierapolis. The caravan that was robbed near the pass belonged to Titus Flavius Zeuxis, the famous merchant. He was traveling to Rome and is outraged by what happened. For the first time in his life, Flavius Zeuxis canceled his trip. He turned his caravan around and went home. We think he's preparing a formal complaint against the magistrate of this city. He probably intends to file the complaint with the authorities in the provincial court in Ephesus."

Amos leaned forward and looked straight at Anthony for the first time. "Titus Flavius Zeuxis? He's my best client! He's been with us several times since we bought the inn. It was his idea to give it a new name. He said, 'I feel welcome here. I always want the road over the mountain to be open, free, and safe. If I were you, I'd change the name to Inn of the Open Door. It sounds more appealing.' I agreed, and business is growing. Having the right name is important."

Anthony glanced at the deep lines on Abigail's face. Dark patches under her eyes made her face look old and sad, and her arms were folded tightly across her chest.

Miriam suggested, "Anthony, we need to let Uncle Amos return to his work."

"I'll be gone in a minute," he said in a cheerful tone. "I apologize for coming without notice, but I wanted Miriam to know that I would be out of the city for several days. Felicior wants my team in Hierapolis to learn what happened. Perhaps we can determine if these are some of the same criminals that we encountered last year. I will be on city gate guard duty until midnight for the next two days."

Anthony searched for some way to connect with Amos apart from his military task. "Uncle Amos, do you like horses? You do? The garrison has given me a horse called Brutus to use while I'm here. He's a lovely horse, one of the best I have ever ridden."

He walked to the door and gathered his soldier's gear. "Miriam, I will be leaving now, so please come outside with me to say goodbye." She picked Grace up and followed Anthony.

Anthony walked to the door and gathered his gear, and then he went with Miriam and Grace to the courtyard, where his horse was waiting. He turned around, gave them a gentle hug, looked back at the closed door, and mounted his horse.

"I got the impression your aunt doesn't like me."

"Your impression is correct," she answered good-naturedly. She pinched her husband's leg lovingly and patted the horse's neck. "Brutus," she said, wrapping her long, slender arms around the dark brown horse's neck, her fingers combing his mane, "take good care of this soldier, do you hear?"

"Miriam, I need to talk with you, but I couldn't do it in there. Commander Felicior told me that I can retire in four and a half years. We can go to my farm in Philippi, raise our family, and settle down. But there's something else...."

"It's not serious, is it?" Miriam's lip quivered.

"Commander Servius has made an accusation. He says, 'Anthony Suros refuses to declare the Solemn Oath as it is to be declared: "Caesar is lord and god."' Miriam, I will *never* say all that."

His jaw was tight with determination as he took the reins in his hands. *I won't tell Miriam that Servius has other claims, some of them serious and perhaps enough to cause me a lot of problems.*

She felt her chest heaving. "I remember when Grandpa Antipas told you, 'Following the covenant will be dangerous. It may bring you great danger.' Be careful, my love. I will have one of the servants bring me to the inn Saturday morning at daybreak to say goodbye. I want you back soon."

Anthony turned to go. "As soon as I can. I'll try to get a message to you somehow when I return, but it will be difficult since I have no access to messengers. I will tell Felicior to go ahead and send the wagon to Thyatira to bring Ateas and his family. Felicior says he will also talk with Amos to work out a job for Ateas at the inn. Since Amos didn't say a word about Arpoxa and her boys staying here, will you see if you can get that to happen? I was afraid to push them for an answer the first time I met them."

The cold response to his visit caused him concern. *If Ateas stays in Philadelphia, where will Arpoxa live? Can she fit into the Ben Shelah home? Abigail obviously doesn't accept outsiders. If Ateas is at the Inn of the Open Door, Arpoxa could only stay at the Ben Shelah home if Abigail allows it.*

As Miriam returned through the front door, the rest of the family came downstairs and gathered for breakfast. Most expressed disappointment at having missed meeting Anthony during his short visit.

As soon as Miriam went outside to see Anthony off, Amos turned to Abigail. "Anthony won't be back in Philadelphia for a while, so you won't have to trouble yourself with him. Now relax, my dear. Anthony is on horseback and will be gone for days, and if this Ateas fellow comes, he will be at the inn."

"I don't want that soldier in my house *again*," she said, "but you may tell Miriam that if the woman with the two little children comes, she can stay here. I need children around me."

Amos looked up at the ceiling. *How can I keep Anthony away? He should not come anywhere near Abigail, and he must never share salt with me at a meal. My wife has changed so much since those terrible days, first in Alexandria and then in Jerusalem. She used to be the life of every gathering, calling for instruments and music, but that was before the legions surrounded our city, before the temple was burned.*

Chapter 4
Dedicated to Destruction

A CAVE OVERLOOKING THE COGAMIS VALLEY

As evening shadows crept over Sasorta and Philadelphia, the bandit Craga sat on a large rock beside a cave. Watching the evening come to the Cogamis Valley, he stretched his left leg and squeezed the scar below the knee. The pain was always worse at this time of day.

Instead of his former soldier's tunic and armor, he was dressed as a standard auxiliary, his brown tunic coming down to his knees. He kicked the ground in annoyance, sending a small stone tumbling over the cliff in front of him. As he rubbed his knee, he pulled at the long, leather strip wrapped around his shin. More than twenty years ago, he first put on a pair of military sandals, lacing them up with long, black leather strips.

A long sigh slowly escaped through tight lips. Craga closed his eyes, watching outstanding achievements and glorious adventures pass by. *Ah, those days of grandeur! In Upper Germania, I was the lead centurion in the legion,*[13] *the youngest "primus pilus," or "first spear," in the legion. I commanded my cohort in battle. But then came that awful day!*

He rubbed his leg, deciding what to say to Taba, Harpa, and Maza when they returned. His forehead was lined with deep creases as he remembered those days of glory and thought of how they contrasted with his present shame and failure.

Since joining the army at age seventeen, Craga had been known for his skills in battle. Legion XXI, the Predators, was one of several legions pacifying barbarian tribes in the north.

His commanding presence was fearsome. His protruding chin; a large, puffy red face; hazel eyes; and a voracious appetite for victory made him a fearsome warrior. A hazardous operation against a

---

[13] Upper Germania corresponds to present-day Southwestern Germany and Northern Switzerland.

barbarian village on the west side of the Neckar River led to his being promoted to First Centurion.

He closed his eyes again, remembering. *Those days were days of glory!* He savored the success of being elevated to the "'first spear." Unlike his present situation, that was something to dwell on, but today he was in agony.

When I gave instructions, eighty legionaries obeyed my words. Instantly! I was the ablest centurion in Legion XXI. But then came that fateful day—the injury to my leg. And here in the province of Asia Minor, I should have had success. It has only been one failure after another. I should not have been hurt that morning by my enemy. The downfall started when I was stabbed by that scout!

He walked to the edge of the cliff, examining the narrow ledge on the side of the hill where he and his three friends had made their hideout after the recent robbery. Turning around, he eyed four bundles of merchandise taken from the camel train. A broad smile spread across his face. *We will rebuild our little army, and 'The Faithful' will rise again.*

He threw small twigs on some coals and stoked the tiny flames, preparing for his three friends. Smoke curled up toward the overhanging rock that formed the roof of the cave, winding its way out into the open and up through green pine branches. Here, on the steep hill overlooking the vineyards and fertile southern Cogamis Valley fields, he felt safe.

An hour passed before Craga heard his friends. Taba arrived first, a tall man with a long neck and thin arms. Coming to the top of the steep climb and sweating profusely from the exertion, he lowered a large skin bag of wine.

Harpa, the next to arrive, brought a basket of dried figs, also stolen from a shop in the nearby city of Castolius.

Maza, who carried meat draped over his shoulders, had killed a stray sheep and then dressed it. It brought him an instant sense of euphoria and well-being.

They relaxed together at the sound of meat cooking and fat dripping into the coals. Flames consumed the sizzling drops, and the men congratulated themselves for success in their afternoon raids. All four knew their discussions this evening might well decide their future.

With the meal over, Craga rose. Limping, he walked to the back of the cave and rested his sore leg on one of the bundles taken from the camel train. A shiver of excitement passed down his back. This was his moment to renew the motivation that brought them together.

"My friends," he said, "we *will* rebuild our army. 'The Faithful' will rise again. Look at our success!" His hand repeatedly bounced on one of the four bundles, and he laughed. Stealing that merchandise had been so easy. "If only more faithful ones had been added to our ranks, we could have made off with the whole caravan!" Craga could boast and exaggerate with ease, among other abilities, two skills developed during childhood in Bedriacum in Northern Italia.

Taba looked doubtful. He prided himself on handling a sword, but three hours earlier, he had barely escaped being discovered as he took the wineskin from the back of a merchant's store. His lips were drawn tight, and his breathing was irregular, something not experienced before. In the army, he had brought many barbarians into submission. Soldiers in Legion XXI talked about him with awe, repeating the story of his fight against four tribesmen who sprang from behind a wide tree trunk. He had escaped with only a few cuts. However, here, farther south than he had ever been, his sigh was that of an ordinary, lonely, fearful thief.

"Two months ago," he accused, "we were in the process of delivering one hundred slaves to Adramyttium.[14] What went wrong? Why are we down to four members from an equivalent of a whole platoon with auxiliaries?"

"The time has come to restart our rebellion," Craga said, avoiding Taba's question. "We have learned from our recent setback in Prosperity Village. Such an opportunity only comes once in a lifetime!"

"What opportunity?" asked Taba, "We arrived in Prosperity Village with twenty auxiliaries, but where are they now? Captured!" He spat on the ground in disgust.

[14] Adramyttium faced the Aegean Sea. It is known today as Edremit. This city is mentioned in Acts 27:2. Mines in the mountains close to the port supplied industries in Asia Minor.

"I agree, but let me open my heart to you, my three loyal tribunes. We lost twenty auxiliaries in that village, yes, and learned that our other twenty had also been arrested. I assure you that a defeat like that comes only once. But 'The Faithful' will prevail."

Maza, the smallest of the four, was the toughest when it came to wrestling or hand-to-hand combat. He was also wavering, wondering if a life spent taking from others was going to lead to his arrest. He shuddered, thinking of what had happened to his six companions. Rome's justice was severe against convicted criminals. Especially deserters.

He complained, "Where are our tribunes: Arta, Tissa, Baga, Ota, Tira, and Spithra? All captured! A year ago, you and Mithrida convinced us that we could do anything we wanted, go anywhere we wanted. 'Soldiers' uniforms give us protection'—that's what you said. We anticipated the sale of many more slaves to the mines near Adramyttium!"

Craga cut him off. "A temporary setback, that's all."

Taba interrupted. "No, we have been beaten! Craga, how many times have you *almost* been arrested? When you recruited me into this gang, you promised to tell me how your leg was almost cut to bits. Start there, and tell us how we can be victorious against Rome."

Waiting for Craga to respond, Taba reminisced, watching sparks darting upward. He stared into the flames and tossed another log on the fire. He had trained eight robbers in Sardis, and they took treasures from the finest houses. Yet all had been arrested two years ago. He was the only one who had escaped during the dawn raid on the mountain close to the oak tree. Then, in Hypaepe, he had recruited another three men, and they were also captured.

This year, one hundred slaves were being taken to Adramyttium in four shipments, and this little group of four tribunes had been the only ones to escape the army's trap. Who had infiltrated their ranks? Could he still trust Maza and Harpa? He was considering a return to the Bosporan Kingdom, north of the Black Sea. There he would be beyond the reach of Rome. Yes, it was cold and dreary in that northern land, but he would be safe.

Craga looked around at the three faces illuminated by dancing flames. "Sit back! It's time to talk about 'The Faithful.' I'm going to remind us why we are here. It all started with my father, Claudius

Carshena Datis. He was a legionary assigned to Upper Germania in Legion XIV, Gemina, before I was born. During that time, his legion was utterly loyal to Nero, but after the emperor's suicide, as a year passed, there was too much infighting among the troops. Father served under Commander Vitellius, and his legion defeated a pretender to the empire. General Otho lost the First Battle of Bedriacum.

"After that, my father's troops were ordered home until Vitellius's claim to govern Rome was challenged by the legions Vespasian had stationed in the east. They formed a siege around Jerusalem. As the city was about to collapse, the generals proclaimed Commander Vespasian as Rome's new emperor.

"A battle to control Rome followed. That is when my father saw his commander suffer a crushing defeat. We called it the Second Battle of Bedriacum. Father was wounded and died three years later. He was angry that Vespasian became emperor and not Vitellius. I hated the way Vitellius was executed.

"I will not forgive Emperor Vespasian and his family, his son Emperor Titus and now Emperor Domitian. That anger never leaves me; it courses through my veins. My father gave me his name and political opinions. I was convinced that the empire would be better served with Nero. Back then, I did not believe that Nero had committed suicide. Instead, I sided with people who claimed that he was preparing to return to Rome at the head of a rival army. Now, twenty-six years later, I know that Nero did commit suicide. It wasn't someone looking like him who was buried, as some say.

"Fighting barbarian tribes—and there were a lot of them—Legion XXI joined with another legion. We overcame barbarians. But Emperor Domitian wasn't satisfied with merely extending his reach over barbarians in Upper Germania. He wanted a more significant victory. He would take control of Dacia. That meant defeating King Decebalus.[15]

"My tribune back then, who is now our leader, Mithrida, learned that the two legions were going to be separated. Our troops were to

---

[15] During the Roman Empire, Dacia was equivalent to Romania and Moldova, with portions of Bulgaria, Hungary, Poland, Slovakia, and Ukraine. Several wars were fought against King Decebalus, starting in AD 85. The final victory over and death of Decebalus came after two prolonged campaigns under Emperor Trajan in AD 101–102 and 105–106.

be relocated. As *'primus pilus,'* I was the first centurion to be informed. We bent our heads close together, planning how to oppose Domitian's decision. We kept it quiet because such talk was dangerous.

"Mithrida is Flavius Memucan Parshandatha; he was First Tribune. Like me, he is descended from an ancient Persian family. The second tribune was Sesba Bartacus Sheshbazzar. He also has Persian blood running through his veins. They called me over to their table in the officers' tent after learning that I, too, had an affinity with Persia and explained the emperor's decisions. We three objected to Rome's plans, and we wanted to prevent the two legions from being separated. Now I see that those conversations laid the foundation of our uprising. We left the army, becoming deserters, and formed 'The Faithful.'

"We had just finished building a bridge across the Neckar River, and we heard of plans by barbarians to burn it. That was eight years ago. It was late at night, and we had been drinking in the tribune's tent. Unknown to us, a scout entered, or perhaps we simply did not notice him giving a report to one of the other officers. The legionary heard us talking. We were making plans to keep the legions together. Of course, it was forbidden to have a political discussion. A couple weeks later, he lodged a complaint with our general. He said, 'Two tribunes and one centurion are acting with political motivations.' Under the *Law of Offenses against the Empire,* that would have meant demotion or even execution. So we had to get that scout out of the way."

Taba interrupted, as he often did when listening to others. "Clear this up for me, Craga. Was the scout you tried to kill back then the same soldier who shouted up to us when we were on the top of the cliff behind Prosperity Village? Was he the one who left you limping until today? A month ago he said something about your wounded leg. How could he know your real name, Claudius Carshena Datis, and your rebel name, Craga?"

Craga nodded. "Yes, that scout is Anthony Suros. He was well known in Legion XXI, the Predators. Twice he saved our troops from falling into traps set by Germanic tribesmen. But when he reported us to the general, we had to get him out of the way. I had one of my legionaries make a false report, claiming that a barbarian was seen under the eastern end of the bridge. Along with Suros and eight others, I crossed the river where 'the enemy' was supposedly sighted. I was the last one under the bridge, and in the dim light, I prepared to strike Suros. At the last second, he turned around. I struck his face, but as he fell, his sword ripped my leg open. Afterward, while giving a report to my tribune, I said that the barbarian had escaped. The men in the squad took us back. We were both bleeding badly.[16] I heard later that Soros didn't wake up for several weeks. A report said he didn't remember anything that happened. Since then..."

He pointed to his left leg.

"Later the legions were separated, and we faced King Decebalus. Enemy troops crossed the Danube River one night and raided our camp. It had frozen over. My cohort was on duty that night. Who would believe that enemies could cross a river in the dead of winter? A Dacian army regiment killed many in our camp, and we would have been held responsible. After that, Flavius, Claudius, and I escaped by 'borrowing' one of the navy's ships. About a dozen of us abandoned the army, an act punishable by death. From the mouth of the Danube River, we went to the north along the Black Sea coast. We arrived at the northern extreme of Rome's influence at the capital of the Bosporan Kingdom."[17]

Maza asked, "Is that when you started capturing young men and women to sell as slaves? We know why you recruited us to help get them to the slave market."

Craga nodded. "The idea of entering the slave trade happened unexpectedly. Flavius and Claudius took a young woman. She was a cripple, deformed feet I think it was. They sold her as a slave. They

---

[16] This event and others in Craga's speech are recorded in earlier volumes of this series of novels.

[17] The Bosporan Kingdom, with which Mithrida and Craga are associated, was an ancient state on the northeast portion of the Black Sea. It was located on the Crimean Peninsula and the Taman Peninsula in southern Russia. It was a client state of Rome and served as a buffer between the Roman Empire and Central Asia's lands. In AD 64, Nero sought unsuccessfully to gain control over the Bosporan Kingdom. He wanted to bring it under the Province of Moesia (approximately today's Croatia, Serbia, Bosnia and Herzegovina, Kosovo, Macedonia, and portions of Bulgaria).

didn't get as much as they wanted but saw the potential in illegal slave activity. Soon afterward, we got our own transport ship."

The evening was not chilly, but Craga stood by the fire, warming his hands. "At the same time, many in Rome were still expecting Nero to return. Many *wanted* him back. So that's how our army, 'The Faithful,' came into being. We were faithfully preparing the way for the return of our former emperor. Obviously Nero would need a small army to support him to return. Nero is not alive—he did commit suicide—but it took me years to accept that. My friends, our little army will rise again!"

He saw them lean forward as he gradually regained their trust. "What an endless supply of fine young men and women in Scythia! All those people with fair hair and blue eyes. They don't speak Greek, so it's easy to control them! Poor things, their eyes brimming with tears as they dig in their heels, refusing to be put up for sale in the slave market. Now we've found an easier way to lure them here. We simply say, 'Attention! Sign up for four years of service in Asia Minor, and then you can return to your homes. You will know both Greek and Latin. It will make you a valuable person in your town. You'll earn lots of money!'

"Of course, they don't know our real intentions! After being taken away like this, they have no way to return home! They don't know they are going to be sold as slaves."

Maza had never heard how the first decision was made to use nicknames obtained from the ancient Persian satraps who ruled Asia from Sardis. "Who first thought of returning to our Persian roots?"

"That was our leader's idea. We needed false names, something shared, known only among ourselves. He chose 'Mithrida,' Sesba became 'Sexta,' and I liked 'Craga.'"

Again, Maza spoke. "How did you arrive at your names?"

"Our leader's name, 'Mithrida,' is a combination of three names: that of an ancient king of Bithynia and Pontus; the name of our god, Mithras; and the name of his ancestor. We call him 'General,' and he works in the lands north of the Black Sea.

"My name comes from Cragus, the highest mountain in Pamphylia, far to the south. It is held to be a sacred place, the home of Zeus. My Persian ancestor, Datis, was a nobleman five hundred years ago. He destroyed the enormous fleet of Greek ships when the invasion went up against Athens. So I'm 'Craga.' I am responsible for selling our illegal slaves and wild animals to the south. I'm in charge of our fleet, like Datis, my hero."

Taba stood up suddenly to object. "We don't have a fleet! It's only one old, battered ship! It almost sunk when it slammed against a rocky shore in a storm. It stinks because it has been carrying slaves. And we don't have an army! How many of us have been captured? By my count, forty-five out of a total of ninety! Most 'disappeared' after the Prosperity Village disaster. We need to recruit more, so why are we hiding at the edge of a quiet valley known for vineyards?"

Harpa's comrades often made fun of him for speaking slowly. Now he stumbled while describing his adventure. "I was almost discovered when I was stealing the fruit we enjoyed with our meal. I was pressed against a wall at the back of that store after escaping the building. I heard the owners talking. Listen! Families are desperate. There are no jobs anywhere. Income is down. To meet Domitian's orders, half of the vineyards were destroyed to plant grain late last year. It will be over four months before there is any work during the harvest. Let's talk to discontented farmers. Why not recruit them to our side and have them become part of 'The Faithful'? This is a good place to be to restore our strength. We don't always have to just be trading in slaves."

Craga scratched his head, concealing his thoughts. *Only three recruits left! Taba, Maza, and Harpa helped me escape from Prosperity Village. Harpa and Maza agree with me. No problem there. But I must convince Taba. He sometimes sounds like he's ready to quit...or just get mixed up in highway robberies.*

He stood up, resting his foot on a flat black stone. Their illegal slave trade from farms in Scythia, north of the Black Sea, had been disrupted. Craga would not be in good standing with Mithrida when they talked again unless this group showed some success.

"I think Harpa has the right solution. This is our moment for action. Let's convince people throughout Cogamis Valley that Domitian seeks his own well-being, not theirs. The mood of the people out of work in the valley is 'We must survive by hook or by crook.'" He laughed at his description of the tense atmosphere and added, "The public is in a mood to rebel. But remember, we must keep the slave trade as our main purpose."

Craga finished by saying, "That wealthy merchant who 'shared' his goods with us last week is only one of many that travel through the Door. Soldiers from Philadelphia will, of course, try to prevent raids on the highway. Just let them try! With our talents, we will open and close it at will!" They laughed together, and Craga believed that he had won their approval.

"Next week, I will go to Smyrna, then to Chalcedon by boat, and then north to where Mithrida is staying. I'll get further instructions. You three, stay here and recruit some valley farmers for our local army. I intend to return here in April, and you will find me in this cave. It's well hidden."

Three of the ten tribunes he had recruited for the Faithful were still alive. These three were the best of them, the most capable, imaginative, and daring. They would recruit desperate farmers and peasants and begin to regroup. Having narrowly escaped the soldiers sent to Prosperity Village, they shared a common purpose. All four were ready to continue activities that brought wealth to them at the expense of others.

He concluded, "Remember, never use our real names. We'll use our assigned names of Persian satraps, the Zoroastrians who governed here long ago. If anyone uses a different name, trying to impersonate one of our 'army,' we'll be able to spot the deception."

THE TOWN OF SASORTA, THE PROVINCE OF ASIA MINOR

On Thursday morning, Rastus arose early to start the fires in the bakery ovens. He worked with two helpers. One was a poorly paid freedman, and the other was a slave. Following the riot, Philadelphia's mayor, Aurelius Manilius Hermippus, had released rations of wheat and barley to the bakeries under strict supervision. Still, the amount of bread that Rastus could bake each day was insufficient to meet the demand.

Midmorning, after the rush of customers, Rastus climbed the stairs to his apartment. Selene was waiting for him, and she had asked Thelma to join them. They had let Thelma stay with them for two nights, but they needed to tell her when she would have to leave.

Selene asked, "Thelma, what do you plan to do? As you can see, we have little room here, and I'm expecting my baby in three months. Did you make friends with anyone before your husband died?"

Thelma looked around the apartment. She could not impose on the only people who had been kind to her. "I don't know what to do!" she sobbed, rubbing tears from her eyes. "Where can I go?"

"Return to Silandus, to your family, and ask them..."

Thelma shuddered and put her elbows on her knees. "I can't! I just won't!" She could not face telling these friends about her past.

"Well, where are you going to live? Who will feed you? You can work a few hours here each morning kneading dough, but how can you live on such a small wage? If the city cuts back any more on the grain rations, we won't be able to do that! Even working men don't have food for their children now that so many vineyards have been cut down."

The young widow's voice was hardly more than a whisper. "I can't return! You don't understand what happened there."

Anguish was spread across her face. *No one knows what I went through at the hands of my uncle. Hera, please take away the memories! How can I go on living?*

Her friends guessed that something dark, perhaps even sinister, lay beneath the expression on Thelma's face. The happy, joyful, extrovert Selene had met at the bakery several weeks before, didn't want to go home.

"No, I despise those men! My father died after an accident during a building construction. I have only a few memories of him. Only a few months later, my mother died too. I was eight, and she had another baby. She was in labor so long, and soon after, both died, my sister and my mother. I was brought up by my uncle."

"Your uncle took you in?" Selene looked at Rastus, and both rolled their eyes. Abuse in such a situation was too familiar.

"Yes, but I don't want to talk about it." Thelma shuddered.

Her hand held her throat, and then she started to cry. "I was an orphan in the home of a cruel man. I ran away from there and got married. My husband was," she paused and sniffled, "a runaway slave from Hierapolis."

Selene hugged her. "A runaway? Weren't you afraid that he would be caught? Don't you know what happens to runaway slaves?"

"I didn't have a choice. I met my husband at the marketplace while buying vegetables. Both of us wanted to get away from Silandus. He was so cheerful and whimsical. He said, 'We'll work in Sasorta, earn some money and go away. Let's start a new life!"

Selene spoke to Thelma, patiently yet firmly. "It's terrible how he died, and now you're a widow. But I'm going to have a baby, and we don't have room for an extra mouth."

"May I stay for a few weeks?" Thelma asked hopefully. She prayed to her goddess. *Demeter, goddess of women who mourn, I can't imagine going back to Silandus. Help me!*

"Maybe ten weeks? I'll sleep in the bakery. I won't be a burden, I promise. And I'll work hard."

Selene and Rastus talked about the request during the day, and in the late afternoon, they gave her an answer. Rastus said, "All right, but after ten weeks, you'll have to go."

Rastus could not imagine what his young wife, Selene, would do if he had been the one crushed by that horse. He looked out the open narrow window and longed for a breeze. Any movement of air, no matter how slight, was welcome during this season of the year.

He calculated, "Ten weeks. I'm a lucky man because I wasn't a vineyard worker. We have food, so you can keep working in the bakery, but afterward, you will need to find somewhere else to live."

Chapter 5
Friday

THE CITY COUNCIL, PERGAMUM

As the week ended in Pergamum, a large city many miles to the west of Philadelphia, Marcos Pompeius, chief counsel to the Pergamum city council, left his meeting with the highest city officials. He had urgent business at home, and the sun was low in the western sky.

A shimmering red reflection from the Aegean Sea colored the sky. He walked down the acropolis, stepping carefully. Once past the steep steps, Marcos crossed the lower portion of the city and then walked up a low hill to his home. He and his wife enjoyed a rooftop view that looked down on the Roman Forum at the city center.

"I'm home!" he called to Marcella, his wife. Their dog came scampering to meet him, its tail wagging joyfully. He paused, playing with its ear and stroking the dog's chin.

"How was the meeting of the council?" Marcella asked.

"Tiring, as usual. The city fathers cannot decide how to get those cheating merchants in the Forum to pay their full share of taxes," he replied. "But I must finish writing a letter to Miriam before we get ready for this evening's House of Prayer meeting."

He reread the communication from Miriam, a sealed letter that had arrived the previous day. She had written it before leaving Thyatira.

May 30, in the 13th year of Domitian
From: Miriam Bat Johanan, in Thyatira
To: Marcos Aelius Pompeius, in Pergamum

I should have written more often. Anthony was recently reassigned to Philadelphia due to the social unrest and bandits on the roadways. We leave for there tomorrow by wagon. Uncle Jonathan will dispatch this letter to you tomorrow. You can send letters to me through my uncle, Amos Ben Shelah, in Philadelphia.

Kindly send my next disbursement of Eliab Ben Shelah's estate to the Bank of Philadelphia at the beginning of November. Thank you for handling our affairs in Pergamum since we left.

He picked up a pen to write a response.

June 5, in the 13th year of Domitian[18]
From: Marcos Aelius Pompeius, in Pergamum
To: Miriam Bat Johanan, in Philadelphia

If you are well, then I am well. I greet you with the Name above all others.

The next payment from your grandfather's estate will be available at the beginning of November. I will send your portion of the inheritance to the Bank of Philadelphia as you requested.

Pergamum's city council needs additional taxes for many new construction projects that have grown since you left. First, for the Great Red Temple, which will be dedicated to many gods, not only Egypt's. Also, Egyptian priests are demanding an expansion of their bridge over the Selinos River. They want it to be broader, thus enlarging the entire Red Temple area. Second, the council requires repairs for roads into and out of the city. And lastly, urgent structural changes must be made to the acropolis. A new Imperial Temple, which some hope for, will require additional revenue.[19]

I have information about your family's legal case, now known as "Conflict of the Wills." One lawyer always opposes me. This young man tried to again press for the expropriation

[18] The date of the letter from Marcos is June 5, AD 93.

[19] The ancient Red Temple is in the broad valley at the center of Pergamum. Today the city is known as Bergama and is located about two hours north of Izmir (ancient Smyrna). Now, two thousand later, the bridge over the Selinos River is still in excellent condition. The Red Temple is in ruins and undergoing a process of restoration.

of Antipas's property. He argues that Pergamum should acquire the entire Ben Shelah estate, consisting of thirty-eight houses, several workshops, and two stores. Fortunately, Manes Tmolus soundly denounced the lawyer, noting that the argument against expropriation had been decided by the courts and accepted two years ago. There was an overlap between your great-grandfather's will and that of your grandfather, Antipas. The conflict was resolved at the Senatorial Courts in Ephesus. Thankfully, there will be no further attempts at the expropriation of the Ben Shelah estate.

Marcella and I feel your loss of your grandfather. We, too, lost relatives, in a terrible earthquake.[20] *We know what grief is, and we hold you, Anthony, Grace, and the Ben Shelah family in our hearts.*

THE SYNAGOGUE OF PHILADELPHIA

Friday afternoon, the Amos Ben Shelah household prepared to leave for the synagogue for worship with friends.

Miriam hummed a tune. During the previous year in Thyatira, many painful experiences had left her feeling empty, and she wanted to meet other families here.[21]

Wagons from Amos's farm carried farm products to the city. Merchants purchased milk, cheese, eggs, and seasonal crops from Amos. They had now become business friends. Coming back, the wagons sometimes brought building materials to the farm.

The best wagons, the cleanest ones, provided the family's smoothest ride over the rough farm road to and from the city.

The sun had dipped halfway down from the noontime peak, and cool breezes brought some relief from the heat. Miriam looked around, gazing at mountain ridges that stretched far to the north. To the east, she saw the broad valley. It was beginning to be swallowed up in the shadow cast by the mountain.

---

[20] Marcos lost four brothers, their wives, and all their children in a massive earthquake in Nicomedia. This story is told in *Through the Fire: A Chronicle of Pergamum.* Nicomedia is known as Izmit, a large city in Turkey near Istanbul.

[21] Miriam's experiences in Thyatira are told in *Purple Honors: A Chronicle of Thyatira.*

An involuntary sigh accompanied her thoughts. *Such a wonderful time of the year! The sky above is a yellow-blue tinge. Tiny patches of white snow are still at the top of the mountain, but they will soon be gone. And the Cogamis Valley, to the east, is peaceful and quiet. This would be an excellent place to settle down, to raise our family. Grace will be the first of many children. I can live here with Uncle Amos and Aunt Abigail while Anthony does his job.*

Miriam joined the family in the large wagon. Amos and Abigail sat on one side with Obed and Isabel. Obed made sure that his mother felt comfortable. Ruth, aged nineteen, sat next to Jesse, her husband, who was a year older. He placed his hand on her stomach, and she leaned her head on his shoulder. Ruth smiled, for she would soon be a mother.

"Be careful," said Isabel to her daughter, sitting opposite her. "I'm concerned about your precious little baby. Only three more months. Are you sure you can stand these jolts and bumps? Everyone will understand it if you decide to stay home."

Sarah, the seventeen-year-old, beamed, sitting beside her older sister. "I'm so happy for you, expecting your firstborn! For my marriage, a year from now, I want a gorgeous day, just like today!"

Watching the family members talk together, Miriam felt her heart soar. She wondered how long it would take to become familiar with each one's dreams and struggles.

The guards at Mountain Gate knew the Ben Shelah family well and waved them through. After all, no Jew had ever been involved in a riot. Jews were model citizens occupying the northwest portion of the city around their place of worship.

They went a short distance along the Avenue of Temples. Turning right, they stopped in front of their destination, the synagogue. It served both as a place of study and worship. Frequently, family events were also held in the portico at the sanctuary entrance. They had arrived early and talked with friends before entering.

Oil lamps lit the dim interior. Almost fifty families had gathered to commemorate the arrival of another Sabbath. Men sat on the right and the women on the left in the well-constructed building. Its high roof with vents provided good air circulation in the hot weather.

"Every household in the congregation is here for worship," whispered Abigail to Miriam, signaling her to sit down.

Zacharias, the beloved elder, turned his face upward as he began the service. Leading in worship meant more to him than anything else. His profitable gold jewelry business, for which he was blessed with exceptional eyesight, supported him financially. All week long, he carefully fixed precious gems onto intricate gold rings.

His hand smoothed his long, white, bushy beard. A white and blue linen prayer cloth with elaborate embroidery covered his head. His eyes were half-closed, and a rich, deep voice rolled effortlessly up from deep down in his chest.

Zacharias lifted his voice and his heart through prayers. At age fifty, the father of five sons and grandfather to four girls and three boys was known for godly desires. His eager heart passionately desired to obey every one of Adonai's instructions.

The service began with "Hear, O Israel, the Lord our God is One. Love the Lord your God with all your heart and with all your soul and with all your strength."[22]

Ancient psalms were intoned, the earliest prayers, which spoke powerfully to Jewish men and women. The cantor called out the well-known and loved words: "Blessed are you, O Lord our God and God of our fathers, the God of Abraham, the God of Isaac and the God of Jacob, the great, mighty and revered God, the Most High God who bestows loving kindnesses."

The congregation knew the prayer by heart, and everyone followed Zacharias as he opened his spirit to the Almighty.

"O Lord, I call to you. Come quickly to me. Hear my voice when I call out to you. May my prayer be set before you like incense; may the lifting up of my hands be like the evening sacrifice. Set a guard over my mouth, O Lord; keep watch over the door of my lips. Let not my heart be drawn to what is evil, to take part in wicked deeds with men who are evildoers; let me not eat of their delicacies. Keep me from the snares they have laid for me, from the traps set by evildoers. Let the wicked fall into their own nets, while I pass by in safety."[23]

---

[22] Deuteronomy 6:4–5
[23] Psalm 141:1–3, 9-10

He stepped down from the low platform, and a reader took his place. "We will sanctify your name in this world just as it is sanctified in the highest heavens, as it is written by your prophet: And they call out to one another and say…"

The congregation responded, "… 'Holy, holy, holy is the Lord of hosts; the whole earth is full of his glory.'"

The reader continued, "Those facing them praise God…"

Again, the congregation joined in: "…saying, 'Blessed be the Presence of the Lord in his place.'"

The reader said, "In your Holy Word it is written, saying…"

The congregation added, "…the Lord reigns forever, your God, O Zion, throughout all generations. Hallelujah."

Amos looked longingly at his wife and remembered their days in Egypt. *My dear Abigail, after the birth of each of our children, you threw a great party. How we loved our home in the Jewish sector in Alexandria! You even wanted the dockworkers at my father's business to join in our festivities! And we served enough food to feed an army, but now you hardly eat a thing. Your sweet face, your gorgeous smile, drew me to you. Oh, you are so thin and drawn! It's so difficult for me to say, "Hallelujah," when I see you like this.*

The reader's final section was a joyful declaration: "Throughout all generations, we will declare your greatness, and to all eternity we will proclaim your holiness. Your praise, our God, shall never depart from our mouth, for you are a great and holy God and King. Blessed are you, O Lord, the holy God. You are holy, and your name is holy, and your holy ones praise you daily. Blessed are you, O Lord, the holy God."

All gathered for the service loved the way Zacharias led worship. His recitations of the psalmist's prayers brought people into the divine presence. It was so easy to concentrate on the things of God when the short man with the thick neck and chubby face sighed with a deep longing for the Temple of Jerusalem. How he longed for ancient traditions to continue!

At the end of the service, Zacharias began interceding, praying for the ill, and asking for wisdom. However, this evening, his final words were different from his usual benediction.

"During the present difficulties, O Lord of the universe, remember Rabbi Haim, our leader who is in Antioch. Guide him and others. Thanks be to you, O Sovereign Lord, for the arrival of news from our dear leader, Rabbi Haim." He had planned the prayer at the end of the service to let them know that he had unusual news.

With the service over, the men mobbed Zacharias. Typically they would gather in small groups for conversation. But this evening, they formed a tight circle.

"What news have you heard? When is Haim returning? Our rabbi went away almost two years ago!" The speaker was dressed in garb typical of Syria, showing him to be from Damascus.

"Does Haim say anything about the weakening of our faith by false teachers?" asked Michael Ben Akkub, another elder.

"No, the letter is short, unlike his previous ones." His rich, deep bass voice vibrated with excitement as Zacharias answered the questions. "He says here, 'The Council of Rabbis will pronounce a deliberation on spurious groups. I ask for your prayers. We will decide before May.'

"This letter was written on April 2 and came by ship, taking two months, so we may hear his advice about foreigners worshiping in our midst. Another letter should be here at the end of July or by mid-August."

A third elder, Daniel Ben Helkai, wanted more detailed information. His strong hands and arms skillfully shaped wooden planks into furniture. He had earned a reputation as an industrious, talented carpenter who paid attention to the tiniest details. Daniel was descended from a long line of scribes and was waiting impatiently for Haim's decisions.

Daniel and his wife, Dorcas, never missed a worship service. They disregarded the inconvenience of the heat in the summer and cold evenings in the winter. The main joy of his life was to join with others for worship. Although only thirty-nine, his long beard was specked with white streaks, fitting for a man expecting his first grandson. This evening he was pleased to see Jesse, his son, talking with Ruth. He closed his eyes, thinking ahead. A year from now, he anticipated a second marriage. It would join his younger son, Mith, to Amos Ben Shelah's daughter Sarah.

Standing at the entrance, Daniel watched young people gathered in a circle. He reckoned he was fortunate to have the Ben Shelah family as his in-laws. The carpenter admired their large home and wanted a home like that, one large enough for Jesse and Ruth to live with him one day. Daniel promised himself to build such a house. Secretly, he was jealous of Amos's library, and this evening he had once again prayed for forgiveness for his secret sin, the envy only he knew about. He wanted to return to his studies, to keep the Ezra and Nehemiah tradition alive, following the scribes' strict rules and those of his forefathers.

Daniel hurried over to talk with Zacharias. "Did Rabbi Haim mention which scrolls they are accepting? Have any books been pronounced 'unholy,' as not true scriptures?"

Zacharias said, "No, no news about that."

Then, in a surprise move, Zacharias drew Daniel and Michael close. With both hands resting on the friends' shoulders, the three men huddled close together. He whispered, "Listen! About Amos and Abigail... Their niece Miriam has arrived, and I heard that she married a legionary! Servants tell me that Anthony, her husband, came into their home for a visit."

Daniel turned around, staring at Amos and Abigail. His knees had gone weak as a horrifying realization hit him. His son, Jesse, was married to Ruth, and Mith was betrothed to Sarah. Amos's sons lived in a home where Amos had recently welcomed a Roman soldier!

Chapter 6
Friends

THE SYNAGOGUE OF PHILADELPHIA

On the other side of the congregation, Dorcas was watching her husband talk with Zacharias. Dorcas was Daniel's wife and a midwife, one of the few Jews known to visit the homes of non-Jews. She did not refuse to assist when expectant mothers called for her. Much to Daniel's displeasure, she helped pagan women by delivering their babies.

Recently Daniel had argued with Dorcas. "This is serious talk! I do not want you attending to those women. It has to stop."

Dorcas had greeted his words with a burst of gentle laughter, and Daniel's face had turned a darker shade of red. He had never been able to respond to her mirth because she had left him without a comeback.

Ruth and Sarah came to talk with Dorcas, their mother-in-law. Ruth began, "Uncle Antipas's granddaughter, Miriam, came, and you'll never believe this. Her husband is a legionary! He will patrol the Southern Road to protect merchants from thieves. He was at our house early this morning but left before I could meet him. I'm so happy that Miriam is here. She seems to be a kind person! And guess what. Miriam has a little girl; her name is Grace. She's two and a half years old. She's not here, because tonight she stayed at the Ben Shelah home with the servants."

With a dark look covering her face, Dorcas said, "How are you feeling, my child? Ruth, your time will soon be here. Our first grandchild!" Dorcas held her arms together like a woman carrying an infant close to her chest.

Suddenly the meaning of Ruth's words hit her. *My son, Jesse, is in a home where a Roman soldier came to visit? Sparks will be flying over this when we get home!*

Martha, Michael's wife, joined this small circle. She had married Michael after he arrived in Philadelphia. Martha was strict in her beliefs but not in the same disagreeable way Michael was known for. When Martha was not supervising their servants, she visited her friends' homes or invited them to her house. She had just turned sixty.

Her great-grandfather, a scripture copyist, had been brought up in an Essene home near Jerusalem. During the Roman siege, he had avoided capture by fleeing across the rugged desert of Judea one night. Then he found safety by sailing from Joppa to Attalia on the Mediterranean shore. He and others left scrolls bound up and carefully sealed in clay jars, hidden in the Judean desert caves. "If the Romans conquer Judea, they will not find those scrolls," he declared. "We even covered up the entrances!"

Martha's grandfather had lived in Rome for a short time until Tiberius Caesar demanded that all Jews leave the capital. He had moved to the province of Asia Minor and later married. Martha was born and brought up in Philadelphia.

Martha's mother was the daughter of a Jewish family from Tarsus who was open to the varieties of Jewish beliefs and showed kindness toward poor families. She died of a stroke when Martha was fifteen. Her daughter was determined to live with the same generosity toward others that she learned from her mother.

People commented on Martha's love for prayer and discipline from her father's side of the family. Generosity came from her mother's side. She brought both qualities, generosity and discipline, to her marriage long before Michael was elevated to an elder's position. However, now that he was in leadership, tensions had sprung up between them.

Martha was still emotionally close to Michael, who took a very conservative approach to worship through observing the commandments. She had told him, "Michael, in my home, I want things to be the way my mother taught me."

Her husband, two years older than her, stroked his long beard and shook his head. "Someday," he growled, "you will learn that I am right. On that day, you will *want* to obey me."

Michael longed to return to his youth. His most cherished memories were of days when he looked down on Antioch from a high mountain ledge. On days of meditation above the city, watching the Orontes River flow out to the Mediterranean Sea, he had sat on a rocky crag, memorizing the Torah, the psalms, and long passages of the historical books. Michael loved the outdoors.

On those days, he contemplated the great enemy of the Jews, Antiochus Epiphanes IV.[24] Instinctively, he knew how superior any godly leader was compared to that powerful, terrible dictator.

Martha, the older woman, and Dorcas, twenty-two years her junior, supported many Jewish congregation programs. No one imagined doing anything without their approval or at least before getting their opinion. Both women were soon going to hear disparaging remarks about Amos Ben Shelah for allowing a soldier to come into his house.

Before leaving for home, Martha drew near to Miriam, close enough to whisper, "Hello, I'm Martha. Did I hear that your husband is a legionary?"

She wanted confirmation of this new information.

"Yes, he is away on a special assignment. He arrived recently to help at the garrison."

Outwardly, Miriam's face glowed with a broad smile, but her smile was calculated, no longer spontaneous. A picture came to her mind of vineyards. She pictured vines with leaves bursting on spreading branches. Grapes would quickly mature. She blinked for a second, saw other small groups still talking in the portico, and knew that gossip would spread quicker than tiny tendrils sprouting on green vines. Everyone would know all about her within a short time.

Miriam watched Martha's eyes, knowing other people were already talking about her. She did her best to be pleasant. "I'm happy to be here, Martha. I've always heard about Philadelphia, the city of brotherly love, and I want to enjoy every day Adonai lets me stay."

Her fears were well founded. Within a few hours, the gossip began circulating. Such talk traveled fast. "Did you hear the latest about Miriam? She is Amos and Abigail's niece! A young mother, she came from Thyatira two days ago. Remember Antipas Ben Shelah,

---

[24] Antiochus Epiphanes IV, victorious in many battles in Syria and Judea, offered a sacrifice of pigs' blood on the Temple's altar in Jerusalem in 167 BC. The Maccabees, a Jewish family, resisted Greek influences and revolted because of this and other atrocities. They won many military victories and renewed Jewish faith and practices.

the merchant killed for being a follower of Yeshua from Nazareth? Well, get this.... Antipas's granddaughter, Miriam, married a Roman! A legionary! Oh, such stains on the reputation of Amos and his family!"

AMOS AND ABIGAIL'S HOME

The family returned to the Ben Shelah home. The sun had set, and the sky radiated a faint purple glow. As soon as they arrived home, Isabel lit the two Shabbat candles and placed them on the table. The meal was served in the *triclinium*, the room where they reclined for meals. Although the house was built by a Greek man, it was modeled on the Roman style of dining.

The walls were covered with marble. Large slabs of pastel colors went from the bottom to the height of a person's waist. Above the colored marble, the pictures painted on the wall depicted the outdoors. Painted scenes of animals and sheep with shepherds gave the room a calm, tranquil atmosphere.

The previous family had designed the house with this large room occupying most of the main floor. At mealtime, eighteen people could gather. During meals, servants placed food on a small table. Each of the three couches around the table was made from a wooden frame with leather straps crisscrossing the bottom, giving a solid base. One could support three adults. Stuffed cushions spread over the leather straps and bronze adornments at the ends hinted at a Greek influence. Each person leaned on their left arm when reclining, eating with the fingers of their right hand.

The windows opened onto the splendid valley beyond, which was now starting to darken. "I never tire of that view of the valley," commented Abigail, lowering herself slowly onto the center couch beside her husband. A breeze blew through the open window. "It soothes my nerves on a Friday evening."

Underneath her talk of feeling calm, deeper waters flowed. *Oh, how I wish I could flee the troubles of my life!*

Amos and Abigail were celebrating a memorable day. Fifty-three years had passed since their betrothal. In commemoration of that unforgettable day, Abigail had called for a specific meal. "Butterfly Leg of Lamb" was the dish that had been served in Alexandria when Abigail was twenty. That day, Amos had marked his seventeenth birthday.

After the meal, Amos and his son, Obed, went to the library to discuss the ancient texts read at the service tonight. Jesse, Ruth's husband, joined them. Three generations of men were gathered around the Torah.

Miriam realized that her unexpected arrival had brought apprehension to Abigail's home. Listening to Abigail, Isabel, Ruth, and Sarah, she noted how they formed a tight family group. "I'm going to bed," said Miriam quietly as she excused herself from the table. "I woke up early this morning." She felt as if she were trespassing in her uncle's home. These were her relatives, but already problems were arising.

She went upstairs to put Grace to bed, and the women remained at the table. Abigail heaved a soft sigh, happy that her family was soon to add a fourth generation. She breathed out slowly. She welcomed the comfort of being home, but she needed to talk about events at the synagogue.

"I felt uneasy there," Abigail said. "Did anyone else sense the tension in the air? Martha and Dorcas were not happy to learn about Anthony."

Ruth and Sarah, the two sisters, had talked about it in low voices as the wagon brought them home. Ruth shifted her unaccustomed weight, taking her left hand from under her head. She turned onto her back. The change of position was welcome.

"This baby is getting heavy. I'm going to be uncomfortable this summer. I won't be able to work outside in July and August for any amount of money. Too hot!"

Then she sat up and flashed a sparkling smile, laughing. "Listen, everyone, I have an announcement! I'll take all my meals on the terrace, under the shade of the vines and overlooking the valley. Thank you!"

The others laughed too. They talked about babies and families. Another woman in the congregation was also expecting a baby, and they talked about that family.

Ruth continued, "I know my mother-in-law well. I could see the surprise on Dorcas's face when learning that Miriam is married to a legionary. And Martha is upset too. Don't you think so, Mother? You know your mother the best."

Isabel had the same shape as her mother and was relatively short and plump. She remembered a day when she was about twenty. Someone on the street thought they were twins. That day Isabel knew she had inherited the profile of her mother, Martha, for life.

Coming back to the conversation, Isabel answered, "I don't know what her response will be toward Miriam and her husband."

THE MILITARY GARRISON IN PHILADELPHIA

During his previous assignment, Anthony's team members had included Omerod and Bellinus. They had come to Philadelphia the previous Saturday and were assigned to riot control by Commander Felicior. Early Friday morning, the two of them were sent across the valley to Castolius. A demonstration there led to a call for reinforcements.

Omerod had slightly darker skin than Bellinus and Anthony. One of Omerod's ancestors, the first in his family to become a legionary, was born in Carthage, the capital city of Africa Proconsularis.[25] Later, another ancestor, also a legionary, settled in Damascus. Omerod was born in the capital city of Syria. He chose a career in the army, keeping up the masculine tradition of five generations. His piercing gaze came from self-imposed discipline. His stern face, straight posture, and firm grip intimidated citizens, freedmen, and slaves when he had to confront them. Penetrating questions always brought out the truth during interrogations.

The other soldier was Bellinus. Whereas Omerod's outgoing personality led to endless stories, Bellinus was quieter. Two years before, a large section of the rock face of the Sardis Acropolis had broken off. When the debris destroyed several houses near the Temple of Artemis, Bellinus distinguished himself by working endless hours rescuing people. Despite high winds and slashing rain, he had worked tirelessly, saving entire households.

Anthony described Bellinus, saying, "This soldier says little, but he is essential to catching the thugs. He reminds me of an anchor keeping a ship safe in a harbor during a storm. His face never changes expression, and he doesn't depend on emotions to see a task through to the end. I can't do without him."

---

[25] Ancient Carthage today is known as Tunis, the capital city of Tunisia.

Anthony was waiting for them at the inn when the two soldiers arrived at sunset from Castolius. They dismounted quickly, their horses breathing heavily after a strenuous ride across the valley. Saliva dripped from the horses' mouths after galloping the last stretch.

Omerod pounded Anthony on the back. "In Prosperity Village, we captured almost all the bandits. Unfortunately, four of our vultures flew away!"

"And before that, Bellinus and Omerod, we captured other rebels in Port Daskyleion!" Anthony commented approvingly. "No matter how many criminals we capture, there always will be another creature crawling out to replace them."

"Of course!" Bellinus said. "Rebels up there on the Postal Road and now down here on the Southern Road. It's all the same thing! The same base motives. The same miserable characters!"

Bellinus quiet sense of humor often lightened stressful situations, but he had no sympathy for wrongdoers. "Now it's time for a bath and a hot meal! Then we can get to bed early to be rested for our trip to Hierapolis tomorrow," he remarked, leaving his horse with a servant.

THE CITY OF PHILADELPHIA

On Saturday morning, as Anthony, Omerod, and Bellinus were preparing to leave the inn, Miriam arrived in her uncle's wagon. The driver, a farm servant who worked for Amos, waited while she talked with Anthony.

Two camel trains were assembling to leave. Each animal was tied by a cord to the camel in front of it. Throaty noises, swishing tails, and wiggling necks let the caravan driver know the camels were getting comfortable with the way baggage settled on their backs. All around the inn, merchants were moving heavy bags, preparing to depart.

The first was a caravan of ten animals led by two merchants. It exited through the Valley Gate, heading north. Tonight they would arrive in Sardis. Three days later, their merchandise would be on ships sailing from Smyrna to Athens. In Corinth, they had buyers waiting for them.

The second caravan was headed south toward Attalia, a seaport. It would arrive there in a few days after having passed over the mountains.

Miriam passed a quick eye over Anthony's detachment with their uniforms and short swords. Sometimes she felt jealous of the time that the army demanded of her husband. "Thank you for letting me say goodbye! I came as early as I could," she said breathlessly, standing on her toes to kiss his face.

She whispered so that the others wouldn't hear. "Listen, it's not just the Ben Shelah family who are shocked about our marriage. Last night the folk at the synagogue learned that I married a Roman soldier. There has already been a lot of gossiping. How long will you be away?"

Anthony whispered, "I hope that the gossip will die down. It eventually did when we were in Sardis, remember? I'll miss you while I'm away, maybe a few days or a week. When we return, we may get caught up in another disturbance. Felicior and the authorities must do something to calm the rioters. We can't keep pushing hungry men back, simply telling them, 'Here's a little of the emergency grain; now get back to your farms!' The grain supplies may not last all summer, and long-term jobs will still be needed for the winter. We need better answers. I did get to talk with Felicior about Ateas and Arpoxa. He will send the wagon to Thyatira next Tuesday."

Bellinus watched Miriam speaking with Anthony, and he called out, "Don't worry about your husband coming back too soon! Trying to corner the thieves that we are looking for could take years. Only after we solve the problems on the farms will all of this be over!" Miriam smiled at his attempt at humor, but she really didn't find it funny.

As the three soldiers left, Miriam frowned. She watched them ride through the Valley Gate, join another group of mounted soldiers, turn right, and then disappear along the Southern Road on their way to Hierapolis.

Miriam crossed her arms tightly, and the edges of her mouth hung down. *A year ago, I was riding on a vegetable cart, going alone with Grace to live in Thyatira. This morning I wanted to bring Grace to say goodbye to you, my dear husband, but she's restless and feverish. Oh, Anthony! She's growing up without you, and here you are, off on another assignment. I jump for joy seeing the expressions on Grace's face when you take her in your arms and lift her above your head. Could you not be with us every day?*

A scene came back. Miriam was riding on the back of a vegetable wagon to Thyatira, and that memory made her shudder. Anthony had been away with these men for almost a year after being given his previous assignment.

As she got up onto the wagon to return to Amos and Abigail's home, she looked around. A man was watching her. He stood in the shadows, just inside the Inn of the Open Door. The man was dressed in the green apron used by Amos's servants at the inn. She saw his eyes were fixed on her, and then he turned away. She looked again, but he was gone. The hair on the back of her neck stood up on end.

Cleon! How did he get here from Sardis? Two years before, Cleon worked for Uncle Simon in Sardis as the Ben Shelah shop's salesman. He was behind the botched attempt to kidnap my daughter. I'm sure of it.

The early Saturday farewell to Anthony, which she hoped would be agreeable and without incident, left her heart racing. Anthony had no set time to come back, and he should know that Cleon was working at the inn.

As the wagon moved back through the city, headed for Uncle Amos's home, Miriam looked around, studying the results of the destruction caused by the earthquake many years before. Many buildings toward the lower side of the city, once the pride of previous generations, still lay in ruins. Once supporting the hot baths roof, several tall white marble columns lay spread out haphazardly over the ground. Their jagged edges hinted at former glory. Columns symbolized power and grandeur, but there was little indication of Philadelphia's former splendor in this corner of the city.

Miriam was soon passing through the Mountain Gate, and looking at the farmhouse set on a small hill. As she drew closer, she found herself in a cold, nervous sweat. Security and safety were uppermost in her mind.

That single glance! Cleon faded into the background after seeing me, and now I'm concerned for Grace as well as my husband.

As Miriam came through the farm's outside gate, she paid more attention to details. She studied the courtyard to see how a person might sneak into her uncle's property. That was what Diotrephes had done in Sardis two years ago when he came to kidnap Grace. Thankfully, that evening he had been caught in the act.

She examined the area outside the front door. The courtyard's open driveway was covered with an interlocking pattern of polished, yellow-brown stone slabs. They lay in lines with small stones, some black and some a rich dark brown, separating the slabs.

A thick vine in the courtyard led up past the bedrooms on the second floor to the terrace above. There, vines spread out on thin ropes covering the roof. The vines provided welcome shade from the hot summer sun. No one could get up to the top unless they came over the wall.

The thick outside gate was made of wood. Miriam noticed that the entrance gate was flush with the high wall surrounding the house. The gate was secured at night with a heavy wooden bar to keep out transients. She patted one of the guard dogs. These were probably the family's most effective deterrent.

The house had been built by a Greek family before the earthquake. Twenty years ago, Amos had restored it when he and Abigail came to Philadelphia. The farmhouse had been rebuilt using money from the Ben Shelah merchant business from Alexandria. The large building with stone walls was built into the hillside, and this provided a spacious basement. The family lived on two floors. Bedrooms located on the upper floor were bright, with windows overlooking the valley.

The basement section was reserved for the servants. Some of the basement rooms were also cool enough to be used for food storage.

Miriam found the family already gathering at the table for breakfast. The morning summer heat announced its intentions with a warm breeze.

The day would be hot by midafternoon. She went upstairs and brought Grace to the table, rocking her in her arms. Miriam passed a hand over Grace's forehead, rocked the feverish child, and waited until the meal was over before speaking.

"Uncle Amos and Aunt Abigail, may I speak with you?"

"Of course! Come into the library."

The library was neat and organized. Amos took meticulous care with his precious documents, each one stored in lattice compartments set out slightly from the wall. These were like the ones she had seen in Uncle Simon's house in Sardis and Uncle

Jonathan's house in Thyatira. This type of storage space permitted air to pass along the walls. It helped prevent mildew and humidity from destroying expensive, hand-copied scrolls.

Most documents were scrolls of papyrus; others were the expensive new "codices" made using parchment with pages attached by a thread binding at the spine. One wall of the library was filled with old financial records from Amos's shop.

More recent documents were piled together: the land title of the inn, taxation documents, and notes made during its reconstruction while repairing the damage left by the Great Earthquake.

Other documents filled the space along a second wall. These related to business dealings with Amos's brothers in cities across the province.

A copy of the Greek Septuagint and other scrolls in Hebrew filled the third and shortest wall.

They moved into the library, shut the door, and sat down. "What is on your mind?" said Amos, smiling. He and Abigail sat on two chairs placed in front of a table. Several documents were rolled up. He would not look at them on the Sabbath.

"Uncle Amos, I just came from saying goodbye to Anthony."

"What is it, my child?"

"I saw a man named Cleon at the inn. Is he a good employee?"

A note of incredulity crept into Amos's voice. "You've been here only five days. Are you going to comment on how I run my business? Yes, my brother Simon alerted me to a problem. Simon claimed Cleon caused trouble in Sardis, but nothing was proven, and I value the man. He works well. I put him in charge of hospitality, and he is one of my best assets.

"Every day men come to the inn after walking or riding great distances. The sun is hot. Travelers feel sweaty, smelly, and hungry on arrival. He shows them where to get a bath and food. Their animals are supplied with feed and water. They laugh at Cleon's funny stories, and everyone leaves in a good mood the next day. They come back to the inn the next time they are in Philadelphia."

"How and when did you take him on as a manager?"

"I hired him last year. I needed to turn the business around. The previous owner did not take good care of the place, but now things are clean. We have a good reputation. Perhaps you didn't know this, Miriam, but merchants traveling to the Aegean Sea have two ways to go. One is along the Meander Valley to Miletus, south of these mountains. If they set sail with their merchandise from Miletus or Ephesus, they will miss Philadelphia altogether.

"Or they can take this slightly longer run. It runs through the Cogamis Valley and on to Sardis along Hermus River Valley. It's two days longer for travel, but the food and accommodations are better. If they go to Miletus, the last part of the journey is more complicated since loads must be placed on small boats to reach the other side of the river. In Miletus, the merchandise is unloaded at the port and then put on seagoing vessels. This adds almost two days to the journey, maybe more if the weather turns cold or rainy.

"So I want people to choose this route. It means more customers for my inn, and it is happening in large part because of Cleon. He remembers everyone's name, and he adds a sense of genuine friendship and companionship. That was missing before. Now, tell me why you are concerned."

Miriam hugged her daughter tenderly before saying, "Cleon worked as a salesman for Uncle Simon in the Ben Shelah shop. Yes, he pulls in customers, especially the wealthier sort. You know what he sold in your brother's shop: gold rings, perfumes, olive soaps, clothing, and bronze objects. When it comes to his abilities as a salesman, yes, Cleon is outstanding, but he was caught stealing from the store. He was also a spy for an evil man, Diotrephes."[26]

Amos looked at Abigail, his brow wrinkling and accentuating the furrows of his seventy years. This was an unwelcome conversation.

Miriam ran a hand across Grace's fevered brow. "I bring all of that up because of our daughter, Grace. She became ours through adoption. Adoption papers were signed by the mayor of Pergamum in the home of our family lawyer, Marcos."[27]

Abigail straightened up, now much more interested.

"As I mentioned before, I do not know who the child's mother is, but she gave the baby a lovely Greek name, Chrysa, which means Golden.

"We added the name Grace, and she has been safe with us. At least we thought she was safe with us until about a year ago. Uncle

---

[26] Diotrephes's first attempt to kidnap Grace is recounted in *Never Enough Gold: A Chronicle of Sardis.*

[27] Grace's birth and adoption story is found in *Through the Fire: A Chronicle of Pergamum.*

Simon gave a party at his home for some of the city's poor people. A widow, Lyris, and a widower were married. When the music was loudest, Diotrephes broke into the house to kidnap Grace. That man is a teacher at the Gymnasium of Sardis."

Amos interrupted. "Did a man called Diotrephes come to kidnap Grace? Did he have a connection with Cleon? Was it ever proven that either Cleon or Diotrephes intended to kidnap the child?"

Abigail responded the same way. "Are you sure that Cleon helped the kidnapper? Accusations need two witnesses, my dear."

"No, we never proved that Diotrephes actually came to kidnap our daughter. Why? Because of his high social standing!

"But I am certain that Cleon helped Diotrephes sneak into the wedding banquet. He gave Diotrephes a wedding garment, but it was not finished. It was missing from Uncle Simon's shop. The finishing embroidery had not been completed. For months, our friend Arpoxa embellished the collars of ninety-nine garments by showing two eagles flying together. When Diotrephes came to the wedding banquet wearing that one hundredth wedding garment without the embroidery, he was spotted. It had been stolen."

Amos stiffened, not happy to hear this about his best employee. "Maybe it was just a simple mix-up. Surely there is a logical reason for what happened."

"Uncle Amos, I'm convinced Cleon was behind the kidnapping attempt. Thank God for Ravid, my cousin's husband. He saw Diotrephes go into the house and take a candle from room to room. He followed him upstairs and witnessed the kidnapping as it was about to take place. I believe the Diotrephes Milon and his family, an ancient Lydian family, want Grace taken away from us. I don't know why."

Abigail spoke sharply in a tone Miriam had not heard before. "Miriam, Grace is a Greek. You are married to a Roman! To us, your husband is considered an enemy. Remember this: Roman soldiers caused us—you and me—untold grief! That we know. Now, are you really convinced that Diotrephes took your daughter in his arms? If I follow your story, all that activity happened at night, when things were dark. Did Ravid have a reason not to like Diotrephes?"

The reaction from her aunt and uncle surprised Miriam. She had expected sympathetic support or at least concern, not displeasure, but Abigail continued, "I cannot accept your accusation! Cleon is a fine worker. Our son, Obed, enjoys him. It was Cleon, more than any other employee, who turned the inn around. We are making money, not much but enough. Remember, he entertains merchants, keeps people laughing, and gets even more stories from guests as they pass through."

Miriam hung her head. "All right, Aunt Abigail, I won't say anything more against Cleon. Do you mind, though, if Chrysa Grace stays in this house whenever I am in Philadelphia? I don't want Cleon to see Grace for any reason."

"Now, that's a wonderful change in your attitude, my dear niece!" said Abigail, her thin face lighting up with a smile. "I love children, and Grace is a beautiful child. It has been so long since I sang, and when I am with her, I feel like singing. A few minutes ago, I even forgot for a moment that she is a non-Jew. You and Grace are both welcome in this house."

Miriam noted the abrupt way that Abigail's mood quickly changed. Amos and Abigail clearly did not want Anthony around. Well, at least she and Grace had found a home. God was good to them today. Because Grace was ill, she had not taken her to say goodbye to Anthony. And Cleon had not seen her baby. But he did spot Miriam.

She groaned. *Uncle Amos and Aunt Abigail do not believe me when I say that man is deceitful!*

Abigail watched her niece walk up the stairs, and then she turned to her husband. "Amos, a dark shadow has passed over our home! Miriam married an enemy! How did Antipas permit it? Nothing in our tradition lets her be joined to a Roman."

Her voice rose several pitches, a telltale sign that let him know distant memories were clouding her thinking.

"I don't want Anthony in our home. Oh, just the thought!"

"I'm sure we can handle this, Abigail," he said, putting his hand on her thin arm. "We'll ask Anthony to stay away from our house. Miriam will not speak about Cleon again. I don't want her talking against my employees. Our relations with outsiders are necessary only because we carry on business with them."

Abigail's heart started to beat wildly. "Amos, what are we going to do? That dreadful soldier is going to come again!"

So many thoughts spun through her mind. *Anthony has a breastplate, just like the ones in Jerusalem when Simon's army knocked on our door.*[28] *And Azetas, my son, tried so bravely to keep Simon's soldiers away from our food supply. And now a helmet, a Roman helmet, has been in my house! God, protect me!*

And Ater, my other son...slaughtered outside the wall.

O God! Why me? Nobody cares. Amos brought us to Antioch and then to Pergamum...and from our house in Philadelphia to this farm. He had a shop, and then he sold it, he bought the inn, and now soldiers are in it. They will not go away. They never do.

Here, at last, on this farm, is isolation. And stillness. Avoiding those contacts, I gain control over my temper.

But now Miriam shows up with a Roman, a legionary, on her arm! I thought I was finally over those memories. No, I'm not. The nightmare is coming back. Her husband is a soldier who will stay at the inn—and not just one...many of them.

"Are you all right, Abigail? What are you thinking?" Amos watched his wife, who had broken off the conversation. Her eyes were fixed on the floor. "Shall I get you anything to eat or drink?"

Amos knew the signs that signaled the arrival of another attack. When anxious and vulnerable, she resorted to this high-pitched voice. If she had too much contact with people when she felt this way, she became silent, spending hours rocking back and forth.

Even after twenty-three years, Abigail still felt the desolation of the events in Jerusalem—the siege, the death of each of her six children, and those sleepless nights. Anthony's presence in her home brought all the memories back.

"My dear," she said slowly, "Miriam and Grace can sleep here, but Anthony—no!"

---

[28] While the Roman Army was besieging Jerusalem, a civil war was taking place inside. One faction was led by Simon Ben Giora, the other by John of Gischala. Each general commanded thousands of Jewish soldiers.

Chapter 7
Flavius Zeuxis

THE POSTAL ROAD FROM PHILADELPHIA TO HIERAPOLIS

After leaving Miriam at the inn, Anthony's team met with other mounted soldiers gathered in front of the Valley Gate. Decimus was assigning units to critical locations along the Southern Road. Anthony, Omerod, and Bellinus joined them, but they would continue riding on to Hierapolis.

Uniforms and weapons stirred respect and submission in peasants and merchants alike. Short swords hung from the waist. Protecting the torso was a breastplate, adjusted to the contours of each soldier's body. Metal helmets gleamed in the morning sun as they passed by. Their horses were fit, well fed, and carefully groomed.

Felicior had requested reinforcements from other garrisons. He was concerned because of the out-of-work farmers and the shortage of food in the cities. Additional troops were coming from other towns: Tripolis, Nysa, Antiochia, Mastura, and Aphrodisias.[29] With their arrival, space had run out at the garrison. Amos offered to have them stay at the Inn of the Open Door, using it as a temporary barracks.

The horses ran at a canter until they reached the area called "The Door" on the Southern Road, near the first relay station. The uphill slope called for fresh horses. On their way again, their horses slowed

---

[29] A large garrison in Tripolis, a city on the south end of the Southern Road, guarded the boundary between Asia Minor and Phrygia. Archaeological studies discovered a vibrant marketplace dated to the first century. Ruins indicate that Tripolis was an important city. Nysa, Mastura, and Antiochia, smaller places in Asia Minor, were located on the Menderes River's northern side. Aphrodisias in Phrygia was a center known for sculpture, devotion to Greek gods, entertainment, and sports.

to a walk at the steep part of the hill. Anthony rode beside the centurion and asked, "Decimus, where were you at the end of May?"

"On the day of the robbery, we were supposed to be watching this section of the Southern Road. That's when riots broke out. Commander Felicior sent us to protect the emergency food supplies in three cities: Castolius, Sasorta, and Clanodda. It was the first time in months that we didn't have soldiers guarding the Door. Why did the attack on the caravan take place that day? Just dumb luck for the robbers. Look just ahead. This part of the road up to the mountain pass is called the Door. Rocks rise above the road on the west side. On the east side, the cliff slopes down toward the Cogamis Valley."

They arrived at a switchback. It was here that the thieves had made off with Flavius Zeuxis's merchandise. Anthony asked, "What are the details of what happened here?"

Decimus pointed to the first curve in the road. "Men pretending to be auxiliaries appeared there. They halted the caravan, which was coming down the hill. They yelled to the camel drivers, 'Stop! Wait here! Robbers were spotted ahead. Our soldiers want to make sure the road is safe.'"

The question in Anthony's voice reflected his bewilderment. "At that moment, your men were protecting food supplies in the valley, so the Door was unprotected. Is that a coincidence? Who were they, the auxiliaries who stopped the caravan?"

Decimus shook his head. He had no answers now; he had already asked those questions. He motioned with his hand, and they continued riding toward the Door.

A little farther up, around the second curve, they stopped, and Decimus said, "Here is where Flavius's merchandise was stolen. His caravan was composed of thirty-five camels; only the last two were robbed. Four bundles were taken. I was surprised that they didn't take more. This is as far as I'm going. I will return to Philadelphia now. Remember, swim in that hot water pool in Hierapolis! I enjoyed doing that a couple of years ago."

Omerod and Bellinus dismounted and climbed a steep rise at the side of the road. There was nothing to be investigated except the low-lying scrub brush. Soldiers had inspected the slight cliff and found nothing suspicious. "We'll have to come back to explore," Omerod said. "We know about the trick of having someone 'official' stop a caravan to make for an easier robbery. That is how one of the robberies took place last year south of Prusa. Our team looked into that theft then."

The horses leaned forward, their necks straining at each step as they plodded along the steep incline. Omerod rode beside Bellinus, and they followed Anthony as they made a few comments to one another.

"Bellinus," Omerod said, "you could become rich, earning more than you do as a soldier. Look! Hide in that clump of trees and then jump on my unsuspecting camels! Or emerge from that forest over there and take all my merchandise. Do that a couple of times, and you can retire from being a soldier! I've counted half a dozen places where those human snakes could slither out without being seen until the last moment."

"Yes, I could rob caravans and be rich for a while, but I would probably waste the money. All good for me until you catch up to me. Then execution! No thanks. The life of a highway robber is not for me!" responded Bellinus, smiling.

Anthony looked back over the Cogamis Valley, seeing it from above its southernmost point. As he took a deep breath, he marveled at its beauty. *It is a quiet and peaceful valley, yet menace lurks where people least expect it.*

They stopped for a midday meal at the next relay station, which was a few miles beyond the top of the long incline. As they ate, the station auxiliaries brought fresh horses from the grazing fields. After the meal, they mounted their horses. The sun was directly above them, and their mounts stepped on their own shadows.

With no breeze to cool them, sweat dripped down their faces, necks, backs, and chests as the road leveled out along a broad plateau ideal for raising horses and donkeys. Acres of land had been cleared from the pine forest, and shepherds waved to the soldiers as they trotted by. Flocks of sheep and herds of cattle dotted the broad plateau as well.

After another relay station, they headed down a long slope. Arriving at Tripolis, a city overlooking the Lycus Valley, the sun disappeared behind distant mountains. They checked in at the large garrison and prepared to rest for the night. Omerod said, "This gang acts like predators hiding in these forests. We came through quickly on horses, so we were safe, but caravans move slowly. Maybe several gangs are hiding around here!"

Bellinus countered, "Omerod! Don't make things harder! Trying to flush out one gang of beasts in those forests will be quite enough!"

Anthony sat on the edge of his cot, deep in thought. "Something has been troubling me about the robbery since we left that place in the road. If the caravan had thirty-five camels and only the last two were robbed, why didn't Flavius complete his trip to Rome? Why abandon the whole endeavor over a relatively small loss? Something does not make sense."

The ride to Hierapolis through the upper reaches of the Meander Valley took them through several small villages. By early afternoon on Sunday, the white cliffs of Hierapolis seemed to be hung suspended above a stone curtain of minerals deposited by the water. Countless people were drawn to Hierapolis to experience the healing qualities of the salts in its thermal waters.[30]

The northern entrance to Hierapolis would take them through a cemetery. It was an easier way to enter, but few people used that entrance. The fear of the spirits of the dead was widespread. Entering through the Southern Gate, the city opened before them. On the high hill to their right, with its imposing presence, Hierapolis Theater drew twelve thousand people each evening to dramas and singers, comedies, dancers, and jugglers. Just below the theater were the most significant temples, those of Apollo and Zeus.

The city was predominately made up of insulae. Three-story buildings occupied each city block, and each block was home to four buildings. The whole place was carefully laid out in a grid pattern. Each street was wide enough for two oxcarts to pass carrying furniture or supplies for repairing buildings or for new construction. Ceramic pipes brought clean water from springs higher up the mountain. Under the streets, sewers channeled dirty water out of the city and down to the fields below.

After they entered the garrison, Anthony dismounted, twisting his torso several times; he needed to stretch his muscles after the long ride. He greeted the garrison commander. "We were sent by

---

[30] Hierapolis's travertine basins, warm pools of water, on the white cliffs are known in Turkish as Pamukkale, which means "The Cotton Castle." Water gushes from a spring at the rate of 60 gallons a second (228 liters a second). The evaporation leaves a deposit of calcium carbonate. Many other minerals are also suspended in the water.

Commander Felicior in Philadelphia. He sent us to talk with Titus Flavius Zeuxis."

"You're in luck! You'll get to rest for the remainder of today," responded the commander. "Flavius is in Laodicea, across the valley, but he's coming back tomorrow. Why not bathe in the hot pool? Afterward, please be my guests for dinner. I want to hear how the new commander of the Philadelphia Garrison is handling the problems there. We'll take in a play and entertainment in the theater this evening."

The healing waters of Hierapolis drew people from as far away as Italia to the west and Syria to the east. They traveled for weeks to bathe in the outdoor pool. It was large enough for hundreds of people. Anthony, Omerod, and Bellinus splashed and floated on their backs in the hot mineral water, their minds now free of dangerous roads and hungry peasants.

They splashed water on each other and laughed, and Omerod plunged deep into the water. Hot water spurted from a narrow crack about fifteen feet below the surface. Blistering hot water hit him in the face, and then he pushed himself toward the top, his lungs bursting as he reached the surface.

"That spring has a powerful flow! The water is scorching hot!" he yelled. "And you won't find me tempting that gate to Hades again!"

Tall trees lined the pool. Flowering oleander bushes added to the charm. The clear spring water reflected it all: pink, red, and white petals; the blue sky; and tall, stately green trees.

Anthony walked around the large enclosure, turning his attention to the shallow end of the pool. Friends brought loved ones in need of healing, and he watched four carrying a man on a stretcher. Blind people stood waist-deep in the pool, splashing water on their eyes. Lame men crawled down some steps. One had been wounded at a building site, and others were lame from birth.

Bellinus swallowed the water, but it made him sick. He stopped beside a small tree outside and vomited while Omerod bent over with laughter. "The manager told you not to drink this water! It makes your stomach churn!"

Good-natured ribbing like this was expected here.

The water overflow from the pool was channeled to the edge of the hillside, from where it flowed into scores of small basins. Each pond held clear water, but pure white deposits appeared after evaporation. This gave the appearance of walls resembling cotton balls around the edges.

The vast, fertile valley spread out beyond, and Anthony fell into a silent daydream. *How beautiful! I must bring Miriam here! When I have completed my years as a reservist, Miriam, Grace, and I will sit right here, at this pool, with our feet splashing in the warm water, and we will watch the sun go down, just like this.*

THE CITY OF HIERAPOLIS

Word had been left at Flavius Zeuxis's home that three soldiers from the Garrison of Philadelphia had come to talk about the robbery. The merchant was forty-five years old and had a good reputation in the region.[31]

The businessman's dark brown eyes took in everything at a single glance. His appearance mesmerized every audience. Flavius enjoyed entertaining people. His pent-up energy and vigor made his guests feel fortunate to be in his presence. Zeuxis was famous for wisdom offered freely and unendingly to everyone, whether they wanted it or not. He enjoyed telling stories, switching effortlessly from storms on the Aegean Sea to architecture in Corinth and lavish parties in Rome. After every trip to the empire's capital, he came back with immense profits.

There was a reason why Flavius never fully opened himself up to anyone. In his heart of hearts, he thought of himself as a merchant-conqueror. His Persian ancestors, led by King Darius and King Xerxes, had gained control over Greece, ruling there for a decade. His

---

[31] The tomb of Flavius Zeuxis is a funerary building. The well-preserved chapel is close to the Northern Triple Gate. It is surrounded by a bench. The burial place is made with a rectangular plan and has a gabled roof. The inscription states that Flavius went to Rome seventy-two times. There is a strong possibility that Flavius Zeuxis was a descendent of Satrap Zeuxis, the Persian satrap or governor. The decorative frieze of *metopes* or decorations on the outside of the chapel is evidence of wealth. A sarcophagus in the Hierapolis Museum carries the name "Maximilla." Possibly it was his daughter's. His tomb indicates a merchant of enormous wealth and influence. My story about Flavius Zeuxis is fictitious, including details of his age, house, business, and armband loss.

life and identity were anchored in that distant age six hundred years ago.

Before sleeping at night, he praised his gods, believing that he was more successful than his ancestors. He was milking his profits from Rome and making Hierapolis into a jewel of a city. This was his twenty-fifth year as a merchant. Returning from Rome, he would wink, adding, "After having to hand over bribes and taxes to the authorities, what can compare to the joys of being back at my home in Hierapolis?"

Flavius sent an invitation to the three soldiers to visit his house for breakfast. He met them as they arrived at the front entry, and a slave washed their feet.

Once inside the atrium, their host complained humorously, "I demanded a personal visit from the commander of the Garrison of Philadelphia, but look! He only sends me three scouts!"

He invited them in, putting his hands on their backs and pushing them. "Here, I want to show you my house."

Luxury overflowed from every corner. The mansion was perched above the smaller of Hierapolis's two theaters, providing a panoramic view of the city and the valley below. The view from his terrace was matchless. Tripolis lay to the northeast, and the larger city, Laodicea, was across the valley to the south. The smaller city, Colossae, was tucked into the lower flanks of a mountain range to the southeast. Below the property, a bubbling creek flowed from the high mountains to the east.

Red and purple panels hung from ceiling to floor beside each window. Two slaves sprinkled water on light cotton sheets hung in front of the windows. As evaporation took place, the room, which had a high ceiling, was cooled. Proud of his accomplishments and his ancestors too, he had commissioned painted panels on the walls to illustrate the family lineage. Large murals traced his Persian roots. Priceless objects around the house led to his bragging about achievements.

They arrived in the great room, where breakfast was ready. Flavius leaned back and put his hands high above his head. "I'm only a merchant. Oh, I've lost track of the number of times I've been to Rome! How many times?"

Of course he had not forgotten. It was his way of indicating to his chief slave that it was time to interrupt. The African man performed the same function whenever guests reclined at his table. "Your honor, I believe the number is forty-three trips," he said, bowing. "Master, it would have been your forty-fourth, except that you canceled your last voyage."

After the breakfast, they moved to Flavius's study, a corner room set on the upper floor. It was superbly furnished. Its centerpiece was a white marble tabletop resting on ornate legs made of dark brown wood. A wooden panel around the edge was inlaid with small squares of white ivory and dark myrtle wood. Chairs were made of the same dark wood, but people sat on seats of soft leather. Intricate patterns on the backs of chairs were cleverly woven to point out his favorite animals: horses running, eagles soaring, and lions attacking.

Sitting down, Anthony said, "It sounds as if you enjoy going back and forth to Rome."

"Oh yes, I started going to Rome in the fourth year of Vespasian and have been going there ever since," he began.

Anthony leaned forward, paying attention to the details. Dismounting from his horse an hour before and entering through Zeuxis's gate, he had no idea about how to form a working relationship with the famous businessman. He knew he would have to find a way to cut through the merchant's brash exterior. That shield was a thick hedge keeping outsiders away.

An idea came to him. *All this bragging and his emphasis on outward things may be hiding something fragile, precious, and personal. The fourth year of Vespasian...hmm, that's when my service began in Legion XXI, the Predators, twenty years ago.*

While sailing past Greece, Flavius chooses to travel along the most dangerous sea route, going south around Achaia and passing Cape Malia. He dares the elements. How many ships have floundered there because of sudden winds and crosscurrents?

Other merchants travel over land, going through Corinth. Does he see himself as a demi-god, defying the fiercest forces of nature? Flavius withholds his real identity by bragging and sounding self-important.

How is it that someone so fearless is stopped by someone stealing four bundles of merchandise from his camels?

As Flavius talked, Anthony tried to form a pattern from his thoughts, a plan that would put the puzzle pieces together.

Flavius craved recognition. Beyond wealth and an appreciation of his possessions, he longed for something more profound beyond the endless round of social events in Rome and Hierapolis. He was a mixture of Persian, Greek, and Roman qualities.

Anthony guessed that this desire for recognition led Flavius to challenge fierce odds, even daring the power of nature.

Flavius walked into the next room to talk with a servant about details involving a conflict between two slaves earlier in the morning. During the silence, Anthony whispered to Omerod and Bellinus, "Let me do the questioning. Don't, under any circumstance, ask him directly about the stolen merchandise!"

Their wide-open eyes showed that they thought he was crazy to suggest such an approach. Bellinus whispered, "We're going to be here for a month, not a day!"

"Could you slow down please?" Anthony asked when Flavius returned to the table. "Of course we are here concerning the robbery, but let's start at the beginning. When did you decide to go by ship around Cape Malia? Why not go through Corinth, over the land route? We have lots of time and want to hear the whole story. As soldiers, we want to know details, to know what makes you famous and what you think real wealth is. You know many things about wealth and importance that we don't."

Omerod and Bellinus stared at Anthony without blinking for several seconds. Slightly bulging eyes communicated unspoken disapproval.

Flavius had been walking, almost running, toward their goal as he first showed off his treasures, and they were now on the verge of learning about the robbery. But Anthony was slowing Flavius down to a crawl! They had not even talked about the robbery; instead, Anthony asked Flavius to tell yarns about his travels!

Flavius loved details, those found in tapestries as well as the complexities of winds and waves. He told about ships sailing from Smyrna and Miletus. He painted pictures of ports in the islands off the coast of Greece and marketplaces in Rome. As he talked, he puffed up like an empty water bag being filled to be carried on a camel. All his trips ended with glorious events in Rome. His were the most thrilling guests, the most exciting parties, and, of course, sales completed at enormous profits. He described golden birdcages, silver jugs, and lavish tapestries. A young woman walked into the library dressed in a stola made of fine yellow linen. He introduced her as Maximillia. "I'm so proud of my daughter. Maximillia, these are the legionaries sent to learn about the robbery. Soldiers, Maximillia is married to Donatus Aelianus, the older son of a fellow merchant."[32]

"Happy to meet you," she said. "Soldiers are supposed to protect Daddy as he travels, but you certainly failed in that task. Daddy doesn't permit failure in any form."

Maximillia found the scroll she was looking for. It was written by Polybius, one of the most famous early Roman historians. "Do your job better next time," she called over her shoulder as she swept out of the room. Something of her father's character came through in her words. Where her words were meant to hurt, her father's comments inspired admiration and wonder. The merchant made judgments without sounding condemning.

More details flowed out about Rome. Omerod's glance showed he was unhappy and wanted to make better headway toward their goal of learning about the robbery.

Following the midday meal, Flavius said, "Time for our baths!" He led them to another part of his house, the *caldarium,* where they stripped and sat naked in the steam on cedar benches along the walls. Above them were mosaics of wild animals in forests looking down on them.

When they could hardly breathe any longer because of the heat, they moved to the *tepidarium* with sweat pouring from every pore in their skin. They lay down on yellow marble tables. Strong African slaves massaged their backs, arms, legs, and feet. They had not seen these slaves before, even after counting a dozen in the previous five hours in Flavius's mansion.

"How many slaves work for you?" asked Bellinus. He grimaced as he asked the question. "Are they all as strong as this man?" The strong hands of this slave from far up the Nile River massaged every muscle.

"I need twenty slaves working in my house. Another thirty care for my horses, donkeys, and camels. A few care for the pets. Many

---

[32] The Museum of Hierapolis boasts a sarcophagus with the name Maximillia on it. It is an exquisitely carved stone coffin. Some assume that this was prepared for the daughter of Flavius Zeuxis. We know little beyond the name. Details in this novel about Maximillia are fictitious.

others work in the city, gathering goods and preparing my next caravan."

He listed the many areas of the city where people worked for him. "Everything except my decisions in business is all done by slaves. They help as servers, cooks, tasters, carvers, entertainers, tutors for other slaves, grammarians to teach new slaves proper Latin and Greek, carriers for the goods going to Rome, and keepers of animals. Others are oven stokers, washers of floors, and cleaners of toilets. My chief steward controls the release of funds and access to food supplies."

"And where do they all live?" asked Bellinus. He was willing to try a joke, so he commented, "Surely they can't all sleep in your house, even if you do occupy half the side of this mountain!"

THE CITY OF HIERAPOLIS IN THE PROVINCE OF PHRYGIA

1 City Hall
2 Garrison of Hierapolis
3 Pool of Healing Waters
4 Temples
5 Market, Gymnasium
6 Frontinus Avenue
7 Fountain
8 Public Latrine
9 Frontinus Triple Gate
10 Zeuxis Family Tomb
11 Northern Baths
12 Cemetery
13 Southern Agora-Market
14 Southern Gymnasium
15 Residential Blocks
16 Theater
17 City Walls
18 Large Sycamore Tree
19 Nicanora's House
20 Modesto's House
21 Flavius Zeuxis's House
22 Coppersmiths' Guild
23 Pools of Water
24 Homes of Poor People
25 Garbage – Refuse Heap

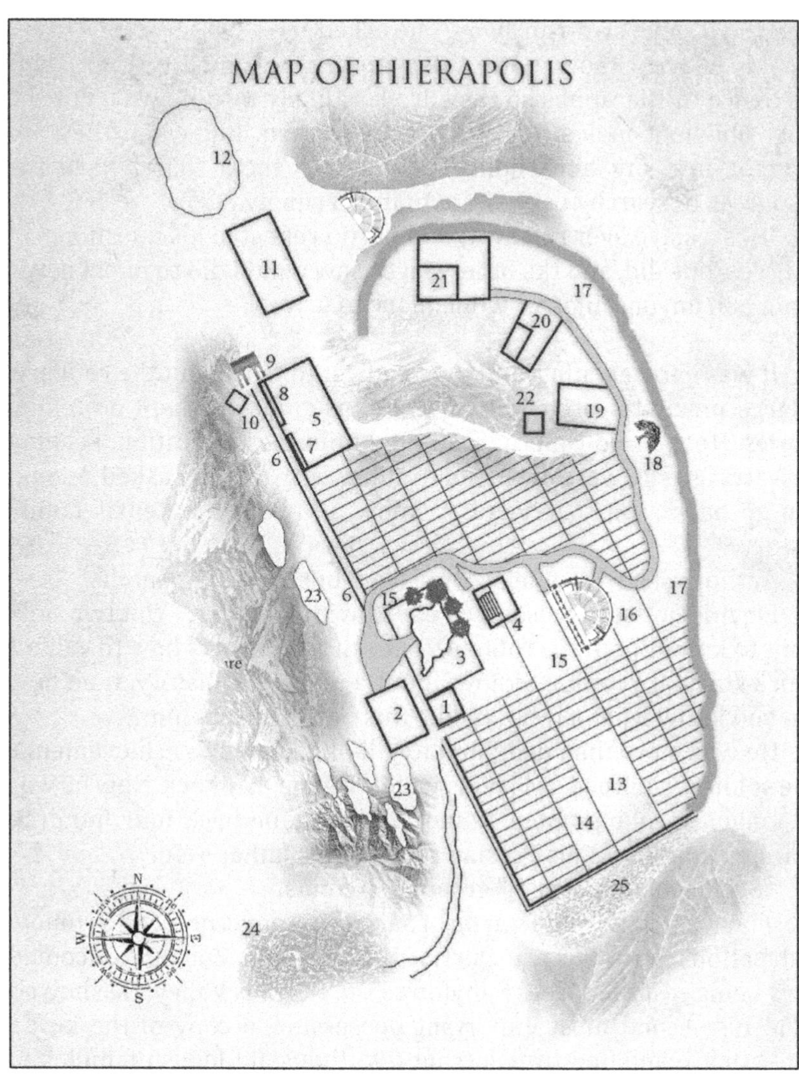

Flavius appreciated the humor, and he responded with a hearty laugh. "No, only twenty sleep in the house! My other sixty-five slaves stay in the insulae below my house. You looked down on them when we stood on the balcony."

Omerod thought back to his childhood when his father, one of the judges in Ephesus, lost a slave. That slave had sailed away on a ship, and when he was returned, he was whipped until he lost his life. "Did a slave ever run away?" he asked.

"My slaves know both sides of my personality. I fix their residence in Hierapolis so they are less likely to run away. For the most obedient males, I buy a young woman. But when they are brought into my household, I explain to them that I have the resources to search everywhere to find a runaway."

"Has a slave ever run away?" Omerod repeated his question.

"Yes, one did, and the other slaves saw what I did to him. I never again had anyone, man or woman, try to leave."

It was early evening, and they had yet to talk about the robbery. A large meal was prepared, and at sunset, Flavius kept on telling stories. He ignored Omerod's and Bellinius's exasperation. Leaning forward, as if he were even more interested, Anthony asked, "Could you go back a bit? We want to know all about the Zeuxis family history."

Anthony heard a squeak come from both his companions.

Flavius noticed it also and roared with laughter. "You two only want to know about the robbery, but Anthony knows how to value a man's story! If you don't know about a man's life history, then how can you know what a robbery like this one means to him?"

He was more than delighted to tell of his family's achievements. The soldiers slumped as Flavius went even further back. Now he was no longer speaking about Rome; he had gone back four hundred years, talking about his Persian roots on his father's side.

"Such a *long* time ago!" groaned Bellinus.

Flavius told how the *satrap* of Sardis, the governor, had to follow instructions from Susa in Persia. His ancestor, Zeuxis, welcomed Jews being resettled from Babylon to the Hermus Valley. He showed them his second most important possession, a copy of the king's letter that mandated transferring two thousand Jewish families to this region.[33]

---

[33] Persians dominated much of Asia Minor from 550–333 BC. Jews came from Persia perhaps as early as 520 BC. Under Antiochus III the Great, General Zeuxis, in 214 BC, relocated two thousand Jewish families to Asia Minor from Babylon as a new colony. The king's letter said: *Letter from King Antiochus to Zeuxis, his Father, sendeth Greeting: If you are in health, it is well. I also am in health. Have been informed that a sedition is arisen in Lydia and Phrygia, I*

Flavius's story rolled off his tongue. "My ancestor, the governor of Sardis, provided trees for lumber, and he gave the Jews food and whatever else they needed. From Sardis, they spread out to places like Philadelphia then to Hierapolis and Laodicea."

While the fruit was being served, Flavius explained how Alexander the Great's military campaign changed the Persians' fortunes.

"The Persians had taken over this area from the ancient Lydians, dominating for two hundred years. Under Alexander's amazing skill, Greek forces twice pushed back a superior Persian army. After his death, this region was fought over. At times it came under the Seleucids in Antioch, but ultimately it became part of the emerging power of Pergamum."

Flavius went to the latrine, and Anthony suffered a quiet rebellion as they were left alone. Omerod's face was red with impatience. "Ask him about the robbery! He's suffocating us with stories of his past! I don't want to hear one more comment about family connections or battles between Greeks and Persians. How can anyone brag so much about his ancestors?"

"You don't know how to deal with such a man," scowled Anthony. "When I was a scout in the black forests of Upper

---

thought that matter required great care; and upon advising with my friends what was fit to be done, it hath been thought proper to remove two thousand families of Jews, with their effects, out of Mesopotamia and Babylon, unto the castles and places that lie most convenient, for I am persuaded that they will be well disposed guardians of our possessions, because of their piety towards God, and because I know that my predecessors have borne witness to them in that they are faithful, and with alacrity do what they are desired to do. I will, therefore, though it be laborious work, that thou remove these Jews; under a promise, that they shall be permitted to use their own laws and when thou shalt give every one of their families a place for building their houses, and a portion of land for their husbandry and for the plantation of their vines; and thou shalt discharge them from paying taxes of the fruits of the earth for ten years; and let them have a proper quantity of wheat for the maintenance of their servants, until they receive bread-corn out of the earth; also let a sufficient share be given to such as minister to them in the necessaries of life, that by enjoying the effects of our humanity, they may show themselves the more willing and ready about our affairs. Take care likewise of that nation, as far as thou art able, that they may not have any disturbance given them by any one. King Antiochus's letter, quoted in Josephus's Antiquities: Book 12, Chap 3, Section 3, lines148–153.

Germania, I had to follow the terrain through forests and swamps. I had to learn the best way to sneak up on little villages. But this is a big city. It's a different world.

"What motivates Flavius? Why is he so confident that he prefers dangerous sea routes to an overland trip? Why doesn't he take the safe route across the Corinthian isthmus? He goes to Rome two or three times a year. Any person who wants safety wouldn't make the trip he takes even once! Think! What is his motive for so often staring danger in the face? When we learn that, we might find out..."

Their host returned, and Anthony asked Flavius about his business in Hierapolis.

"I wanted you to ask that!" he responded with the glee of a twelve-year-old. "Have you noticed how this city operates? In addition to beautiful buildings, we sponsor a school of sculpture and bring in people from all over. I give generously toward it. Young men vie to get into our school.

"What else do you witness here? Efficiency! The insulae are laid out in a grid in one hundred city blocks—each building with plenty of space around it. Every city block has ceramic pipes bringing clean water in and sewers taking dirty water out. We invest heavily in terracotta pipes. Insulae buildings fill each block. How many impoverished people are there in this city? Only a few, because we give them all work."

Bellinus recalled laid-off men shouting at the Valley Gate in Philadelphia. "Did you say that there are only a few people without work? What kind of employment do you give them?"

The great room was illuminated with several oil lamps now, and Anthony saw the gleam in his host's eyes. Bellinus had touched on a subject of pride to Flavius. The visitors looked at each other and almost sat up straight on the couches where they had been reclining.

"I have created a kind of competition. People here belong to any one of many different tribes. Heavy, soft black wool from the sheep is woven into cloaks. Rainwater doesn't penetrate these cloaks because the weaving is so tight. Excellent quality. I make tons of money selling them in Rome. Other tribes produce carpets. Some specialize in spreads to cover a bed, and others weave blankets.

"My biggest competitor is Modesto. You passed his house coming here. Nicanora, the widow of the previous mayor, owns the other mansion you passed by, and she is a pleasant lady but not a competitor of mine."

Omerod realized what Anthony had done by asking Flavius to talk about himself. Anthony wanted to understand the man's soul, hear his dreams, know his fears, and be aware of what gave the man his deepest joys.

Spying out a man's soul was more difficult than spotting enemies in a dense forest. Determining a wealthy man's inner motivations called for careful stalking, silently pursuing and waiting for the right clues.

Omerod asked, "What do you mean by competition between the tribes?"

As Flavius spoke in a quieter voice, the lines in his face softened; he was proud of his contribution to the city's welfare. "Tribes compete against each other. They are something like the guilds in Thyatira, but each is not so specialized as a guild is. Each ten-section block in the city chose a name, and that 'tribe' competes against the other fourteen. All fifteen tribes in our city take their names from cities, gods, and ancient rulers. They each have their own banner, and we stimulate pride in their group. The nine from which I buy products for my business are Apollonias, Tiberiane, Rhomais, Eumenes, Seleukis, Laodikis, Attalis, Stratonikis, and Antiochus. Others provide useful items but not good enough to sell in Rome."

He listed the other six merchants and then told his guests about poor people who lived in the insulae below the city, beyond the travertine pools of water. Flavius loved his city. He would speak about Hierapolis for the whole night if given a chance.

"A dozen slaves grade the products before I buy from the workers. Five keep track of the improvements each tribe is making. I'm not the only businessman doing this either. Once a year, in April or May, we hold a massive celebration. The tribe with the best-quality garments, blankets, carpets, tunics, or cloaks takes the prize as the winners."

"What are some of the prizes?" asked Omerod, realizing he was on to something.

"I give them gold ornaments."

Omerod leaned forward. "What kind?"

"An armband, a little bit bigger than a bracelet. Persian governors also awarded people this way, but they were really a symbol of authority at that time."

His big, puffy face suddenly changed as he remembered the pain of the robbery on the Southern Road. Suddenly his eyes were moist. "So you are guards for the Southern Road? The most important thing stolen from me in the robbery was an armband." Flavius had dropped his guard.

Anthony replied. "No, as we explained before, we are not trained like the special guards from Italia. We are simply a small detachment sent to help the 'Keepers of the Door.' We're not members of that elite force."

Flavius turned toward Anthony. "Your humility honors you, which tells me that you three are better fighters than those troopers brought from Rome to keep the Door open. You've been through a fight or two as well. I can see that from your face."

It was the first time that Flavius had mentioned the long red scar. Flavius was a man of adventure and risk. The welt that stretched from Anthony's right eye down to his jawbone, almost to his ear, indicated that he was talking to a man who had fought battles of life and death.

"If the armband was ever found, how would you recognize it?" Anthony's question was innocent. He did not ask how it had initially been stolen, and he did not promise it would be restored. Still, the possibility of its return was implicit in his words.

"It is an heirloom from my ancestors, my most precious treasure. No one knows of its importance except my daughter and now you. She will inherit it upon my death. Something like that has no price. Yes, it's made of gold, but its value lies in its history. It came from Persia's capital city many generations ago, 310 years ago to be exact. My ancestor, General Zeuxis, who served Antiochus III, became the satrap of Sardis. It was his symbol of authority. That armband connects me to Persia and the Seleucid Kingdom.

"My ancestor was Persian. He was dedicated to a Persian god on his father's side but dedicated to Zeus on his mother's side. That is why I told you about my ancestors. The gods protect me as long as I carry the armband with me. They have safeguarded my family for past generations. This robbery was a tragedy. For the first time, I do not have my armband. Without it, I do not have the protection of the gods. It combines my Persian, Greek, and Roman characteristics, all of them together! Without it, I will not be shielded from danger when my ships confront the winds and currents around Cape Malia."

They held their breath. Flavius was about to describe his precious treasure. He had just indicated that its power enabled him to face such peril on the seas.

"It's this big." He placed his right hand around his upper left arm to simulate what the band looked like. "Around the top and bottom edges, there are red rubies. Along the side, it opens on a hinge. Several other gems are lodged in it: jasper, topaz, beryl, and a large jacinth. I am known to many Roman senators by it. They love to run their fingers over my armband. When it was stolen from the camel train, I turned around and came straight back to Hierapolis. My only physical link to my ancestors has been broken. I have nothing else so powerful to protect me from the many threats during my travels."

Suddenly Flavius wanted to talk about the robbery. He told them how it happened, where he was standing, and how the sun was shining through a fluffy white cloud near the end of the day as they walked down the long hill toward Philadelphia. For the first time since they arrived, tears clouded his eyes. His loud voice was now down to a normal tone. Gone was his pomposity.

"We were walking down the hill through the Door. We came to a bend in the road. Two auxiliaries arrived, rushing up the hill on foot, sounding desperate. 'Robbers ahead!' they shouted. 'Our soldiers are chasing them. Stop here. Gather all your people here, at the head of the camel train. We are going up the hill to warn the next caravan.' One of them brought my camel drivers to the front, and we huddled for protection. He then left to join the other auxiliary.

"We trusted his word of course! Our camels had stopped and knelt, waiting for someone to give the all-clear. Well, you know what happened. I was the first one who realized it. 'That man is part of a bandit gang!' I shouted. 'They are robbing us while we wait here! Around the curve, where we can't see them, they are unloading the camels at the back of the caravan!'

"They had taken four bundles from two camels at the rear and disappeared! When I realized that my personal possessions had been stolen, especially my ancestor's armband, I was horrified. I could go to Rome without my special clothes and jewelry. I could simply buy more but not without that treasure. In Rome, without that armband, I would feel naked and completely powerless. So I came back. Yes, I'm almost ready to go on my next trip, but how can I go without that amulet to empower me and explain who I am? Wealthy men fall silent when they see the first visible link to their ancient enemies, the Parthians and Persians. Yet I come to them as a friend and take more money from them than a dozen robbers ever could!"

Anthony asked, "Did any of your drivers see anyone other than the 'auxiliaries' who stopped the caravan?"

"One of my caravan men ran to the back of the train, but they were already gone. Four bundles were lost. Since it would have been difficult for a man to carry more than one bundle, we think it was only the four auxiliaries in the gang."

Omerod broke in. "When the thieves left the road with the bundles, did they go higher on the mountain or down the slope?"

"We think that they had to go higher up. Down the slope, no, because it is almost a sheer cliff. We couldn't be sure how many were up there or how they were armed, so we didn't try to chase them. So now you know my dilemma. I fear the thought of travel until I recover that armband! My business is at a standstill. I do not trust that those specially trained soldiers from Italia, Guardians of the Door, will return my armband and thereby keep me from being ruined."

He stared at Anthony. "Anthony Suros, I was not going to tell you about my most precious possession. Somehow you led me to explain the whole story. It perhaps seems silly that I am so profoundly dependent on that armband for safety in travel, but it has fended off evil for so long that I genuinely believe in it. Now it is lost. There is nothing I can do about it. I can only pray that the gods will do the impossible and return it to me. I have considered hiring my own guards, but the expense for such a long trip would be immense. I may have to do that just to ensure that I keep my presence in the Rome market. I would also go over land through Corinth in Greece instead of going only by sea.

"I intend to write a letter to my friends in the Roman Senate and those in Ephesus to tell them how displeased I am that the Southern Road is so poorly secured. Perhaps I can get an investigation started that will end up with better guard capability. This kind of theft needs to be stopped immediately before whole caravans are stolen. I think a lot of the problem is centered in the Bouleuterion of Philadelphia."

Anthony sensed that a new topic was about to be raised. *Flavius is about to tell us what he thinks of Philadelphia. Still, he has been careful not to directly criticize that city. I believe that is about to change.*

Flavius had regained his composure and was ready to say more about Philadelphia. "Tell those fools in Philadelphia a word or two. It would appear the city maintains broken walls as a monument to the past! To an earthquake! Why? Old buildings lie broken across the town. Who attempts to repair them? No one! I look forward to staying at the Inn of the Open Door. But the city? It's a disaster! Its very condition indicates that the robbery should be no surprise. They obviously have no pride, so why shouldn't they tolerate a few robbers? I see the situation as only getting worse.

"Look at Hierapolis! After the earthquakes, we repaired everything, put ordinary people back to work, and paid them. Look across the valley. Laodicea is more glorious now than before the earthquake! Didn't Colossae return to its former glory? Hierapolis has a larger theater, better streets, and a growing population. We rebuilt the central avenue and named it after Frontinus, the governor. We dedicated it to Domitian. It required some upfront expenditures but has paid off in the long run with higher productivity and resulting taxes.

"So tell me, why is Philadelphia so slow to see the advantages of rebuilding?" Flavius looked at the soldiers one by one. "Now, I think this conversation is over," he said. "It's late, and you will want to be on the road back to Philadelphia in the morning. You've got what you wanted from me, haven't you?"

The four men talked a little longer, and Anthony's mind was racing to think of what else he needed to ask before they left. Flavius had opened his soul only after probing.

Flavius walked with them to the front door of his home. "Come back at the second hour tomorrow. Have breakfast with me before you return to Philadelphia. I think you are men I can work with, and perhaps overnight, we can think of something useful to do to help with my problem."

At breakfast the following day, Anthony asked a question. "Supposing that people in the Philadelphia area also produced cloaks, garments, blankets, or anything like that, would you buy products from those people?"

Flavius had returned to his acquisitive, overbearing self, and he was dreaming of future profits. "If the quality is good enough to take to Rome, then yes, I would buy from them. I pay a fair price, and I always make a profit. Here is a secret, but please keep it to yourselves! Your question is very timely because I am finding that other merchants here are jealous of my success and are cutting in on my business! I need new suppliers, but they have to make good merchandise."

Flavius chuckled. The conversation's twist might expand his business sources from an unexpected place, the Cogamis Valley. But he was also covering up the worry caused by the loss of his prized possession. To senators in Rome, the armband was a curiosity and a trademark identifying the merchant. Still, these three scouts had learned that to him, it was his gift from the gods, his guarantee of protection from dangers by sea and by land.

As they left through the impressive hand-carved door, Anthony turned to their host. "I want to bring your treasure back to you. If it's humanly possible to find it, we will do that. I ask that you delay sending any letters off to Rome regarding the robbery. We three were sent to Philadelphia just because of your robbery. I am requesting that you give us some time to allow us to catch the gang responsible and possibly return the armband to you."

Flavius looked skeptical for a moment. "Anthony Suros…I do tend to trust you after our discussions here. Right now, you men are the only ones in a position to return my treasure. To be totally truthful, I think any action provided by Rome would be a long time in coming. My complaining would make me feel better but probably accomplish nothing. Send me a report occasionally and tell me of your investigations. I will wait until sailing season next year before starting another caravan. Remember, it costs me profits to wait."

Lines showed on Anthony's forehead. *I'm prohibited by Felicior from saying anything about you to the soldiers. But I call upon your Name. It is more effective than threats, deceptions, and even Servius's accusations. Almighty One, what a contrast between your glory and the fleeting grandeur of objects made with human hands! Perhaps Flavius will come to see that.*

Chapter 8
Motives Revealed

THE POSTAL ROAD AT THE DOOR, NEAR PHILADELPHIA

A day and a half later, with the sun at its highest point, the three soldiers arrived back at the curve on the hill known as the Door, where the robbery had taken place.

Omerod observed, "Thugs don't disappear. Remember the proverb, 'A vulture flies overhead'? Doesn't it imply that bandits preying on the weak will be observed before landing on their victims? Let's come back to explore this area another day. Felicior needs to know right away what we heard from Flavius Zeuxis."

A caravan was coming up the hill with camels walking at their usual slow gait. They had an unending, mesmerizing sway to their necks and grinding jaws, their front teeth clearly visible. Two merchants walked beside their animals, talking little and conserving strength as they plodded toward the top of the pass. The next day, they would be into the next valley and on to Hierapolis.

"Hail" and a nod was all they could manage for Anthony, Omerod, and Bellinus.

Soon the three soldiers were back at the garrison. Under their hot armor, sweat prickled their skin. A small but noisy mob had gathered at the city gate, shouting and demanding faster action from the authorities. In the heat of the day, no one on either side was about to do anything violent.

The team reported to Felicior's office just as the commander returned from the city hall meeting. "Glad to see you back. What did you learn from the merchant?" he said, making room for them in his office.

Omerod explained what had happened. "Truth be told, we didn't learn much that we didn't already know. Flavius Zeuxis confirmed previous hearsay reports. Two unknown men, dressed as auxiliaries, stopped the caravan. 'Stop! There are robbers ahead,' they shouted.

They gathered the travelers at the head of the caravan 'for safety.' Then the gang, hidden by a bend in the road, stripped the last two camels. That is not new information, but we did learn about Flavius Zeuxis's most precious treasure. His ancestor's armband was stolen. He considers it to be an amulet offering travel protection."

Anthony took over. "It's why he didn't complete the trip to Rome. He fears travel disasters without it. Zeuxis decided to not send any grievance letters to Rome after we told him that we are working specifically to capture the robbers. He is praying to his gods that we will return his amulet."

Following their noon meal in a nearby thermopolium, Felicior gave Omerod and Bellinus their next assignment. "I want you both in Clanodda tonight. It's the same problem—unemployed men hammering at the gate." They left immediately to gather some belongings and get across the valley before dark.

Felicior nodded to Anthony to dismiss him.

Anthony turned to leave then stopped in mid-step. "I have something to talk about, sir. May I speak alone with you?"

"Speak, soldier."

"May I talk openly, sir?"

"Permission granted."

Anthony felt his heart beating rapidly. "A clever gang carried out the robbery, sir. Most likely it was the four rebels who escaped us at Prosperity Village. They will carry on until they are captured. But right now there is a more immediate problem. There are hundreds of irate peasants justifiably protesting. Philadelphia's authorities should do more for the families without food."

"But do what for them?"

"Men at the gates are causing disturbances. Why? They need work, food, and money. They would rather be at home with their families, be in the fields, or doing anything else but rioting. If nothing is done, it will worsen, and we won't find enough soldiers to control the riots. Men whose children are hungry will do desperate things."

"I suppose you have a suggestion. Is it something to do with your trip to Hierapolis?"

"Yes, Flavius Zeuxis might help in unexpected ways. We spent a day with him, and his long stories gave us an idea of how we can put these unemployed farmers to work."

"To work? How?"

"Flavius told us how Hierapolis rebuilt its ruins after the earthquakes and how they got the city to function normally again. May I make specific suggestions, sir? It will require you to request another meeting of the city hall."

Felicior sat down at the table and motioned. "Sit down, Suros. Now explain the details of what you are thinking."

"Large portions of this city still have to be rebuilt. That is true in the surrounding towns as well. Starting with public buildings, the city could obtain loans from local bankers, maybe request emergency funds from Ephesus, our provincial capital. We must open our storehouses and distribute food rations. We can't have people dying of starvation. During the coming weeks of summer, the provincial government can bring additional food supplies from other cities where grain fields were not converted to vineyards.

"The city could bring in stonemasons to direct construction and give work to hundreds of small farmers, those who have wagons and horses. They would clear off the existing ruins, save the usable stone, and start to rebuild. That will give hope and income to farmers until the local grain harvest occurs in the fall. If you give those people a reason to stop rioting, things will calm down."

Felicior looked skeptical. "But that would still leave hundreds of families in a desperate situation later on."

"Sir, Flavius gave us something unexpected. A promise. He said, 'I will buy garment goods from households in the Cogamis Valley if their quality is good enough.' He can't expand his business anymore in Hierapolis because other merchants compete for the same goods from his local sources. The man needs new suppliers of high-quality items: coats, cloaks, blankets, perhaps jewelry...anything else that Rome might want to buy.

"I think it all fits together, sir. As new buildings are restored, they would be available for use as workshops. Then we could teach the townspeople how to manufacture the goods Flavius requires. We might improve this valley's economy by developing the quality weaving and garment making that Flavius will buy. I know a man in Sardis who has the expertise needed for setting up looms. Others could teach townspeople how to use them."

Felicior leaned back in his chair, sipping a cup of water. Obviously Anthony's suggestions gave him something to think about. "Huh. Let's see now: Call a meeting of the city hall, borrow money from the banks, distribute food from emergency storage, hire some stonemasons, organize the out-of-work farmers as construction workers, start repairing the ruins, and set up training workshops to teach people to make garments. Then sell the merchandise to Zeuxis. And at the same time, capture the robbers on the Southern Road and get Zeuxis's amulet back so he will continue going to Rome."

Even his eyes began to radiate the smile working its way onto his face. "I'm not sure what will be more difficult: to get the city council and the Bank of Philadelphia to cooperate with all that or to capture the rebels."

He leaned back. With his eyes closed, he talked about the next day. "Suros, it doesn't sound impossible…just difficult. A meeting should include Mayor Aurelius Manilius Hermippus; Giles, the wealthiest banker; Headmaster Damian from the gymnasium, and High Priest Spiridon from the Apollo Temple.

"Earlier this morning, all forty-two councilors plus those four men were shouting at me, 'Felicior, call more troops!' They swear that Rome brought on this crisis, but no one dares to complain about Domitian. So as the commander of the garrison, I'm the one declared to be at fault!"

He stood up suddenly. "How quickly can we get men put to work? Will there be enough food available to get started?"

Decimus entered without knocking at the door. "It's not urgent, sir, but there's been another robbery."

"Where?"

"A hundred peasants confronted us at the Valley Gate. Lots of noise, so our attention was focused on them. Meanwhile, six others climbed over a section of the broken-down wall close to the Mountain Gate and got into the emergency storage units."

"What did they take?"

"Not a lot—four sacks of wheat from the storehouses. Four men threw the sacks onto their mules, but we caught them before they could get away. What do you want to be done with them?"

Felicior drummed his fingers on the table and looked up. "Take the sacks back to the storehouse. Give each man a single sharp stroke with a rod on the left palm. No bone breaking. Tell them next time they might get hanged instead."

Decimus looked puzzled. "Is that all you're going to do to these thieves?"

"Someone recently reminded me that men whose children are hungry will do desperate things. Decimus, after you finish with those thieves, go back to the Southern Gate. Suros, take a guard position at the Valley Gate tonight. Both of you meet me here tomorrow afternoon before going to the baths."

For the first time since Felicior had arrived in Philadelphia two weeks before, he walked with a light step. A half-smile played at his lips as he left to set up an emergency city hall meeting.

THE ACROPOLIS IN THE CITY OF PHILADELPHIA

The next day, the sun's rays had weakened a little. Decimus and Anthony followed Commander Felicior from the garrison to the Upper Baths. The acropolis, the upper portion of the city, had undergone substantial restoration decades earlier. After the earthquake, rebuilding the Upper Baths was one of the first projects. Everyone commented on how little reconstruction had been attempted in the city's lower section.

All nine buildings on the acropolis were now grander than before the earthquake. Each building boasted new pillars erected at great expense. And now the city council was both paralyzed and polarized. They could not agree on a list of priorities, on which improvements to make next.

Decisions made by these men affected the welfare of this city and the surrounding towns. Councilors often tended to approve improvements to the places important to *them*. The theater, the garrison, and the baths were in fine shape. So were the four temples, those of Athena, Zeus, Apollo, and Artemis. The gymnasium had also been refurbished. The school for boys provided education in literature, history, government, rhetoric, and physical training,

Two hours later, Decimus and Anthony sat in the sweltering heat of the *caldarium*. Felicior was explaining what had happened at the emergency meeting held that morning.

"Mayor Aurelius Manilius Hermippus received me at his home last night. At first he refused to hear any idea about putting men to work. I reminded him that the riots were getting worse and we were losing control. We discussed the realities of that, and then he changed his mind and agreed: 'I think we can get approval from the city council. But the Bank of Philadelphia may not agree to my financial terms. It's the only one with sufficient resources to support the whole project. It's worth a try.'

"When the meeting opened, the mayor spoke with a passion I haven't seen for weeks: 'Welcome to the City Hall of Attalos and Eumenes. Those two ancient kings inspired people to show brotherly love. Remember this. They worked well together. Mutual respect strengthened them and everyone around them. What was their most significant achievement? Was it merely laying this city's foundation stone? No! A thousand times no! They spread the Greek language. Culture and wisdom were the footprints they left behind.'

"'Did they argue? Do you have a single example of them vying for preeminence? No! Our city isn't named for a god, not for a single person like most places. Attalos and Eumenes shared each other's honors. Let's learn from our past. To make it through this crisis, we must strengthen our relationships. I do not want more bitter comments like we had yesterday.'

"The mayor continued, 'Last year, farmers obeyed imperial instructions: Cut down half the vineyards, plow up the ground, and plant grain crops. Peasants are now marching. They're tired and hungry, and many lost jobs due to the reduction in vineyards. They need to work until harvest time later this year. Families need food. Mothers are weeping, and babies are crying. And last evening, Commander Felicior told me that he does not have enough troops to control more angry mobs.'

"'So,' the mayor continued, 'I have a plan. Today I am declaring a state of emergency. I will send an urgent request to Governor Marcos Atillius Postumus Bradua in Ephesus for funds. I'm also requesting reduced taxes. I will ask for permission to release emergency food supplies from cities to the south of us to feed our people.'"

"Then he addressed Giles, the head of the Philadelphia bank: 'Next, I want your bank to loan funds for a three-year rebuilding program. I'm thinking of public buildings here and in surrounding towns. Rebuilding will provide immediate wages to the jobless until harvest time. The building will continue into winter and next year.'"

The soldiers were stretched out on three white marble tables with Felicior in the middle and Anthony and Decimus on either side. As the slaves massaged their backs, Felicior continued telling them about the meeting.

He laughed as he remembered the negative response from the Bank of Philadelphia. "Well, that was how the meeting started. Giles, the banker, interrupted, but for once, the mayor put him down: 'You will have a chance to speak later, Giles! Today our city is in a crisis, and we, as civic leaders, must respond responsibly. Your bank is the largest in the city, and you must support what has to be done for our people to survive.'

"'Merchant Flavius Zeuxis, from Hierapolis, has committed to buying fabrics made here if they are of good quality. A year ago, in Rome, the emperor organized a public display of woolen fabrics from Phrygia. Domitian honored Zeuxis at the Games in the Coliseum. With his popularity soaring in Rome, Flavius has a huge market. He wants to purchase goods from our future weavers and clothiers. All of us will profit from a stronger relationship between Philadelphia and Hierapolis.'

"'Here's what we will do: rebuild the old, damaged workshops to create the initial construction jobs for our citizens. The spaces in the refurbished workshops will be used for training citizens as weavers and clothiers. Their early work can be sold locally. When they are improved enough, they can sell their products to Flavius. Higher-quality goods will end up in Corinth and Rome. This will generate both wages and taxes.'"

Felicior laughed. "That's when Giles tried to butt in again. He stood up in the meeting and was recognized to speak. 'Put people to work? It's not easy! Even if we loan our money to the city, who can we trust to distribute food to half-starved people? I cannot see this working. Moreover, will Flavius Zeuxis exploit us? Will his agents pay sufficiently for the work people do here?'

"When Giles started complaining, I heard council members whispering, 'Bankers always want higher returns for themselves. He is putting up arguments now so his bank can charge high interest for loaning money to the city.'

"Now, this is where the meeting became interesting. Calisto, the Greek teacher, is almost deaf. He whispered a little too loudly, 'I hope Zeuxis comes here to do business. Giles and his bank will face competition from Hierapolis's bankers, who are more willing to take risks. Giles's bank will be forced to reduce interest rates. Better quality garments will begin to appear too.' I looked at Giles. The expression on his face showed he didn't like the idea of outside competition coming to his bank!

"The mayor finished by saying, 'Our first three rebuilding projects will include structures destroyed seventy-six years ago. They are inside the city wall near the Valley Gate. Close by is the crumbled portion of the wall. Hundreds of men will be needed to reconstruct those buildings and the wall. We'll pay workers fair wages. This will inject money back into the city's economy.'

"'Now for the details. An old building called the Workshops faces the square near the Inn of the Open Door. We should rebuild it first for immediate use and put weavers' looms there to teach weaving and to sew garments for Flavius. We will also rebuild the old Lower Bath. It will generate revenue and reduce the crowds coming to the Upper Bath.'

"Old deaf Calisto had the last word. He said, 'Mayor Aurelius has backed Giles and his friends into a corner! If they don't join in, everyone will blame them for the protests in the surrounding cities. They will demand a higher rate of interest, but they won't get it. Instead, they will be forced to cooperate. In the end, they will be hailed as heroes.'"

Their afternoon bath was over, and Decimus felt refreshed as he put on his soldier's tunic. "So Giles accepted the mayor's plan?"

Felicior answered, "Yes and no. As I was leaving, the banker was leaning back with his eyes half-closed. He had his thumbs inside his fancy, wide leather belt. He replied, 'We will examine this proposal. Some ideas are worth carrying out. The others will be discarded.' Hearing a banker talk like that, I think things can change for the better. But we'll have to watch out for their deceptions! His bank will try to squeeze as much money as possible from the rebuilding."

Entering the garrison, Felicior said, "Suros, for the next two or three weeks, while we're waiting for those robbers to show themselves again, I want you at the Valley Gate. Decimus, you will continue duty at the Southern Gate."

THE CITY OF THYATIRA

The day before coming to Philadelphia, Ateas and Arpoxa were staying at Jonathan Ben Shelah's home in Thyatira. Arpoxa was crippled. She needed rest because her legs, feet, and muscles were so sore today. The young mother wanted quiet, so Ateas took his two young sons outside into the front garden area.

Recently Ateas had spent three months helping the Roman military track down a gang of criminals. His assignment included spending several weeks with an escaped Scythian slave. His translation of a slave's experiences confirmed what Anthony and his squad had suspected about the criminal gang.

Ateas had come back from the military assignment in Prusa the previous week. The young man loved his sons dearly. He often made humorous comments about using crutches even while helping his crippled wife. His first son darted about almost uncontrollably, and he rocked their baby boy in his arms. "There you go, Saulius. We'll sit out here with your baby brother. Let's give Mommy a rest."

As Ateas cared for his children, a military wagon pulled up in front of Jonathan's home. "I can see you are lame," the driver observed. "Are you Ateas, the Scythian?"

"Yes, I am. You must be going to taking us to Philadelphia. My wife told me you coming." Ateas, unlike his wife, had difficulty speaking Greek. He still needed a lot of help in this.

"I am under orders to bring you to Philadelphia. Commander Felicior wants all of you—you, your wife, and your two sons—and your belongings. I will take you there tomorrow."

Slave traders illegally seized many young men in Scythia. Four years ago, Ateas was one of them.[34] They had captured him near his home city of Bilsk,[35] north of the Black Sea, and had bound him and taken him to Phanagoria to be shipped southward.

Before being captured, he had worked as a guard to protect merchants on the Silk Road. He lamented the day he was injured

---

[34] Ateas was named for King Ateas (429–339 BC), one of Scythia's most famous and influential monarchs. He unified many of Scythia's tribes. King Ateas died in battle at the age of ninety while fighting the Macedonian king, Philip II. After his death, the mighty Scythian Empire fell apart.

[35] Bilsk is today a small village in the District of Poltava in central Ukraine. Archaeological research has shown that it was a large city of forty square km. It was one of the world's most important trading centers during the height of its influence, the 7th – 6th centuries BC. Its ramparts, constructed as earth-walls, rose fifty feet (16 m). The wall extended twenty-one miles (33 km) and wholly enclosed the massive city. Bilsk was constructed beside the Vorskla River; trade from Europe reached into the steppes of Asia.

when the earth caved in on him while digging a well. Because there was no one to set the broken bone, he was crippled for life and walked with crutches.

Ateas fell in love with Arpoxa, a Scythian captured for sale as a slave. When walking, Arpoxa needed help because both feet pointed inward. She had to walk on the outside of each foot. They, along with other slaves, were transported to Asia Minor by ship from Phanagoria. That was the last time they had seen the far-away northern port on Lake Maeotis, close to the Black Sea.[36]

In Chalcedon, on the way to the slave market, they promised to love each other for all their lives. Their marriage was conducted by a priest of a local deity.

Thinking he could only get low prices for the cripples, the slave master at the Pergamum New Forum left them until the end of the auction. Antipas Ben Shelah purchased them together, a kind act that let them remain as one family. After that terrible experience of being bought and sold as human flesh, they became part of Antipas's village. There, they became followers of the Jewish Messiah.

People learned to love these two enthusiastic young people. Each one brought new skills to Antipas's workshops. Ateas and his young wife had blue eyes and hair the color of straw, and their boys looked like them.

THE ACROPOLIS IN THE CITY OF PHILADELPHIA

In the Upper City of Philadelphia, Damian and Calisto, the two most prominent men in the gymnasium, walked down the hill. Having passed the theater, they turned left at the Avenue of Philadelphia, heading toward the school. Hundreds of boys gathered each morning for studies and physical training. The building had been rebuilt with splendid pillars and columns.

Damian appreciated the abilities of Calisto, the demanding Greek teacher. If boys complained, it was because they had to memorize too many Greek words and expressions. Damian liked hearing this kind of criticism. No one ever complained about a lack of discipline in Calisto's classes. The Greek teacher, who was decidedly deaf, was known for his sharp eyes. He always noted any act of disobedience.

---

[36] Lake Maeotis is known today as the Sea of Azov, between Russia and Ukraine.

Damian, the headmaster, stepped over a sleeping dog on the street. He pulled at his short goatee, puzzled. "Do you know what I can't figure out, Calisto?"

"What's bothering you?" Calisto asked.

"Flavius Zeuxis always goes to Rome at this time of the year. Well, this summer, he's not in Rome. He's still in Hierapolis! Something in the mayor's speech this morning doesn't make sense. Flavius makes huge profits when he sells good, quality merchandise made in Hierapolis. Why would he start doing business in the Cogamis Valley, buying products from our district? Until now, he always turned up his nose at 'Philadelphia's backward towns and cities.'"

Damian continued, gambling on a plausible reason. "Maybe Flavius sees this as an opportunity to increase his business sources and expand his influence."

Calisto did not answer. He was not about to speculate on Zeuxis's actions. His mind was occupied with something closer to his heart. The famous Greek teacher was increasingly worried about his home. A conversation from the night before kept going around in his mind.

His son, Timon, who had recently completed his studies, was complaining more and more. "Father, why should I spend all my life learning about poets, historians, and ancient authors? Be practical! I want to be more business-like! I do not like learning about philosophers and writers like Thucydides or Herodotus of Halicarnassus, Manetho, or Berosus! I want a different career."[37]

THE HOME OF ALEXINA, IN THE CITY OF SARDIS

While Damian and Calisto were making their way back to the school in Philadelphia, Diotrephes, a teacher in Sardis, was starting to write a letter. He taught boys between the ages of twelve and sixteen. The teacher's straight back and upright posture showed his determination to be the best Director of the Department of History that the Sardis Gymnasium had seen.[38]

---

[37] These historians' dates were Herodotus of Halicarnassus, 484–425 BC; Thucydides, 460–401 BC; Manetho 305–282 BC; and Berosus, c. 290 BC. Halicarnassus was an ancient port now known as Bodrum, the famous holiday resort city in Turkey. These writers were studied as part of the education in gymnasia in Domitian's time.

[38] Diotrephes is a significant person in each of the three preceding volumes.

His desk, the most expensive in Sardis, was purchased at the Western Agora. He enjoyed shopping at the furniture shop beside the Temple of Hera. Sitting down, he took his quill, dipped it in the black ink, and wrote to his mother, Lydia-Naq, the well-known high priestess of the Altar of Zeus in Pergamum.

June 11, in the 13th year of Domitian
From: Diotrephes, in Sardis
To: My mother, Lydia-Naq, in Pergamum

If you are well, then I am also well.

I have two reasons to be joyful. Last week, I reclined at Mayor Tymon Tmolus's table. Across the table was Cynthia, Tmolus's daughter. I impressed her family with my charm and wit. Then I woke up this morning after a dramatic dream. In it, I ended an ancient quarrel through my marriage with Cynthia. It's the conflict between the Milon and Tmolus clans.

Could this dream be a prophecy? Should the Milon clan, since so few of us are left, still hold a grudge against the Tmolus family for claiming our land? Who could predict the Hermus River changing its course back then in the Year of the Many Storms? It was the reason we lost our vineyard. How unfortunate that a conflict engulfed our families for generations! A marriage could put a permanent end to the quarrel.

Secondly, please tell Uncle Zoticos that yesterday I received word from Cleon, my friend in Philadelphia. He wrote me. Miriam and Chrysa are staying in the home of Amos Ben Shelah. I will find a way to bring the baby back to the bosom of our family, where she belongs. They call her Grace, leaving off her birth name, Chrysa.

A year ago, in Sardis, I got past all the guests and entered Simon Ben Shelah's house but only saw her.

Then, recently, I nearly kidnapped her in Thyatira. Once again, I was unable to hold her in my hands. I arranged for the Sardis acropolis guards to grab Anthony and Chrysa in Thyatira, but those four men bungled their attempt. Mayor

Tmolus forgave me for my angry outburst when I heard of their failure.

Now, finally, I think we have a new chance.

He grinned as his seal left its mark in the soft red wax.

Chapter 9
The Survivors

AMOS AND ABIGAIL'S HOME

Thyatira, sixty-one miles northwest of Philadelphia, required two days of travel by wagon. With fresh horses replacing tired ones at each relay station, the military wagon bringing Ateas and Arpoxa arrived at Amos Ben Shelah's home. The lame Scythian let himself down carefully.

Hearing her two Scythian friends' voices, Miriam ran out to the wagon, lending a hand to help them. Arpoxa beamed, her face mirroring the joy filling her heart. The twenty-three-year-old mother with soft lines around her face and an attractive figure was beautiful. She spoke Greek well now, four years after being redeemed from the slave auction.

As Miriam helped her walk to the house, Arpoxa said, "I am so happy. You said Philadelphia means 'City of Brotherly Love.' I have my husband, Ateas. He is such a good man. What is the Greek way of saying, 'The City of the Love of My Husband'?" They chuckled. Arpoxa often asked funnily worded questions.

Once inside the front doorway, Miriam introduced her friends. "Uncle Amos, this is Ateas. Arpoxa is his wife. Grandpa Antipas redeemed them and gave them their freedom papers. Arpoxa embroiders cloth. Ateas made gold rings for Uncle Simon, and he decorates pottery. They are like family to me. Both are artists. These are their sons, Saulius and Madis."

Abigail, who had been waiting to see the children, turned her face away when she saw Ateas. His eyes were blue, and his hair was like straw on the ground after harvest. She knew Ateas would stay at the inn with the soldiers, but his very presence was unnerving. He was a non-Jew, and he used crutches.

Her clenched jaw hid many emotions on the arrival of a Scythian family. She felt compassion for the mother with club feet. Small children nearby brought back the memory of her sons when they were little. Then came the ever-present loss of six children. She turned and opened her arms to the two boys.

"Come," she said. "I want you to see my house."

As Abigail talked with Arpoxa, Amos, Miriam, and Ateas went back to the wagon. Amos directed the servants to remove Arpoxa's few belongings and take them into the house. Some items remained on the front steps. Ateas would stay at the inn.

Amos then addressed the new arrival. "Ateas, Commander Felicior wants you to work at my inn. We have not determined precisely what work you can do yet, but the commander will talk with you about the tasks and salary. He particularly wants you to speak with the Scythian caravan slaves.

"We are giving you a secret name. You will be called Zarrus. You are to pretend that you are the crippled son of a rich client of mine. At the inn, you will be working for my son, Obed. He runs the daily affairs there. Tell people your father is paying for you to have this job. You want to work 'in the world of business.' You will not recognize or speak to Anthony when another inn employee is around. Your relationship with him and Miriam is to be secret. Can you do this?"

"Yes, if it helps Felicior and Anthony and catches rebels."

"Good. If Cleon or any other man at the inn asks questions, you must say you don't know them. You should also take notice of Cleon's activities and report anything unusual to Obed. You can confide in him at any time, and he will determine your work at the inn and carry messages for you. Anthony will talk with you when no one is around.

"Obed has spoken to Anthony about this. Anthony says he never actually met Cleon when he and Miriam lived in Sardis. Of course, Cleon will know Anthony from his scar, but Cleon will almost certainly not mention that he was ever in Sardis."

With that, Amos had the military wagon driver return to the city garrison. He had one of his servants bring a smaller farm wagon, and Ateas went to the inn. Obed had already worked out where Ateas would be sleeping at the inn, and he had been expecting the arrival of the cheerful man who used two crutches.

Two weeks after the emergency meeting at City Hall, grain was being rationed into the hands of needy families and the city bakers.

Confrontations outside city gates subsided significantly but continued with lower intensity. Anthony was instructed to meet Felicior midafternoon. He calculated that he could visit Miriam at Amos's farm and still be back in time to meet Felicior, so he left the garrison and sped up the hill on Brutus.

Anthony clapped his hands at the gate to Amos's courtyard, and a servant opened the door to let him in. He left his helmet and breastplate in the patio area outside the front door. His sword was laid on a high shelf at the entrance, for he did not want any of the children accidentally cutting themselves.

The Ben Shelah family was reclining with their untouched noon meal on the table before them. The women had their long black hair done up over their heads to keep their necks free in the hot weather.

"Da-da!" screamed Grace after she saw him. She raced across the floor, and he took her up in his arms, holding her high. She shrieked again. Her face lit up with joy when Anthony hugged her again. Miriam came close and kissed him on both cheeks.

Seeing Anthony, Abigail sat straight up. She had been reclining, and she made sure he saw her look away.

Anthony noticed and sucked in his breath, thinking, *Aunt Abigail is still threatened by my presence.*

He kissed Miriam on her cheek and whispered, "I can't stay long...just a minute."

"I was so afraid for you, my dear. Did you catch the criminals?"

Anthony spoke cheerfully, loud enough for all to hear. "We talked with the wealthiest man in Hierapolis. We haven't caught the rebels yet, but we will!"

"I'm happy to see you, my dear, but do you know what this day is?"

"No, what is today?" he said.

Tension filled the room, and Anthony did not know what he had done to cause it. They were sitting silently, and the expression on every face showed he was not welcome.

Aron explained, "Today is Tzom Tammuz. It's the day on the Jewish calendar when Nebuchadnezzar's army first broke through Jerusalem's walls. We sit at our table but leave all food untouched. We remember the bitter day with tears, silence, and repentance. Twenty-one days later comes Tish'a B'Av."

Anthony already knew about those events from his many conversations with Antipas. "Yes, I know about *that* date. Nebuchadnezzar's army... The temple on Mount Zion was destroyed." But occupied with his trip to Hierapolis and the uprisings, he had forgotten about Amos and Abigail. Their sensibilities today took them back hundreds of years.

He reached back for memories of events at Antipas's home. *So many occasions to keep track of on the Jewish agendas! New moons, festivals, and fasts! Something new every day! ...My father led a detachment, climbing over Jerusalem's outside wall, the first Roman trumpeter*[39] *over the walls...and he died there.*

Aunt Abigail, you have much pain from those days. I want to hear your story, but I want you to hear mine too!

"I'm terribly sorry about the destruction of the walls of Jerusalem," he stated simply. "I am sure you have much to say about it."

He heard Abigail mutter, "Yes, and I have a lot to say to you!"

The rude comment was meant for his ears. Anthony stayed for a few minutes and then explained why he had to leave. "I have to report to Commander Felicior, and I must not keep him waiting."

Grace cried as he left the house, and she was screaming as he left the courtyard. She wanted her daddy because she had not seen him for many days. Anthony felt terrible tearing her away as she clung to his neck. Miriam took their daughter into her arms and tried to comfort her.

THE INN OF THE OPEN DOOR, PHILADELPHIA

Never had Philadelphia's city hall worked so hard. Mayor Aurelius was up early. He worked late, calling citizens together: judges, lawyers, architects, engineers, and advisors. Carpenters and stonemasons were sent to surrounding towns to estimate the cost of repairs.

While everyone hoped to see historic buildings rebuilt, stonemasons began drawing up plans for restoration. Reports were

---

[39] In the Roman army, a trumpeter directed troop movements in battle by sounding various note combinations from his trumpet that were easily heard over the noise.

being submitted about improvements needed for public edifices in Castolius, Clanodda, Temenoth, Malonia, Silandus, and Sasorta.

Many complained bitterly about the delay. "Why is the city council waiting so long? We want work, not simply handouts! Can't city hall see how desperate we are?"

However, food distribution was better organized. Officials were posted at each gate, and the word was racing through the countryside: "Philadelphia is doing something! Even better, many will have work paid for by the authorities!"

Ateas, now called Zarrus, was assigned a room in the inn in the area where caravan slaves were quartered. He understood his instructions ably and responded to the name Zarrus. When casually tested by Obed, he ignored the name Ateas.

Zarrus was to care for the needs of caravan employees. Many lower-level caravan workers were either Scythian or Persian. Slaves could usually talk to each other, so Zarrus communicated with both using the Scythians as his interpreters.

Anthony found that Cleon had a regular time to go to the Upper Hot Baths late in the day. He and Zarrus arranged that when Cleon was seen walking up the Avenue of Philadelphia, they would meet in the stable and talk briefly.

Due to the continuing general disorder, Anthony could not return to spend time with Miriam and Grace. Felicior demanded constant vigilance of his guards. No one had a day off.

Anthony frequently crossed paths with Obed at the inn. He hoped that Obed could become more than an acquaintance. Still, Anthony noticed a tendency for the inn director to avoid him. Anthony was leaving for his duty early as Obed arrived at the inn. They normally greeted each other with merely a word or two, but today Obed started a conversation.

"Anthony, the workers tell me that the wall outside our inn is going to be rebuilt!"

"I heard the same story," replied Anthony, preparing to mount his horse.

"Miriam says she is missing you very much."

This was the first time that Obed had acknowledged Anthony's marriage. "I've been watching you since you came. You've only been here for nine weeks, but I see something in you that I haven't noticed in the other soldiers."

"How many soldiers do you know?" A smile crossed Anthony's freshly shaven face.

Obed pointed to the inn where two large rooms were occupied by soldiers. "I watch them all. Extra soldiers from cities appeared as reinforcements. There is something different about you. You don't swear, and I see how you treat others. Small gestures show you are a generous person.

"If you ever want to send a message to Cousin Miriam, I'll be a messenger between the two of you. I'll also contact you if our friend Zarrus needs to talk with you."

"Thank you, Obed. I didn't mean to interrupt your family gathering yesterday."

"Never mind. It was a short interruption, and you left right away. My mother is sensitive to soldiers at the best of times, but when we remember the destruction of Jerusalem…"

"I won't offend that way again. Perhaps I will accidentally insult or hurt you in other ways but not intentionally!"

Obed had another concern. "Terrible news! Last evening, our cook was injured. He was attacked by men who were turned away at the Valley Gate. He had been to Sasorta to see his parents on his day off. Some attackers arrived late at the Valley Gate but were turned away. They took their anger out on our cook, whom they mistook for someone else. His leg is badly hurt, and he may not be able to stand. It's not good news for our business. A good cook who can handle a lot of people is hard to find."

Anthony remembered previous times when he had faced difficult situations. A prayer came to mind. *"I will lift up my eyes to the hills. Where does my help come from? My help comes from the Lord, the Maker of heaven and earth."*[40]

"Penelope." The name escaped his lips before he knew it.

"What did you say, Anthony?"

"Penelope—the first word that came to my mind. She is a widow who needs work. She has five small children and makes the best food I have ever tasted. Her husband, Nikias, was a friend of mine, but he was recently killed by highway bandits. He ran a farm for your Uncle

---

[40] Psalm 121:1

Jonathan along with his four brothers, all from Stratonike.[41] Ask Miriam if she thinks that Penelope would be a suitable replacement cook. However, if Penelope comes, she'll need a place to live."

"How did Nikias die?"

Anthony looked at the floor, the terrible beating passing before his eyes. "Nikias fell into the hands of bandits. He visited a village that was their lair. They beat him to death while asking questions about my military squad. I promised Penelope to pray for her. Could the Lord be giving an answer?"

Obed was startled. "Do you always pray for people?"

"Well, not always! Antipas taught me to think of others, believing all things are under the Lord's control. Yes, I pray for people, but Penelope slipped away from my thoughts during the last weeks. Too much work trying to control the chaos. Her name came back to me just now."

Encouraged by Anthony's honesty, Obed went further, asking for an opinion. "Cousin Miriam will not come if Cleon is here. He's an excellent worker. His stories and humor turned the inn into a happy place. But Miriam distrusts Cleon, saying he caused you trouble in Sardis. Tell me, is the man really a threat?"

Anthony looked around at the kitchen and eating area. How could he accuse Cleon if he had not been a witness to any misdemeanor? He had only heard Ravid's story, and Cleon was sure to deny anything he said.

"From what we think he did in Sardis, I believe yes, he can cause problems. I avoid talking to him, though I'm sure he knows who I am from my scar. I never actually met him in Sardis."

"What kind of problem could he cause here?"

"Obed, look, you have only seen a man named Cleon who talks to everyone, laughs a lot, and makes jokes. He remembers everyone's name and makes everyone feel important. I did not witness the things he's accused of, so I'm not a reliable witness, but I personally do not trust him.

"I'm staying at your father's inn with more than a dozen other soldiers. They will be here until the disturbances have died down, which might take longer than we think. Now I must be off."

---

[41] The story of Nikias and Penelope and the other four families at Olive Grove farm is told in *Purple Honors: A Chronicle of Thyatira*

Obed watched Antony leave. He looked down at his shaking hands and leaned forward, trying not to lose his balance. Everything seemed to be swimming around him.

Anthony said that the soldiers will stay on. I was hoping they would go away soon. God, the pain of what happened! Ten thousand soldiers are out there…or maybe twice as many. I can see them surrounding us. And now the Jerusalem city gate is open for just a few minutes. We rush out, panting with fear. There! Jerusalem's death is behind me. Now I am safe! We as a family are outside, walking toward the army, which has come to kill us. No strength left. I am starving. Limping. And now I fall on my knees to ask my enemies for mercy!

Oh no! These memories returning from twenty-three years ago! It's happening again. I see myself looking back, the gate slamming shut, being pulled shut from inside. We lost everything because of soldiers. But it was the Roman army that gave us food. Mother is right. I should not talk to Anthony. Just his being here makes me go back in my memories.

I could not get him to tell me anything about Cleon. What really happened between Cleon and Miriam? What did he really do?

AMOS AND ABIGAIL'S HOME

Abigail waited until everyone had gathered around the table. She watched Jesse help Ruth, his wife, to her place. Amos and Abigail, Ruth and Jesse, Sarah, Miriam, Grace, and Arpoxa and her two little boys were ready for the evening meal. Abigail nodded at Amos. Her family members were all reclining on the couches waiting for his usual prayer.

Amos prayed, "King of the universe, blessed be your name for this day and for this food."

Food was brought to the table: boiled eggs, a vegetable stew, flatbread, honey, goat cheese, and fruit.

Obed was slow to begin. "My thoughts kept me awake for hours last night. We need to replace our cook at the inn. He was attacked at Valley Gate yesterday and confirmed late this afternoon that he would not return to work. Then, this morning, Anthony suggested that I invite a woman to replace our cook. Her name is Penelope. She lives at Uncle Jonathan's orchard."

Miriam's pressed her hands tightly against her heart. "A good suggestion. I know her. She would be a good help at the inn."

Obed continued, "If she were willing to come, we could send a couple of wagons to bring her and her children."

Abigail shook her head. After several weeks, the children were getting on her nerves. "It would never work. How could a woman with small children come to the inn?"

Miriam watched Abigail's hesitation. "Penelope would be a great help, but you are right, Auntie. Her children should not be allowed to be near soldiers, merchants, travelers, and men we don't know. And of course she can't stay here at your home."

Amos turned to Miriam. "What do you know about the widow?"

"She is about thirty-eight years old. Nikias, her husband, oversaw Uncle Jonathan's farm, Olive Grove. She has five children. Evander is the oldest, fourteen, and he has a brother, Hamon, who is nine. There are two girls: Rhoda, eleven, and Sandra is seven years old. Her baby is about seven months."

"Is she a good cook?" asked Amos.

"I only had her food during one stay at the farm. That was when we were coming from Pergamum to Sardis. Yes, a wonderful cook and a good mother too."

Amos scratched his nose. "I don't think she should come. What would she do with the little children?"

Abigail also put her foot down. "She's a widow, is that right?"

"Yes, she is," answered Obed.

Abigail's dark look hid a trace of revenge mixed with a subtle accusation. "Aren't all soldiers the same? Why would Anthony want a widow to come to work where he is living?" A slight tremor shook her shoulders with the thrill of questioning a soldier's faithfulness to his wife. She saw Miriam's face turn a darker color, red flooding her cheeks.

Obed said, "There was something a little strange about how this happened. I told Anthony that we needed a cook, and he replied, 'Penelope.' I asked, 'How did you think of this woman's name?' He said, 'I've been praying for this widow and her children. Her husband, Nikias, was my friend at Olive Grove.' Anthony says he was praying for her to find a place to live and bring up her children."

Amos turned to his son. "Really? Did Anthony say that he was praying for this widow?"

"Yes, Father."

Question marks showed on the old man's face. "Abigail, a man who prays for a widow and her children is not a 'normal' soldier!"

"A soldier is always a soldier!" she shot back. "You're not going soft on Roman legionaries, are you? Next thing you know, you'll be asking him to share a meal at our house!"

"Yes, after hearing this, I *would* like to ask Anthony a few questions. What kind of prayers does he pray? I've never heard of such a thing."

Later that day, Abigail agreed to let Amos send for Penelope. She was still reluctant but conceded that the inn would desperately need a cook for the guests. But they would have to find a place for her to live. Just as Cleon had helped improve the general atmosphere, the kitchen could also use some improvement. Amos wrote a letter to his brother Jonathan Ben Shelah in Thyatira.

July 14, in the 13th year of Domitian
From: Amos and Abigail
To: Jonathan and Rebekah

If you are well, then I am well—peace and grace to you.

Cousin Miriam is staying with us. Thank you for taking care of Miriam during the past year. Both she and Grace are well, but we are disturbed by the Roman soldier's arrival.

Ateas and Arpoxa arrived with their two young boys. Abigail warmed up to the boys and loves watching the older ones play and baby-talk with the younger ones.

As of yesterday, the Inn of the Open Door needs a cook. When Anthony learned about this, he told us about Penelope. He highly recommends her as a cook. If she is willing to come here, we will find a suitable place for her and the children to stay. She will work in the kitchen, and her two boys can enroll at the gymnasium. I will pay their school fees. Rhoda and Sandra will help their mother. We will also find someone to care for the children when needed, especially the baby while Penelope is working.

Ruth is expecting her first baby toward the end of September. We will tell you about the baby when the happy day comes.

Miriam read the letter and approved. Obed also read it. He sealed it, impressing his ring into the hot wax, and took it to a courier, paying for rapid delivery to Thyatira.

That night, upstairs and unable to sleep, Abigail enjoyed a new secret thrill, a forbidden pleasure. *What I'm thinking of is not revenge. I just want Anthony to learn about the pain his army caused. Murder, grief, and trauma! Oh, how I want him to feel my pain! Lord of the universe, when I said the word 'revenge' just now, I felt something new, not genuine pleasure but a hidden delight.*

I want to inflict pain on Miriam's husband. I have never stopped hurting from the loss of my children. When I close my eyes, I see them as they were twenty-three years ago.

Abigail sighed silently. Her husband's comments had helped her formulate a plan. She had now found a way to hurt a Roman soldier.

The following day, she planned to say, "All right, invite Anthony Suros to our house. I want him to see how we suffer because of Tish'a B'Av."

Chapter 10
Revenge and Consolation

AMOS AND ABIGAIL'S HOME

Abigail continued to struggle with thoughts of revenge. Seeking to put them aside was fruitless. She was grateful for the other women's companionship during worship and longed to be cleansed from the frightful memories. On the one hand, Abigail yearned to empty her memory of those appalling scenes. But on the other, she wanted Anthony, the Roman soldier, to know how much she had suffered.

Leaning her head back, the old woman felt perspiration tingling her skin. Kindness was what she felt toward her family, but she had none for the soldier who had married her niece.

"Miriam, Anthony can come tomorrow evening."

"Auntie, you are getting soft! You know that this means he'll be here on Tish'a B'Av." Miriam hugged her aunt, hanging onto her for several seconds.

"Do you feel my pain? Is that why you hugged me?" asked the older woman in a gruff voice. "Things are getting worse, not better. Obed says Penelope should come to the inn, but I still think it's a bad idea! Obed says good things about your husband. To me, he is a Roman. Any soldier is my enemy."

The pleasure of seeing a soldier suffer brought a sweet sensation. *He will learn about absolute devastation during his visit: "the terror of night and the arrow that flies by day."*

A gleam shone in her eyes. Miriam realized that not kindness but something else, perhaps sinister, lay hidden in her words.

THE MILITARY GARRISON IN PHILADELPHIA

Felicior called Anthony to his office to give the latest news. "Word arrived today that the city council is going to finalize the first of many reconstruction projects."

"That is good news, sir. May I leave my post early this afternoon? I received an invitation, and I don't want to turn it down."

"Yes, permission granted. I think the gates will be quiet tonight."

Anthony was pleased that Felicior had given him consent to not stand guard tonight. He left his armor at the inn. Walking up the hill to the west side of the city, he found Amos and the family waiting in the synagogue portico. The soldier waited until the Sabbath service began and then entered, sitting beside Miriam, who stayed near the door. Grace played, climbing up on his knees and then jumping down. No matter how many times he told Grace to be quiet, she kept moving around, joyful to be with her father.

This Shabbat was meant to prepare the congregation for a day of mourning to start at sundown tomorrow. The rich voice belonged to Zacharias, and he could easily be heard outside in the portico. He spoke loudly and slowly.

"We will mourn the destruction of Bet Hamikdash, the Temple of Jerusalem. We will fast and lament the day when Nebuchadnezzar caused that to happen. Our mourning is more acute though. Titus brought about the same catastrophe on the same day 656 years later.[42]

"Mourning helps us examine our hearts and interpret sad events in our lives. The loss of fathers or mothers, brothers or sisters, children, relatives, and friends is never just a personal event. Death always impacts us as a community."

He spoke about the destruction of the Temple of Solomon, explaining the causes of God's wrath. "Our people became idolaters, imitating outsiders around them, and they no longer lived according to the Law. The consequences experienced in the Exile were felt across many generations. And here we are, a second diaspora."

He came to the end of his exhortation. "We used to worship together at Herod's Temple in Jerusalem. How blessed we were to stand shoulder to shoulder, coming from every part of the world! O Lord, all of that is gone. We must now cultivate an attitude of the presence of the Holy One. He comes into our midst, into our lives. We cannot return to Jerusalem since it is occupied. We cannot take an offering. Instead, we bring sacrifices of thanksgiving and prayers. Our ancestors carried out rituals but forgot justice and

[42] Solomon's Temple in Jerusalem was destroyed by the troops of Nebuchadnezzar in 586 BC. Similarly, Herod's Temple was burned by Titus, the son of Emperor Vespasian, in AD 70. Both events occurred on the same day of the month in the Jewish calendar, on the ninth day of Av.

righteousness. They intermarried with families around them, learning their ways. Uncleanness must be taken out of our midst." He ended with these words: "Think on this as we remember starting tomorrow at sundown. Recommit to following the Law of Moses."

Zacharias looked around the crowded sanctuary, his heart overflowing with compassion. Grown men rocked back and forth, tears streaming down their faces. Women had aching hearts, remembering friends suffering sicknesses and thinking of their deceased, beloved family members.

Listening to Zacharias, Abigail felt she could breathe more easily. *This is my Sabbath of Preparation. Zacharias touched my heart, and I want those blessings, thanksgiving, and prayers. But no one here knows the resentment I feel toward those who hurt my children. I cannot even mention it. Only Amos knows my agony and how I toss and turn at night.*

Afterward, as the congregation left the building, several families brushed past Miriam. Scowls and disapproving looks came naturally after listening to Zacharias talk about disobedient people.

Martha stood with Isabel and Ruth, three women spanning three generations. Thinking about her great-grandchild soon to be born, Martha had not listened carefully to the message.

Dorcas tapped Martha on the shoulder, whispering, "See there, the man with the long scar on his face. I think he's Miriam's husband, the soldier we heard about!"

Not meaning her words to be overheard by Abigail, who was standing close by, Martha said a little too loudly, "Anthony is here!"

As the wagon took them back to their farm, Miriam wished she had not encouraged Anthony to join them in the portico.

Abigail shut her eyes on the way home. *How much damage will this do to us in the congregation? Why did Antipas agree to Miriam's marriage? O Lord! You permit too many enemies to come into our lives!*

MICHAEL AND MARTHA'S HOME IN PHILADELPHIA

Word spread quickly during the next hour. At home, Michael cleared his throat before making an announcement. "As long as Amos permits contact with that soldier or any other non-Jew, I will not allow anyone in my family to speak to anyone in the Ben Shelah family."

Martha rushed to Dorcas's house, which was close by, and standing outside the door, she heard Daniel's loud voice inside before she knocked. He was yelling, "Amos must rid himself of the soldier and other outsiders!"

In a softer voice, Dorcas replied, "And what, my dear husband, will you do?"

"To start with, I will not permit Mith to go to their farm to visit with his brother."

"But Daniel! Ruth and Jesse will soon have our grandson or granddaughter. If Ruth and Jesse have a child in their arms, how can you stop me from going there if Amos still has those people in his house?"

Their voices became softer, and Martha left. She strolled back to her home. The evening message had faded away, and in her mind, an ill-defined fear was forming.

AMOS AND ABIGAIL'S HOME

The time of remembrance, lasting from Saturday night before sundown through Sunday to sunset, was a day of fasting and contrition. The Ben Shelah family gathered around the table, but no food was brought. Little children were only allowed to eat "unpleasant" food: dry bread and water.

Grace tried to feed something to Miriam. "Mommy wants to eat?" she kept asking. Anthony tried to keep her quiet but was not successful.

Even Arpoxa participated in the fasting, and Abigail had begun to accept her. The young woman's two little boys magnified happy memories of Abigail's long-gone children.

She looked around the room at the long faces. *I've been living with grief for twenty-three years, from before the fall of Jerusalem. I cannot remember what it was like to live without pain. Ruth will give birth to my first great-grandchild. Perhaps a new baby in our family will revive my spirit.*

Isabel sang in a quiet, mournful voice, slowly, with a Jewish rhythm. "This is my song for today," she said. "It's my sad song." Her words were more of a chant, a mellow voice with an alto pitch.

By the rivers of Babylon, we sat.
We wept when we remembered Zion.

There on the poplars, we hung our harps.
There, our captors asked us for a song.
Our tormentors demanded songs of joy.
They said, 'Sing us one of the songs of Zion!'
How can we sing the songs of the Lord
    while in a foreign land?
If I forget you, O Jerusalem,
May my right hand forget its skill!
May my tongue cling to the roof of my mouth
    if I do not remember you!
If I do not consider Jerusalem my highest joy.
Remember, O Lord, what the Edomites did
    on the day Jerusalem fell.[43]

The words "what the Edomites did on the day Jerusalem fell" took away Isabel's breath, and she could not finish the ancient song. Tears welled up, and she gasped for breath.

Hearing the beloved psalm, Abigail felt faint. *Those words bring back the death of each of my children. I want my enemy to know what it is to lose them. To lose life's most precious gifts, my sons and daughters.*

The worship recalled all of their deepest feelings—rejection, pain, anger, and loss—with a recognition of God, the Almighty. The Lord was always present in history, knowing their pain yet sometimes seeming far away. All these sentiments came together in the quiet moments as the sun began to set behind Mount Tmolus.

Amos concluded with another prayer. "Ancient of Days, King of the Heavens, God of Jacob: He is our comfort." For a moment, silence filled the home. The observance was over, the oil lamps were lit, and flickering beams of light revealed deep creases on Abigail's face.

This was the moment Abigail wanted. Amos would ask her enemy to speak. "Do you have any thoughts for us on our day of mourning, Anthony?"

Anthony was dressed in an old, torn tunic. It was the closest garment to sackcloth that he could get. Since arriving two hours before, he had kept silent, his eyes downcast. However, encouraged

---

[43] Psalm 137:1–7

to speak up, he sat up straight said, "Amos Ben Shelah, your brother, Antipas, taught me what true worship is."

"I want you to know my deepest thoughts. I lived in Rome, and I saw endless worship at various temples. Animals were sacrificed in the names of many gods and goddesses. It was so different from what I learned from Antipas. He taught me about the Temple of Jerusalem and Jewish festivals. He explained how God is to be both feared and adored. He said, 'Endless sacrifices of animals could never permanently remove the sins of the heart. We who trust in the Messiah never need another sacrifice. There was only one sacrifice, and it was *sufficient for all.'*

Family members raised their heads and looked at Anthony. It was not at all what they had expected.

"Through your brother, I came to understand that both Jews and Gentiles can come to the same God. He explained that Yeshua Messiah gave himself up as a sacrifice. He told me, 'The purpose was to destroy the dividing wall of separation making peace where there was enmity between Jew and non-Jew and to forge reconciliation with God for both where there had been hostility.'[44]

"This kind of teaching was completely new to me. All I knew about Jews was what others said, such as, 'Those people are selfish,' or 'They only think about their own nation.' And there I was, learning the word 'reconciliation' from the mouth of a Jew. Antipas lived it each day. He told me, 'Yeshua brings reconciliation between Jewish and Gentile believers.' He changed my life."

Anthony looked at Amos, whose eyebrows were raised, each little line crowding out the one above it.

Abigail's mouth was half-open.

The word "reconciliation" did not sound right coming from a legionary. Anthony looked at Miriam, and she gave a slight nod.

He closed his eyes and recalled the moment in Sardis, two years before, when he had first learned of the pain that Abigail had suffered. The recollection came of the prayer he had made.

Lord, I think this is the moment I have been asking for—to speak with Aunt Abigail—but now I don't know where to start!

He took a deep breath. "May I tell you my story?" He looked around the room and saw heads nodding. "I joined my legion at

---

[44] From Ephesians 2:14–17

seventeen, and I have been a legionary for almost twenty-one years. I am now a reservist and will be a reservist for four and a half more years. After that, I'll be free."

Light laughter rippled around the room. Here was a reservist counting down the days.

"I will tell you something that I never thought I would ever tell anyone. I never could admit it to myself until I became a follower of Yeshua. The reason that I volunteered for the military was because of my hatred and desire for revenge."

He heard several members of the family suck in their breath.

"In our home, I was taught by my father about the worst defeat that ever happened to the Roman army. Three legions were swallowed up in Teutoburg Forest. Arminius was a Germanic nobleman who obliterated three Roman legions: the seventeenth, eighteenth, and nineteenth. That was in the thirty-fifth year of Caesar Augustus,[45] the lowest point of our army's history.

"I thought, 'If ever I get the chance to take revenge on Germanic tribes, I will do so.' Everyone expected me to enlist in my father's legion, to continue Legion V's heroic actions. I hesitate to tell you this, but my father fought against your city, Jerusalem. He was the head of a detachment of eighteen men, the first to go over the wall. He was a trumpeter, and he directed the initial charge. Shortly afterward, Herod's Temple was burned, and your city was completely destroyed."

He had their complete attention. Tish'a B'Av was for mourning the loss of their temple, not for hearing details about the army's siege and destruction of Jerusalem. Never had this day of observance captured them so.

"I'm taking a risk telling you what my father's legion did to your city. You may never want me back in this house. Well, my father was killed there, one of the first to die in that direct attack. His friends raised a plaque in Damascus in his honor. The memorial says, 'Legion friend, Syrian Septimus Vibianus, presented this memorial to trumpeter Aurelius Suros, who lived for forty years, a pious and

---

[45] The Battle of the Teutoburg Forest, between the Lower Rhine River and the Lower Elbe River, happened on September 9, 9 BC. The battle was described by four ancient historians. It became an essential point of reference in Europe during the wars against Napoleon. The battle site continues to draw visitors.

faithful servant of Legion V, in the second year of Emperor Vespasian.'"[46]

He looked at the floor. Tenderness for his father whelmed up from somewhere deep in his heart, a sensation he thought he had forgotten.

Abigail's mouth was open again.

"I wanted to become a legionary, but Palestine was far from my mind. 'Judea is an obstinate province,' we were told. 'It will never bow its neck to Rome.' I was determined to make the stubborn tribes in Upper Germania submit. Those fierce, wild tribesmen! We call them barbarians. My commander said, 'Anthony, you are a good archer. I want you trained to be a scout.' It involved dangerous work. Every day in those dark forests could have been my last."

He had never spoken this way before, opening himself up. The army had trained him not to be vulnerable. Yet here he was, letting them into his heart, knowing he would undoubtedly be condemned by Aunt Abigail.

He continued, "I longed for vengeance. I lived for it. I hated barbarians for what they had done to the honor and glory of Rome. Perhaps you think that I killed lots of people, but I did not. I led a particular scouting unit and gathered information. We pacified small villages. Upper Germania is now an organized province where people pay taxes and are submissive to Rome.

"Most of the time, we captured villages, making them understand Rome's demands. We let them live. Because of that, they were more likely to accept our rule.

"But something changed in me after I became a scout. I realized it after one village was burned by our cohort. Villagers refused to submit. I had been a scout for five years and noticed something changing in my mind. I had come to want villagers to stay alive.

"At first, I was convinced that the only enemies I had were 'those rebellious people out there in the forest glens' and that I was always surrounded by friends. However, I was almost killed. I will not tell you why or how, but an army man tried to kill me. It happened under a bridge; my face was cut open here. I almost died, but the army brought me back to Rome then to Philippi, where I recovered.

---

[46] The tombstone, housed in the Istanbul Museum of Archaeology, refers to July 5, AD 70. I appropriated this historical plaque to work it into Anthony's story.

"I have a farm there, not nearly as choice or inspiring a location as yours, Uncle Amos. My small farm is on a fast-flowing creek, sheltered by mountains near a valley.

"So I became whole again, except my face was scarred. I could no longer fight, so I was sent to Pergamum to train future scouts. While there, I met Antipas. When I was a child in Rome, my mother had become a secret follower of Yeshua. She wanted me to learn about the Jewish Messiah. It was her dying wish. I had been in Pergamum almost six months when I saw Antipas. Your brother was at the Agora slave market when he ransomed Zarrus and Arpoxa, the last ones to be sold that day.

"Somehow Antipas realized these two belonged together. He paid as much for two cripples as a highly prized slave that day."

For a moment, the attention was on Arpoxa as the group had a new understanding of her background. Two Scythians, the young man and his wife, were redeemed from the hands of a slave master. Arpoxa's eyes were moist, and she hugged her sons tightly.

"I started going to 'The Cave,' the place where Antipas brought people in his village together for worship. Over the next few months, I learned to see myself differently. His way of life conflicted with all I had learned and practiced. Miriam's songs stirred something in my heart that I hadn't felt since my mother died. Antipas taught me to be a follower of Yeshua of Nazareth. He invited me to be part of a group and trained me to be a leader. My army officer, Commander Cassius Flamininus Maro, erupted with anger. When he heard that I was interested in that crucified Jewish teacher, he changed my assignment.

"When I was in Upper Germania, danger lurked behind every tree. Coming to Pergamum, I wanted to be free from peril. However, Antipas explained, 'To be a follower of the Messiah is costly. You must be willing to die daily to your fleshly desires, the natural way you live every day. This new way of life is going to cost you everything. Anthony, it starts with repentance.'

"Antipas didn't have an easy time. Troubles abounded. First, he was excluded from the synagogue by the Jewish elders. Next came a boycott of his shops. Financial troubles followed. He was rejected by the Pergamum city council, the priests, and the military. No one wanted him teaching anything about Yeshua. Antipas's belief in our Messiah led straight to his death.

"But he taught me about agape love. Antipas both taught it and lived it. He ransomed Zarrus and Arpoxa and built houses for all the ransomed and freed slaves. He cared for widows: three Jewish women, two non-Jews, and one Samaritan. He said that the conflicts that broke out between the six widows were more than enough to keep him and several other people busy!"

Wry humor broke the tension, and he saw weak smiles. Abigail was sitting straight up, her backbone rigid and a blank expression on her face.

"I thought life in the army was dangerous, but Antipas was living a more uncertain life. In Upper Germania, my squad was attacked many times, but the legion was close by, ready to back us up. However, when Antipas suffered public opposition and that painful execution, no one spoke up for him. No one had the power to prevent the city government from lowering him into boiling oil.

"Now I have talked too much about myself. I serve under Commander Felicior, and I am in Philadelphia to arrest four harmful, loveless creatures. They threaten peaceful commerce on the roads. Because of the riots, we keep public places secure. Since we left Pergamum, I have developed a new desire for wherever I am posted. Outwardly you see a soldier, but inwardly I want to serve God, the Almighty, the Creator of the earth and the heavens, the God of Israel."

Anthony heard several people suck in their breath, never expecting this. Miriam gave a slight nod, as she had done half an hour before, so he went on. He had never made such a confession. But if he were going to live in this city, there had to be a moment of truth.

"I'm taking a risk. Possibly you as a family will not accept me. Maybe, to you, I am the enemy. But I know who your enemies have been. I know Jews suffered in Alexandria and that twenty-seven years ago more than fifty thousand were killed there. I know about the more recent destruction of Jerusalem. People suffered terribly. Up to two million Jews were killed during those awful days.

"These are things I *know*, but such atrocities are beyond my *understanding*. Each person who died left a hole in a family, a gap that can never be filled. I know entire families perished.[47]

---

[47] The number of Jews killed in the destruction of Jerusalem was about 1,600,000. This estimate comes from Josephus and his famous books, *Antiquities of the Jews* and *The Jewish War*. His eyewitness accounts form the basis of much of the wars' history against the Jews in the first century.

"Uncle Amos and Aunt Abigail, I have only one request. I am telling you about things I know. My plea is that *you know*, even if you can't understand it, that my innermost desire is to serve God first and foremost. Because of Antipas, I found life in God, the 'God of gods and the King of kings.' For those words, Miriam's grandfather, Antipas, died in boiling oil. I might be subject to a court martial for saying these words if my commander ever heard me.

"Please know that between you and me, there is no wall, no division, no hatred. I do not want to harbor sentiments that bring shame. Worshiping the God of Israel taught me this. I will never bring an animal as a sacrifice. I gave myself to Yeshua three years ago. On this day, such a sad one for your home, this is all I can say. I am sorry for your loss. I thank you for asking me to come to your home to share this day of grief with you."

He sat back, perspiration glistening on his forehead. A tremendous burden had been lifted from his shoulders. No one spoke, but they looked wide-eyed at each other. Who could have expected such words on this day of all days?

Across the room, Abigail was deep in thought. No one moved or said anything. Silence prevailed. Then she raised her head. "Please, Miriam, you were going to sing for us tonight. Please go ahead. I can't find the words I want to say."

Miriam began, "I composed a mournful song for this day. We know of your grief, Aunt Abigail. I can't say anything sufficient to console you. However, I can share a song called 'The Cup of Consolation.'

"Aunt Abigail, I was with you during those terrible days in Jerusalem. I was only five years old. What fearful memories: sharing frugal, joyless meals; the piercing cries when another neighbor's child died from starvation; breathing pain; and witnessing destruction together. How many times did you hold my little hand? I can't remember, but you were there with me. Then we escaped on that fateful day. My father died, shot from behind by our archers, those defending our high walls. I can only imagine your anguish."

It was Miriam's first song in Amos's house, a dirge. It started off high, like at the death of a child, when a mother mourns the loss. Her voice descended slowly and then finally rose, ascending to where her high, clear soprano voice had first begun the dirge.

You understand and care for me, O Lord.
Give me joy again! Please remember me.
I trust in your eternal, matchless Word.
Help me! I bring my pain to you, a plea.
  I drink a cup of consolation!

You are longsuffering. Our hope's in you.
Did you, our God, forget your covenant?
We called, 'Come! Our enemies, please subdue!
How long must we endure such punishment?'
  We wait in pain for your compassion.

I looked for healing. Why did none come near?
We mourn. Our ancestors sinned against you.
Lord, would you turn away your ear?
Terrorized children starved. Anguish ensued!
  All around us, nothing but destruction!

You scattered us with your winnowing fork.
The Temple! Our city lies in ashes!
Mothers imprisoned, saddened, forced to work.
Children wailed. Maidens cried out. Fires flashed.
  Our hearts are overwhelmed by frustration.

But your Word brings joy. Spirit, I invite:
Come search this repentant heart. Restore me.
Your redemption is my utmost delight.
Prevent further cruelty. Keep us free.
  This prayer is my cup of consolation.[48]

Miriam stepped behind her aunt, putting her arms around Abigail's shoulders and hugging her. Amos, Obed, Isabel, Ruth, Jesse, and Sarah—the rest of the family—moved from their places. Tears flowed as they surrounded the old lady. Words were not needed. In the silence of this day, their love touched a deep well of yearning within a mother's broken heart. That oasis, once so inviting and

[48] Miriam's song is based on Jeremiah 14:19–16:7

deep, had been stopped up for years. Like an abandoned well, it had filled up with litter and debris.

Anthony stood to one side. Though he wanted to join in the family's demonstration of affection, he knew that time would be needed to create trust.

Amos also knew this was not the moment for bringing Anthony and Abigail closer together.

Tish'a B'Av had always been their day of sackcloth and ashes, mourning and repentance. Tish'a B'Av meant soul searching and asking questions. This was also a day of recognizing mercy and redemption, a day for thanksgiving because the Almighty had preserved their lives through one more year of danger and threats.

Jerusalem was a pile of rubble and dust, but they had come away alive, although bearing scars that would never disappear.

Miriam did not want to break the magic of the moment. She realized Aunt Abigail was not the only one who had lost a loved one. Penelope had recently lost her husband. And then there was that new widow they had seen in Sasorta.

She said, "I've just thought of something. On our way to Philadelphia, we came through a town north of here. In Sasorta, a young woman was screaming because her husband was just killed in an accident. She's a young widow, and she probably needs a home. And a job. Perhaps she could be the one to look after Penelope's little baby."

Abigail said nothing, but her thoughts were whirling. *I would tell him my story, but how can I do that after what he has just said? I wanted him to know my loss, to feel my empty heart, but he said things that I must think about.*

I won't speak today.

How does he have the courage to speak this way in the home of a Jewish family? He's a Roman. He had tears in his eyes when talking about an army trumpeter killed on the walls of our city. What other personal things is he going to share?

Chapter 11
Two Letters

THE INN OF THE OPEN DOOR, PHILADELPHIA

Six weeks had passed since Tish'a B'Av. The family enjoyed pleasant, relaxed evenings, and the mornings were cleaner and crisper. Tonight the inn was quiet, and all the guests were asleep. Although Cleon was tired from the long day's work, he did his best thinking under a clear sky with stars twinkling above.

He pulled one of the small tables in the inn's food court under two oil lamps and began his letter.

August 27, in the 13th year of Domitian
From: Cleon, at the Inn of the Open Door, Philadelphia
To: Diotrephes, Gymnasium of Sardis

If you are well, then I am well.

Burn this letter after reading it. Two years ago, I lost my job in Sardis after helping you enter the wedding banquet at Simon Ben Shelah's house. No one told me that eagles were to be embroidered on the collars of the wedding gowns given to the guests. The tunic I gave to you was sufficient to enter as an invited guest, but you were caught upstairs in the house. After I was wrongfully dismissed from the Ben Shelah store, your letter of recommendation helped me find this job at the inn. Thank you for that.

I have important news about Anthony, Miriam, and the child. I will need to form a plan to take the child away from them. Miriam stays at her uncle's home most of the time. The child is never brought here into the city.

Anthony Suros and other soldiers are busy with an uprising. Unemployed farm laborers threatened to break into the city's emergency food storage center. Six weeks ago, emergency actions were passed, and now food is being delivered to the populace. In nearby towns, we hear less about grumbling and riots. The city council approved repairs to the city walls and public buildings. The wall close to the Inn of the Open Door had collapsed many years ago but is being repaired. The inn is packed each night. Not only are caravans coming through but also many soldiers are housed here.

The first building project is the restoration of an old, abandoned building. "The Workshops," across from the inn, was one of the least damaged original buildings. They tell me that it will have many areas for weavers' looms. Talk is going around, something about selling clothing to a merchant from Hierapolis. Workers have also started rebuilding the nearby Lower Hot Baths. That will be an extensive reconstruction. From early morning until sundown, I hear the noise of workmen.

The Inn of the Open Door has a new cook, a widow called Penelope, the mother of five young children. A young woman, Thelma, also a widow, is taking care of Penelope's children. They are staying in the livable portion of the partially reconstructed workshop building. Penelope, her children, Thelma, and some other people call that place home for now. I am sure Miriam will bring Chrysa to play with Penelope's children from time to time. This might provide the chance to take Chrysa back to your family. We could plan this during the construction activity. Shouts from workers and the constant sound of hammers would cover up a child's screaming.

The girl's father, your uncle, Zoticos, will be happy to raise her in the bosom of your family.

Finally, thank you in advance for your generosity in providing for my financial needs after sending you this confidential information.

THE POSTAL ROAD AT THE DOOR, NEAR PHILADELPHIA

After almost three months of Anthony and his team on various guard duties while waiting for the robbers to show themselves, the criminals struck again. A caravan of camels belonging to a merchant was robbed. Only a small amount of merchandise was taken. Still, the word that the Door was not safe due to highwaymen would spread quickly. Merchants and travelers were deciding to use the southern route along the Meander River.

That resulted in less traffic moving through Philadelphia and Sardis. Commander Felicior was flooded with complaints from the affected merchants. Anthony's team and other soldiers left the garrison to explore the latest banditry site.

An hour later, they began examining the area. To the west, the mighty Mount Tmolus dominated the horizon. A small river ran along the base of a steep cliff forming the southern flank of Cogamis Canyon.

"So this is where the robbery happened. How was it done this time?" asked Decimus.

A soldier had interviewed the camel driver. "I was told that the robbers went to the side of the road, over there. Then they vanished—poof!"

"Were they dressed like auxiliaries?" asked Bellinus.

"Oh no! He said that these men looked like simple peasants marching down the hill. They passed him as he was traveling up the hill. The driver became suspicious when he heard unusual noises. He walked back to his last camel to check and arrived just in time to see one of the bandits disappear carrying a bundle of goods."

Omerod and Bellinus searched the area and then called to Decimus and Anthony, "We found how they did their disappearing act! Watch us!" They vanished behind a rock.

A large rocky outcrop had bushes growing up to the road's edge, but a small tunnel was hidden behind the bushes. Inside, steps were carved into the rock so a person could climb down. Once inside, the four soldiers squinted in the dim light. They stood in a small underground cavern. A natural fault in the rock had been enlarged, serving as an exit. Stepping outside, below the road and not visible to travelers, they saw how well the cave was hidden. Both the entrance far below the cliff at the edge of the road and the tunnel were almost imperceptible.

"We didn't catch any snakes, but we've found where they slithered away and hid," said Omerod.

Bellinus muttered, disappointed, "How will knowing about this cave help us to find them?"

By evening, they were back at the inn. Cleon filled their cups with beer. He listened as they talked about robberies. Anthony was aware that the inn's employee was eavesdropping, but nothing was being said that was critical.

"Well," said Omerod, "at least we found their tunnel. After they attacked, they could hide things quickly. Perhaps their real hideout is close by."

"Let me pour you some more beer," Cleon said, leaning across the table.

Anthony added, "We now know they used the tunnel to escape. I would have to guess that they spent much time scouting out that area."

They had discovered their first significant piece of the puzzle. At least it was something to report to the wealthy merchant in Hierapolis. Later that afternoon, after reporting their findings to Felicior, Anthony found the garrison scribe. He dictated a short letter to Flavius telling him that the robbers were still in the area and that the team intended to apprehend them. The letter from the garrison was sent to Hierapolis for delivery to Flavius.

ZACHARIAS'S HOME IN PHILADELPHIA

While Anthony and the other soldiers were searching the area where the robberies had taken place, a letter arrived from Haim, Philadelphia Synagogue's respected rabbi. He had left Philadelphia two years earlier to join other rabbis in Antioch. Their conference debated issues about their faith and practical daily life.

The letter arrived on the Sabbath at the goldsmith's office. Always an observer of regulations, Zacharias could not open it until after sundown. The letter was addressed to the synagogue elders, and he sent a servant to the homes of his two closest friends: "Daniel and Michael, come to my house just after the sun goes down. Haim sent a letter to us."[49]

---

[49] In 1871 a scholar named Heinrich Graetz proposed that a gathering of rabbis had occurred in the first century or early second century, called the Council of Jamnia. He believed it confronted issues about Judaism after the destruction of Herod's Temple. Many scholars accepted this thesis. However, there was no proof in documents from that time. Included in the decisions of the postulated Council of Jamnia were: a) the acceptance of the Hebrew language; b) the adoption of Hebrew documents and the rejection of the Septuagint and books

Michael's pottery workshop was closed for the day. At home, he rested from work, and the workshop would be open again on Sunday morning.

Daniel's carpentry equipment remained on shelves every Sabbath. His house was located behind the shop, which opened onto the street. Every tool had its own place: chisel, adze, saws, ruler, caliper, square, and hammers.

Haim's letter had been sent well before the sailing season ended. Four days after the letter was written, a ship carried it from Antioch to Myra, a six-day voyage. Ten days later, it reached Rhodes, where the document was transferred to a vessel on its way to Miletus. A third ship brought it to Smyrna, and a courier arrived in Philadelphia on September 8. The letter had taken thirty-six days to reach Philadelphia.[50]

With Rabbi Haim's letter before them, they covered their heads with their prayer shawls. This was material to guide their future steps.

Zacharias lifted his prayer shawl over his head. "It is fitting that we would receive news from Rabbi Haim one week before the blessed day of Rosh Hashanah. Surely such an important letter

---

known as Apocrypha; c) an acceptance of life after death; d) a rejection of the Sadducees and their doctrines; e) a rejection of the Jewish Christians; f) the dismissal of all *minim,* or promoters of heresies; g) the adoption of the Eighteen Benedictions; and h) the addition of a twelfth paragraph, which would have prevented Christians from attending the synagogues. However, the idea of a Council having been held in Jamnia is controversial. Was every issue about the future of Judaism settled there late in the first century? Until 1960 this concept was widely accepted. However, increasingly, many scholars cast doubt on Graetz's thesis. In this novel, I proposed a gathering, before Jamnia. I imagined fifty-two rabbis in Antioch from Asia Minor and other nearby provinces for a meeting called over these issues. Rabbis arrived at their own conclusions, followed by a larger Council including rabbis from the entire diaspora. In history, Jamnia is referred to with variations. The "Council of Antioch" in these novels is fictitious. Nevertheless, something similar may have been a logical prelude to the events at the Council of Jamnia.

[50] The time needed to sail around the Mediterranean Sea is explained in *Biblical Turkey: A Guide to the Jewish and Christian Sites of Asia Minor* by Mark Wilson, page 90.

arriving before our New Year's Day was of the Almighty." He read the letter.

August 4, in the 13th year of Domitian
From: Haim in Antioch
To: My beloved friends in Philadelphia

Greetings in the name of Him who brings us true Shalom.

Having sought the will of the Almighty with many other rabbis about recent and unwelcome disturbances in our houses of worship, we send this admonition to the faithful gathered to worship his name.

We resist those who twist the truth. These people wish to change the covenant. Many treacherous ideas are circulating. The most dangerous of all are those that say the Messiah has already come. We cannot accept that a crucified Galilean from Nazareth was our Messiah. Was a crucified carpenter really our promised Messiah? Impossible!

We have a guiding principle found in Hosea: "It is love I desire, not sacrifice." This must be our guiding light until the temple is rebuilt. All our decisions will be based on love for God, sincere hearts, and renewed discipline. We must follow the Torah and the tradition of the elders.

The sacrificial system and the priesthood cannot continue. Since we do not have an altar, animals can no longer be sacrificed for sins. Instead, loving deeds expiate sin. We will seek justice and purity. We will not tolerate heresy. Prayers in houses of worship and in our homes replace the ancient pilgrimages to Jerusalem. Uniformity must be maintained through common prayers. Hebrew will be the language of our prayers. As Jews, we are committed to holding the same beliefs.

The following is a listing of the new regulations adopted by our council. True worship begins with at least ten men present. A new synagogue may be formed wherever sufficient families form a Jewish community. The covenant will be preserved in diverse locations. We will not tolerate those who divide us by false teaching or pagan philosophies.

Those who teach that the Torah is not from God must be cast out. First, Sadducees and those who are the descendants of Boethus[51] *must be cast out. Next to be excluded are the outsiders, the heretics, the dissidents, the apostates, the traitors, those who deliver Jews to pagan authorities, those who separate themselves from the Jewish community, the Hellenized, the Essenes, and the Nazarenes. Some in the Parthian East subscribe to elements of Zoroastrianism. Some in the West have been Hellenized. All these groups are considered anathema.*

The grain has been harvested, and we, like Ruth, who laid down at the feet of Boaz, await the final harvest. Our redeemer will reclaim us. Adonai will remove the shame of our widowhood. Just as the wind blows the chaff away, blown to a place where it is never found again, leaving grain for bread that preserves the body, so we, too, hold tightly to the truth.

Our task is to separate the truth from falsehood.

Our meetings continue here in Antioch, and we call upon you for prayer.

After hearing these words, Michael and Daniel sat with Zacharias in his library, comfortable with a long silence. Strict leadership had spoken in far-off Antioch, and the implications for their little community in Philadelphia were enormous.

Zacharias broke the silence. "We must talk with Amos Ben Shelah. The season of the High Holidays has begun. Let's visit him on Monday night. In only two more weeks, Yom Kippur will be here."

AMOS AND ABIGAIL'S HOME

Amos welcomed his friends on Monday evening, happy to see them. They left their sandals at the door. Each man had a long black beard ending in a point over his chest. They all wore long black tunics with tassels around the hem. Arriving after the evening meal, the visitors sat in the library where Amos conducted his business.

---

[51] Boethus was the founder of a family that cooperated with the Sadducees for decades before Jesus of Nazareth was born. His beliefs included a rejection of life after death.

Abigail asked if she might listen in, and they agreed to her being present.

"Yes, you may listen, but you will not speak," Zacharias decided. It was not normal for a woman to be present for such matters, but this was a decisive moment.

"Amos, do you know the fast that will occur next week?" asked Zacharias.

"Yes, I do. The Fast of the Seventh Month. It follows Rosh Hashana."

"And why do we remember that day?"

Amos replied, "It marks an unjust assassination. We tell the story each year to remind us of those terrible days."

"My dear friend, you remember some but do not maintain all the fasts. I talked to many of our friends in the congregation and found that you do not observe the fasts of the fourth,[52] seventh,[53] and tenth[54] months. How is it that you depart from our traditions?

"Next week, you should celebrate the Fast of the Seventh Month like the rest of us. Do you not value the contribution of Gedaliah to the peace of Jerusalem during a time of calamity?"

Amos looked at Abigail, and he shrugged. "I keep the fasts and celebrations that our Holy Scrolls command us to remember. We keep all the days designated in the scriptures, three feasts in the spring: Passover, First Fruits, and Pentecost. In the summer, we mark Tish'a B'Av. Like you, we still mourn Solomon's Temple's destruction centuries ago and Herod's Temple more recently.[55]

"There are three more in the Law, celebrated in the fall: Rosh Hashanah, or New Year; Yom Kippur, which is the Day of Atonement; and the Feast of Tabernacles. Building little shelters and sleeping outside takes us back to trials in the desert. We celebrate Chanukah in the winter and Purim in the spring.

---

[52] The Fast of the Fourth Month commemorated the day Nebuchadnezzar breached the outer walls of Jerusalem (2 Kings 25:3–4, Jeremiah 39:2, Zechariah 8:19).

[53] The Fast of the Seventh Month reminded Jews of the assassination of Gedaliah (Jeremiah 40:7–41:3 and Zechariah 7:1–5; 8:18).

[54] The Fast of the Tenth Month reminded them of the day Babylonian troops began their siege of Jerusalem (2 Kings 25:3–4, Jeremiah 39:2, Zechariah 8:18).

[55] The Fast of the Fifth Month memorialized the burning of Solomon's Temple (2 Kings 25:8–10, Zechariah 7:5).

"Nine special celebrations altogether. The Lord himself directs our calendar and the times of celebration for his people. But in Alexandria, our elders decided the extra four fasts were non-compulsory, so I, too, consider them optional."

Amos looked at Abigail again. Her eyes darted from one visitor to another. From experience, he knew that this verbal ordeal would mean she would lose sleep.

Nothing tonight will comfort her. This will drive her further into herself. She is no longer the happy woman I married.

"Amos," Zacharias's deep voice reverberated slightly within the stone walls of the Ben Shelah house, "you should participate in these four fasts. You must observe thirteen memorable events. But let us not be divided by your non-observance.

"Something more urgent brings us together. It has come to our attention that your niece, Miriam, is married to a legionary."

His logic was straightforward. Amos would be condemned, not only for his association with an outsider but for Anthony's willingness to continue working for Caesar.

Zacharias had taken control. "Think of the families in our congregation grieving because of what Rome's army did. Who burned the temple? Who destroyed Jerusalem? Who committed those evil deeds? Who robbed our treasury? Who stole our gifts, lovingly given to the Lord but robbed and used to construct the Coliseum in Rome? Amos, that was Jewish gold and silver! Ours! We had dedicated it to the Lord! Look what pagans did with it! Don't you see that Rome's army is our enemy?"

Amos nodded. The use of the treasures of Jerusalem to beautify Rome galled him, but he stayed silent. Even now, Domitian was adding another level to the Coliseum in Rome. His brother, Titus, had used Jewish treasure to build the grand building. But Amos would not be drawn into an argument over Anthony.

Michael spoke next, and his words cut deeply. "I heard it said the other day, 'Is Amos Ben Shelah a real Jew? If so, how could he permit Anthony, a non-Jew and an enemy, into his home?' But things are worse, Amos. We understand Miriam's baby is an outsider. And now a crippled woman and her sons live here! How can you allow Scythians to set foot in your house?"

Amos felt his heart beating rapidly. "Am I being rejected by our community because I offer hospitality? We are a true Jewish family!

For more than a thousand years, in an unbroken line, my family has been true to the covenant!"

Daniel cut him off. "Then listen to us, Amos! As teachers of infants, we come to your house. Let us be a light for those who walk in the dark. I would not want to leave here knowing I was an unwelcome instructor of the foolish."

"Go ahead, my friends, Zacharias, Michael, and Daniel," said Amos, crossing his arms. "Call me what you like, 'foolish' or 'one who dwells in the darkness.' I'm completing my seventh decade, and although I'm older than you are, perhaps you are wiser, so I will listen to whatever you have to say."

Hand gestures made by Zacharias seemed to fill the entire room. "Amos and Abigail, our dear friends, look around you! I think this wall contains copies of the new scrolls. Am I correct? Do you have the writings of that so-called 'scribe,' Matthew? Or the 'righteous Pharisee,' Saul? What about the outsider Luke?"

Amos pointed to a portion of the wall where several scrolls were bundled together. "Yes, I bought well-made copies."

Zacharias exploded. "Should the Ben Shelah clan accept the writings of non-Jews?"

Amos knew he could not win this argument. Still, he asked, "I know you don't give hospitality to outsiders, Zacharias. But don't you sell gold rings and ornate jewelry to them? Michael, who buys your pottery? And your furniture, Daniel..."

Zacharias pounced, infuriated. "Doing business is different from worshiping with them! How did our father, Abraham, become wealthy? And Isaac and Jacob and Joseph? I will never open my home to an enemy or listen to his false doctrines. Those who influence our children lead them astray."

Michael added, "Your niece married a Roman! What could be worse? That goes beyond all bounds of honor! Shameful!" He said the word twice, forcefully spitting it out.

An intense conflict was mirrored by expressions forming on Daniel's face. Both his sons were closely related to Michael's granddaughters. "Amos, my son Jesse is married to your granddaughter, Ruth. We would celebrate a wedding bringing our families even closer together if my second son, Mith, marries your second granddaughter, Sarah. Must I now tell my wife that our sons,

Jesse and Mith, would live in a home where non-Jews come and go freely?

"Are not our regulations about food, the way we pray, our calendar, and our circumcision rites intended to keep us separate from pagans? Amos! The precious gems of your birthright are disappearing faster than snow melting on the mountain in summer. What is left after the snow is gone? Only bare rock void of vegetation! Your life will be barren too."

Deep-seated lines on his face seemed to intensify as Amos asked, "What do you want from us? What must Abigail and I do?"

Fingering his long beard, Zacharias smiled. His warm personality bubbled up again, and he spoke kind words. "Amos, let go of these new beliefs. Yeshua was not the Messiah we are waiting for. He was killed as a criminal! Cleanse your library of every translation. Use only Hebrew. The Septuagint scrolls of the Torah, those you brought with you from Alexandria—burn them. All the writings of Matthew, Luke, Paul, and other heretical authors must be destroyed. Deal with non-Jews only in business and never in your home."

Sarah knocked on the door loudly. "Come quickly, Grandmother! Ruth's water has just broken, and she is going into labor! You are going to be a great-grandmother tonight!"

Amos offered his hand to his three guests. "I think our meeting is over." He took a deep breath, feeling the sudden urge to make a sharp, nasty reply. Instead, he bent down, picked up their sandals, and gave them to his visitors. It hit him that this was the action expected of a slave. He followed them out to the wagon and watched them prepare to return to the city.

With a heavy heart, Daniel sat down in the wagon's bench seat. He had so much more to say to Amos, and he wanted to go over the letter's contents from their friend and rabbi, Haim.

Amos was a dear friend. He was the carpenter's in-law through the marriage of his son, Jesse. And here Daniel was, in the house the very evening Jesse became a father. He was to be a grandfather for the first time. And hopefully many more times. Daniel wanted Amos to put aside all the ways of outsiders. The diaspora could not be splintered into smaller and smaller fragments. Disunity and division left broken pieces, like the useless shards scattered outside Michael's pottery shop.

Instead of declaring what was churning in his heart, Daniel turned to Amos, saying, "I am happy to know that my son is to be a father. I will tell Dorcas to come right away. She will help with the delivery."

Abruptly, Daniel added a hurtful parting comment in desperation, hoping to shame Amos. Unkind words might bring his friend back onto the path of the righteous. As the wagon began to move, he called out, "Amos, I will talk with my son Mith. Should he break his commitment for the wedding next May? After all, how can my son continue in fellowship with your family?"

Since the wagon was already moving, the shock of Daniel's comment did not allow for any kind of considered reply. With a slight bow of his head, Amos bid them goodbye: "May the blessing of the Almighty follow you. Walk in the paths of peace."

He watched them leave in Michael's wagon and pursed his lips. *I feel as if something has fallen and been lost. It's as if I were outside in that storm last winter. I saw how much damage it did. The gale broke branches from my fruit trees. Now my friends demand that I refuse hospitality to outsiders. How can I? In Zarrus, Arpoxa, and Anthony, I have found people who love the God of Israel. The effect of the elders' decision on both sides of our family relations is like walking into a dark cave without a candle. We don't know what we may stumble over next.*

Chapter 12
Ruth, Jesse, and Asa

MICHAEL AND MARTHA'S HOME IN PHILADELPHIA

Rushing home and running through the front door, Daniel shouted, "Ruth is going into labor!" He took Dorcas as quickly as was safe on Mountain Road and then along the bumpy farm road up to the big house. She stayed all night with her daughter-in-law, making sure that Ruth was resting well. As a midwife, she brought baby Asa into the world; as his grandmother, she witnessed the next generation's arrival.

As the morning sun was rising, laughter and joy reverberated throughout the home. Abigail sensed more energy than she had for years. Ruth held her precious little boy then gave him to her husband. Jesse held the small child high over his head and lowered him into his arms, repeating the action three times.

"My little Asa! My little boy, you are so precious! Your name means 'healer.' I want you to bring healing every day of your life!" The young father lifted the baby above his head again. "I'll never lose my hold on this lovely little boy!"

Dorcas beamed while talking to Ruth and Jesse. "Well, your little boy will be circumcised next week on the Fast of the Seventh Month! What a wonderful day for this family! I love being a grandmother. I've waited so long for this day to hold my grandson. Here, Jesse, may I hold Asa again?"

Miriam could not hide her smile. "You are so brave, Ruth! A long, hard delivery, wasn't it? But look! You have forgotten the pain of giving birth, and here, right in your arms, lies your first-born son! What a lovely name! Asa, the king of Judah. He was a good king. Isn't his black hair sweet? I never get tired of letting tiny fingers grab my hair!"

Dorcas asked, "Miriam, you don't have any children of your own, do you?"

Miriam's eyes became misty since this was her most sensitive topic. *Arpoxa has two children, and Penelope has five. Thelma told me that she wanted a baby right away. I want to give a child love and care. I cannot tell Dorcas my most intimate thoughts. God, why have you not given me a child?*

Miriam bent forward. "Aunt Dorcas, the answer is 'No, the Almighty has still not given me such joy.' But my answer to the question you did not ask is 'Yes, God did give me a lovely child. Anthony and I adopted Grace, and she's healthy and intelligent.'"

AMOS AND ABIGAIL'S HOME

On Wednesday, a day after Asa's birth, Daniel went from his carpentry shop to the inn. He asked for Obed and then spoke in two short sentences. "Obed, we are coming to your home tomorrow midmorning. Please give this message to Amos immediately."

"Are you only going to meet with my father?"

"Yes, six of us from the council are coming to talk with him. Not your mother though. She will not be in the room with us."

Obed rode home on his horse, taking the message written on a small piece of papyrus. Michael's most delicate penmanship was written in Hebrew. Before receiving Haim's letter, everything he wrote had been written in Greek.

The note said, "We will follow up on the topic of our conversation on Monday, the evening when Ruth's labor started. Please be home tomorrow midmorning."

It was signed by Zacharias, Michael, Daniel, and three others.

Amos's house was full of guests when the elders arrived. Now, two days after the new arrival, Penelope's children wanted to see the baby. Thelma had said she was happy to go with them to the Ben Shelah farm to help control the children. The wagon was full, bringing ten people: Penelope's five children, Thelma, Zarrus, and Arpoxa and her two boys, Saulius and Madis.

Penelope stayed at the inn to prepare the meals.

The happy sounds of children playing filled Amos's home when Daniel came to the door. He stood speechless upon seeing so many in the room. Arpoxa was breastfeeding Madis, her younger son. Three-year-old Saulius was giggling and playing with Sandra. There were several women as well, the wives of Amos's servants.

Dorcas knew why they had come, and she hid a smirk when she saw her husband. A dark scowl covered Daniel's face.

Abigail saw the other five men arriving, but she ignored them while lost in her thoughts. *Asa, two days old and so healthy! For the first time in many days, I'm not saying to myself, "I have no hope!" Since Asa's birth, the light seems brighter. God will preserve us. I feel joy with all these children around me!*

The visitors walked toward Amos's library without saying a word. Six men were dressed in flowing black tunics and fingered long black beards. The mood changed in the home and was now tense, foreboding. Once inside the library, the visitors stood in a semicircle. Amos offered them chairs, but the men stayed standing next to each other.

"Who are all these people in your home?" asked Zacharias.

Amos felt his muscles tightening. His chest was tight. Breathing was a struggle, but he knew what the outcome of this morning's meeting would be, and it helped to calm his heart.

"Five children belong to Penelope, a widow, who now works as a cook at the inn. She came from Olive Grove, my brother's farm. Thelma, the young widow from Sasorta, looks after Penelope's children. Arpoxa and her husband, Zarrus, are former slaves from Scythia. I hired him to work at the inn. They and their two boys moved into the partially renovated workshop building. Penelope and her children are staying in another room in the same building. Both families will be moved elsewhere when the workshops are completed and ready for use."

Zacharias observed, "Zarrus and Arpoxa are the cripples. And just to make sure, those are Scythian names, aren't they?"

"Yes, they came on a ship from far up north."

With his face turning a shade darker, Zacharias asked, "Is Penelope a Jew?"

"No, but she is a God-fearer. She believes in our Messiah."

"Are any of these children, hers or the Scythians'...are they circumcised?"

"Well...uh...I really don't know, but I doubt it."

"Is Thelma a God-fearer?"

"No. We brought the young woman to help Penelope."

"Tell us more about the crippled people, the two Scythians."

"My brother, Antipas, redeemed them. They were being auctioned on the slave platform at the market in Pergamum. Very soon afterward, they became followers of Yeshua Messiah; they are now God-fearers."

Zacharias sighed, lowering his head. "Amos, how far you have fallen! How sad! You open your home to evil influences! A child's name should point to the God of Glory! Look! Your friends are pulling you down! How can we have fellowship with you?"

Responding quickly, Amos answered, "Besides being a follower of the Messiah, Zarrus is an expert craftsman. He makes pottery. People appreciate the designs he paints on vessels. He is going to teach those skills to the people in Cogamis Valley."

"And the crippled woman, what does she do?"

"Arpoxa is an expert with a needle and thread. The city hall wants families throughout the valley to produce high-quality clothing. The women she teaches in workshops will improve their work. As people sell their products, there should be more money in the cities, more food, and less social dislocation. She wants to teach people good habits, share her life with them, and be a light to the Gentiles."

Zacharias wiped his forehead. Sweat was glistening, a sign of increasing distress. "Amos, you permitted another young woman in your house! She will corrupt men here as surely as yeast causes bread to rise!"

"You are talking about Thelma, aren't you? She lost her husband three months ago in a riot in Sasorta. She needs a place to stay, so she helps Penelope, who requires someone to look after her children. Thelma will learn about our Lord. We are teaching her, and she will learn to worship with us."

As Zacharias found harsh words to express his anger, his deep voice resonated in the room. "Your situation is worse than we feared. By taking in widows and orphans, you allow corruption! Do you not understand? Compassion must not be extended to everyone. You need to be faithful to your heritage, as we are.

"Think about the five elders standing with me. Michael was named after his ancestor. Five centuries ago, that faithful man loved Jerusalem so much he returned from the Exile with Zerubbabel. He was one of ten loyal elders that Zerubbabel could count on. Michael is the same age as you, sixty-nine years old. I want to see you being like him, faithful to the covenant.

"Now look at Daniel Ben Helkai. He's a generation younger than you. You and Abigail are great-grandparents and related to him by marriage. Remember the faithful men who returned to Jerusalem from Babylon with Zerubbabel? Daniel is named for the prophet who refused to bow down to an evil king. And what do we find in your home? You are not a faithful follower. You refuse to observe all the traditions of our ancestors. In twelve days, we celebrate Yom Kippur, the Day of Atonement. We want you to confess your pride and to be cleansed."

He straightened up as tall as his forty-eight years would permit. Arriving at the main reason for their visit, his voice was little more than a whisper. "If not, you and your family will be excluded from our fellowship. You must carry out the actions demanded of you.

"We told you not to open your home to outsiders, but look! Your house is worse than an anthill. Can't you see that the place is crawling with pagans? Their males are uncircumcised. Just as bad, a pagan woman cares for children under your influence! What will she teach? What did she learn as a child? She knows only stories of pagan gods! She is ignorant of the covenant."

Amos tried to interrupt. "We are going to teach her, and she will learn that the Lord is One, the God of Israel."

However, Daniel broke in with "Do you refuse our demands?"

Amos crossed his arms. "The temple built by Solomon was called a 'House of Prayer for All Nations.' Everyone was to come and worship there, people from all–"

Zacharias held his hand up to stop him. "Amos, the council met last night. We decided that you will make a choice. Light cannot have fellowship with darkness."

Amos felt his stomach tighten. From the large room came the happy laughter of little children and mothers—this sharp rebuke contrasted with his joy of being a great-grandfather.

An acute pain traveled along his left arm and down to his wrist, and he quickly lowered his arm, holding it in his right hand.

"How long do I have to decide?" Amos asked quietly.

"In twelve days, we celebrate Yom Kippur, the Day of Atonement. The Feast of Tabernacles begins five days later. After that feast, you will be subject to our rules. Do not disregard this warning. You and your family stand to be excluded."

The meeting was over. It had taken longer than the elders had anticipated. Sitting in the wagon and fingering his long beard, Michael groaned, "I kept telling him four years ago, 'Don't sell your shop!' and then 'Keep away from the inn. Those people will lead you astray.' But Amos bought that broken-down place. I knew it would seal his fate. The man completely refuses to listen!"

Standing beside the wooden gate at the entrance to his property, Amos watched them leave. He felt buffeted by forces beyond his control, like strong winds sweeping down from the mountain in wintertime and gusting against the trees. A tradition was like a blustery gale, something beyond his powers to influence. How could he stand against families who were longtime close friends? What could he tell them to convince them he was sincere and not living in rebellion?

He held his left wrist in his right hand until the pain in his arm eased, and then he closed the gate.

Abigail moved slowly and groaned quietly as she rested her head on her husband's chest. Amos wanted to sleep earlier than usual. In their earlier years, her being close to him like this raised her passion and desire for his love, but tonight she felt little strength.

The old woman had too much going on in her mind to fall asleep. She felt refreshed. People were constantly coming to visit Ruth and Jesse. Children were running around the house. Oh, the noises children made when they were having fun!

"Can't you sleep?" Amos asked, rolling over in bed. "You told me a long time ago that you wanted revenge. Is this what keeps you awake?"

"Oh yes! I wish it on all my enemies! Of course, I don't have the strength to hurt anyone, but I would like to."

"Can we talk about a couple of things? Before Anthony told us his story, you wanted him to sense our people's pain. What did you think after he spoke to us?

"Today the elders demanded that we reject all friendship with those who were in our home. Sometimes we are surprised by who is being honest with us and who wants to hurt us."

She cut him off. "Amos, you have no idea what goes through my mind. Thinking about Anthony's story or seeing the dark looks on the elders' faces as they came in this morning..." She stopped speaking.

Thoughts that tormented her every day could not be expressed. *Everyone is against me—Romans and Jews! Those in Jerusalem and now those we counted on as being our friends. I can't trust any of them! My mother and father, dead from starvation...and my lovely boys too. Soldiers surrounded our city! But who killed Annias? Oh, my son! It was John's army. Fellow Jews murdered him! Annias was taking a lamb, the last one we had. That was our offering! He carried our prayer that peace would come to Jerusalem. He was shot and killed on the way to the temple.*

And our son Azetas! Simon's army killed him after they broke into our house. They were fellow Jews, and they took all our food!

Help, Lord. I cannot continue hating like this. No, not loathing everyone, just Anthony. He must know how much pain his army brought me. With that, I have only one person's face before me. And in his scar, I will see all the people I detest.

THE SYNAGOGUE OF PHILADELPHIA

On Sunday evening, Jews gathered for Yom Kippur readings and prayers. On this holiest day of the year, every space in the Jewish house of worship in Philadelphia was taken. Zacharias called on the God of Abraham, Isaac, and Jacob, and his soothing voice brought comfort.

He sounded the shofar, the ram's horn trumpet, to signal their freedom and to gather their exiles from the four corners of the earth. He prayed, "Blessed are you, O Lord, who gathers the dispersed of his people Israel."

Next he prayed for the righteous reign of God on the earth. The provision of the Lord in former times brought judges and counselors. In those times, sorrow and sighing had been removed. He prayed for the loving-kindness and compassion of the Lord. Again he praised the name of God. "Blessed are you, O Lord, the King who loves righteousness and justice."

The next part of his prayer was a new paragraph. It was the first time any of the worshipers had ever heard it, for he was implementing Haim's directions. He specifically asked God for the destruction of apostates and the enemies of the Lord.

In his voice, grief and passion were mixed with a sincere desire for true holiness. He prayed that the enemies of God's people would be left without hope. All wickedness would perish, and the dominion of arrogance would be rooted out. Enemies would be smashed, and the arrogant would be humbled.[56]

As he led the people in prayers for the righteous and for proselytes, he remembered Thelma. He paused while worshipers meditated on their sins, and an unfamiliar concern stirred within. The picture came back of happy children at Amos's house and the news that a twenty-year-old widow cared for them.

His eyes were closed as he thought about that moment. *For an instant, I believed it might be right for Amos to pray for someone like Thelma, the young widow. Might she hear of Adonai and become a proselyte, like Rahab the harlot? But no, that is impossible.*

The idea flew through his mind, but instantly it was gone.

Continuing his prayer, Zacharias asked for the Lord's compassion on the righteous, the pious, and the elders of the house of Israel. Included were the remnant of their scholars and proselytes. He wanted a reward for all who trusted in the name of God, asking that they would never be put to shame. "Blessed are you, O Lord, the support and stay of the righteous."

His deep, rich voice filled the building. Zacharias had found a new depth, a new meaning in praying for the rebuilding of Jerusalem. "Return in mercy to Jerusalem, your city, and dwell in it as you did in days long gone by." He finished his prayer by praising God. "Blessed are you, O Lord, who rebuilds Jerusalem."

His congregation was always inspired by the way he uplifted the name of the Lord. Every request for the benefits they might receive depended upon the Almighty One.

---

[56] This phrase has long been discarded. It was used in prayers at the end of the first century. Significantly, it marked the beginning of the division between Jews committed to the Torah and followers of the Jewish Messiah.

Chapter 13
Abigail

AMOS AND ABIGAIL'S HOME

On Saturday, the sixth day of Sukkot, the Jewish Feast of Tabernacles, many people made their way to Amos and Abigail's house. Comments made the rounds in the Jewish community that Amos was deliberately setting out to cause a division. After all, wasn't he leading prayers for a group of people who were not close family members?

By late afternoon, their home's large central room began to fill as the many visitors arrived. Abigail looked around, content in her new role as a great-grandmother and anxious to use the right words. She still wanted Anthony, her enemy, to know about the many painful events in her life.

Outside, one of the servants guarded the wagons in the courtyard. Two others led the horses down the hill to the farm's stable, where they munched on fodder while swishing their tails. Their skin jerked involuntarily to keep annoying black flies away. Away from the city, all found relief from the persistent pall of smoke. The haze was caused by the after-harvest burning in the fields.

Jesse sat beside Ruth, and little Asa was asleep in her arms.

Dorcas looked at Ruth and Asa and then at her sons, Jesse and Mith. She hid a smile when she heard someone whisper, "Isn't she the grandmother? Look how happy she is!"

Family members wore their best clothing, with men dressed in tunics that came just above the knees. The light brown clothing helped them recall the experiences of desert sands. Their ancestors wandered for forty weary years, facing hunger and thirst.

The four women—Isabel, Ruth, Sarah, and Miriam—each wore a *peplos,* a long tubular garment. Fastened by a pin on each shoulder, it hung straight down, covering the toes and just skimming the floor. A cord was attached at the middle, just below the bust. The resulting fold in the one long piece of cloth appeared to form an upper garment being worn over a skirt.

Isabel's *peplos* was a light blue, while Ruth's and Sarah's were dyed a light pastel red with dyes from the madder plant. Miriam preferred a darker blue.

A wagon arrived bringing Penelope and her children. Her work was done for the day, and the meal was being served at the inn by other servants. Her three oldest children stayed downstairs while Thelma went upstairs to care for the five younger children: Penelope's two youngest, Grace, Saulius, and Madis.

Servants who typically took care of the farm had been invited as well as their families. The sweet scent of olive soap filled the room. This was an evening for their best clothes. For once the smell of farm clothes was gone, and an expectation of a good evening brought out their best manners.

Always one to note details, Anthony, the last to arrive, whispered to Miriam, "I counted thirty-two people in this room, two more with you and me."

He sat in a corner, his rough light brown military tunic clearly marking him as belonging to a profession no one else had chosen. Thick carpets covered marble floors. A carefully prepared meal was served, and for more than an hour, people talked with each other, their heads close together. The din slowly increased in volume.

When all were satisfied and the empty bowls and platters returned to the kitchen, Amos asked them to sit down. People found a place to sit, mainly against the wall where they could lean back, and the room became silent.

"This is a special day for us," Amos began. "When we lived in Jerusalem, throngs crowded narrow streets. We inched our way toward the temple, and we were as close then as we are to one another right now. Every year at this time, we built small tents using branches and blankets. I slept with my children outside on the roof. Questions come to mind when you look up at the stars, especially during nights out in the open. Darkness is overwhelming, so real you think you can touch it.

"That was our way of remembering our ancestors. After leaving slavery in Egypt, they struggled for years in a vast desert. Every day they asked the same questions: 'Where will we find water? What will we eat next? Where are the herbs for healing when we feel sick?'

About 1,500 years ago, my ancestors wandered along dried-up streams. Many died of thirst, hunger, war, and illness.

"Tonight, unlike other homes in this city, where entertainment follows an evening meal, you will hear a simple story. It's our story. Abigail and I passed through what we call our 'desert experience.' It was her idea to call you together for a meal and to hear her story. She has not been feeling well, but the birth of her great-grandson gave her a renewed strength. That's why she invited you here."

He sat down, and people cheered, grateful for the tasty food and happy to listen to Abigail. Her white linen *peplos* gave her thin figure a younger look. She was more invigorated and did not appear to be seventy-three years of age. Miriam whispered to Anthony, "I've never seen her look so beautiful. She looks more alive tonight than ever. She is usually so pale and fragile."

For two weeks, Abigail had wondered how to describe her family's journey. She was not used to speaking to a crowd, and many were men. But smiling at Amos calmed her racing heart.

"Welcome to our home and to this celebration of the arrival of my first great-grandson! As my husband said, tonight is the time to tell the story of our family. My father, a scribe and a son of a scribe, would have been thrilled to see our new great-grandson, but the Almighty was pleased to take him...far too early."

She stopped to catch her breath because she would not let her emotions show. She blinked several times, forcing back a tear.

"My ancestors helped the translators of the Torah, our Book of the Law. For generations, they lived in Alexandria, Egypt, and they were proud to aid the specialists in the Hebrew language. They produced the Septuagint. That Greek translation of our writings is what we prefer in our home. My ancestors became friends with the Ben Shelah family many years ago, so our families have been associated for a long time.

"My ancestors had not always lived in Alexandria. They moved there almost two hundred fifty years ago when fear of the heavy-handed Seleucid kings in Antioch drove many people away. In Egypt, they made new relationships and found a permanent home. Ours was the eighth generation born there. My father, Jorah Ben Eddinus, loved the Law of Moses, and he spent Sabbath days discussing the Law.

"Near the end of Nero's reign, our whole family, including my mother and father, prepared to move to the city we spoke of so lovingly. We wanted to return to Jerusalem. *Pax Romana* made it safe to live in any province of the empire. Our seven children were all born in Alexandria, and they came with us. There were five boys—Annias, Ater, Azetas, Obed, and Arah—and two girls, Leah and Agia. Annias was twenty-two years old when we boarded a ship sailing to Joppa. Agia, our youngest, was five.

"Before we packed our baggage, my niece, Miriam, was born. Stand up, Miriam, so everyone can see you!"

Miriam stood up and looked around the room. People clapped and cheered. Then Miriam sat down, her shoulder pressed tightly against Anthony's chest.

Abigail waited for a moment. She knew everyone was attentive, wanting to hear her story. *Telling them about my family in Alexandria took away the butterflies I felt in my stomach. I'm ready to tell them what happened in Jerusalem.*

"There she was, a baby girl, born just as we were about to leave Egypt! Her mother, Tamara, said, 'I'm going to call her Miriam, like the sister of Moses, who led our people out of Egypt.' That is how we all came to Jerusalem. We were an extended family of eighteen people. How happy I was to get on the ship with Amos and our seven children! My father-in-law, Eliab Ben Shelah, and his wife, Ahava, came with my brother-in-law Antipas and his family.

"How we longed for our first glimpse of Herod's Temple! After decades of work, it was finished. A majestic, beautiful structure! No more builders, workmen, artists, or scaffolding! No noise. None of that! And the celebrations as people flocked into the city! People commented on the enormous stone blocks and the beautiful colonnaded walkways.

"I thrived in that hustle and bustle. Our money came from the family business in Alexandria. Amos bought a house inside the city walls while Antipas and his family lived on a farm near the town of Bethlehem. Each of us wanted that peaceful atmosphere to last forever, but storm clouds were forming.

"After a Zealot rebellion broke out up north, Rome's army arrived to crush the uprising. More soldiers arrived. No one could stop them. Our enemies came in three legions: the fifth, tenth, and fifteenth. They captured cities, towns, and villages, one after another. Jotapata fell, then Taricheae and Mount Tabor.

"Thousands died, all agonizing deaths. Insects stood a better chance of survival since they could hide in small places. Wherever there was a Jew, Roman soldiers' swords shed blood. We shuddered to hear that the Jewish resistance had been annihilated in Joppa, the city on the coast. Even worse was the news of the terrible assault on Gamala.

"Antipas and his father sold their olive farm near Bethlehem. The next day, the house next to ours in Jerusalem became empty. The owner said, 'All is going to be lost. We refuse to stay here to face death. The Romans are going to surround Jerusalem and destroy it.' Amos and Antipas bought that house at a reasonable price. For weeks, we prepared for a long siege. Our boys dug a big storage area below the floor, making a large storage room. We stocked it with food from Bethlehem.

"Having been defeated in the north around Galilee, a Jewish army took quarters inside the city walls. This militia was led by John of Gischala, an inflexible man full of strong talk. John commanded a group called the Zealots. For years he had been causing problems for peace-loving Jews. My husband said, 'Watch out for him! He'll set himself up as the king of Jerusalem!'

"But then another Jewish army arrived! This one was led by Simon Ben Giora. Next we heard that the gates were opened to his militia from Hebron in the south. It was a sad day because we knew suffering was upon us. Both men, John of Gischala and Simon Ben Giora, came to dominate Jerusalem. My fears were realized. Everyone inside the walls would lament their actions.

"Weeks later, Roman legions arrived. Tents sprang up on hillsides like mushrooms, except mushrooms last only a few days. Legionaries were like iron, firm and unbending. We watched eagle standards standing beside encampments. Colorful flags identified the various cohorts and divisions. Trumpets sounded as even more soldiers appeared from another legion. From the top of the city walls, we watched soldiers going in and out of their tents. We were surrounded as battle equipment spread over hills to the north, east, west, and south.

"Inside the city, a war of our own making was underway. John's army fought Simon's. Our community was split in half. Suddenly, there was not enough food for everyone.[57]

"We prayed desperately. One day Amos asked Annias, our firstborn, to take an offering to Herod's Temple. Perhaps the Lord would look in kindness on his people. He took a lamb in his arms, but just as he gave the lamb to a priest, he was killed by an arrow shot by a soldier in John's army at random. The arrow went over the temple wall, and...Annias was...killed in our temple...our twenty-five-year-old! A priest came to our house, and I screamed when he said, 'Your son is dead, killed by his own people.'"

Guests' eyes filled with tears as Abigail wiped her eyes.

"His body was placed outside the wall on top of thousands of corpses. The fighting was fierce. We could not have a funeral. That was another tragedy, which still galls me.

"A few days later, *Jewish* soldiers burst into our house, demanding our food. A jealous neighbor had told Simon's army about our hidden resources. Ater, who was twenty-four years old, stopped them at the door. They knocked him out of the way, rolled up the carpet, and discovered our hidden storehouse.–Azetas protested, but a *fellow Jew* stabbed him in the belly with his short sword. The soldier screamed, 'This food belongs to us. You cannot have it, because it has to be shared with everyone!'

"My third son died an hour later. We lost our food and my twenty-two-year-old son. Again I wailed in agony. Since the city gates were closed, Amos had to drop Azetas's body over the wall on top of the several thousand rotting corpses of the city's dead. Many

---

[57] This account of events in Abigail's story is taken from the extensive narrative written by Josephus. Much of the city was controlled by Simon Ben Giora. John of Gischala led a bitter fight against Simon and his forces. John's Zealots sought to overthrow Simon, who had gained control of the temple and other city sections. John's leadership was known for both tyrannical orders and charming words. Some of those resisting him brought accusations that he planned to be king after a future victory over Rome. Josephus reported that John's militia shot arrows at random from below Herod's Temple into the temple precincts. Jerusalem was destroyed in AD 70 after the wall was breached. Days later, the temple burned to the ground, with the treasures being taken and sent to Rome. Then the entire city caught on fire. The two houses Abigail mentions are fictitious. I imagined them living in the northwestern sector.

others died that day, and I wept many tears. However, nothing could bring my son back."

While listening to Abigail, many were crying openly. A servant who worked in the kitchen had heard all the stories before. She, too, was wiping her eyes with the back of her hand. Abigail heard several people blowing their noses. She looked at the floor, her eyes misty.

I don't want to do this, God! I hurt to talk about Ater...but Anthony must hear the whole story. I think the expression on his face shows me his feeling of shame, and I see humiliation.

"The army was constructing earthen ramps to cross over onto our walls. I'm now going to tell how our other son, Ater, was killed by the *Romans*. Their siege preparation was complete. Soldiers were on every side of the city. One night, Ater became so angry he went out of the city with many young men. Their intention was to burn the enemy's war engines. They did destroy one of them, but they were caught before returning and..."

She struggled to say the words. "My son was...slaughtered ...along with five hundred others who had gone out from the city that night. I didn't sleep for days after that."

The story brought gasps from around the room. While speaking of how Ater died, Abigail looked penetratingly at Anthony. A dark intensity glowed in the old woman's eyes. The bitter memory worked like poison after being bitten by a snake. Venom would spread through the bloodstream and infect the body. Abigail's passions flowed freely; her mind was lucid and her words descriptive.

Abigail glanced at Anthony and studied his face in the flickering light from the oil lamps. *Anthony has tears in his eyes. I hope my son's death is touching something deep inside.*

"People began dying of starvation. One woman's child died, and she ate her own son. Neighbors smelled meat burning, and when they broke into her house, they saw what she had done. They ran away, screaming in horror. Was there ever such darkness?

"My son, Arah, was only eleven when he died, such a sweet boy. He loved music and wanted to sing right up to his last day. He died in my lap, overcome by starvation. Leah died next, also famished. Agia had always been a sickly child, and she also died from starvation. I held her close to me, and I cried, 'Lord, take my life, but spare hers. I cannot take another death!'

"Where could we put the dead but drop them over the city wall? The stench of decaying bodies made it hard to breathe. Famine crept in, a silent killer. How many perished? One million? Two million? Hungry fighters were up against well-fed Roman legions. People went crazy while fighting against hunger, fighting to live. But it made no difference. Death was everywhere."[58]

Abigail could hardly carry on, for her energy was being sapped through recounting such sad memories. *I will have nightmares tonight. O God, why such a loss?*

Isabel came to sit close beside her and put her arm around Abigail's shoulders. This helped the elderly woman to gather strength to continue. "After each one died, Amos took their little bodies out to the city wall at night, said a prayer, and then laid them before the Lord. To prevent people from escaping, the enemy cut down trees and built a separate wall around our city. Three weeks later, we were utterly imprisoned. No longer could young men slip past the Roman guards at night to bring in extra food. Without hope left, we were merely a weak and dying family. My father was so ill he could hardly walk.

"One day a small group of priests decided to leave the city. They had been praying for deliverance, searching the psalms and the prophets. They quoted Jeremiah, one of our prophets. Centuries before, when Babylonians invaded from the north and Jeremiah was dying of hunger, he pled with the people to surrender. 'Whoever stays in this city will die by the sword, famine or plague. But whoever surrenders...will live.'[59]

"So Father said, 'I am going to surrender with the priests. Better to be killed by enemies than to stay in the city. Here, we will die at the hand of our own people.' Mother pleaded, 'No, Jorah, my dear, God will keep us safe. Only a few more days, and then the Romans will be defeated!"

"But my father, Jorah Ben Eddinus, convinced my mother. It was July 17. He knew the city could not hold out much longer. We had arrived four years before, awestruck by the glory of the temple, but he said, 'We must leave or all die of famine.' We were nothing but

---

[58] Josephus gave estimates of deaths in each city and town. After the destruction of Jerusalem, he estimated the number taken as slaves, those killed for entertainment in Caesarea Philippi, and those sent to Egypt as slaves.
[59] Jeremiah 21:9

skin and bones. Only five of us were left now: my parents, Amos, Obed, and I. Antipas and those in his family also left. We stumbled through the gate early in the morning."

She sobbed quietly. No one moved, and slowly she built up the courage to finish. "Perhaps a hundred escaped that day; I can't remember. If more had shown humility, they would have lived. Joseph and Jesus, the high priests, got out in time. The three sons of Ishmael and three sons of Matthias and their families were given safe passage.[60] Matthias, a priest, was killed by Simon. His fourth son wanted to escape with us, but he was killed just outside the gate. Some of the nobility also left. There were no more animals for sacrifices, and those priests stayed until the last possible moment.

"Once out of the city, there was only one choice: face the army, fall on our knees, and cry for mercy. Death looked us in the face. Either it was *Jewish* cruelty or *Roman* brutality."

Half an hour before, she had been relaxed, but now lines of tension showed on her face. *I can't go on.... I can't tell them how Mother and Father died from gobbling down the food given to us by the soldiers. Within a day, they were bent over with pain, never to rise to their feet again. Of the eleven in my family when we left Egypt, only five of us crossed the Jordan River. How I hated everything Roman: their fearsome weapons, giant ladders, endless siege equipment, and shining shields. Dear God, I don't have the strength for another word.*

Her shoulders slumped, and she finished her story simply. "I keep repeating the words of Naomi to her daughter-in-law: 'The Almighty has brought misfortune on me.'"[61]

As silence filled the room, she hung her head and wiped her eyes. *But God kept a remnant. We are alive, and he gave me a place to live. I want an end to this tragedy. My sorrow hangs on me like this garment, covering me completely. Why did I do this, telling them of my*

---

[60] Josephus recorded the death of the fourth son of Matthias, killed by Simon probably while leaving the gate. Many of the nobility and some priests also escaped on July 17. Titus, who later became emperor, promised to return their possessions. Nonetheless, he left the city with thousands enslaved. Many were taken to Antioch, where they dug the famous canal to protect the nearby harbor at Seleucia. Thousands died while fighting wild animals in the arenas of Caesarea Philippi. Tens of thousands were sent to mines in Egypt, where they perished.

[61] Ruth 1:21

pain? Will my friends and my community understand? Obed and Isabel; Jesse, Ruth and Asa; Penelope and her young ones; our servants and their families; Miriam; and even Thelma—that's my community. But Lord...Anthony can never be part of my community...and now he knows why.

Miriam stood up as Abigail finished. Her new song was set to a tune often sung in the city. She had first heard it while watching workers remove decades-old rubble. She said, "I want to thank God for keeping me alive. I was five years old when my parents rushed me through that open gate."

She paused. *The prophet said two-thirds would be struck down and only one third left.*[62]

Sarah sprang to her feet. "May I go upstairs to care for the children? I want Thelma to come down and hear your song! I've already heard it." Without waiting for an answer, she was on her way.

"This song is called 'That I May Declare Your Praises.' It's about forgiveness, a word that softens my heart. Our hearts are heavy from suffering."

"Aunt Abigail didn't tell you this, but when she fled the city of Jerusalem, I was with her."

Thelma came downstairs, and Miriam said, "Oh, come here, Thelma! Take the place where Sarah was sitting. We've just heard Aunt Abigail describe her feelings of torment and pain at the loss of her children in Jerusalem. God wants to heal her broken heart, and we want to see her healed too. So let's think now about Ruth's new baby. Asa knows nothing of fear, abuse, hurt, or any of the things Aunt Abigail described. We realize that tragic things like these do happen. Amid conflict and pain, God wants to restore joy.

"That terrible day still lingers in my memory, even though I was young, only five. Those walls, so big and strong. The noises! Terrible shouting and cursing. I was so afraid. As we left the gate, my father fell. An arrow from our soldiers had struck him in the back, and he died right there. We stopped to help Daddy, and my mother was hit by the next shot. Mommy died a year later after poison moved up her leg and infected her body. I watched her being buried in Antioch.

---

[62] Zechariah 13:8

"I still struggle with those memories, but often God gives me joy. I get afraid until I remember that God is teaching me to look to him. The song I will sing is about people who lived a long time ago, before and during those forty years in the desert.

"Aunt Abigail asked me to write a song for tonight. I want to make sure that the children learn that God calls us to praise him in every circumstance, especially when things seem to go wrong. Each of the stories in this song has to do with people who lived through what I call a 'desert experience.' As we celebrate the arrival of little Asa, we want to bless him with a blessed life despite the difficulties he is sure to face."

Penelope's children accompanied her on instruments.

Abraham has lived long, well into many years.
Sarah cries at night, bitter with her tears.
She has one hundred ways to turn this phrase:
"When will I see and hold my baby boy?"
She's ninety now. And look! She jumps for joy!
God answers. An old woman sings his praise.

Isaac is gloomy, searching for a wife.
Rebekah's sad, her twins in constant strife!
Esau seeks revenge; Jacob overplays
His luck and runs. Rebekah sends her boy
Away and prays, "Bring Jacob back with joy."
God answers. Hostile sons can learn to praise.

Joseph stands so handsomely. He looks down
To view his brothers, strangers to the town.
Ten brothers bow, pay cash and take their maize.
Jacob mourns at home. "Dear God, where's my boy?"
Then, together again, Jacob weeps with joy.
God answers. Dejected men can learn to praise.

Mothers in Egypt fearfully give birth.
Killing Hebrew baby boys brings the Pharaoh mirth.
Moses's mother is due, prays with hands upraised:
"Preserve his life, Lord. Keep my little boy.

Bless this trick, for a basket we'll employ."
God answers. Bond slaves sing a song of praise.

Praise is better than blood and sacrifice.
Feel sorrow if temptations have enticed.
Learn the worth of life, now and all our days.
Lord, purify by means that you employ.
Forgive our sins, restore to us our joy.
God answers us! We want to sing Your praise.

"Now, I'm going to sing it again," Miriam said, "and this time, you can sing along with me. Then you'll have it in your mind for a long time."

Before their guests left for home, Thelma whispered to Miriam, "I liked your song, Miriam. I know the tune and can teach the words to Penelope's children. Who were you singing about? I've never heard those stories before."

"Those are the stories we teach our children."

"Are the people in the song your relatives? Where do they live?"

Miriam laughed. "They lived long before my parents were born, but I think of them as being alive!"

Thelma looked wistful. "I know so little about my parents, and I don't want to talk about the town I came from. Miriam, I remember everything if I hear it in a song. Will you teach me about your family? You used special words—praise, purify, forgive, and restore—and linked them together. Those words made me feel clean inside for the first time in a long time. You want to teach much more than just these stories, don't you?"

"Yes, Thelma, we will share things together! I want to spend a lot of time with you."

As he listened to Abigail, Amos also found unwanted memories flooding in. He cringed when thinking about the pogrom in Egypt. *My three sisters were consumed in that terrifying fire.* Amos closed his eyes against the memory of those vicious flames hurtling up, swiftly destroying the Ben Shelah house.

A more recent event came to mind. Amos thought of Eliab on his bed, dying in Pergamum, an old man of eighty-seven. Before his death, Eliab had blessed each of his sons in the order of their birth. He pronounced personal benedictions.

His father's last words came back intensely and vividly. *Amos, my third child and my first son, your sisters were burned by the flames, young lives whose loss still leaves me distressed. You will always feel that grief because you loved each of them. But Amos, my son, you will be healed, and you will bring healing to others. You will rise above the level of our enemies. The weapons you will use will be words of peace. They will pierce deeper into men's hearts than a double-edged sword. You will avenge your enemies when your door is open. Hospitality will make you an overcomer.*

Amos kept every word in his heart. His weakened father's quiet voice could yet be heard, for the impact of that blessing had not faded. Eliab died the same day.

Four years had passed since those words were spoken, and Amos continued to ponder their meaning.

Chapter 14
Arguments

THE THEATER OF PHILADELPHIA

Three men sat down on the seats of honor at the theater. They had come to watch musicians practicing and had a clear view of the stage. At the drama rehearsal, the actors and chorus members argued, still not ready for the evening's performance. Damian, the headmaster of the gymnasium, leaned back, humming quietly. In charge of the school's Greek literature and language program, Calisto sat next to Timon, his nineteen-year-old son.

Eight aisles divided the audience into nine sections. Ordinary people would be sitting on seats farther back, packed shoulder to shoulder in the theater. Only during a rehearsal like this could these three individuals occupy the prized seats of honor. Damian rubbed his hand along the smooth white marble carvings of the armchairs.

Later, during the evening's performance, Mayor Aurelius Manilius Hermippus and his seven guests would revel in their high social standing. After they occupied the seats of honor, the drama would begin.

Calisto looked around the theater before bringing his attention back to the actors on stage, who were ready to rehearse.

"There's only space for ten thousand spectators," he said with a frown. "Hopefully funds will be provided for more spectators. It would not take a lot of work because the slope of the mountain favors installing more seats. Improving this theater would greatly enrich the city."

Timon, the youngest, snapped, "We can't enlarge the theater at this time, Father! Declaring an emergency meant releasing funds to repair buildings, rebuild the fallen city wall, provide job training for the peasants, and ease the sense of anxiety. This is not the time to propose an enlarged theater!"

Calisto's thin neck and slight build were topped by a patch of graying hair around his bald head. Hundreds of former students pictured his austere image when reminded of Greek literature.

He observed, "Our city will forever keep alive our Greek heritage! The Festival of Dionysus begins soon. During the season of harvest, we'll drink endlessly to the joy that Dionysus brings. In taverns and along streets, celebrations will flow with wine. But tonight, we will witness a production of Aeschylus's *Agamemnon*! Watch how the actors play the gods, climbing the steps to the top of the wall behind the stage. They appear up there, portraying Zeus and the other gods."

Timon shared his father's thin neck and torso. From his mother, he had inherited his sharp cheekbones and long black hair. Some considered the nineteen-year-old good-looking, but most girls found him too frail. "He should eat food instead of drinking in Greek plays!" was one of many mocking comments.

With a close-cut black beard, Timon's face had an innocent look, as if a sculptor had not quite finished his workmanship. He protested, "Father, Philadelphia will never be rich like Hierapolis unless we work to restore our commerce." Today he was determined to speak about a topic weighing on his mind. "And I don't want to learn anything more about Euripides, Sophocles, or Aristophanes."

For years, Calisto had tried in vain to convince his son to become a teacher. He explained that a man wasted his life if he only aimed to earn money. "Remember how old these dramas are, my son! Will your wages be intact five hundred years from now? No! But Aristotle's words will still be discussed by schoolboys."

It was disrespectful to argue with his father, but this was serious to Timon. "Father, please don't try to sway me with immaterial thoughts! I will not follow your career! Don't insist on sending me away to Athens! I don't want to study drama or Greek literature! I will be a businessman!" The young man's flushed face looked reddish and tense.

The chorus leader walked past the musicians, leaned over, and addressed them for the third time. "I'm sorry to ask you to leave! I've already warned you. Damian, I know you are the gymnasium director and Calisto is the head teacher for Greek literature, but do you have to speak so loudly? How can we complete our preparations for the drama when you do not stop arguing? We are here to repeat the words of the gods and heroes of old, not argue about a young man's profession!"

He raised both hands, extended his arms, and pointed to the two exits. "I don't care which side you choose to leave through. My, you're worse than little boys! Don't you realize the slightest sound carries to all corners of the theater?"

They left, and Calisto unconsciously scratched his balding head. "Timon, my son, how could you not want to be a teacher of Greek plays?"

Damian put an end to the debate. "Calisto, I'm ashamed to be asked to leave the theater because of your arguments! Give the lad a chance. Why won't you accept his word? He doesn't want to go to Athens or Corinth or anywhere else. Timon will not study six-hundred-year-old dramas or memorize a single play. He is not stubborn. Your son simply wants his own career."

Damian placed his arm around the shoulders of his defeated friend, one of his best teachers.

THE SYNAGOGUE OF PHILADELPHIA

While Calisto was trying to accept his son's decision not to train as a teacher, Zacharias talked with the synagogue elders.

It was late on Sunday afternoon and the seventh day of the Feast of Tabernacles. "I want a quick decision. Three weeks ago, we told Amos to decide how to live in our community. However, I did not calculate the dates correctly! My five sons and their wives invited me for a final Sukkot meal. We'll have to go to his house another day, not tomorrow."

The threat hanging over Amos jolted them. Only a lost, wayward soul would refuse their correction. These elders were descended from Jews who were deported from Jerusalem under Nebuchadnezzar 680 years earlier. Some fled Judea before Roman General Titus invaded with his hosts.

They trembled, thinking of the two dreaded words Zacharias was implying. *Midduy* was a temporary exclusion from fellowship for thirty, sixty, or ninety days. Worse was invoking *hçrem,* which cut a person off from the synagogue forever.

"When will *midduy* begin?" asked one of the men. He knew less about the events of the previous three weeks.

"I think we should pronounce *hçrem* on Amos, cutting him off right away," stated Michael adamantly. He was the oldest, and he wanted the penalty enforced immediately. "Amos is stubborn and insists on violating the tradition of the elders. You won't believe how many pagans were at his house! He uses the Septuagint and collects erroneous scrolls."

"He's from Alexandria," observed another. "Jews there are different. Look at their dress and beards. Listen to their accents. I never heard of a person being threatened like this before. Surely after the blessing of these days and remembering God cared for us during the Exodus, we can treat Amos mercifully."

"Not at all!" interrupted Zacharias. "Wickedness is like a diseased limb on a wild olive tree. Once it is corrupted, it does not bear fruit! Nothing good grows from deliberate rebellion."

Three different opinions were heard over the next hour.

Two of the men were descended from the Babylonian captivity through transplanted colonies to Asia Minor. They suggested a softer, kinder approach, rejecting both *midduy* and *hçrem.*

Another group, eight heads of families descended from scribes and teachers of the Law, wanted Amos cut off without delay.

In between these two positions, two elders attempted another solution. It included mercy while also requiring Amos to keep the Torah's strict demands.

One prevailing concern kept them talking, even when they disagreed. All wanted the Synagogue of Philadelphia purged of any element that might bring contamination.

Zacharias ended the conversation abruptly. "Then we are agreed. We will meet with Amos, giving him a deadline. If he does not follow the tradition of the elders, then he must be cut off from our congregation."

As usual, his wise counsel was accepted by the others. Leadership in his community meant avoiding the confusion of too many options when deciding on issues. Being a leader also meant taking a solid position.

They met again as a congregation on Monday, this time for worship on a day of joyful celebration. "Shemini Atzeret is unlike any other holiday," said Zacharias to the congregants before prayers. "After the Feast of Tabernacles, we spend one extra day with the

Lord. God has been merciful to us, giving life and health, work and food, in a never-ending circle."

New wine would soon appear, for this was harvest season. During the Feast of Tabernacles, most families shared the tradition of living in small makeshift tents or huts outside with their children. They were imitating their ancestors who lived in the desert during the Exodus from Egypt. After seven days, Sukkot was over. Shemini Atzeret was an extra eighth day for worship and rest intended for intimate communion between the Lord and his people. This most critical day marked the completion of reading the Torah.

The next day, Simchat Torah, was when the congregation would return to Genesis once more. The men joyfully walked around the sanctuary. They smiled with delight, taking turns carrying the Torah. Older boys who could take the Torah without dropping it also made a circle around the sanctuary. The youngest children found it too heavy, so small copies of the Ten Commandments in Hebrew were given to them.

Zacharias called children to the front and offered a prayer of blessing. Each one was growing up so quickly! Some were about to begin studies, while others were finishing and would enter a trade. One young man was about to leave home for Smyrna. He wanted to become a rabbi, and he expected to study under a well-known scholar.

DANIEL AND DORCAS'S HOME IN PHILADELPHIA

Arriving home, Daniel sat down, still grinning and relishing the joy of the evening. Dorcas followed a few minutes later, and she approached him with a dark look in her eyes. "Daniel, I heard something that distressed me terribly. This is supposed to be a day of joy, of exuberance, but I came home sad. Martha told me what is going on."

"What are you talking about?" asked Daniel, knowing what she was about to say.

"You plan to discipline Amos and his family. There we were, singing and dancing, going around and around, enjoying the moment and celebrating the covenant and the Torah. Then someone whispered in my ear, 'Do you know why Amos and Abigail are not here? Did you hear that they will never come to Simchat Torah again?'

"I was stunned when I heard it. 'No, what are you talking about?' Martha looked shocked. 'Oh, they are keeping it from you because of little Asa, your grandchild!' So I asked, 'Keeping what from me?' She answered, 'You aren't supposed to know, but Amos is going to suffer *hçrem*. He's going to be cut off from the community.' Is it really true, Daniel?"

It seemed like such a good idea when the council was debating the penalty. Now, hearing his wife's shrill voice, Daniel knew Dorcas would not be satisfied with his reasoning. "I'm sure something will be worked out," he said lamely, trying to avoid a conflict.

"No! Amos and Abigail must be with us next year! Be reasonable. Amos is your friend, even if you can't agree with him! Everyone must have a chance to mend their ways."

"I agree," he said, hoping to avoid an argument.

"Then convince Zacharias to reconsider this decision. At least give them a warning of thirty days!"

"Perhaps," he said, trying to imagine if a conversation could change either Zacharias or Michael's minds.

"'Perhaps?' That's not good enough for me! Yes, Amos has pagans coming to his home, but this is not the way the Council of Elders should do things!" She put on a light cloak.

"Where are you going?"

"To speak with Martha. We will have a meeting!"

"Two women may not resist the decisions of the council!" he said, raising his voice.

"Learn what mercy is!" she retorted, anger and frustration in every word. At the door, she turned and glared. "Do you not realize what being disciplined, being completely cut off, means to us? It means you will never see your grandson. You have not gone to see him. Not once! Why?" She was shouting now. "Whose laws do you follow? The laws of God, who gave us a grandson? Or do you think Zacharias knows best? He's good at what he does. He fixes a gem to a ring, and after it's in place, no one can dislodge it. But he should not decide if you and I can go to see family members!"

As Dorcas headed to Martha's home, Daniel felt hot and dry inside. He thought of a pot of water heating up until it boiled away. *The elder's decision is going to prohibit family members from visiting the Ben Shelah home! Perhaps we can convince Ruth and Jesse to come live with us.*

AMOS AND ABIGAIL'S HOME

Abigail knew why Amos had not taken them for Shemini Atzeret and the Simchat Torah services. "If we had not been kind to Miriam, then we wouldn't be under a threat of discipline. How much more can I put up with?" A tone of bitterness flowed through her question.

Amos rubbed his sore arm. "Without Miriam and her friends, you would not have children hiding around your legs, running up the steps, and bringing us laughter."

She turned away from her husband's weak attempt at humor and went upstairs to lie down. It felt good to close her eyes and lie on her back.

IN THE CITY OF PHILADELPHIA

Many families were now better off in the cities and towns around Philadelphia. Wages began to appear for work done in rebuilding and restoring the buildings damaged by the Great Earthquake.

Bankers spoke quietly among themselves, calculating how to increase their profits on money loaned to the city council.

Accountants had just handed the mayor the initial reports for the first three months of the emergency project. Unable to swallow with a dry mouth, he almost choked.

The mayor's face turned red when he learned the actual cost of rebuilding. "When I agreed to 'restoration,' I did not say, 'upgrading and enhancing' the whole city!" he shouted. People in the outer office rolled their eyes. They had predicted deception by contractors before the reconstruction had even begun.

A HUT ON MOUNT TMOLUS

Outside the city, another dispute was taking place. The three rebels whose hopes were raised after their first successful escapade experienced gnawing pains in their stomachs. Dark lines had formed on Maza's face as he paced back and forth in the small hut they occupied. For weeks, they had survived in their hidden cave.

But in July they found an empty shepherd's hut. Flocks, which had been plentiful all summer on the upper slopes of Mount Tmolus, had recently been moved to lower pastures. They had shelter but little food. Today the three men had only bones for a thin soup.

Maza growled, "When Craga left us in June for Smyrna to sail back to Mithrida at Tanais in the Bosporan Kingdom, he left specific instructions. But we haven't found even one peasant willing to join the Faithful. Now look at us! Heating up dried bones!" He spat on the floor.

Harpa nodded, also frustrated, but he tried to put a better spin on events. "Things are going to work out, Maza. You will see. Those garments we sold fetched good prices at the market!"

"You got more money than I did selling that stuff," Maza shot back. "I'm not good at bargaining. You and Taba, both of you are a great success."

Talking to prospective customers was not in Maza's blood. Wrestling, hand-to-hand combat, and swordsmanship—those made life worthwhile. They were activities he excelled at even before joining the army. But selling merchandise was not a job for him.

"Look," said Taba, butting in, anxious to stop the quarrel. "I've been thinking. Last night, cold winds blew, and it won't get any warmer in the coming months. We can't sleep on empty stomachs, and there is no food around here. We can't spend winter in this miserable place, so let's go eastward to the province of Galatia."

He looked at his friends, realizing afresh that a tiny sliver of hope, even if it sounded impossible, could calm his comrades. "Craga told us about that family living in a natural stone castle close to Lystra. It's a half day's march to the west from that small city. They've caused headaches for travelers for decades."

Maza squeezed his hands against his empty stomach. "The army is watching that family. Too many of them were highway robbers in Galatia. How could they help us?"

Taba had not been chosen as the leader by Craga for nothing. An idea popped into his mind before Maza had even finished his question. "Remember what Craga said about them? The extended family promised the army they would never again rob travelers in the *province of Galatia*. However, the *province of Asia Minor*, now that's a different matter! Let's invite half a dozen, maybe more, to join us in this province."

Maza stuck out his lips. He rubbed his hand against the ten-day growth on his face, glared at Taba, and then nodded his agreement.

"Right. Are we over our little spat?" Taba continued. "We'll return in March, when Craga said he would be back. We'll find better opportunities when merchants travel again. The gods will show us which day to gain treasures at the Door again."

He slapped his sides, laughing with joy and savoring the moment he had opened his bundle. "Each of us got a bundle from that caravan. Huge rewards, weren't they?"

Taba's face lit up. He leaned back on a poorly made wooden chair. His prize from the summer was well concealed, a hidden "something" that neither Craga, Maza, or Harpa knew about.

My prize! The treasure of a lifetime! That golden armband is mine. Appropriate payment for me leading a brave troop of men. An exceptional approval from the gods. We promised each other to share and share alike, but that didn't include something as beautiful as that gold armband.

Chapter 15
October

THE MILITARY GARRISON IN PHILADELPHIA

On the second day of October, the rebels disappeared from Cogamis Valley. Their eyes shone as they dreamed of riches in Lystra.

The same day, Felicior called Decimus, Anthony, Omerod, and Bellinus together as soon as they arrived at the garrison. "Before explaining your new assignments," he said, "let me bring you up to date on what happened at City Hall yesterday afternoon. Mayor Aurelius Manilius Hermippus was relaxed earlier, at the end of the summer, but not now."

Decimus asked, "What changed?"

"Well, you know how we have to wait for things to get started at that kind of meeting. Obelix, the high priest of Apollo, sacrificed a sheep with flair, full of color and mystery. While prayers were being made asking for protection from further earthquakes and destruction, I saw Giles whispering to his banker friends. I could see from the expression on their faces that something had agitated them.

"The mayor tried to be diplomatic, wanting to put off a confrontation at the meeting. He said, 'First, let's hear a report on progress being made in Philadelphia on the restorations.' He turned to me. 'Commander, are you ready to give a summary on the security of the Southern Road and the surrounding towns?'

"I glanced out of the corner of my eye. Horace, the Supervisor of Public Works, was resting his arms across his ample belly, and I didn't like the smile on his face. If you think the mayor embellishes his speeches, you haven't heard anything until Horace tries to cover up his shenanigans. I won't repeat his exaggerated phrases, but I'll let you know the increasing financial concern. He said, 'The city council approved a three-year plan.

"'The outer wall's collapsed places are being reconstructed, and scores of men are working on it. The workshop building did not require extensive repair to make it functional. However, the Lower Hot Baths and the old gymnasium will need new stone blocks, something we had not counted on. We previously estimated that we could reuse the old materials, but much of it was found to be too damaged. The foundation stones are badly fractured and out of alignment. Many need to be replaced. Men working in quarries across the valley will bring replacements. In the other cities and towns, as many as a thousand men need to be employed on buildings, sewers, and water drainage ditches for the mountain runoff.'"

Felicior had dealt with imposters, slaves, and even thieves on the open roads. Unexpectedly, he had learned how bankers found secure means to accumulate wealth. Giles worked under-handedly with contractors. All attacked the public purse by demanding higher interest rates.

"'It's a bigger risk than we first thought,' Giles explained.

"And this was followed by Horace. 'Overall, it has become a bigger task than we initially estimated.'"

Felicior shook his head. "I think the mayor wanted to yell at them. Veins in his neck throbbed as he listened to their demands. It was about higher interest rates and more money. My contribution at the end of the meeting was very brief though. I told them the distressing news that vagrant slaves on the eastern side of the Cogamis Valley, around Malonia, Silandus, and Temenoth, are camped on a mountain without supervision. If Silandus's population is desperate now, then we can expect more trouble there during the winter when those slaves get hungry. We are also hearing that the people in those cities are outraged, with lots of malcontents.

"So, Anthony, in the morning, I want you to cross the valley to Malonia and Silandus. Take Omerod and Bellinus and a dozen soldiers from the Italia Regiment. Examine the situation among the vagrant slaves and within those cities. What does the district council need to do? During the trip, you will be supported by a wagon with auxiliaries to set up camp. Are there any questions?"

"Yes sir. Since many of those slaves will be Scythian, can I take Zarrus as an interpreter?"

Felicior agreed, and they saluted their commander and left the office. Anthony notified the other soldiers to be ready to cross the Cogamis Valley in the morning. Zarrus was told that he would come more slowly, traveling in the wagon carrying baggage, supplies, and a few auxiliaries.

AMOS AND ABIGAIL'S HOME

Early the following day, a light haze hung over the vineyards near Philadelphia. Wheat and barley fields, which were already harvested, lay interspersed among the vineyards. Stubble poked through dry land. In the early morning, blackbirds gleaned seeds from the leftovers.

Obed rushed into the house, and Abigail stood up. "Why are you back so soon, my son? Is there a problem?"

"Where is Miriam?"

"Upstairs with Ruth. Little Asa has been colicky. Ruth didn't sleep well last night."

"I need to speak to her." Obed dashed to the staircase and called for his cousin.

When Miriam came down the steps, he led her by the arm into his father's library. "I was given a message for you from Anthony. He has left the city with more than a dozen soldiers."

"Where is he going?" Miriam's heart started to pound.

"He's to be away again on another assignment."

"Another one? So soon? Where to?"

"Across the Cogamis Valley, to a city called Silandus."

"That's where Thelma comes from!"

"He gave me a message for you. 'Tell Miriam to be careful of Cleon. Grace should not play again at the workshops with Penelope's children, even with Sandra.' Several times Anthony has seen him listening to the soldiers' conversations. The man insists on pouring more beer and then stands around listening. Cleon is always sly while asking for information from soldiers. I think he wants to know their schedules. It would seem to be all in the name of making sure rooms will be clean and ready for them when they return. I don't like the sound of it, Miriam. I'm beginning to believe that he is a problem like you said."

"Yes, I don't like that man either." She added, "I hate the way Cleon looks at me when I go to talk with Penelope. Is there anything else?"

"Yes, Anthony also said runaway slaves on the other side of the valley are creating a disturbance. He asked Felicior for Zarrus to help with translating since Scythian slaves are likely involved in those disturbances. With Zarrus gone from the workshop, please give Arpoxa extra attention. Zarrus and Anthony may be gone for a couple of weeks.

"Sorry that he is gone again, Miriam. On a personal note, both Father and I have been talking about your husband. He is...how can I describe a soldier this way? It sounds strange...but he is a kind man. Maybe one day Mother will see him that way too."

Miriam groaned as she turned away and went back upstairs to help care for Asa. *I'm supposed to be happy that my cousin likes Anthony and...some distant day...Aunt Abigail may change her mind about Anthony. But the news of a "disturbance" among runaway slaves makes me afraid.*

THE REPAIRED WORKSHOPS IN PHILADELPHIA

The morning sun was on the eastern horizon. Arpoxa had been up half the night, and her light-colored hair was disheveled after a restless sleep.

Strangers who saw her riding in a wagon and did not realize she was lame stopped to take a second look at the twenty-three-year-old woman. The soft lines of her face suggested a peaceful spirit, but people cringed watching her try to walk.

She wanted to forget the trials of last night. Awakened by Madis's crying, she had wiped his little gums, whispered in his ear, and then rubbed his back. Her son had gone back to sleep, and both boys were sleeping.

It was a bad dream that startled her. She raised herself on her elbow and thought, *This is my own home, our first home! Things are improving for us here in Philadelphia. Ateas and I are together. We have two lovely boys. Other women are learning from me. They don't look down on me like people used to do. All that is gone. I'm not a slave anymore.*

She lay back, closing her eyes and realizing that her husband was not in bed beside her. He had returned from the inn last night after she had gone to bed. Hearing him moving around in the front room, she called out, "What are you doing?" When they were together, just the two of them, she spoke in Sakas, her tribal language.

He answered in Pahlavi, a similar dialect spoken in Scythia. "My love," he said, entering their room on his crutches, "last night Anthony asked me to help the army again."

"Where?"

He pointed. "We're going to Malonia and Silandus. The soldiers' supplies are being loaded, and I will be riding on a wagon with auxiliaries."

She placed her hands on a chair and leveraged her weight, slowly getting to her feet. Hobbling on club feet across the room, she closed the curtain that set their bedroom off from the room that served as their living space. In the darkness, she held Ateas close and kissed him, marveling at the love they shared.

Two lame slaves had been thrown onto the same slave trader's ship in the far-off city of Phanagoria. Weeks later, they were married in Chalcedon. She recalled all those events endlessly.

Next door, Arpoxa heard weavers talking and remembered they would be expecting her to teach them again today. She also realized she was late to work. In the bigger part of the building, she heard Thelma's voice: "Don't let the baby play with that pot. It will break!"

Penelope lived with her children in the larger of two workshop rooms turned into temporary apartments.

"I don't want you to go!" she said, holding Ateas close. "Remember how long you were gone the last time Anthony asked you to help him?"

Ateas's golden hair and blue eyes matched hers, and he bent over to stroke her hair. "Anthony is taking me just to the other side of the valley, two weeks at most. Roman soldiers need me! Also, I will be getting extra pay, and we can use that for many things we'll need for the children."

Arpoxa did not share her husband's enthusiasm. "What about your work with the potters? I don't want you to go, my love!" She wanted to keep him there.

"Anthony has already arranged for other potters to instruct new apprentices while I'm gone."

She watched him go. He crossed the city square to the inn, and she wiped a tear from her cheek. *How am I going to care for two children with you away, Ateas? I don't want you going there! Women in the workshop speak of fights breaking out in Malonia and Silandus. Soldiers' work is dangerous! What if something terrible happens? I couldn't stand it when you were gone last year, tracking down those brazen thieves! My days are so difficult without you to help.*

THE HOME OF LYDIA-NAQ IN PERGAMUM

In distant Pergamum, the daily morning sacrifices at the Altar of Zeus were over. Lydia-Naq, the high priestess, was back in her house. Many small scrolls lay side by side on a little black table. The last message she received was open, with metal objects weighing down the four corners. Like the others on the table, this was a letter from her son. She passed her hand over her hair, overflowing with pride for his achievements.

Lydia-Naq called a scribe to write her return letter.

October 2, in the 14th year of Domitian
From: Lydia-Naq
To: Diotrephes, my dearest son

If you are well, then I am well. May the power of Zeus be yours in this new year of classes with your students in Sardis! May you have continued success!

Your efforts to bring back my niece, our baby girl, are praiseworthy. Continue in your attempts! Bring her here for the sake of our family and our legacy. How I look forward to holding my brother's daughter in my arms!

Be careful in dealing with Cleon. Do not let him make a fool of you again, but remember, our best chance of success lies with him.

THE CITY OF PHILADELPHIA

On that same morning, Calisto had been awake for a long time. Today was the first day of classes after the harvest season. Some boys would begin studying Greek literature for the first time.

He ran his hand across the top of his head, his fingers trying to make his wispy hair lie down. The teacher patted water on it, but the effort was futile. His hair was more stubborn than a lazy schoolboy. He opened the shutters and looked out. A clear sky above and a low haze on the fields spoke of a sparkling fall day.

Only a sliver of the moon showed as it entered its last phase. *I don't want my son storming out of here, running away, and sailing to a distant city. I might never see him again! Timon is the only family I have. The Festival of Dionysus is coming, and I want my son to stay here in Philadelphia. The only way for that to happen is for him to get a job. When he finds one, I'll celebrate with a great party for him and his friends.*

"Good morning, my son," he said. A new warmth sounded in his voice. "I want you to stay in Philadelphia. Can you find a job here to learn the skills needed for business?"

Timon looked at his father with wide-open eyes, but he was even more surprised to hear the rest of his greeting. "Of course, my son, not everyone has to study Greek literature. Yes, you should become a businessman, and then later, when you have lots of money, and if I'm still alive, I will teach you more of the great masterpieces!"

The young man blinked his eyes several times and then slapped his father on the shoulder. "Father, I should have known! You can never admit failure, and in your last days, you will still be talking about the great writers of the past. Anyway, thank you for your openness to my desires."

Chapter 16
The Warning

MICHAEL AND MARTHA'S HOME IN PHILADELPHIA

The Sabbath was over, and three friends huddled together at Michael's home as they shared a late evening meal. Their conversation was "private," but Martha knew what it was about. She excused herself and went to bed.

Daniel leaned forward eagerly, his face gray and haggard. "Dorcas has been unusually cold toward me," he explained. "She doesn't want Amos and Abigail removed so quickly from our fellowship. She says to give him thirty days to repent. My friends, would this not be a better way to deal with Amos?"

Zacharias responded, "Our reasons are clear. By pronouncing *hçrem*, no one else will be tempted to reject our demands for a pure expression of our faith."

For a moment, there was silence in the room. Michael considered the verbal bonfire set ablaze in his home the previous evening. Martha's words still rang in his ears.

Think about this during your meeting tonight, Michael. After your nasty words to them on your last two visits, do you think Isabel and Ruth want to hear you speaking like that again? How will you improve our relationship with Ruth and Jesse? Divided loyalties, people fighting each other...I won't have any of it!"

Michael rubbed his chin and shifted in his seat. "You know my wife. Martha prefers a softer approach. I met the Ben Shelah family twenty-three years ago as refugees from Jerusalem. They originally came from Alexandria, Egypt. We befriended them. I saw that young Obed was a good match for Isabel, and later they were betrothed and married. She has been a wonderful mother to our grandchildren.

"Ruth and Jesse have been to our home twice since Asa's birth. On the first visit, I said, 'Please come and live with us. We'll make room for you. I don't want you staying in the Ben Shelah house with outsiders.'

"On their second visit, I insisted that Jesse leave Amos's place. But the young man stood up to me. Imagine that, Daniel! Your son yelling at me. What is worse, Martha sided with them. I will not tell you how that family visit ended, but Jesse's words hurt me. He said, 'I am not coming here again. Look how my wife's grandfather treats me as if I'm a child.' My friends, I don't want this to go on."

Michael had a tender spot for his wife of forty-two years. "Our first two grandchildren died here—little Gershom and Jacob. Gershom would have been twenty years old now, except he died at birth. Jacob would have been nineteen, but he died in that farm accident. That leaves our third grandchild, Ruth. The baby means so much to Martha. She talks of Asa constantly."

Zacharias shook his head. He was as immovable as a block of stone. "If we permit Amos to continue in good standing, then he will pollute our friendships. Look at what's happening right now!"

But Michael was not finished. He shook his finger at Daniel, the younger man. "Your younger son, Mith, is to marry Sarah. Martha and Dorcas have reason to be upset about all this. All they talk about is marriages, children, and grandchildren."

Zacharias had obviously had enough. His cheeks turned an angry red. "You should be ashamed of yourselves, my friends! The desires of family members cannot work against the principles by which elders live!"

He studied his friends' faces then took a deep breath and sighed, "Let us pray on this for a few days. We will not be hasty. If we are so led, we will grant Amos until the end of Chanukah to repent and to change his ways. That is another sixty days. If he does not repent in that time, we will give him a final ninety days before he is dismissed. At that point, his name will be removed from the Book of Life. I will require that he make a public apology to the whole congregation when he repents."

AMOS AND ABIGAIL'S HOME

On Thursday morning, Amos was called to the gate. The steward from Michael's workshop handed him a letter. "Please read this. I will wait to take an answer back," the man said.

Amos read the short note. It was Michael's careful handwriting, again in Hebrew, saying, "The elders will come to your home at noon today." He nodded to the servant and said, "Tell Michael I am happy to welcome him and his friends."

The sun was hidden by clouds, making for a gloomy day when the three men arrived. "Please, enter my library," Amos invited. Abigail entered with him, standing beside him, her head covered.

Zacharias took the lead. "Amos, we advised you against changing your loyalties. The Torah does not allow you to show overt hospitality to pagans. And you cannot have them as close friends. That path goes against our laws. For us to survive as a people, all in the diaspora must submit to the same rules. Will you submit to our leadership?"

Abigail leaned toward her husband and took his hand. Her eyes were big with fright. Amos looked at his visitors steadily without saying a word. He nodded and said nothing.

"Your silence accuses you. Know this! The elders demand a turnabout on your part. Beginning tomorrow, we are placing you under temporary discipline until the first day after Chanukah. If you do not repent of your ways during those sixty days, then, because we are merciful, we will offer you a second chance. You will be given an additional ninety days to amend your ways and to implement all the changes. If you do not comply, then we will be forced to cut your family off from our fellowship."

Abigail's eyes were brimming with tears, but she set her jaw, determined not to let them see her crying. Amos went to the door to show his friends out. He put his arms out, ready to give them his customary hug, but Zacharias, Michael, and Daniel turned away. They refused eye contact or to touch him with their hands.

Before Amos closed the gate, a piercing pain shot down his left arm. He caught his breath. *Even my arm is showing me the pain of being severed from my community.*

Inn of the Open Door

A Chronicle of Philadelphia

Part 2

October AD 93

Forgiveness and Reconciliation

Chapter 17
Hidden Fears

THE CITY OF PHILADELPHIA

Having received his father's blessing, Timon walked along the city's highest avenue, searching for a job. He started at the top, near Mountain Gate. The Jewish house of worship was on his right as he began to stroll along the avenue. Here, the homes of wealthy citizens overlooked Cogamis Valley. Farther on, Timon passed the Temple of Artemis with its massive pillars. Seven white marble steps led up to the temple.

He asked for work in the shops between the Temple of Artemis and the Temple of Zeus. Shops up here were more spacious than in the agora halfway down the hill. That was where he usually shopped for bread, fruit, and vegetables. On the acropolis, higher up, jobs brought in the highest income but only for those with the required skills: civic employees, the superintendent of buildings and construction, bankers, lawyers, and magistrates. However, no one offered him work.

Timon turned back to make sure he had evaluated every possible occupation there. *Father says I can pursue any profession, but what trade do I want to take up?*

Next he walked toward the civic center. Sounds of young voices could be heard from the gymnasium. He smiled, for he had no interest in becoming a teacher. The young man walked past the agora. He knew most merchants in the marketplace, but their crooked ways were against the principles taught at home. Those older men would take advantage of him. More importantly, Timon knew he would not enjoy selling trinkets all day long.

The Upper Hot Baths, where he went every afternoon, did not hold any appeal for him either. Only slaves and their supervisors worked there.

At the primary intersection, where the Avenue of the Temples intersected with the Avenue of Philadelphia, he turned left, gradually descending the long thoroughfare. Ropemakers, potters, and basket makers busily went in and out of their businesses. *These people live near their work. Each building has space for animals and wagons. Will I ever have enough coins to start a business? Oh! I don't know what I want to do!*

Along the main street, he saw people working in other professions: perfume makers, butchers, candle makers, and jewelers. A wagonload of olives passed by, being brought in from an orchard. He stopped to watch a merchant weigh the fruit. Olives were precious because the oil was used for food, lamp fuel, and medicine. Soap made from the fruit left a pleasant scent. *I don't want to work with olives, pomegranates, apricots, melons, apples, oranges, or raisins. Farming and food, that's not for me.*

In one shop, carpets were for sale, and at another, men sold spices. Timon's interest picked up. He would like to do something with merchants, but he did not want to be limited by a shop's narrow space. *I enjoy working with people. I'm at my best when I meet people and hear about real problems. Probably that's why I don't like Father's old stories. I want tales of adventure, of people who have been to faraway Arabia. I like cosmetics, myrrh, perfumes, anointing oils, frankincense, saffron, aloes, and calamus too. Ah, cinnamon! I love food flavored like that!*

Stores and offices lined the next block. Parchment makers, scribes, and ink makers worked together. A tax collector greeted him, a young man who had finished his studies two years before. His "friend" was already respected...and hated.

Timon came to the end of Philadelphia Avenue, and the Valley Gate was not far off. Before him, workers were busy clearing out the rubble from damaged, collapsed buildings at the center of the city's rebuilding program. The pavement at the city entrance was being torn up and refitted with dressed stone.

"Watch out there!" yelled an engineer. "We don't want this slab to fall on you while we're taking it down!" He yelled again, "Is that man deaf? Why isn't he paying attention to me? Get out of there!" The man had trouble hearing, and a fellow worker pushed him away just in time, saving the worker from a bruise or something more serious.

Timon watched workers preparing to take down the main lintel over the caldarium entrance of the old bathhouse. A stonemason bellowed, "I want this to be an exact replica of the original building before the earthquake! Every detail should be the same. We're restoring the original lines of the building!"

"Not at all!" shouted the superintendent, waving his hands. He disagreed with both the engineer and the chief stonemason. "This is a chance to improve our city. Reconstruct it! But make the design more like the hot baths I visited in Miletus! A little bit more expensive and much sturdier. It should also have a space alongside the building for a wrestling and fighting arena."

Timon knew the superintendent in the employ of Horace.

"We were told to renovate, reconstruct, and restore!" shouted the engineer in contradiction. "We were not commanded to design a new city!"

An argument broke out, and Timon walked on toward the Valley Gate. He looked up and saw the Inn of the Open Door before him. *Now that's different! Merchants pass through here bringing their packed animals. They gossip over meals and tell tales of far-off places—mystery, stories of adventure, hospitality, and travelers. I wonder...is there something for me at this inn? I will talk to someone to see if they need help.*

Around the outside of the inn was a tall, stone security wall. Outside windows were placed on the second-story office. Its main gate was wide open with two wooden doors secured at night by a large oak beam. Both halves of the wooden door were attached to the stone walls by iron hooks. Above the door was a high arch that opened into a broad courtyard.

Two women walked past him, leaving the inn. One woman was older than the other. Between them were five children. The younger woman carried a screaming infant. They left and walked out onto the street. *Probably a merchant's family. The woman has six children, and the oldest daughter is about my age. Now, where is the manager?*

"Hello, can I help you?" asked a young man wearing a blue apron. "My name is Cleon. What can I do for you?"

"My name is Timon, and I want to become an apprentice. I would like to work in this inn to learn about the business. I finished my studies and ranked among the best who left the gymnasium."

"Well, you would have to talk to Obed about that. He's the manager. Come this way."

Timon looked around the courtyard. It was open to the sky and was swept clean. He followed Cleon. *My, what a pleasant man! I hope I can get hired here. This has the right feel!*

Cleon led Timon up a flight of stone stairs attached to the inside wall facing the inner courtyard. Obed's office was on the second floor. Timon noticed the windows looking onto the street, the ones he had seen from the outside. Other windows opened on the other side into the courtyard. The office had plenty of light.

"Sir, someone wants to talk to you," said Cleon. "His name is Timon."

Obed looked at the young man standing in front of him. He could not decide if this visitor was good-looking or not. His neck was thin and so was his body. His hair, longer than that of most boys, softened the sharp lines of his cheekbones.

He estimated Timon to be about twenty years old. His complexion was tanned, so obviously he had been outside a lot during the recent summer weather. His sandals were worn more on the inside than the outside, the mark of a man who loved to ride horses.

"Come in. My name is Obed Ben Shelah."

"That's a Jewish name, isn't it? My name is Timon."

"How can I help you?"

"Cleon says you are the manager of this inn."

"My father, Amos Ben Shelah, is the owner. I am his chief steward and responsible for the business. I make sure everything is done well. We take pride in our work. Tables, rooms, and stables must constantly be cleaned. Our food is good for guests, and animals are well cared for. We want our guests to feel welcome so they will return."

"I am asking for a chance to work here, perhaps to be an apprentice manager."

Obed looked at the young man. The moody atmosphere at home, his mother's crying spell after the elders' visit last night, and a recent shortage of fodder for the animals left him in turmoil. When he came from the farm this morning, he dreaded another full day's work. Obed could not concentrate and was concerned about the many aspects of the inn's hospitality.

He knew he needed help for the inn to cover minor details. Perhaps someone could help with the accounting, yet he was fearful of making a mistake in taking on the wrong worker.

On any other day, my answer would be an immediate no! But I'm getting too far behind in the accounts. I don't know what has to be paid for first. Besides, I've been getting headaches. I need someone to help with light jobs. I never thought of taking on an apprentice. It's precisely what my father-in-law, Michael Ben Akkub, was so adamant about. His words echo in my mind: "You are getting too close to non-Jews!"

"Why should I give you an opportunity?" Obed asked, trying to buy time.

Timon leaped at the chance. "I love animals. I would make sure that the animals are well-groomed, brushed, fed, and cleaned. I enjoy meeting people, and hearing their stories makes me feel like I'm part of something bigger. I can read, write, and do mathematics if needed. I work hard, and I'm honest."

"You finished classes at the gymnasium, right? What were your best subjects?"

"I did well in all the studies. Mathematics and geometry were my best classes. Well, not really. Greek literature was my best. That's supposed to be a joke because my father teaches Greek, but I don't like literature. I really want to learn to manage a business. I am strong but not good enough at sports to run, jump, or wrestle in the Games."

Obed smiled, enjoying the young man's forthrightness. But Michael's words came back, and the thought of taking Timon on as an apprentice brought a frown. He halted between two desires. One was the need to satisfy the men threatening his family's participation in the congregation. The other was his worry about his growing inability to do a full day's work.

"I do need help, and it would be a good way for you to learn the basics of inn management. I cannot pay you if you come to work here, but I will provide your meals. My family…our financial situation isn't all that good right now."

"Don't worry about pay, sir! I'll gladly work as an apprentice just for the business experience. Later I hope to be a merchant. I want to travel and see Rome, Corinth, and Athens."

Obed was convinced that he had a bright young man who wanted to learn with each additional question and answer. But what kind of influence would Timon bring, especially if he knew so much about Greek literature? He had to make sure.

"Timon, will you require holidays and feast days off for worshiping the gods?"

"Oh no! The temples are simply where priests make lots of money from sacrifices and the sale of the meat. I prefer money earned from buying and selling things. My father knows all about the gods, but I don't care for such talk. It's not practical."

Obed made up his mind. Timon could become a merchant. He wished Timon was a God-fearer, like Anthony, Zarrus, Arpoxa, and Penelope. However, he needed help now. Ever since soldiers had come to stay in the inn, Obed had been feeling worse. He had not told his parents, but sleep had left him the last two nights. Even now, he felt dizzy.

"Come tomorrow, Timon. For a start, you will work under Cleon. The hours are long. Sometimes you will be bone-weary. In your work, you will meet merchants from many lands. Don't be taken in by too many tall tales though!"

He called Cleon. "I decided to let Timon work here as an apprentice. Show him what it takes to run an inn. Also, I want you to know that my cousin Heber, from Sardis, is coming in two weeks. His father, Simon Ben Shelah, is a brother to my father. The city has hired Heber to set up weaving looms for the peasants. They will be learning in the reconstructed workshops."

"Very well," said Cleon. "Timon, come with me, and I'll show you around."

THE INN OF THE OPEN DOOR, PHILADELPHIA

Timon had been working at the inn for two days. Menander, the inn servant charged with buying the food, wanted Timon to learn about purchasing food. He sat down with Timon and went over a list of the different menus. They calculated the food quantities to be purchased at the market to meet those requirements.

"Timon," said Menander, "our guests have walked a long way during the day. Upon arriving here, they want a satisfying meal, a clean spot to lay down their bedroll before a good rest, and a clean toilet area. Naturally, they want a bath, so we send them to the Upper

Hot Baths. All this takes ongoing work from us. If they leave with a full belly after the morning breakfast and their animals are well cared for, we can count on them coming back. Now, take this list to the marketplace so we can provide those meals."

It was a Saturday morning, and Timon was on his way out to the agora to buy food. He dropped the list and bent over to pick it up.

A giggle came from a young woman. She had a pleasant laugh. "You dropped something," said Thelma good-naturedly. She was holding Penelope's youngest child in her arms. The baby turned her head, trying to see the young man.

"Yes, I'm kind of clumsy! I am supposed to learn how much food to buy for the kitchen. This is Menander's food list that I dropped."

"Are you buying food at the market for Penelope?"

"Yes, I'm the new apprentice."

"Good luck!" she called over her shoulder. "Running an inn is hard work!"

Timon stared as she walked out of the inn, past the construction sites, and turned right, entering the workshops. *A woman with such a pretty face, olive-colored skin, and those deep brown eyes...and that soft laugh! She carries herself and her little sister with confidence, probably taking care of the baby since she was born!*

"I saw you drop your notes," called Obed, standing at the overhead window and looking out over the courtyard. "So you've just met Thelma?"

Timon's mouth was open in astonishment. He did not realize how much Obed could see from upstairs in his office and how much control that gave him over the property.

Thelma! He repeated her name again. *Penelope's daughter, but she does not know my name yet.*

THE CITY OF PHILADELPHIA

As summer started to cool, Philadelphia experienced more comfortable weather. Many men were still working, even if wages were low. Food was being released to families as decreed by the council. Under the emergency agreement, no taxes received in Philadelphia were to be forwarded to Ephesus for two years. People even cheered when hearing the governor's name when the decision was announced.

Besides, two holidays would soon occupy the attention of all, rich and poor alike. The god, Dionysius, rewarded them with excellent grape harvests. Half of the original vineyards were still operating. In many parts of the city, men and women crushed grape clusters with their feet in huge vats. These activities led to many late-night parties.

A different festival was celebrated on the fourteenth of October. It was only for women. For many, this time at the Temple of Demeter was the best day of the year. The Festival of Thesmophoria commemorated their story.

Hades, the brother of Zeus, had kidnapped Persephone, the daughter of the goddess Demeter. Hades kept Persephone in the underworld for months. This story satisfied people about the reason for winter's arrival.[63]

Day-long celebrations included a play. Zeus and Demeter persuaded Hades to release Persephone, causing the end of winter. Her release was for half a year and brought about spring and the growing season for the year. It brought flowers back to life and made the fruits appear. Before she had to return to Hades, harvest time had to take place.

This festival was unlike any other. All married women, rich and poor, gathered for one day. No one bothered about social differences. All married women could come together as sisters bound by everyday struggles.

After the tax relief decision was released, influential citizens joined a procession to the Temple of Artemis. A special dinner was held in the evening at the mayor's home. "We've come through the first part of the emergency program," Mayor Aurelius stated, raising his cup. His servant had provided last year's best wine for a toast.

"Mobs are no longer at the gates howling like hungry dogs. Ruins are being reconstructed. Let's raise a toast to the bankers! Those in Philadelphia and Ephesus! We owe them much gratitude. They have cooperated in response to the crisis, keeping their interest rates as low as possible."

---

[63] More complete descriptions of the Festival of Thesmophoria are given in *Through the Fire: A Chronicle of Pergamum* and *Never Enough Gold: A Chronicle of Sardis*.

The toast was gladly accepted, but Mayor Aurelius wondered why he noticed a cunning look on Giles's face. He caught the banker smiling slyly at two of his friends. Then Aurelius looked across the table and saw a man winking to another of the bankers.

"Well, everyone," he said, "winter rains will begin soon. We hope our plans to keep law and order succeed. And of course, Giles, we will make our payments on time, every three months, just as we promised."

But while everyone was leaving the party in a good mood, he pursed his lips. *What is that rascal, Giles, up to? I smell a rat! I thought he was helping us by keeping the interest payments as we agreed. Is he planning something that I don't know about? He can't be! I studied the plans and examined every detail.*

AMOS AND ABIGAIL'S HOME

Abigail was turning seventy-four. "Isn't Abigail's birthday the most significant family event of the fall season?" asked Amos.

For a moment, she seemed to regain the outgoing generosity of her youth. This was what she was known for in the first years of marriage. As the three Jewish families became increasingly connected with one another through marriage and friendship, all accepted that Abigail's birthday would be a special day to celebrate. Few women were as old and alert.

Whereas the women in Philadelphia celebrated their Festival of Thesmophoria on Wednesday, the Jewish women would be invited to a birthday celebration at the Ben Shelah farm on Thursday. A heifer would be slaughtered, providing fresh meat.

Previously, Amos had sent invitations to Zacharias, Michael and Martha, Daniel and Dorcas, and others. However, the invitations were returned. The steward brought them back to the farm. Undeterred, Amos tried personal visits to his friends, but each attempt to talk with them was met with a closed door.

"Well," he said, "tomorrow evening is Abigail's special celebration, number seventy-four!" He used the exact phrase each year, and only her age changed as he announced the event.

After a magnificent birthday meal on Thursday afternoon, platters and bowls were taken away to be cleaned by servants. Amos and the other family members took turns telling their favorite memories of Abigail.

Later, as they got ready for bed, Abigail told Amos, "I really enjoyed myself. Tonight you had us laughing at your funny stories. I forgot a lot of those things about Alexandria. When did you put all those tales together?"

"I wanted to go over happy memories for you, my darling. Our best days were those in Alexandria. We were young, remember. Everything is so different now. Tuesday I was met with a closed door at each home I visited. I'm sorry to tell you this, but our pain is not over. The elders meant what they said."

"Amos, my dear husband! Did you think funny stories would take Isabel's mind off our problems if her parents were present? Did Jesse wonder about Daniel and Dorcas and what they would say? But you did the right thing. We laughed tonight, and I will chuckle again next year. Then I'll be seventy-five."

Several days later, while talking to Miriam, Abigail started to drift in and out of the conversation. Closing her eyes, she saw the faces of her children. She looked puzzled.

Why are they getting thinner?

She tried to remember the sound of their voices, and she wanted to talk with them.

My darling Leah! How I miss you! I would do anything to have you with me again. So... "Why don't you come back..." *to me? Let me hold you again, my little girl...* "so I can hug you?"

Miriam tried to continue the conversation. "Aunt Abigail, you were starting to say something, and then you drifted off. You didn't say anything for a while. Are you feeling all right? What did you mean by saying, 'Why don't you come back?'"

"Yes, Miriam, I'm fine. I'm just..." *thinking about my little girl, about Leah. I never told you about her.* "...thinking about all the trials. I realize now..." *I'm bitter and angry, but I cannot forgive...* "because of all the things that happened."

Over the past weeks, Abigail had started drifting in and out of sentences but never to this extent.

"Miriam, I am" ... *even more upset because of the recent arrival of Anthony, your husband. And now, because of him, I am losing my friends...* "not feeling really well today."

Miriam curled her legs under herself. She waited for her aunt to speak a complete sentence.

Grace ran up and down the steps, and Miriam watched her. A tiny kitten lay asleep on one of the couches. Grace went to it and petted its head and back, putting her index finger to her lips to make sure her mother did not wake the beloved household pet.

Obed arrived at home early the next day, but no one was expecting him back before noon. "I'm not feeling well," he said. "I'm out of energy. This is our last busy stretch of the fall, and I need more hands to help the merchants and travelers. My new apprentice is watching the business for me just now, but I don't want to trust him to do all the necessary things when I'm gone."

Abigail looked at him, waiting to understand more.

"I'm not feeling well these days, Mother. We don't have enough feed for the animals."

He put his hand on his mother's shoulder. Increasingly worried about her worsening condition, he glanced at Miriam, raised his eyebrows, and softly murmured, "I need help too, Miriam. What shall I do?"

"What about asking Heber to stay three weeks, not just a few days? He's used to running Uncle Simon's store," Miriam said. "He's coming to set up the floor looms for Arpoxa. Perhaps he'll agree to stay on for a while. You need a few days to rest."

Obed nodded and whispered, "Agreed. Mother is acting strange, and I want her watched. Heber sent a note to me at the inn, explaining that he was delayed in leaving Sardis. We had asked him to round up another two looms for the new venture, so he needed extra wagons."

A smile indicated Miriam's joy. "So villagers will learn weaving techniques!"

"Yes, and two men are coming with him to set them up. Since Heber knows how to manage a business, I'll ask him to help at the inn. I'm going to lie down for a while."

THE REPAIRED WORKSHOPS IN PHILADELPHIA

It was midmorning on Friday when Cleon sent Timon to the Ben Shelah farm. "Tell Obed to come to the inn! Heber has arrived, and he's brought the looms."

Obed returned to the inn just as the men started moving loom components into the workshop building.

Giving his cousin a hug, Obed communicated his relief. "Heber, I'm so glad that you arrived safely. Could you stay a little longer than you planned? It will take two or three days to set up the looms. You won't be working tomorrow because the Sabbath begins tonight. You were expecting to stay Sunday and Monday, but I have a special request for you. Mother needs me. She has several problems at home...and she isn't well. I need someone to run the inn for a couple of extra weeks or more, at least until traveling merchants go home for the winter."

Heber threw his head back, laughing. His family in Sardis always counted on him to see the lighter side of challenging situations.

"I thought I was coming for two or three days to work, but I see it's more like weeks. Or will it be two months? I'm certainly open to doing that. I'm sorry to hear about Aunt Abigail. How is this for a plan? I'll go back to Sardis, spend a day or two at home, and explain why I am needed here. I'm sure it will be all right with Father. I would enjoy doing something different and no longer taking care of the family store in Sardis!"

Obed steadied himself, feeling faint. "Come, I'll get you and your men placed in the inn. They can continue working on the looms this afternoon. Meanwhile, I'll take you to see my father and mother at the farm. They will be happy to see you."

Bowing his head, Obed thought, *I'm glad you are here, Heber. I don't want to see any more soldiers. Their voices, words, games, and coarse jokes have worn me out. Seeing them every day during the summer...I feel like I'm falling into quicksand.*

Chapter 18
Arrivals and Departures

AMOS AND ABIGAIL'S HOME

Abigail stood beside her front gate, waving to Heber as he left on his way back to Sardis. Miriam and Isabel were beside her, their arms around the older woman's waist. Ruth held her son, waving his tiny hand. They watched Heber's wagon head down the hill toward the Mountain Road and saw a horseman coming toward the farm.

He was a courier and asked, "Is Miriam Suros here?" Several fingers pointed at Miriam, and he handed her a document.

A moment later, Miriam was grinning. "I'm called to the Bank of Philadelphia!" said Miriam. "This is the best news."

"It's the payment from great-grandpa's estate. I'm sure that means that Uncle Amos's deposit came in at the same time. Marcos, our lawyer, sent the money here, and I am required to register as a client at the Bank of Philadelphia. I need to hurry to the city and get that done now! The Sabbath starts in a few hours."

Miriam returned after a successful trip to the bank, arriving just before noon. Abigail declared, "I must get my mind off the threats from the elders. While we have our meal, tell us what Heber meant during his visit when he said, 'Miriam changed our lives. Two years ago, she got us to think about the poor people living in the insulae. Our family is selling clothing and simple rugs made by those people in workshops that she started.'"

Miriam chuckled. As servants brought out the food, she told her story. Many individuals had become part of the Ben Shelah business ventures in Sardis and Thyatira.[64]

Tears welled up in Abigail's eyes. After the meal, she commented, "Miriam, you're the first person outside our immediate

[64] Miriam's involvement with the poor people of Sardis is found in *Never Enough Gold: A Chronicle of Sardis.*

household who can understand this. Leah, my daughter, was born like Aulus in Thyatira. You told us about Melpone, a mother who was ashamed to take her son outdoors. People immediately knew that he couldn't learn like the others. I had a special love for Leah.[65]

"But Miriam...about my son Ater...I'm so angry and distressed! Slaughtered...with five hundred others who were captured. Oh, Ater! My son! My son! You will understand about Leah, I think." *My never-ending memory of when Ater was killed...*

She held her elbow over her eyes, her shoulders heaving.

Miriam moved close. "I'm here, Aunt Abigail. I can't understand what you meant, but I'm here beside you, and I'm not going to go away. I'll stay with you."

Later that evening, Isabel called Abigail aside. A cold draft had started to blow through the house, and they drew their scarves tightly around their shoulders. With Grace and Saulius running circles around the couches, the only place they could meet for a quiet conversation was in the library.

"I'm worried about the threat of being rejected by the elders," Isabel stated, furrows crossing her brow. "Thirty days have gone by, but Amos won't change his mind, will he? I'm scared that my father will reject me. And..."

"What else is on your mind, my daughter?" Abigail asked.

"Obed is not well. Every morning, my husband wakes up saying, 'I'm tired.' He doesn't sleep, and he won't talk. Since Heber left after the noon meal, have you seen how quiet he is?"

"Yes, I've been watching. What's making Obed act this way?"

Isabel walked around the library. She stopped at a shelf and picked out a scroll. "He remarked to Heber, 'Father is threatened with exclusion. On December 8, the elders will come again. If he doesn't comply, then they will come again in early March.' After that, he's hardly said two words."

Abigail was sitting at the table. "I know my son well, Isabel. He calculates numbers, prices, dates, and calendars. But he doesn't do well if he's losing control. He's like me. The soldiers at the inn are rowdy and rough. I believe it's upsetting him."

---

65 The story of Melpone and Aulus is found in *Purple Honors: A Chronicle of Thyatira.*

"Mother, I'm going to guess what the real issue is. After the elders' first visit, he laid down on the bed. He would not even reach out to touch me. I asked him what was bothering him, and he groaned and said, 'Our daughter Sarah is betrothed to Mith. If Mith's father tells him to call off the marriage, will he obey his parents?' He previously thought that we were the perfect family union. The union of two sisters and two brothers meant that our children and grandchildren would always be interrelated. Now Obed is afraid that the family's loving associations will be lost."

Abigail took her daughter-in-law's hand. They shared such deep emotions.

Later, when they went to bed, Abigail told Amos about the conversation. He said he would prepare a special event for the beginning of the next Sabbath.

Seven days later, Heber had returned from Sardis to help at the inn. Amos gathered his family, the families living on the farm, and his servants for the beginning of the Sabbath. Soon the room was crowded.

Amos looked around, joy bubbling up and radiating his face. Abigail carefully lit the Sabbath candles. Obed was with Isabel. Jesse and Ruth were together too, proud of their little boy, who was sleeping.

Sarah, though, hung her head. Amos thought of the terrible possibility. *Could Sarah's marriage be called off?*

Miriam held Grace, although the child was too energetic to stay in her arms for long. Standing around the room were several farm employees. Menander, the inn steward, had joined them as well.

Amos gathered his thoughts, carefully choosing his words. "The Lord our God is One," he declared.

They made their regular prayers, the same ones they would repeat if they were seated with the congregation. Amos had always led worship for his family, but Miriam noted a new resolve this evening. It came through in his voice.

"The Holy One of Jacob tells us not to fear. He says to us on this Sabbath evening, 'Do not be afraid.' How often do we find these words in the Scriptures? Hundreds of times! Why? Think of when our forefathers were afraid. Remember the cloud that was a light to the Israelites as they were leaving Egypt by night? It was also a cloud of darkness and confusion to their enemies. Moses proclaimed, 'Do not be afraid. Stand firm, and you will see the deliverance the Lord will bring you today.'[66]

"Today we face a threat. We didn't create it or want it. We have not sought a confrontation with friends. Instead, we seek peace. We ask, 'What will the elders do? Will they reject us?'

"I want us to remember these words: 'Do not be afraid.' Every time this phrase came from the Lord, he provided a way of escape. We heard the same words from Yeshua Messiah: 'Do not be afraid.'"

Amos looked at Sarah. Tears and worry had appeared in his granddaughter's eyes. He guessed that she was concerned about the wedding. Would Daniel and Dorcas force Mith away from the family? Jeremiah's prayer came back to him: "O Lord, I'm worn out from groaning, and I find no rest."[67]

After everyone had gone home, Miriam tossed and turned, unable to sleep. *Anthony is still away. I miss him so much, Lord. What Uncle Amos said helped, but it won't take away Sarah's fears. Whenever Anthony is on an assignment, my memories of being a little five-year-old come back. I'm all alone again...and I see Daddy falling to the ground, an arrow in his back. I'm afraid of bad things happening to Anthony. I want to trust you, but...I'm also scared.*

THE INN OF THE OPEN DOOR, PHILADELPHIA

By the middle of November, things at the inn moved at a slower tempo. The last caravans of the season made their way from the coast to the inland cities of Laodicea, Hierapolis, and Colosse.

Obed and Heber shared the management of the inn, and all the workers were happy. Heber created a cheerful atmosphere, something Obed had not been able to do, mainly because he avoided conversations with the soldiers staying at the inn.

As the sky began to darken one afternoon, Cleon decided to write a second letter to Diotrephes in Sardis. Looking around and making sure that everyone was working, he turned to the apprentice. "Timon, go and help wash down the stables. Today is the first time in many days that caravans are not expected to come for the night.

---

[66] Exodus 14:13–20
[67] Jeremiah 45:3

Only the soldiers' horses are here. Work with the stable boys, and stay with them until they are finished."

Heber went upstairs to work on the accounts, and satisfied that no one would see him, Cleon took out his writing supplies.

November 16, in the 14th year of Domitian
From: Cleon
To: Diotrephes, at the Gymnasium in Sardis

If you are well, then I am well.

As I wrote to you, the child Chrysa remains at Amos Ben Shelah's house. Heber, who was the manager of Simon's shop in Sardis, helps manage the inn. I don't know if Heber will leave after his commitment. He has extended his support until the end of March. The reason for this: Obed is not well, but the issue is not physical.

I need to be careful because Heber suspects me. He thinks it was through me that you got the wedding garment that allowed you into Simon's house. Since Heber came, everyone is less friendly to me, even Penelope, the new cook. However, the inn earned a lot of money, more than last year, so I will ask Obed for a bonus.

The inn is the perfect place for me to be your lookout. If you want me to continue being your eyes and ears, a tangible gift will help. Kindly let me know your response quickly. Destroy this letter.

It was not a long letter, especially for Cleon, whose complicated stories kept people chuckling for hours.

His deepest wish was to own a horse. He studied the steeds as they came each day and decided he would like a lovely mare. It would permit him to go up the mountain, explore the forests, and occasionally get out of the city. Even with one free day every two weeks, he was determined to see Cogamis Valley from high up on Mount Tmolus.

Cleon put his writing materials away. His letter was sealed with his own ring when Anthony, Omerod, and Bellinus appeared at the inn's door, having been gone for weeks.

They left their personal things and rode to the garrison. Returning to Philadelphia in the supply wagon with the auxiliaries, Zarrus stopped off at the inn.

THE MILITARY GARRISON IN PHILADELPHIA

Felicior's office was cold, and a brisk wind attacked the cracks around the windows and door. "Welcome back, soldiers. What is your report?" The commander was happy to see them return.

"Six weeks spent in Silandus, Malonia, and Slave Mountain. Do you want a full report now or later, sir?"

"Give me a summary now. We'll write the details tomorrow."

Anthony motioned, and Omerod began. "Very well. The unrest in those four places started a long time before this food shortage crisis. We walked around Silandus first. There are no jobs there for the men. But women do their usual work, taking in the harvest, gathering grapes, caring for children, and running the few businesses. Everyone seems disgruntled. It doesn't take much for people to start speaking against the authorities. None of the reconstruction projects authorized by city hall have begun. Minor restoration has been done on buildings damaged in the Great Earthquake."

Bellinus added, "In Silandus, young women are routinely sent to brothels in Sardis. Few jobs, little money, and men having few women to marry all create frustration. More confusing is this: Marble blocks and timber were sent from Philadelphia for reconstruction projects, but emergency work funds were stolen. They protested and stopped working.

"We looked into a crime in Malonia. Eight people died in a riot. One man killed another during an argument. It was thanks to Zarrus that we learned the initial cause of the dispute. One man suspected that his daughter was in love with a young man from another family. Bad words were spoken, and then anger resulted in an honor killing. The young man's father killed the daughter's father. All very foolish and messy, but it was serious business to those people."

Omerod picked up the story. "After that, we went from Malonia to the Slave Mountain area. We waited for a week while Zarrus went up the mountain. He encountered slaves hiding there, having come from agricultural towns across the valley.

"When he returned, we learned why so many try to escape. Slave owners deny them the chance to marry and form a family. Some never have a day to rest. Many would rather be hunted like animals and have a short burst of freedom than continue in those houses."

Anthony summed up the situation. "There are not a lot of bright spots in those towns, sir. The eastern side of Cogamis Valley says it was abandoned by Philadelphia."

"Thank you, soldiers. Come to this office tomorrow. I will have a scribe write down your detailed report. You are all off duty for this evening. The garrison barrack is still full, so you will continue to stay at the inn."

AMOS AND ABIGAIL'S HOME

Anthony, Omerod, and Bellinus rode back to the inn. They were to stay there while the state of emergency was in force. Wanting to see Miriam and Grace, Anthony washed off the dust from travel, left his armor at the inn, and rode to the farm.

Arriving at the house, he stepped inside, surprised to find a celebration underway. A servant said, "Today is Ruth's twentieth birthday."

Miriam gave a little scream and ran to him. "Anthony, you're back and so sunburned!"

"I'm fine. Did Zarrus come here?"

"Yes, he's been here for an hour. He said you were probably still at the garrison office."

"Well, I can't stay because I don't want to disturb Abigail, but I'll be at the inn tomorrow afternoon. Come then."

"No, no, it's not necessary to leave! Aunt Abigail and Uncle Amos want you to stay for a bit. Imagine! She is curious because Zarrus started telling them about the people you talked with. She heard about people on the eastern side of the valley. Anthony, she is living in a daze."

As they sat for the meal, the conversation centered on people who initially had no work. They were now learning weaving and embroidery. Of course, it might be a year before their work reached the workmanship standards wealthy families demanded.

Heber commented, "In my opinion, people should start at a younger age if they want to become master weavers."

Amos asked Anthony to describe the journey to Malonia and Silandus. Speaking cautiously because he did not want to say too much, Anthony outlined their work.

"Zarrus," he said, "why don't you tell them about your Slave Mountain adventure?"

The younger man beamed. He had so much to tell, and soon the family was asking questions about his encounter with the runaway slaves living in caves in the mountain.

Anthony asked Heber about his plans. "How long will you stay in Philadelphia?"

"Until spring."

"Is everything going well?"

"Not really, well...but, yes, Arpoxa is teaching women how to embroider, and that's going well. But something new happened. I became an enemy of Horace. He is the supervisor of the reconstruction project. I approached him, commenting, 'You are spending far more than you need to!' He tears down more of the existing walls than he needs to and then discards some reusable building materials. The workshop building doesn't really require many repairs to make it functional. He fired back, 'Stay out of my business!'

"He charges the city for better quality bricks. New stone blocks cost more than reusing the old ones. Giles and the bankers are happy but corrupt. They wanted to start working on the Lower Hot Baths first because the restoration there will make them tons of money."

"Would Horace ever cause trouble?"

"I don't know. I told the mayor that Amos and I could make repairs quickly on the workshops where Penelope, Zarrus, and Arpoxa are staying. He agreed to pay for the materials, so I put a small team together to repair the workshops. Leaning walls are now back into place straight. We didn't have to tear the whole building down to rebuild. Most of the blocks are reusable. Once the walls are straightened, the roof will be put into place. Horace's original estimates were over-inflated.

"Some of Amos's servants will help with our repairs. We'll have some of the poor people involved, those who have worked with Zarrus. He's made a lot of friends. When Horace learned what I was doing, he became furious but didn't seem to have any power to stop us."

They talked for a few minutes more. Then Abigail said loudly enough for Anthony to hear, "This soldier is interested in people, not like the other soldiers, but...the long scar on his face!"

She finally turned her back on him, but she continued to listen to their conversation.

Anthony turned and whispered to Miriam, "I should leave now. Later, tell her my response: 'My scar, which you can see, doesn't hurt very much now. However, I know the scars that remain on your heart, those that bring the worst pain of all. No one can see them, but we know they are there, and we care about your terrible loss.' Tell me what she says after she hears that."

Chapter 19
Willing Volunteers

THE BANK OF COGAMIS VALLEY

At the end of November, Amos asked for a meeting with the Bank of Cogamis Valley's managers. They were a smaller bank in Philadelphia, so they had decided not to compete in contracts for the large rebuilding project.

Miriam went with Amos but said nothing. He explained to the bank managers that several villagers as a group would want to purchase weaving looms. "I encourage you to look favorably on loans for these people. They started a new commercial effort to spin wool, dye it, and then weave carpets and make clothing. As part of the city rebuilding program, our friends have been teaching villagers and townspeople from around Cogamis Valley. If you grant them loans, you will be making a secure investment in a project supported by a great merchant, Flavius Zeuxis."

The three managers listened carefully to the business plan he presented but sat stone-faced and thanked him for his recommendation. They did not want him to know that they had discussed the topic the previous day. Having received several loan applications, they had already decided to invest in the new venture. Keeping the friendship of a seventy-year-old Jew was what they wanted. They would soon learn that many looms would be set up around the valley.

THE CITY OF PHILADELPHIA

Amos and Miriam left the bankers high on the acropolis. He rubbed his arm as they strolled down the Avenue of Philadelphia, and Miriam commented on various products and shops. As they approached the end of the avenue, Amos felt the stab in his arm again. *I'm getting old and slowing down a lot. Who would have ever thought I would need to be helped by my niece while looking for opportunities and encouraging new ventures!*

At the bottom of the long avenue, they walked around the workshop building. For decades, it had lain in a damaged state. The usable twenty percent of the building had been cleaned out and made into apartments for Arpoxa, Penelope, and their children. Heber and his small crew of workers reset and braced the walls. Next they hired a few more men to put the roof into place. This improvement made the inside waterproof and provided room for several looms to be set up. Some of the sewing and loom training was starting to provide the critical skills needed for supplying suitable goods. All hoped that Flavius would soon be selling their products outside of Asia Minor.

At the far end of the building, an area for pottery training drew in men who wanted to improve their skills.

The mayor had recruited two potters to teach here. Zarrus was the decoration instructor and showed them how to place unique designs on the plates, pots, cups, and bowls. Between this and his other job at the inn, he was kept busy every day.

Penelope and her family continued to live in the section closest to the inn. Arpoxa and Zarrus remained in the smaller area with their two little boys.

Amos and Miriam walked into the loom workshop and met visitors from Castolius, Clanodda, and Sasorta. One said, "After I learn how to use a loom, I want to return home and set one up. But how can I if I don't have the money?"

Amos told him, "Why not ask for a loan from the Bank of Cogamis Valley? I'm very sure that they would be interested in helping if you made a good proposal."

Sitting at the end of the building in the pottery area, Zarrus gave instruction. Five young men were learning how to fire-harden clay pots. "Let the pot dry completely before putting it into a kiln. If the clay has any moisture remaining in it, the heat of the kiln will turn it into steam that will destroy the wall of the pot."

Zarrus explained how to determine when the kiln had reached the proper temperature for the pottery to be finished. Such details were crucial to producing a sturdy product. They included how many hours to allow the kiln to cool before opening it to remove the finished pots.

"If you try to take them out too soon, uneven cooling may cause them to crack. Letting the kiln cool overnight is easiest and safest."

"Tell us about being a slave. How were you freed?" asked a man. "I never heard of someone like you being given his freedom. I thought maimed slaves stay slaves forever."

Zarrus said, "I was digging a well, and a boulder came loose and fell in on me. I guess I was careless." He explained how he had been forced into slavery and how Antipas has purchased both him and Arpoxa. The two Scythians were given their freedom in Pergamum.

Miriam heard the conversation and closed her eyes, remembering. *Ateas...there in the slave market...and now he speaks Greek...not too well, but even strong men listen to him. He volunteered for this and fits in with these men even though he is younger than many of them.*

Miriam tugged Amos's arm. "Let's see what Arpoxa is doing."

The roof over the women's workspace was restored. Strong timbers supported red ceramic roof tiles. Young girls stirred squash mixed with pieces of chicken in a giant cauldron, preparing the noon meal. Miriam knew some of the names of the women learning to embroider. She spoke to each one, inspected their work, and encouraged them.

When the women learned that the lady with clubbed feet had been a slave, word spread quickly. Her stories amazed her students. Even though another lady worked with Arpoxa sharing valuable skills, many had been turned away because of a lack of teaching space.

Thelma ran into the workshop, calling out after Sandra, Penelope's seven-year-old daughter, "Come back, little rascal! You know you can't be out on the street where all these men are working. Horses run by, and people come and go. Come back home with me!" Her arms were held out wide, but Sandra playfully rushed past Thelma.

Leaving Arpoxa's workshop, Amos and Miriam watched Horace and Quintus. The two construction superintendents arrived with a loud clatter of horses' hooves. The mood at the workshops changed quickly. One moment, men had been chatting and laughing as they did their job on the construction site, but now workers worked silently.

Miriam stood beside Amos, watching. *The workers are afraid! I can see that these two are up to no good. If someone complains, he gets laid off. Unemployed men...unhappy homes.*

Amos leaned over and whispered, "Miriam, I know these superintendents. The assistant, the big fat one, tries to be nice, making workers feel good. The one with the twisted nose and the dark expression on his face threatens the men. These two rascals work together! And they get away with it. City hall approved the work, but Horace, the one with the broken nose, is changing the plans. Just as he got his face rearranged after a fight, he says he is 'redesigning the project *just slightly.'* Those are his words. Each change results in bigger profits for the banks. The bankers and these rogues are thick as thieves."

Horace turned his head and saw Amos beside the workshop building. It was the one restoration area not under his control. "Hello, sir," he observed, "you need to let me help you improve the work on this building. I see flaws in what was done here. The roof probably leaked after last night's rain. Oh, that wall truly needs to be torn down. It isn't perfectly straight and may fail later, but I can make it strong and reliable. There really needs to be a pillar here under the entrance. Hmm, I could get my architect to redesign the whole building. Would you like a beautiful arch?"

"As far as I'm concerned, the building is adequately refurbished," Amos asserted calmly. "As far as your offer to help is concerned, no, but thank you for asking. The mayor provided space for men and women to learn new skills to support their families. The work is complete. By the way, there was only one place where water leaked after last night's rainstorm, and it can easily be fixed."

Miriam and Amos went across the square to the inn and talked with Penelope. Amos wanted to stay a little longer, but Miriam preferred to get back to Grace at the farm.

Heber called to Timon, "Here, drive the wagon back to the farm and take Miriam. On the way back, stop at the market and get these supplies."

On the way home, Miriam heard a woman singing. The song, 'Willing Wagoneers', paid tribute to farm laborers. In the music, workers earned a pittance while those who bought the food and sold it to others gained all the profits.

As the wagon rumbled over the bumpy road, lyrics came to Miriam. The words fit the tune she had just heard. She called it "Willing Volunteers," and the words poured from her heart. She would sing it to the family later, perhaps at the evening meal.

Our overseer's face is full of sneers,
He grabs more pay than all his peers,
Earns his wage from men with plush careers,
Meets his friends and whispers in their ears,
"Avoid that bunch! They're only volunteers."

Proud to be a friend of profiteers,
His pockets clink, thanks to financiers.
Another shares secrets with racketeers.
At night, they're sloshed with wine and beers.
"Let's drink! Come, ignore those volunteers."

This man works hard. Each day, he perseveres.
He paints designs made to last for years.
That woman's students give her friendly cheers.
Her work's first-rate. She ignores the leers,
Smiles at those who hate the volunteers.

With friends like these, I'm rich beyond my peers.
Fortunate slaves were saved from auctioneers.
Joy is their pay, and no one interferes.
Their joy brings life, like that of pioneers.
We need more like them. Willing volunteers!

Miriam dashed into the home. She greeted Abigail, did a little dance, picked Grace up, twirled around, and sang her melody. Grace laughed and wanted the song again. Saulius joined in, and the two children squealed and danced. They tried to make the kittens dance too, but the cat family wanted to sleep.

Abigail smiled then, laughing, asked, "What did you do to bring on such a happy song?"

Miriam answered indirectly, "My heart is with Israel's princes, with the willing volunteers among the people. Praise the Lord."[68]

"I have no idea what you are talking about." Abigail smiled, glad to have her niece home in such a happy mood. For the rest of the day, she hummed the new song Miriam had taught her.

"Chanukah begins in four days," Miriam commented. "We need volunteers to light the lamps each evening! Would you mind if we invited Penelope, her children, and Thelma? I'd love to have them learn what Chanukah is all about."

In a gesture of goodwill, Abigail assented.

THE REPAIRED WORKSHOPS IN PHILADELPHIA

Early on Saturday morning, Miriam returned to the workshop. Thelma was caring for Rhoda, Sandra, and Melody.

"Hail, Thelma! I've come to invite you to the lighting of the lamps tomorrow evening. Can you come to Aunt Abigail's? But first, how are you enjoying Philadelphia?"

"I like it a lot. I love taking care of these children."

"How many family members live in Sasorta?"

"None. I didn't always live in Sasorta."

"Really? How long were you there?"

"Only a short while before my husband died. We had been married only two weeks."

"I'm so sorry about that. I heard about your husband's accident. Where did you live before?"

"Have you heard of Silandus? Yes? Well, I was born there."

"And is that where you met your husband?"

"No, I met him in another place, in Malonia, a small city."

"You moved around a lot! From Silandus to Malonia and then married in Sasorta. Your relatives in Silandus must be sorry about your loss, Thelma."

Something in Miriam's voice touched Thelma's heart. "Oh no! I was glad to leave. Such a dreadful place! My mother died when I was nine, and I had to stay with my uncle. When I try to remember my mother's face, all that comes back to me is my uncle...that horrible man." Her eyes watered, and she turned red.

---

[68] Judges 5:9

Miriam took Melody from Thelma's lap. "Oh! So you had a miserable time in Silandus?"

"Yes, the way men treat women there… It's a sad place. There is a saying there: 'The pipe leaks.' You know how ceramic pipes bring water from mountain springs? 'The pipe leaks' means money intended for our city never gets to the people who need it. Many girls my age end up in brothels. They are normally sent to Sardis."

"But you didn't go to Sardis."

"No, I heard my uncle talking with a trader. He said, 'She's the age to be sent to Sardis.' That night, I ran away. I didn't want to live in a brothel."

She wiped her eyes before adding, "I asked for a ride with a family I knew. They didn't know I was telling them a lie. I said I had an aunt in Malonia. Once there, I went from one house to another looking for work. One lady accepted me, and I was treated like a slave. I slept on the hard floor outside the door of my master's bedroom and worked for food but no wages."

"You left Malonia. How did you get to Sasorta?"

"One day I was shopping in the Malonia market, getting food for the household. I met a young man who was going to Sasorta. We often talked at the market. One morning the young man urged me, 'Come with me. I want to marry you. We'll get married at the Temple of Artemis in Sasorta. I'll protect you and care for you all your life.' You see, I had already told him about my uncle."

"So you were married in Sasorta."

"Yes, but we didn't realize the work situation was so bad. In Malonia, the crops are different. More fruits and vegetables. Here in the valley, it's mostly vineyards. Many were plowed up for grain fields, so men had no work or food at home. A baker gave me a job and took me to the public protest. That was when my husband confronted the soldiers. He took the baker's horse, determined to get to the storehouses. The next thing I saw, his horse was rearing up. It fell backward, crushing him. I tried to get the soldiers to help me, but they didn't pay attention."

Miriam's mouth flew open as she remembered the incident. "Thelma! Anthony and I were passing through Sasorta from Thyatira when that happened. Anthony ran over to the scene to see if he could help but he said the man was already dead. He was there for only a short while, so you two would not have remembered each other.

"He told me about what happened when he returned to our wagon. When we needed a person to mind Penelope's children. I remembered the 'young widow in Sasorta' who would be needing help. That was when Uncle Amos sent Obed to Sasorta to find you."

"You must be shattered! So much has happened to you."

Thelma wiped her nose and nodded.

"I see you caring for these little ones: Evander, Rhoda, Hamon, Sandra, and Melody. They are quite a handful."

Thelma looked up. Her eyes expressed an earnest desire to understand. "I'm trying to figure something out. My friends, Selene and her husband, Rastus, the baker, were so kind. They were there just at the right time. They let me stay ten weeks. Rastus wanted me to go back to Silandus, but I couldn't!

"I didn't know what to do, so I prayed to Hera, the goddess of the home, 'Goddess, find me a place to live.' Then, the day before I was to move out, Obed arrived. He asked a shop owner in town, 'Do you know the young woman whose husband was killed in the riot? Of course, everyone knew about my situation. He invited me here, so I came the next day. It was the day I had to move out of Rastus and Selene's home!"

"So what are you trying to figure out?"

"Don't you think it is odd? My prayers were answered just like that. I didn't have to go begging. Now I'm in a safe place. I love taking care of children, and I don't want anything bad to happen to Rhoda. She's the same age as I was when..." A sob shook her shoulders. "I'm sorry. I didn't mean to cry!"

Thelma took Melody and walked around the room, rocking the baby, loving the child, and comforting the little one. In return, Thelma was heartened with the warmth of a child's body safe in her arms.

"I'm coming tomorrow afternoon to bring you, Penelope, and all the children. You're going to spend an evening at the farmhouse. It's the first day to light our lamps for Chanukah."

Miriam walked to the door of the workshop where Arpoxa was working. Arpoxa called Miriam over, whispering, "Miriam, there's a plot being planned for Saturnalia. A three-day riot is being planned to get at the food supplies here in Philadelphia. That will make guards rush here from Sasorta, Castolius, Clanodda, and Temenoth. It will then be easier for people to break into storehouses in those towns because fewer guards will be left there. So, the danger is actually across the valley. The riot is planned to start the second day of Saturnalia."

"I'll tell Anthony," said Miriam. "He'll know what to do."

Miriam left quickly before anyone might be aware that Arpoxa had passed on important information. Arriving at the inn, she found Penelope working with Rhoda. They were preparing turnips and vegetables for the noon meal.

"Penelope! Tomorrow evening we want you at the farmhouse again. You'll get to see the first Chanukah candle as it is being lit."

THE MILITARY GARRISON IN PHILADELPHIA

Anthony sped to the garrison. He knocked at the door and entered immediately. "Commander Felicior, I need to see you. Sorry for the interruption."

"Suros!" said Felicior. "What's up?"

"I just learned about a plot. A disruption is planned to take place on the second day of Saturnalia celebrations. An attempt will be made here to loot the city food storehouses. Reinforcements presently in Sasorta, Castolius, Clanodda, and Temenoth will be called to keep these food stocks from being ransacked, but it's a diversion. Men in those four towns intend to attack the food storage facilities when fewer soldiers are guarding them."

Worry lines showed on Felicior's face. "How do you know?"

"Miriam heard it from Arpoxa. A woman at the workshop classes explained her husband's plans. Rioters intend to reduce your security forces in the towns around the valley. Bringing more guards here means fewer guards watching over the food storage areas. The woman explained that she doesn't want her husband getting hurt when protesters try to force open the food stores."

"Good work, Anthony. We'll deal firmly with people. They should take their complaints to the administration. We'll be ready for Saturnalia. I will need reinforcements from garrisons in the Meander Valley: Nysa, Neapolis, Harpasa, Mastaura, Antioch, and Aphrodisias.[69] Anthony, well done," said Felicior, using his first name.

---

[69]These cities were located close together in the Meander River's upper reaches to the south of Philadelphia. Laodicea, the largest city in this region, is known

It had been a long time since Anthony had received that kind of appreciation.

---

today as Denizli. It is a center for textile industries, and tourists flock there because of magnificent ruins. Aphrodisias, also known for its ruins, was a growing city close to Laodicea. This city receives fewer visitors because it is off the main roads.

Chapter 20
Winter Events

AMOS AND ABIGAIL'S HOME

Chanukah brought the Festival of Lights, a welcome change after the stress of the past months. But hovering nearby was an ominous deadline. It cast a shadow over the Ben Shelah home. Amos invited Michael, Daniel, and their wives to join them for a meal, but the men refused to come.

Daniel voiced his annoyance when Martha and Dorcas accepted the invitation. "You are disobeying me again!" he said, exasperated. "Why are you going to their home?"

"I'm going to see my grandson," Dorcas replied calmly, her chin set at an angle. She adjusted her cloak and a long, red woolen scarf against the cold wind.

"Light the first lamp here at home," he urged. "Please stay!"

"As usual, your Chanukah meal will be served. You will enjoy it here." Her voice carried the sound of a final decision.

Dorcas and Martha arrived at the farm in the middle of the afternoon, anxious to see Asa. He held his head up, looking around. "Look, Asa! Such bright eyes and a strong little neck! My, you're growing every day!" the two women exclaimed.

Penelope arrived with her children, and Thelma was holding Penelope's baby. Rugs were spread across the floor, covering the mosaics.

Amos looked around the room and raised his voice as the families prepared to greet the special evening. "Hear, O Israel, the Lord your God is One."

The center 'servant' lamp was filled with olive oil, and the wick was lit. Amos called the center lamp "The Light of the World." It was time to use it to light the first lamp of Chanukah.

Each night during the next week, another lamp would be lit. God's triumph of light and holiness over darkness would continue.

The oil reminded them of God's faithfulness. The Maccabees were the courageous family who reclaimed their temple from King Antiochus IV, "Epiphanes." His name meant "Divinity Incarnate." The use of the word "divinity" for Antiochus told all that he claimed to be a god.

Abigail pondered the threat of being barred from further fellowship. *If Anthony hadn't come into Miriam's life, then we would not be facing such shame. He brought untold troubles to our three families. Oh, how I love to remember that fabulous party in Jerusalem! Amos purchased our house inside the city walls, and I prepared food for scores when we moved in. We danced and sang songs until the early hours of the morning. Now, after the deaths of my children, what is left? We face the loss of our community and our relatives. Oh, Amos, what are you doing to us?*

Mentally, she was back in Jerusalem, watching Ater walk confidently out of their home. "I'm going to destroy those war machines tonight, Mother," she remembered hearing him say. "Don't worry about me. We young men know how to destroy the Roman army! I'll be back tomorrow morning." *Why didn't he listen when I shouted, "Ater, don't get hurt!"*

Abigail took the central lamp and lit the first Chanukah lamp. Slowly, the wick grew hot, and a tiny flame burst upward. She moved her hand back an inch as the wick held its heat and grew bright.

She breathed again. The first lamp of Chanukah was aflame. It burned, shedding a soft yellow-white glow on the faces of an old man and his troubled wife. The light also touched men and women, boys and girls, rich and poor, Jews and Gentiles. The light was overcoming the darkness once again.

But Abigail frowned. She had not been able to find a quiet moment with Penelope. *Tonight children were dancing around. All those happy voices, children seeing the lamp being lit—that made it worthwhile. I will find an answer to my question about Anthony's real character another way.*

None of the elders came to Amos's home for Chanukah, even though they were all invited. On Tuesday, Amos waited for his visitors to announce the next period of exclusion. He heard them enter the gate, the soft sound of horses' hooves clip-clopping on the paving stones in the courtyard. The winter rains had started, and only three elders arrived: Zacharias, Michael, and Daniel.

Zacharias had a simple message, and he alone got down from the wagon to deliver it verbally.

"Amos," Zacharias began, his voice betraying both sadness and distress, "sixty days ago, we cautioned you against straying from our customs. Yet you have not obeyed our counsel. Why did you not attempt the changes the congregation requires of you? Because the Almighty is 'generous, slow to anger and plenteous in mercy,' we will treat you similarly. Reconsider your paths, my friend. Lead your family in the paths of truth and righteousness. Tomorrow is the beginning of a period of grace—ninety days. There will not be another extension."

He hurried back to the wagon.

Amos bowed his head and then fell face down on the floor. *Dear God, why this separation? Must everyone suffer because of my decision? These are my relatives by marriage! Michael didn't even ask about his great-grandson, Asa! My worst fear, Lord, is that my granddaughter will be hurt by all this. But for Sarah's marriage to be called off, Mith would have to write a certificate of divorce.*

THE REPAIRED WORKSHOPS IN PHILADELPHIA

At Anthony's suggestion, Heber collected several of the most recently woven garments. Proud of the workshop's students, he sent them to Flavius in Hierapolis. He hoped the sample of the goods being offered would result in purchases being made in Philadelphia.

Heber also sent some of the garments embroidered by Arpoxa and her students. In the letter accompanying the shipment, Heber noted that these were made by people recently trained. He expected the future quality to be even better.

SATURNALIA IN THE CITY OF PHILADELPHIA

Philadelphia throbbed with excitement and laughter. Nothing could dampen the celebrations, gift-giving, and enthusiasm. As was the custom in Rome, the Feast of Saturnalia started on December 17 and ended on December 23. The festival coincided with the shortest day of the year. The week was an extravaganza greater than at any other annual celebration.

Gifts of every kind were exchanged: sausages, parrots, writing tablets, pipes, pigs, spoons, masks, dice, hunting knives, lamps, balls, knucklebones, hats, perfumes, toothpicks, tables, cups, items of clothing, statues, combs, moneyboxes, axes, books, and pets. Everyone was expected to give at least one small gift to another person. Some presents were new and brought squeals of delight, while others had been exchanged repeatedly. Some friends knew what was coming, so they guffawed loudly as the same gift showed up one more time.

The name of the festival came from the Temple of Saturn in Rome. It was celebrated with joy in Philadelphia, where many gods, both Greek and Roman, were respected. The Master of Ceremonies took his place on a couch in front of the Temple of Saturn.

The day before the festival, two ropes were tied from the statue of Saturn to the couch. Everyone knew that custom dictated moderation. But on this first day of the weeklong festival, as the mayor untied the ropes, social restraint was thrown off. School holidays brought joy. On the last day, they would be tied again during the Feast of the Ropes. Frivolity was over for another year.

In the home of Mayor Aurelius Manilius Hermippus, according to custom, the head slave came to tell his master that the household was ready for annual rituals. The head slave managed the provisions and directed the activities of domestic servants. Today it was his responsibility to offer a sacrifice to the *penates*, the household deities. He threw a small offering onto the flame in front of Vesta, the virgin goddess of the home. Each festival day, the family honored slaves with a dinner prepared as if they were the master.

Only several days later was the table set again for the head of the household. They laughed loudly because today the master acted as a servant.

Across Philadelphia, the new wine was served. Throngs walked back and forth between the temples of Dionysius and Zeus. Streets were crowded, and when the weather permitted, groups of friends walked arm in arm. Orgies were whispered about. A different market was set up where even slaves could gamble. Repeatedly, tumblers of beer complemented laughter at the taverns. For a week, no one wore a toga. Instead, the colorful, informal "dinner clothes" and the *pileus*, a freedman's hat, were worn by all. Everyone was "free" for one week. Slaves would not be punished but were treated as ordinary people.

Even the bankers gave up their positions, with slaves taking their place of honor. In Giles's home, the head slave took the place of honor. At each meal, he gave a prepared speech, imitating his wealthy owner.

Each slave knew his limits. No one overstepped the boundaries that marked them as inferior in social position. In all homes, families roared at the humorous reversal of roles, so utterly different from how society usually operated.

In Silandus and other cities across the Cogamis Valley, the festival was not a happy time of joy and frivolity. Cynicism and grief, long years of neglect, and sustained exploitation dampened the enthusiasm for Saturnalia's public holiday.

THE MILITARY GARRISON IN PHILADELPHIA

The Solemn Oath on the first day of the year allowed Commander Felicior to explain its importance across the empire. Standing before his soldiers lined up in rank and file and marching back and forth before them, he felt honored. His command mainly had kept the Philadelphia public safe for the last seven tumultuous months.

"Everyone knows why this day is special. From Britannia in the west to the Persian deserts in the east and from the green forests of Germania in the north to the hot white sands of the African deserts in the south, there is only one authority."

The sky's pale colors were gone. Hovering over the canyon and the hills to the south, a low, dark mass of clouds blew in. Another rainstorm was about to arrive, so he shortened his speech.

"Rome is 845 years old. This empire will last forever. You must recognize that and make the imperial cult central to everything. That's why you declare, 'Caesar is lord and god.' No other belief has ever united the world this way. Caesar holds the power of life and death."[70]

---

[70] The founding of Rome and its eventual development resulted in an emperor being the single final authority. Scholars differ on the extent to which Caesar's worship as a god was a formal imperial cult or how much the cult was bound up in the general population with sentiments of devotion. It is undisputed that

Raindrops fell, and a sudden blast of wind struck them. "Caesar is lord and god!" he declared. Their pledge of loyalty was repeated like this on the first day of every year.

"Caesar is lord and god!" they shouted in return. Heavy raindrops ran down their faces.

Felicior looked at Anthony's mouth and noticed, once again, that stubborn refusal to acknowledge Domitian as "god."

Suros is obstinate. His ways will be his undoing.

Soldiers ran into the garrison as the storm hit. The ceremony known as the Day of the Solemn Oath was over before Felicior delivered the speech he had prepared.

AMOS AND ABIGAIL'S HOME

While Felicior was running into his office to escape the pelting rain, Obed called his father, Amos, aside. It was the kind of rain that might return, on and off, for two or three days.

"Father, I want to thank you for spending the first day of the New Year close beside me. Even if we had been welcomed to worship today...if we were comforted by our friends, I could not hide this from you anymore. I am in deep distress."

"What is causing this misery, my son?"

"I worry about our family. We will be cut off. Is it only because of Anthony? Or is it because outsiders work with us? You are well, Father. Look at your recent meetings with the mayor. You always plan new things. You're successful, helping, promoting, and encouraging. Zarrus makes pottery and teaches; Arpoxa works with clothing and teaches embroidery. And the latest project has begun, making bags to transport the harvest grain."

He paused. He knew it wasn't really these things that bothered him. "But I have questions and no answers."

Amos leaned forward. "What questions, my son?"

"Look at our family. Mother still suffers because of what happened in Jerusalem. It's going to get worse for her if we are forced out of our community! I'm caught in the middle."

Obed continued, "I cannot take it anymore, Father. Everyone talks about Mother. They say, 'Seven children were born to the Ben

---

Caesar unified the empire in the power of one person, whose command was absolute.

Shelah family, but poor Abigail, she only has one son left.' That son is me!

"Why does no one ever ask me what it was like in Jerusalem? I watched Annias leave. He went to offer a sheep at the altar, and his limp body was brought back home. I helped you to carry him, remember? We had to drop him over the wall onto that pile of bodies. Have you forgotten the stench? Azetas was stabbed in the stomach by Simon's army, and I helped you carry him out. I cried for days. And then another brother, Ater, was slaughtered by the Romans! Arah and Agia fell ill, their frail bodies consumed by hunger."

He looked up. "But no one thinks about me. No one says, 'Maybe Obed still feels the pain.' Mother feels it of course. She gave birth to us."

"My son, thank you for telling me this."

"Father, I need help! I cannot be your manager at the inn. I am not sleeping at night. Two more months, and then what will we do? How will we worship? The elders will ban us from the congregation in early March."

He was not finished. "Tonight they are gathering for worship. Why can't we be there and sit at the back of the building? I have asked myself, 'What will I say to Isabel?' This division between our Ben Shelah family and her Ben Akkub family rips her apart, although she doesn't say much. I don't know who to be loyal to: you and Mother, our Jewish traditions, or my individual family. I need help!"

"What can I do for you?"

"I can't work at the inn every day. I can't think. I get confused. I'm...broken inside...and feeling isolated. I just can't carry on."

He left quickly and went to his room.

Chapter 21
Thelma

THE CITY OF PHILADELPHIA

A postal messenger from Flavius Zeuxis handed a letter to Felicior. The famous merchant thanked the garrison for Anthony's message concerning continued efforts to eliminate the robberies. Still, he was concerned that the villains who had robbed his caravan continued to roam free. But nothing in the businessman's letter referred to his priceless gold armband or the stolen merchandise's value.

The messenger carried another letter from Flavius, also written five days earlier. It was delivered to Obed. Since the rider was a personal messenger from Flavius, Obed requested that the messenger rest and have a meal before returning to Hierapolis.

January, in the 14th year of Domitian
From: Flavius Zeuxis
To: Obed Ben Shelah

If you are well, then I am well.

Of all the businessmen I talked with during my previous visits to the Inn of the Open Door, I want to work with you. You struck me as the one least likely to "dip your hand into the fruit bowl," as people say. I want you to represent your local garment workers. You will work with my agent, who will stay at your inn for one week. His task is to purchase clothing and classify it according to our standards. If you do not have time for this, I am willing to accept an alternate person.

The garments and other items sent last month by Heber Ben Shelah are acceptable to me for exporting. I am sending my agent to inspect what is available to purchase for my enterprise. He will make journeys to Philadelphia in late January and early March.

I will accompany my agent in late March. My plans are to pass through Achaia on my way to Italia. As usual, I will leave at the beginning of the sailing season. I have decided to make the trip with several guards for security.

Be prepared for a large caravan to stay one night on March 28. Give my greetings to the crippled lady about whom people are speaking. Her embroidery and the choice of patterns and colors is suitable for even my own elaborate tastes.

Reading the letter, Obed groaned. *Oh no! Another intrusion of Gentiles. So many more people that I have never met before.*

He quickly wrote a note to Flavius explaining that Heber Ben Shelah would represent the garment makers. He sealed the letter and handed it to the messenger to return to Hierapolis. Then lines appeared on his forehead as he wondered how best to tell Heber of the great man's plans.

Three weeks later, the inn was prepared for the arrival of Flavius's purchasing agents. The weather had turned blustery, cold, and wet. In late January, the road traffic was minimal, so the staff had no problem settling in the smaller-than-usual caravan.

When the caravan from Hierapolis arrived at the inn, Flavius's men were soaking wet. Heber called, "Obed, let's take all these men to the kitchen to warm up by the fire. They will want the best food, so let's see what we can serve them."

In the kitchen area, Flavius Zeuxis's men, two buyers and one burly guard warmed themselves by the large oven. Penelope sat at a table chopping vegetables and throwing them into a cauldron with lamb meat cuts. Thelma had been called in to help her with the guests.

Doing his best to be cheerful, Obed forced a smile as he stood with the travelers. "Welcome to the Inn of the Open Door! We appreciate your business and hope to make you as comfortable as possible. A meal will soon be ready. Heber has sent messengers to Sasorta, Castolius, Clanodda, and Temenoth to let them know they need to bring their products. Winter is not normally busy, so we can provide you with generous accommodations for your visits over the next few months."

Looking around, peering into the kitchen, Obed seemed to be very nervous. "Penelope, I'm asking Heber to look after the inn. Let him know when the meal is ready for the guests. We will treat these guests exceptionally well since they will be returning twice more in the next two months. Make your best hot meals for them."

Penelope's knife clicked rapidly on the cutting board. "Look at you and Heber! Both the same age and as thin as a rake. Time for you men to eat up!"

She continued cutting turnips, onions, and beans without raising her head. The new cook was intent on keeping the dining room a happy, healthy place. "You've got to start eating better, both of you! Thelma, we have to do something to fatten these men up."

THE INN OF THE OPEN DOOR

Early Friday morning, Flavius's agents packed five camels with numerous garments. Overall, they were content with their purchases from the workers in Philadelphia and the outlying cities. As was expected, the workmanship of items presented varied significantly. Flavius instructed his representatives to acquire all but the more defective items and pay according to quality. They were sure there was a market for each item. At times, they gave suggestions about how workers could improve their goods.

After they paid their bill for rooms, meals, and animal care, the men from Hierapolis informed Heber that they would return late on the last day of February. "At that time, we plan to stay five days. It worked well for this trip."

The only visitors at the inn this early in the year were these agents and soldiers, so Heber had no problem acting as the local sellers' representative. He also handled the inn's operation. Working on Amos and Obed's behalf, Heber requested and got a small commission from each seller for hosting the sales. He told them all to be prepared with new stock to sell on the last day of February, when the agents would return.

AMOS AND ABIGAIL'S HOME

Grace's birthday fell on the second Tuesday in February. The atmosphere in the home during the previous weeks mirrored dark winter skies outside. Still, Miriam was determined to have a lighthearted event. No one wanted to speak about the threat of exclusion.

The center space on the main couch was given to Grace. The child sat between Amos and Abigail, keeping a kitten beside her even when Miriam told her to put it down while eating. "Grace, how old are you?" her mother asked.

Grace held up four fingers.

"No, sweetheart, you are three years old today. February 9 is your special day. Every year comes and goes, and then you add one more number. So next year you will be four, like this. Now, how old are you this year?"

Grace grinned and again held up four little fingers.

After the meal, Miriam retold the story of how Grace had come to her. Penelope and Thelma had never heard the story, although Arpoxa and Ateas knew it well.

"So, there I was, a single woman twenty-four years of age, waiting for Grandpa to choose a husband for me!" Miriam explained.

"Chrysa Grace was left beside the Pergamum City trash heap. The mother had sent a messenger the previous day telling me to go there.[71] I took her up and held my baby in my arms. She was sleeping as I walked through the agora on the way to our house. I thought everyone would shout, 'Thief!' or 'Whose baby is that?' But, of course, they did not.

"When Grandpa saw me bringing a baby girl into our home, an expression came on his face I had never seen!"

She and Anthony had been married one day and adopted the baby the next day.

"What a lovely story! An exposed baby finding a family!" Thelma said, a wistful look in her eye.

---

[71] Throughout the Roman Empire, many unwanted girl babies were left in the open to die. The term used was "to be exposed." Frequently the girl children were taken in and raised by another family, but untold numbers died.

"Now, Thelma, tell us your story!" said Isabel, inviting the shy young woman to join in the fun of the evening. "Would you like to tell us about your family?"

"Some other time," said Thelma, glancing at Penelope and Miriam.

Later, after the birthday party was over, Thelma left with Penelope and the children by wagon. A lantern showed the way down the hill and into the city. "Penelope, do you know who was the only one missing at that party?" Thelma asked under her breath.

Penelope murmured, making sure her children did not hear. "Yes, Anthony wasn't invited. I was cooking in the kitchen when I heard Heber and Obed talking. Heber said, 'At first when the family stayed with us in Sardis, my parents refused to have Anthony at the house. Then the army required him to stay with us under house arrest. After a while, my parents accepted him. Later he could come and go, even when he was working for the garrison.' Thelma," she confided, "they invite us to all their events, yet they never call for Anthony."

"I feel sorry for Miriam," whispered Thelma. "Abigail doesn't let Anthony sleep at their house. It all seems so sad." Tears filled her eyes. Thelma knew what it was to lose her husband. She wanted to wrap her arms around Miriam and say, "I understand you, and please, Miriam, understand me too."

THE INN OF THE OPEN DOOR

Thelma was leaving the inn as Timon came around the corner from his home. "Hello, Timon," she said. "I'm just leaving. Melody hasn't been well, and she wants to be with her mother here in the kitchen. But she is sleeping now, so I'm taking her back home."

"That's nice," he said. "Was Melody sick for a long time?"

She paused before answering. *Timon is interested in the child. Otherwise, he wouldn't ask questions about her!*

"No, Melody came down sick two days ago with a cough and a cold. I think it's not unusual since we have this cold weather."

"Are you all right? I didn't see you for a few days."

Her heart was pumping hard. *Timon is interested in me too! Why else would he ask me that?*

"I had a fever during those January storms. We all got colds. It's hard to care for children when you're ill. Apart from that, I've been as well as anyone else here in the inn. Now that the worst part of winter has passed and the first buds are out on the bushes..."

Timon looked around to make sure no one heard his concern. "Well, I probably shouldn't say this, but I think there is someone here who is really sick."

Ever so slightly, Thelma leaned forward. "Who is that?"

"Thelma, have you noticed? Obed is ill, but there is nothing physically wrong. He came with Heber this morning then went to talk with Menander. Suddenly, in the middle of a sentence, Obed stopped talking. I'm glad Heber is here to help run the inn. Heber knows what he is doing, but Obed... Thelma, I'm worried about him."

Thelma could feel her heart rising in her throat. *Timon used my name, and he is talking to me about a genuine concern he has about the inn. Yes, he is confiding in me!*

"I noticed. Penelope says that there are some family problems. We spent another evening there last night. and his mother, Abigail... One moment she was with us, listening to everything, taking it in, and then she was looking away, her mind in some distant place."

Timon took in a deep breath. "You know, Thelma, the first time I saw you, I thought you were Penelope's oldest child. I didn't know you were here to watch over her children."

Now she could not breathe. *Timon noticed me the first time he saw me, and he wondered about me. He stopped talking about the inn and the Ben Shelah family. He said he noticed me!*

"Yes, that's why I came here to Philadelphia—to care for Penelope's little troop!"

Believing that Thelma was ready to talk about herself, Timon asked, "Where did you live before coming to Philadelphia?"

A shudder went down her back. *Oh no, I've said too much! I can't tell him anything about myself.* "I'm sorry, Timon. I can't talk anymore. I have to get back to the other children."

"Goodbye, Thelma. Take care of those children! Take care of yourself too."

THE CITY OF PHILADELPHIA

On the last day of February, Flavius's agents from Hierapolis arrived at the inn leading five camels. Heber was waiting for them, and he had the stable boys escort the camels to the animal area for food and water. This time he had set up a closed bazaar area next to the workshop building where the garment sellers would display their wares for the agents.

The sellers now realized the importance of quality for these professional buyers. The merchant's agents found significant improvement since their last visit.

By Wednesday evening, the agents had purchased all the clothing that they could carry. On Thursday morning, they loaded up the camels, preparing to leave. They paid Heber for their stay and told him that their large caravan from Hierapolis with Flavius would return on March 28 for a one-night stay.

Chapter 22
A Decision for Amos

AMOS AND ABIGAIL'S HOME

On the morning of March 8, the family gathered for an early breakfast. When the meal was finished, Amos called the servants and announced, "After the kitchen is cleaned, you have the rest of the day off." He gave each one a coin, stating, "Take one of the wagons, go to the city, and buy something for yourself."

They all knew why he had done it. Today was the end of the ninety-day warning period, and he wanted to be close to his family. After they were alone, he said, "When the elders come, I will give them an answer. Of course, all of us have been thinking about their demands: 'You and your family will be excluded unless you submit to the council.' So I ask, why do we hold to our beliefs? The answer to this question is more important than what I say when they come. I want us to share this day together."

Abigail's eyes were big and round. Obed sat close to Isabel, his arm around his wife's shoulder. Ruth sat on the other side of her mother. Asa, the baby, slept in Jesse's arms, oblivious to decisions that might influence his future.

Amos spoke, his voice conveying a new decisiveness. "Our friends insist on regulations, dietary laws, and the circumcision of all males born in our house or working in our house. They forbid me to give hospitality to non-Jews."

Miriam held Grace in her lap, and she brushed Grace's long black hair, running it through her fingers and wrapping Grace's hair around her thumbs.

"Long hours, night after night, I have thought about this. My decision will affect us all." He began at the beginning, telling how Adam and Eve were made in the image of Elohim[72] and how human

[72] Elohim is one of the Jewish names of God or the Lord.

worth was a gift from their Creator. Then he reviewed the stories of Abraham, Isaac, Jacob, Joseph, Moses, and Joshua.

"The Torah says that our people are to be a blessing to the world,[73] used by God, and dependent on him as our King and Savior. Instead, we became self-centered, focusing on ourselves. To this day, we prefer to look after ourselves rather than bring the blessings of Elohim to others.

"A widow living in Lebanon showed hospitality to Elijah. Later, her little boy was brought back to life by the prophet. The captain of the armies of Syria was healed. Imagine helping that man, an enemy, a foreigner! A little Jewish girl, a slave, blessed her master! Naaman had leprosy, but God used Elisha to heal him. His leprosy disappeared! I want to be like those prophets, being a blessing to others. And Yeshua came to show us how we should treat our neighbors, enemies or not."

Deep feelings called for time to listen to one another, and he turned to Isabel. She was going to suffer significantly because of his decision. "Isabel, your father says, 'Without a temple, we cannot be a nation,' but I disagree. We are a people held together by our language, our scriptures, and our customs. I agree with much of what Michael teaches, but I disagree with one important element. Our Messiah has come through the family of Abraham. However, faith in Yeshua Messiah is not given only to us Jews. Salvation is for everyone who believes, not limited by race, language, skin color, or man or woman. We are called to be a blessing to others."

As Amos spoke, Isabel began to cry. She did not want to make such a decision, but she had to choose. Isabel could stay with the Ben Shelah family, with her husband, daughters, and grandson, or she could return to her father's home.

Isabel told how she wanted to go back to her father's home, but then tears flowed as she explained that she could not face the loss of her husband, daughters, and grandson. After many minutes of starting sentences and then explaining things in different words, she leaned against Obed, covering her face.

Amos continued. "We are scattered again, not only in Babylon but dispersed all over the world. We number more than fifty Jewish congregations here in Asia Minor, Bithynia, Cappadocia, Phrygia,

---

[73] Genesis 12:3

and Galatia, From the Aegean Sea to Cappadocia, they have spread far apart, from the Black Sea to the Mediterranean.[74] Why did the Lord permit this? He has favored us, leaving us as a remnant."

Taking in each family member, Amos added, "We have been scattered abroad to bless the nations. We Jews always move from one place to another. Abraham went from Ur to Haran and from there to Egypt. He saw the land of promise but owned little, only his burial ground. Once again, we are a scattered people. I believe this happened so we can bless the nations."

His words had a serious tone while describing their isolation, but they also comforted his family. Miriam, Abigail, Isabel, and Ruth were wiping their eyes.

Halfway through the morning, Amos declared, "I can see how this sounds strange, but we must bless Miriam and Anthony. They chose to marry. Grace had been rejected by her mother but was found and rescued. Zarrus and Arpoxa were lost, cast aside, but were redeemed and saved from a dreadful future. Now they have two boys. We are called to be a light to the Gentiles. That includes Penelope and her five children, Thelma, and others."

Isabel was still concerned about how their decision would affect the family day by day. "What about the staff at the inn? All those soldiers coming and going and merchants arriving from who knows where? Maybe my father was right. He said if you sold your shop and bought that inn, those pagans would soon have you changing your loyalties."

After thinking a moment, Amos replied, "We will relate to Cleon and Timon, the soldiers, and the merchants with honesty in business affairs. We will be a blessing to each of our stewards. And to Menander, who should work faster and more efficiently. Those who work with the animals on our farm are also included."

They smiled through the tears. Imagine blessing Menander!

Amos stopped talking and lowered his head into his hands. Miriam went to him, placing her hand on his shoulder and feeling the deep sighs welling up. Her voice was barely audible. "I remember the choice Grandfather Antipas made and how much suffering came after he had set his course."

---

[74] See Mark Wilson, *Biblical Turkey: A Guide to the Jewish and Christian Sites of Turkey,* pp. 22–23, Yayanlar Press, Istanbul, Turkey, 2010.

Amos had been in bed for hours and was unable to sleep. He had attempted to describe a vision more significant than anything he had ever experienced and was not sure he had found the right words.

I have made my decision. I thought it would be hardest for Isabel, but I was wrong. Sarah is only seventeen. She will lose her husband because Mith will not be permitted to carry out the wedding as planned. We will be rejected—as my brothers were in Pergamum, Sardis, and Thyatira—but I will not respond in anger. I remember Antipas's words at Father's funeral: "This struggle never ends. It's a war we didn't want, but I will be an overcomer in each new battle."

The sun had been rising earlier each day. Flowers painted the fields with vibrant colors, and fruit trees blossomed. Oleander bushes exploded in reds, pinks, and whites, a river of color along the city's streets. Birds returned, and mornings were a cacophony of twittering. Long before fresh milk arrived from the cowshed, the family was up. The day had come to declare their loyalties.

"Lord, God of the Heavens, blessed be your name," Amos said, beginning the morning meal. "Give us strength and fortitude. May your praises forever be lifted up, King of the Universe."

Michael, Zacharias, Daniel, and nine others arrived mid-morning, avoiding mealtime and conversations. This would be their last time to come to the Ben Shelah household.

Hearing the arrival of horses and wagons, Amos nodded to a servant, who opened the gate. Twelve men descended from three wagons. One horse neighed loudly and tossed her head several times as if she, too, were aware of the conflict. The elders formed a semicircle in the courtyard, standing inside the wall but declining Abigail's invitation to enter the house.

Amos knew each one well. They had spent many days discussing the finer points of the Torah. Members of the Ben Shelah family formed an opposite semicircle. The women's faces were touched up. Rouge on their cheeks, slightly blackened eyelashes, and blue eyelids were something Zacharias prohibited. Amos had trimmed his beard. These were customs common in Alexandria but frowned upon by the elders, all of whom came from other traditions.

The visitors stood stiffly, dressed in long black gowns with tassels at the bottom. Their beards were long and uncut. Each one had a small clump of curly black hair hanging down onto the shoulder.

Amos beckoned with an open hand, "Please come into our home," but he knew the offer would not be accepted. Miriam stood next to her cousin Obed, who groaned softly.

Choosing his words carefully, Zacharias began, "Amos Ben Shelah, we have read to you the conditions of reinstatement in the fellowship, but you declined our advice. You continue to have compromising alliances, which cannot be tolerated." A harsh tone entered his words. "I will speak first, and then each one will deliver the same decision in his own way. Amos, all this began because you sold your shop. I warned it would lead you to evil alliances. Outsiders have deceived you."

The elder turned and glared at Miriam. "It's your fault, Miriam Ben Shelah!" His voice conveyed scorn, disapproval. "Remember the admonition, 'The land you are entering to possess is a land polluted by the corruption of its peoples. By their detestable practices, they have filled it with impurity from one end to the other. Therefore, do not give your daughters in marriage to their sons, or take their daughters for your sons.'[75] You cannot pick and choose, wanting one part of our Scriptures and rejecting another. Doing that in the past brought the sword, captivity, plunder, and humiliation. Look at what your marriage to a soldier has done!"

Zacharias finished with the dreaded words: "For these reasons, we turn you over to the mercy of God. He alone will provide just punishment. I pray the Almighty to redirect your steps."

Michael looked at his daughter, Isabel. Lines in his face hinted at conflicting emotions swirling within. A Jewish family had broken many rules and regulations. Anger was kindled because the Torah was not honored in the home where his daughter lived. Moreover, he had compassion for Isabel, his daughter, and felt the loss of his great-grandson.

Isabel ran toward Michael. "Daddy! Don't leave us! Please don't..."

"Are you going to live here, or will you shake the Ben Shelah dust off your feet?" he asked,

---

[75] Ezra 9:11

"Daddy! Don't leave me please!" she wailed.

Although she was forty-one years old, her voice pleaded like that of a little child. "I love you, Daddy! Please do not do this! Do not abandon all of us—your daughter, your two granddaughters, and your great-grandson! Come into the house and sit down, and let us talk about many things."

Michael made a slight movement toward the outside gate. He thought of Ezra and Nehemiah, the leaders who restored Judah after the Exile, and knew they would approve of his actions.

For a moment, he wavered in his decision. *Isabel married into such a truculent family! Martha tells me that Obed is ill and cannot work. Isabel must leave this family and return home. Come on, Isabel! Tell me, in front of all these elders, that you are not siding with the offenders! My daughter, it is so easy! Just say, 'Yes, Daddy, I'm coming home.' Bring your daughters up to follow our ageless traditions. Come, raise Asa with us, and do not disgrace me!*

Daniel's jaw tightened, and he held his hands tightly against his chest. "Do you see, Amos? You are destroying relationships! You refuse to yield, even at this final moment!"

Ruth stood next to Jesse, holding little Asa. She addressed her father-in-law. Familial love was coming undone, like the knitted shawl the cat had spoiled recently. "Father, will you really turn your back on your grandson?" She always used "Father" when speaking to Daniel.

Daniel's heart beat wildly, and he wanted it to stop. How had he agreed to this form of discipline? He had been convinced that Amos would change. It was a terrible decision to cut him off from the fellowship. Still, everyone in this house had chosen to break from the synagogue's customs. Did he raise Jesse in such a way to rebel against sound advice? He wanted to talk but could not. If he lost his grandson, what would Dorcas say?

His words were exact and softly spoken. "Jesse, I can no longer be with you if you stay in this home. Come home with me. Please bring Asa up in the right way."

Jesse pleaded, "Father, I don't want to choose between the two homes."

Daniel spoke slowly so his words would not convey his churning heart. "My son, after today, neither you nor Asa can be in our fellowship unless you repent. Leave all this behind."

"But your grandson!" shrieked Ruth. "How can you do this?"

Daniel turned his back on them. One by one, each elder slowly and deliberately turned his back. The members of the Ben Shelah family would not see these faces in fellowship again.

Jesse's voice was now layered with anger. "Father, you prayed for a grandson! Mother wants to help bring up our baby, see him learn to walk, and hear him talk! Think about it!"

Each elder had had his say. Their decision was made, so they mounted their wagons and left the farm.

The Ben Shelah family had been excluded.

With the elders turning their back on them and leaving, Sarah grasped the enormity of this moment. She spoke in a whisper. "Mother, does this mean that Mith will not marry me? What's happening? Why are they doing this? Mother, I've never seen anything like this before."

"Quiet, my child," said Isabel. "A human heart is beating inside each one. They will change their minds, bit by bit." She bit her trembling lips, speaking with hope but not with conviction.

Amos watched his friends leave the farm. He murmured, "The Gentiles will hear of the salvation of our God, but we will pay a great price for choosing to be messengers to them."

MICHAEL AND MARTHA'S HOME IN PHILADELPHIA

Martha and Dorcas were at home, waiting anxiously for Michael and Daniel to return. "I hope Amos changed his mind," whispered Martha. She had not slept the night before. Deep, dark lines under her eyes reflected weeks of fatigue and anxiety. Mith, the seventeen-year-old, stood beside Dorcas to hear what his father would say.

The door opened, and Zacharias, Michael, and Daniel entered. "Well, they are excluded. Gone!" stated Zacharias abruptly.

Martha demanded, "Michael, tell us what happened. Every word! I want to hear it all." She ached to cradle her great-grandson, to watch him grow from a baby into a toddler and then into a youth.

Daniel began. "We went to their farm high on that ledge overlooking the city. It is such an attractive place, but Amos...what a stubborn man! How does he control them all? They stood in a semicircle and invited us in, but we delivered our message, turned our backs, and left."

The women sucked in their breath. Martha interrupted, "But we can still see them, can't we?"

Michael wanted to paint the entire picture. "Amos refuses to follow the Torah. He's rejected the traditions of the elders, which means division. Isabel and Ruth pleaded with us, but Amos would not yield."

Neither Michael nor Daniel was prepared for the explosion that followed. "You have cut off our own flesh and blood," cried Dorcas. "Get rid of Amos, only him! But not all the others!"

Martha said the same thing in her own words. "Why not call him aside and talk to him alone? Must you condemn everyone for Amos's hospitality?"

"We offered him warnings, two periods of grace..." Zacharias started to say.

Martha interrupted, "Yes, perhaps Amos should dismiss non-Jews, but why tell them to stop using Greek manuscripts? For centuries, they kept Jewish families true to our faith and traditions in Alexandria!"

"Do you want to know how Amos keeps his faith and traditions alive?" Zacharias asked, sneering. "He entertains a soldier who is married to a Jew! At the inn, a non-Jew widow cooks the meals. Yes, I know that she does not serve pork, but Amos and Obed share their food with pagans, with sinners."

Martha would not be silenced. "If I go to see my great-grandson, will you cut me off?"

Dorcas's face carried dark anxiety. "What about Ruth? Can she come here with our grandson? And what did you say to Sarah about her marriage to Mith?"

The three men exchanged glances. They had not entirely stopped to consider that by taking this action, they were also bringing much pain into their own homes.

"We need to go to our workplaces," said Zacharias lamely.

Mith approached his father, his voice barely a whisper. "You told me not to talk to Sarah. I obeyed you. What happens now?"

Daniel turned to walk away, and Mith asked again, his voice much louder, almost shouting, "Father! What does this mean for my betrothal to Sarah?"

The three friends would get little work done today. Still, it was better to leave quickly to escape the inevitable outburst, so Daniel followed Zacharias and Michael out of the home.

A deeply creased forehead hinted at Daniel's feelings as he walked to his work. He had not given thought to how to explain all this to his son.

Mith is only seventeen. How can he understand purity? What do discipline and respect for the Law mean? Amos had to be stopped before our community is infected with increasingly ungodly ideas.

AMOS AND ABIGAIL'S HOME

Meanwhile, at the Ben Shelah home, Abigail was crying and embracing her daughter-in-law, Isabel. The older woman struck out at Miriam. "Why did you marry a Roman? Before you came here, we didn't have any of these problems!" Shock and anger filled the room.

Miriam did not know how to respond, so she kept silent, tears filling her eyes.

"I don't want my betrothal called off!" Sarah moaned, sitting at the end of a couch. "Mith can't leave me! He would have to give me a certificate of divorce!"

Amos saw the look of distress on his son's face. He took Obed's well-worn hands in his own. Together they wept, father and son, sharing the pain.

"I want to speak to you, my family," said Amos. "South of Jerusalem, close to where the land meets the desert, there is a water well. It's called Beersheba and is the southern limit of our ancient lands. Abraham and Isaac watered their flocks there. Beersheba means 'Well of the Oath.' The Ben Shelah clan lived there during the time of David, king of Israel. My forefathers made pottery, linens, and other fine products, and later Elijah, fleeing from Queen Jezebel, rested there.

"Special events are like that Beersheba water well. They mark a boundary and define our decisions. Today we feel abandoned by our friends, who have the best of intentions. They demand purity in religious practices, food, and marriage. We also want purity, but we define the boundaries differently. Today we are at our 'Beersheba' boundary. We have not crossed beyond that border. We have made a choice to live according to the Kingdom of God."

Miriam looked at her uncle. For nine months, she had lived with Amos and Abigail. Miriam had observed him reaching stronger convictions. Then she looked at her young cousin, Sarah, who was wilting under the tension.

"Amos, the prophet for whom I was named, went to Israel from Beersheba to denounce wrongdoing in his day. He called people back to the Lord, and we can still hear his passion.

"Michael, Zacharias, and Daniel gave me a choice. The core of their understanding is this. First, they do not believe a pagan can become a believer. Second, they do not accept that Yeshua was the Messiah.

"Thinking about this, I remember a centurion whose son was ill. Yeshua Messiah told him, 'You have more faith than any other I have found in Israel.'[76] Here is where I disagree with my friends: I believe God offers his salvation to Jews *and* non-Jews. Remember the commandments given by Moses: 'Love the Lord and your neighbor as yourself.' Messiah said, 'Love one another.' Of course, we must remain pure, but that is not confined to handwashing and keeping the Sabbath. Purity also means dealing with fear, jealously, anger, and gossip."

Isabel interrupted with a loud wail. "My father doesn't love me! He turned his back on me. What does this mean for my mother?" She was upset and could not accept words of kindness from anyone. "I cannot imagine being separated from my father or my mother, even for a day, much less for an extended time."

Obed's face was drawn with deep lines. His worst fears were being realized. That dreadful moment in Jerusalem hit him again.

The stench of dying corpses...food being taken away from our home by force. My two starved sisters...such tiny bodies...throwing them on that horrible heap...unable to breathe for the stench. And now...Father is talking about...Beersheba, ancient prophets, Galilee... Everyone thinks of Mother, the grief she still feels.... Don't they

---

[76] Matthew 8:10

understand me? I can't sleep at night because I can see my three brothers dying. Father, how can I explain this to you?

After a time of silence, Obed stood up and walked away from the family circle. He went to his family's room upstairs and did not speak to anyone for the rest of the day.

By Friday, Abigail knew that her son had been severely affected by the recent events. Obed had not gone out of the house, and his meals were being taken to his room. In the evening, Obed called his mother to the library.

When they were seated, Obed spoke, his head bowed low. "Mother, I want you to know what I'm feeling. Heber will have to take on all responsibilities at the inn. I can't think straight. I keep thinking of...when those men walked out of our courtyard two days ago. They forced open the window on my past—Azetas, Leah, Agia.... I stay awake for hours at night and can't sleep during the day either. If I sleep...I have nightmares. I don't want to talk to anyone."

"My son, you don't have to work," said Abigail, comforting him and giving him a hug. "I'm sure Heber will manage the inn for a while. Get a good rest. Your job is to comfort your wife. Isabel is heartbroken thinking her father and mother have abandoned her."

Chapter 23
Evander

THE INN OF THE OPEN DOOR

For three weeks, Heber watched Sarah, who, like Obed, hardly spoke a word. Ruth kept complaining. She was angry at everyone, especially her father-in-law.

Jesse was more optimistic. "My dear, let them believe what they want to. My father's opinions will change. In a few days, I believe that my father will come back. He will be willing to listen to other opinions. Then he will give another deadline. He'll say, 'Yes, Mith and Sarah can get married.' With only two more months until this happy day, no one is going to stop this marriage.'"

Leaving for the inn, Heber rode slowly, taking in the gleaming sky on one of the most pleasant mornings he could remember. Wildflowers painted the fields with blankets of red, white, orange, and purple. The fresh scent of spring was all around, and he breathed deeply, pausing as the birds chirped.

He waited at the inn's entrance while wagons of fresh feed were brought in for the animals. At the rear of the building, where camels, donkeys, and horses stayed, the floor was already being washed out. Every morning the stalls were cleaned with water and stiff brushes made from branches of plants found up the mountain.

Before noon, Heber walked down the steps from the office to the kitchen. Penelope was working with her daughter. Heber asked, "Rhoda, could you fetch more vegetables? We think extra guests will be here for the evening meal."

Rhoda stalled. "How many extras coming tonight?"

Her mother hurried her up. "Rhoda, you heard the man. Fetch more vegetables from the storehouse, my love." Rhoda sped out of the room, happy to be sent away from the endless repetition of cutting and dicing vegetables. She hated the job of endlessly preparing little cubes for the stew.

"Do we know how many are coming?" Penelope asked.

Heber answered, "No, but one of their riders just arrived from Laodicea to make sure they can stay overnight. I think it would be safe to guess about six more men."

Penelope looked at him. "You know, Heber, you look exhausted. You have not been the same recently, and neither has Obed. The staff is asking what's wrong. Is something up?"

"Yes," Heber said slowly, not knowing how much to confide in her.

This is what Michael is afraid of—too many interactions with Gentiles. This is how it happens, through little conversations. I don't think I should tell her about what happened.

Penelope continued, "I can tell something is going on, and it's serious. Nikias, my husband, had a quarrel with his brothers one time. He was riding all over the land, going from village to village. That caused a terrible quarrel at Olive Grove."

She took a stab at the truth. "If you ask me, which you did not, I think Obed is sad because of Anthony. All this has something to do with Amos and the guests in his house. Obed said something to me weeks ago about his mother being stubborn. It's just a guess."

Heber told a white lie. "That's not really the cause of the quarrel."

He walked out of the kitchen as Rhoda came back in, struggling with two buckets full of vegetables. Hungry men enjoyed second and third helpings. The expected travelers arrived from Laodicea in the late afternoon and left the following morning for Sardis. Three days later, they would be in Smyrna, unloading woolen blankets, cloaks, tunics, bed tapestries, and wall hangings. In another two weeks, ships would be docked in distant lands with their precious cargo. These goods were being taken to Athens, Corinth, and Rome.

The following day, Heber wandered around the inn, feeling restless. Penelope was close to guessing the truth. She assumed there was a quarrel and said it had something to do with Anthony. He resisted the impulse to confer with her, went to the office, and found Timon working on the accounting.

"A lot of money again!" said Timon with a grin, showing results from the first half of March. "It's the Ides of March, and the business is doing very well!"

"You've done a good job, Timon! Tell you what, here's an extra coin. Go and spend it on a new tunic."

If he was going to continue talking with Penelope, he had to have Timon out of the way. Cleon would only be coming back to entertain their guests at suppertime.

Heber took a deep breath and went down the stairs to the kitchen. Penelope seemed to have remarkable insight into the problem. "Can I trust you with something?" he asked Penelope, determined to make little mention of the quarrels in the home.

"Yes, I'm good at keeping secrets. You have no idea the things I hear from merchants and travelers standing next to this kitchen counter. I'd be a rich woman if I were paid for all the things that I've learned here!"

"You were right about the quarrel and the part Anthony Suros played in it."

"I knew it! Miriam comes here and talks with him here for a while, but Anthony never stays at Amos and Abigail's home."

"Yes, Uncle Amos and his friends call him an 'outsider.'"

"You are a Jew, and I'm not. My children are like me. We're Gentiles."

"I think Uncle Amos is rethinking what he used to believe about relationships with non-Jews."

"But Abigail still considers Anthony an enemy, right? After all, he's in the army."

"This latest quarrel was bigger than that." He stopped, not willing to go further in his explanation. Penelope stopped cutting vegetables and looked at him, the knife balanced in her hand. He decided to keep things simple. "Obed isn't going to work here for a while. He wants me to do his job."

"He wants you to take his place! I see. He must have a reason."

"He was very hurt and confused by the door being slammed in his face."

"A door? What door? I don't understand."

"The door of the synagogue! Our family has been excluded." Heber blurted it out before he realized what he had said.

"Excluded? What does that mean?"

"The elders at the synagogue believe the Ben Shelah family is too friendly with non-Jews. They detest Miriam having married Anthony, so they have cut us off."

"So Anthony being here is the cause! I knew it. But 'cut off'?"

"All of us who came from Alexandria cut our beards short. They think that makes us different!" He tried to smile at his little joke.

"I've seen the others. They walk about with long beards."

"Yes, and our women use rouge on their cheeks and have blackened eyelashes."

"And that's enough reason to be excluded?"

The sincerity in her voice made him go further than he had intended. "This means Amos and Abigail can't be part of the congregation. So Isabel will not be seeing her mother and father. Ruth and Jesse can't share their son with Daniel and Dorcas, Jesse's mother and father."

The words were out of his mouth before he realized he had said more than he meant to. "I've said too much, Penelope." He looked away to the rooms where the merchants and travelers slept.

"Then don't say anymore. Heber, I have two requests."

"What do you want?"

"My son, Evander, is fourteen. He took the death of his father very badly. He gets depressed, and at times I am afraid. Anger quickly wells up inside him. He hates the killers who beat his father to death. I don't know if he is overreacting or if this is just the way young boys are. Now he is asking me about where babies come from. He is using bad words too, stuff he picked up from other students. Some questions I can talk to him about. Others are beyond me. Evander is telling me about the odd things he is learning in his class on Greek myths. He's getting rebellious, and I'm worried."

"Tell me more."

"He's fascinated by Greek heroes and all the classes in literature. They fought men with only one eye. In one story, a character wrestled a woman whose hair was a never-ending heap of snakes. He laughs about the story in which Zeus castrated his own father. Now he's having nightmares. Heber, he needs a good male friend he can trust, and I have no idea who to talk to about this."

"I think he's probably spending too much time with the wrong people, Penelope. I would recommend that he have a job to keep his mind on better things. I can find odd jobs for him to do since we are getting into caravan season. Do you think we could get him to work here, in the inn, when he's not at school?"

"Yes, I think he would be willing to help support our family. With five children, we need all we can get. And can you talk with him?"

"Yes, I'll talk with him. Now, what is the other thing you wanted to ask about?"

"Actually, two more things, not just one. I'll tell you later. I have to be getting this next meal together now."

Penelope lowered her head. She blinked several times, biting her tongue not to express deep emotions.

How can I tell Heber I don't trust Cleon one bit? Everyone thinks he is so wonderful making people feel welcome. Yes, his hilarity makes guests happy. But he is after me too. And can I ask Heber if he's noticed Thelma taking a liking to Timon? They are almost the same age. Both are lonely, in different ways of course. She's a young widow, and he feels alienated from his father. No, I won't ask Heber. He wouldn't understand anything about this.

Penelope called after him softly as he left the kitchen area, "Thank you for agreeing to talk with Evander. I am grateful to you for whatever you can do for him."

It was about the tenth hour of the day at the inn when Anthony and his team rode through the large open gate and dismounted. Heber called out, "Anthony, you are back! Welcome! Are you coming or going?"

"We are staying here tonight. We scouted near the Door on the Southern Road and ran into a small caravan coming from Laodicea. We rode most of the way back here with them for protection from any possible bandit attack. They are finally on the safe stretch of road. They will be arriving here in about an hour, so have a good meal ready." Anthony patted his horse's muscular neck. Brutus was his favorite horse.

"Shall I let Miriam know that you've come back?"

"Yes, please do that. I should report to Felicior with Omerod and Bellinus after we get cleaned up. We'll be back in an hour. We'll eat a meal with the caravan drivers."

"I am taking on a helper, Penelope's son, Evander, so I'm going to have him be my assistant, going on little errands. I'll send him to the house to tell Miriam that you're back."

Heber left the inn, walking to the square. He passed the men who had finished lowering a polished column in front of the construction site. Soon the pillar would be in place, supporting massive lintel blocks. It was a vital part of the reconstruction.

He stopped in front of Penelope's temporary home. "Is anyone home?" he called. Thelma came to the door, little Melody on her hip.

"I want to speak to Evander. Has he come home yet?"

Evander heard Heber speaking and put his head past Thelma's shoulder.

"I have a little job for you, Evander," said Heber. "You know the way to our house, right? Take my horse. Tell Miriam that Anthony came back from his trip and wants to see her. He went to visit the garrison but will be ready to see her in about two hours. Come back quickly! You are going to be my errand boy, and this is your first job."

Evander let out a whoop of glee. Heber turned back to the inn, walking with his newest young helper. He let Evander saddle and harness his horse and take off for the farm.

THE MILITARY GARRISON IN PHILADELPHIA

Anthony, Omerod, and Bellinus rode along the Avenue of Philadelphia. It was overflowing with shoppers preparing for the upcoming Festival of Artemis. The festival would bring farmers, laborers, basket weavers, and firewood sellers to the city. Priests, potters, merchants, and perfume makers eagerly anticipated the arrival of another spring season. People of every profession would implore Artemis and other gods to bless the coming harvest.

The meeting with Felicior was brief. Anthony explained their findings: "News came of robberies east of Colossae. From the descriptions we got, it is not the same group that attacked Flavius or the other caravan. We learned slaves escaped and are trying to stay alive. For the time being, the regiment from Italia will continue to keep the Door open."

"Good work," said Felicior. "No one can shut the Door while we hold it open." His long, thin face showed his pleasure. Such a rare expression of emotion was welcome.

Under his breath, Anthony muttered contentedly. *The fingers on both my hands are more than enough to count how often Felicior has shown approval during his entire life.*

MICHAEL AND MARTHA'S HOME IN PHILADELPHIA

Before Passover, heated exchanges erupted in Martha's home. She was distressed by not being able to see their children and friends, but nothing she said could change Michael's mind. "The elders in the council made a decision, and that verdict is final" was his answer.

"But can the elders cut us off from Isabel, Obed, our granddaughters, and our great-grandson?" Dark, puffy bags under her eyes spoke of ongoing tensions in their home.

DANIEL AND DORCAS'S HOME IN PHILADELPHIA

In the other home, Dorcas thought about Mith's betrothal to Sarah when Martha came for a visit. "My son was to be married to Sarah!"

"Is there no way to make the men relent?" asked Martha. She shifted her weight from one side to the other, trying to find a comfortable position for her tired legs.

"You tell me!" said Dorcas sharply. "I've begged and cried, shouted and cajoled. It's no use. Daniel won't listen to anyone."

"Well, tomorrow is the Passover," said Dorcas. "Are you ready?"

"Yes, all leaven was cleaned out. Our lamb is ready."

Dorcas nodded and wiped her eyes. "None of them will be present to share the meal, not Jesse, Ruth, or little Asa! I can hardly wait to see how Daniel handles it. Cutting off his own family! He's so stiff-necked!"

AMOS AND ABIGAIL'S HOME

The Ben Shelah household women cleaned every room, all the floors, and every bit of furniture. Not a speck of dust would be found. Fundamental to the preparation was the act of ridding the home of the leaven. The Feast of Unleavened Bread had arrived.

Amos was talking with Abigail. "I want outsiders to understand the importance of our Passover. That means inviting them here. I'm talking about the non-Jewish people who work for us."

Abigail's mouth hung open. "You're going to invite them to our home? I enjoyed lots of company when I was younger...but now? Non-Jews here so soon after the elders talked with us?"

Amos knew his idea would make Abigail uncomfortable. "Yes, but I am not doing this to make you uncomfortable, my love! The people working for us need to understand the Passover."

"Are you going to invite everyone?"

"Just about everyone."

"A few people must not come."

"Abigail, I knew you would object if I mentioned Anthony, but Felicior won't let him come. This is a busy time for merchants, and he has to protect them."

"Good. He should not be at our Passover Supper."

Further conversation reduced the list by six more names.

Obed entered the library. "Father, I heard you speaking, and I want to say something."

Abigail walked toward him. "How are you feeling today? More nightmares?"

"No, but during the last few days, I've had a change of mind about some things. It costs a lot to follow Yeshua Messiah when one family comes up against another."

Obed ignored his mother's open arms. He walked to the small square table, pulled back a chair, and sat down, crossing his arms. "Mother, I want to challenge you. Following our Messiah means giving up things we value, things we hold closest to our hearts."

"I agree, my son. We are paying that price."

"No, Mother, that is not what I'm talking about. Yeshua Messiah said, 'Forgive your enemy.' In fact, he went much further. He said, 'Love your enemies.'"

He waited. Realizing this was going to be a serious conversation, Amos sat down on one side. Abigail pulled out a chair on the other side of the table.

Obed continued, "If we are going to follow the Messiah, we can't pick and choose which parts of his teaching we like and which bits to toss out."

Abigail's eyes expressed surprise, and she sat straight up. "You haven't spoken like this before!"

Obed had only started and was not going to stop. "Father, you were willing to suffer rejection for what you believe. Mother, by keeping Anthony away, you are doing to him what Zacharias did to us. Avoiding him all the time is a rebuff in the same way the elders are rejecting us."

His voice rose sharply even though he tried to keep it on a level tone. "Why do you keep Anthony beyond your reach? Because he's an army man. But I have been observing him for months. He watches other soldiers, correcting them when necessary. No one has been permitted to make an aggressive move toward Penelope. Of course, he cannot control Cleon, but who can handle that man?

"Anthony is away, keeping the security of the Southern Road, hunting men armed with daggers. He keeps at it even though no one has been arrested yet. His detachment helped to restore peace in two cities on the valley's eastern rim. A lot of troubles were going on."

Abigail started to speak. "But in Jerusalem, the soldiers..."

Obed cut her off. "Mother, do you know that Anthony's ideas helped initiate this restoration program in Philadelphia? It was after he talked with that merchant in Hierapolis that he saw what could be done. He suggested giving displaced farmers and their wives work during the winter in construction, sewing, and making clothing. Clothes being bought here are to be sold as far away as Rome.

"Remember the time when you asked me to climb the steps to the top of the wall with you in Jerusalem? That was before my brother was stabbed and died. You looked over the ramparts. Close by, army tents spread for miles. You felt sick seeing legions spread out so far. All soldiers looked the same. They cut trees to make the siege towers that would bring their battalions up to the top of our walls."

Abigail held her head in her hands, her lips quivering.

"Mother, what has Anthony done to you for you to say *he* is your enemy?"

Abigail sighed. "He is a legionary. That's enough!"

"No, Mother, I'm sorry. Anthony is not *our* enemy." Obed stood up and walked around the library. Then he sat down again.

"Two weeks of rest left me with a clear mind. I remember Father saying, 'We would like to choose who is in the covenant and who is out of it, but the Almighty did that! We will bless Thelma, Penelope, Zarrus, and Arpoxa. We did not choose them; that choice was made for us. The most difficult part is to have a will to love others.' I am only beginning to understand what agape love is. Mother, this isn't easy for me."

He stopped for the effect of his last words. "But I know Anthony is not my enemy." He repeated it vigorously: "I know he is not an enemy."

Abigail looked at Amos and shrugged. "He's a soldier. If you insist, he can come to my house, but he is *not* my friend."

Obed concluded his thoughts. "Maybe not, Mother, but we must show agape love. Yes, to him and the others too. If not, then let us prohibit him from coming here. Tell the elders we are returning to the congregation. We'll be accepted as we always were. That way we'll have our friends again."

Miriam walked in on the conversation, and Amos asked, "Miriam, my dear niece, what would you think if Anthony came for the Passover meal?

Just then, Evander arrived at the door. "I have a message for Miriam," he said.

THE INN OF THE OPEN DOOR

Miriam walked up the stairs at the inn to meet Anthony in the office, and Penelope brought plates piled with food and then left.

Taking her husband in her arms, Miriam gave Anthony a long, passionate kiss. She told Anthony in detail about the troubles at Amos's home, starting from the beginning.

Telling about the council members, she explained the details of the sentence given by Zacharias, Michael, Daniel, and the other elders.

"Uncle Amos says it will work out well. He wants our family to be a blessing to others. Obed isn't sleeping well, and Heber is running the inn." She began to weep. "This is not the first time I've been rejected."

He pulled her head onto his shoulder. "It's because of me," said Anthony. "I'm sorry I had to put you through this."

Miriam drew back. "Listen, Anthony. Passover is almost here. Can you ask Felicior for a day off? Uncle Amos wants you to be at their Passover Supper tomorrow night. He's also invited Penelope, her children, Thelma, and others for this special meal."

Anthony laughed. "Your Uncle Amos is starting to act like Antipas, inviting people like me to special meals! I'll go right away and ask Felicior for a day off."

"You can go to Felicior's office in the morning but not this evening. This is the first time I've been alone with you for so long." She stood close, and he could smell the fresh fragrance of olive soap. Her hands went around his shoulders, and she pulled his head down close to hers.

"Will anyone be coming into Heber's office? Maybe Penelope will be…"

She whispered in his ear, "No, don't even think of it! Penelope said no one will come up those stairs. She said she thinks it is terrible that Aunt Abigail is keeping you away from me. She is staying on extra this evening to make sure Cleon doesn't come up the stairs…or anyone else either."

She kissed his mouth eagerly, and he responded by pulling her close. "So, Miriam, we finally have a private moment together in Philadelphia, the city of brotherly love." He kissed her again and ran his fingers through her long black hair. Her lips felt soft, and he kissed her again and again.

"Yes, this is our own very private moment together. Let's make the most of it." She kissed Anthony again, pulling his hands around her back.

In a moment, he had his arms around her waist, and her lips stayed joined to his in the flickering oil lamplight.

Chapter 24
Penelope's First Passover

AMOS AND ABIGAIL'S HOME

Preparation for the Passover meal at Amos's home included many people. Servants busied themselves in the kitchen. Outside, the sun shone brightly, and wildflowers were at their brightest. Miriam took a long walk, relishing the farm's rich scents. Bees buzzed around colorful blossoms blooming on fruit trees. Walking was her way of venting her anger. Felicior would not let Anthony have even one evening off!

In his library, Amos wondered if he was making a mistake. His family had always celebrated Passover at night, keeping Father's traditions and those of his father's father. There would be a full Paschal Moon tonight, but not everyone coming to his house would want to return home on the rough country road after sundown. Considering the possible dangers to adults and children, he decided to start the celebration before the sun went down.

It was still afternoon when the home began to fill up. Voices of children echoed, aglow with wonder. As oil lamps were lit, something of Abigail's previous love of hospitality returned.

Refreshed, her smile lit up the room as brightly as a lamp. Penelope came with her five children and Thelma. Abigail welcomed her guests at the door and thought Timon looked shy entering a Jewish home.

More than forty pairs of sandals, big and little, were lined up at the door. They extended from one wall of the courtyard to the other. At the door, the waft of food welcomed them.

"I've invited you to our special supper, to the *Pesach,* our Passover," Amos began, welcoming everyone. "There is not enough room for us all to recline on couches."

Evander exclaimed, "Oh, we don't have couches. We sit on the floor all the time!"

Amos smiled at the interruption. "Normally, we would be celebrating this meal, our *Seder*, well after dark. Because some of you will go a distance to get back home, we want to finish our meal before it's too dark. Our family will celebrate as we have always done. The rest of you must follow my instructions."

A few low tables had been rearranged so that the youngest sat at one end. Amos and Abigail were the oldest, so they sat near the kitchen, where they had a good view of everyone. Obed and Isabel sat across from each other because they were next in age. Obed was forty-one, a year older than Heber. Miriam sat beside Isabel.

Ruth and Jesse were next, sitting on either side of the low tables along the center. Because Ruth was married, she would light the two Shabbat candles.

Sarah was seventeen. She prayed that next year, after her wedding, she would touch the flame to the Shabbat candles.

Ateas and Arpoxa were conscious of their inability to walk correctly. Arpoxa did not want Saulius, her little boy, to make noise during the special meal. Therefore, the daughter of one of the farm servants stayed upstairs with Saulius and Grace.

Amos had to make sure that each person in the room had enough wine to drink four times during the meal. "If you are going to celebrate with us, then you must do as I say. You can only participate fully if you already believe in the Messiah. Who of you is already a believer in Yeshua? The others will please just watch and learn, and we'll all have our full meal a bit later."

Penelope said she was a believer, and Evander raised his hand too, as did Rhoda. Harmon and Sandra began to raise their arms then put them down. Penelope looked at Thelma, sitting beside her and holding the little girl, Melody.

"Thelma, Harmon, and Sandra, watch this time," Amos instructed. "Next year, you will know what this means to us."

Timon sat in one corner, timid yet anxious to learn what Obed did at such an occasion. Other men sat close to Timon.

When everyone was ready, Amos blew the ram's horn. Penelope's children loved the shrill sound. Some children imitated the sound of the blast, but Amos told them to be quiet.

Amos stood with his white and blue prayer shawl over his head to begin the event. "Hear, O Israel: The Lord our God, the Lord is One. Love the Lord Your God with all your heart and with all your soul and with all your strength. These commandments that I give you today are to be upon your hearts. Impress them on your children. Talk about them when you sit at home and when you walk along the road, when you lie down and when you get up."[77]

Abigail uttered the well-known words: "I will bring you out from under the yoke of the Egyptians."[78] She looked around and added, "In my hands, I hold the cup of Sanctification."

Heber announced the next part. "I will free you from being slaves to them."[79] He had celebrated this feast with Anthony and Miriam in Sardis, and two years later he was in Philadelphia. "The second cup is the cup of Deliverance," Heber said after a lengthy pause.

Obed knew the following passage of the celebration. "'I will redeem you with an outstretched arm and with mighty acts of judgment.'[80] The third cup is the cup of Redemption."

Isabel groaned slightly as she introduced the next cup. "'I will take you as my own people, and I will be your God. I will bring you to the land, and I will give it to you as a possession.'[81] This is the cup of Acceptance."

Plates were piled with *matzah*. The unleavened bread was made of plain flour and water and had the texture of crackers. Ripples on surfaces and tiny holes punched from the top to the bottom of each piece gave a particular meaning to the meal.

Amos stood and prayed again. "Let us ask God to remove the leaven from our hearts." Most in the room did not know what he was talking about, but they gazed in wonder.

Penelope's eyes filled with tears as she talked to herself. *This is what Nikias told me about. We never had a Passover, but he described it to me. What a beautiful light radiates from the table! Miriam looks so pleased. Where is Anthony? O God, you promised to "place the lonely ones in the bosom of families." I remember Nikias saying that once. He noted that I should be kind to his awful brother, Kozma. I hated that man. My husband said I should be calm instead of complaining about him. I was so mean to my brother-in-law at Olive Grove. I uttered many*

---

77 Deuteronomy 6:4–7. The Passover Seder meal in the following pages is borrowed, in part, from *A Messianic Haggadah* by Chris de Vries.

78 Exodus 6:6

79 Ibid.

80 Ibid.

81 Exodus 6:7–8

unkind words to hurt him because he opposed Nikias's new faith in the Messiah. Why did I say those mean words? Lord, clean my mouth and my heart. Thank you for the invitation to this meal. The candlelight is showing me my dark places.

The women who had lit the candles spoke together: "Blessed are you, O Lord our God, King of the universe, who has set us apart by His Word and in whose name we light the festival lights."

Amos looked up to the ceiling. With the cup lifted as high as he could reach, he said, "Blessed are you, O Lord our God, King of the universe, who creates the fruit of the vine." He said it in Hebrew and then translated it into Greek. He nodded, and the people who were participating sipped from their cups.

Penelope looked on and thought about her widowhood. *Nikias was so good to me. He longed to own a farm, and, oh, how he loved our children. Lord, why was he taken away? I miss him so much! And now I will celebrate a Passover without him beside me!*

Amos washed Abigail's hands by pouring a little bit of water from the jug on the table. He took a small cotton towel and dried his wife's hands. She washed Obed's hands, and Obed did the same for Heber. Then Heber carefully poured several drops of water onto Isabel's hands. The pitcher of water moved slowly down the table, each one washing the hands of a person younger than themselves and drying their hands, each one acting as a servant.

Penelope imitated the action, washing Evander's hands. She reached across to Rhoda and then cleansed each of her children's hands. *How many times have I bathed the children's hands at home? Always, it seems, I am the one preparing meals. Lord. Cleanse my son's life. He is learning such bad words and so many wrong and shameful things with his friends.*

Amos waited while Penelope reached over to Thelma, who seemed lost in her own thoughts. Thelma slowly stretched out her hands, and then her eyes filled with tears. Thelma's hands were wetter from tears than they were from the few drops of water that had been poured from the decanter.

Penelope's heart overflowed. *Even Thelma understands this cleansing. So many scars in her young life! You left me as a widow, but I have five children. Lord, she has no one. She and I, both widows. Both lost our husbands from unnecessary violence. She does such a good job taking care of my children, loving them, guiding them, and singing to them.*

Amos repeated the eternal question: "Who may ascend the hill of the Lord?[82] We remember that Yeshua washed not only the hands but the feet of his followers. He was acting as a slave."

Sarah, the youngest, asked the four essential questions. "On all other nights, we eat bread or matzah. On this night, why do we eat only matzah?" She paused and then asked the second question: "On all other nights, we eat all kinds of vegetables. On this night, why do we eat only bitter herbs?"

No one answered.

She asked, "On all other nights, we do not dip our vegetables even once. On this night, why do we dip them twice?" She imitated the action with her hands reaching over the table.

The fourth question followed: "On all other nights, we eat our meals sitting or reclining. On this night, why do we eat only reclining?"

Amos had no need to teach his own family. They already knew the words by heart. But he sensed this was a moment his servants and their children, Penelope and her children, young Thelma, and timid Timon would never forget.

He delighted in the following words. "We eat unleavened bread, matzah, because we were driven out of Egypt quickly, and we did not have time to allow the bread dough to rise before baking. That was the First Exodus. Now our Messiah has become the Passover Lamb. He is our Second Exodus. He has been sacrificed. We are to be a new batch of bread but without yeast.[83]

"This matzah bread is bruised. Look at it. It looks like the back of someone who has been beaten, leaving it broken with stripes and many holes. Now hold it in your hands. Imagine what it means to be beaten because you did not make enough bricks today. How would you sleep at night if your back had been bruised like this? This bread tells us that we were bruised and broken in Egypt. It also reminds us that our Messiah's back was bruised and broken for our iniquities."

Taking three slices of matzah, Amos called them "Unity." He placed the three flat slices in a folded cloth. The central piece was

---

[82] Psalm 24:3

[83] 1 Corinthians 5:7

removed and then broken, and he put half of the broken part into a small bag.

Penelope kept on with her daydream, mourning her widowhood. *God, this is what happens to all our lives. Broken by circumstances. I'm still shattered by Nikias's brutal death. And young Thelma? Abused...and then she ran away to marry a runaway slave. Is her widowhood worse than mine? I work to support five children. Must all widowhood hurt so much?*

Penelope groaned loudly without meaning to. Everyone looked at her.

Amos continued, "This bag is special. 'Unity' is a promise. It speaks of the Coming One, of the Messiah. Pilate took Yeshua and had him flogged many times."

One of the best parts of Passover was about to happen. Amos left the room and hid the bag in the courtyard. He found a special place beside the vine that gave them shade protection on the roof on hot summer days. The *afikomen* bag was now hidden, and he would let the children find it later. He came back and said, "Joseph of Arimathea took the body of Yeshua, wrapped it in a clean linen cloth, and placed it in his own new tomb."[84]

Amos held his hands out to everyone in the crowded room. "The body of our Messiah was broken and hidden in the tomb. In the same way, the *afikomen* is wrapped in linen and is hidden from us for a while."

The other half of the *matzah* bread was in his hands. He held it up and said, "'He took the bread, gave thanks, broke it, and gave it to them, saying, 'This is my body given for you; do this in remembrance of me.' Tonight, together with those who keep the covenant everywhere, we celebrate the bread of our Passover."

The matzah bread was passed down the table from one to the other. More bread was passed, and everyone waited to get a piece of it to hold. Penelope was unsure if she should give some to Thelma or not, but Thelma reached out quickly. She wanted some. A different look was in her eyes.

"I want to eat this broken bread," Thelma whispered. "I understand it now."

---

[84] Matthew 27:59

Another piece had to be passed from Amos's place all the way down the room. Sarah took her little bit of bread in her hand and gave the sign that all should eat. Everyone ate their piece at the same time.

The Ben Shelah family members said together, "Blessed are you, O Lord our God, King of the universe, who brings forth bread from the earth." Amos heard Penelope and Thelma stumbling on the words, and acting generously, he slowed down so that they could participate. He said, "Now let's all say it together," and they repeated the blessing.

Amos went on to the next part of the meal. "Why do we eat bitter herbs tonight and dip them twice?"

Amos looked at the non-Jewish guests at the Seder, seeing expressions of anticipation on two of them. Penelope and Thelma leaned forward, anxious to see what was next.

On the table were bowls of saltwater. Amos passed around a plate of parsley sprigs, which he called the *carpas* vegetable. He asked each person to take a sprig and hold it. "I want you to dip the parsley into the saltwater and taste it." When all had done this, he asked, "How does it taste?"

Everyone answered, "It's bitter."

Amos said, "It reminds us of the bitterness of slavery. 'The Israelites groaned in their slavery and cried out, and their cry for help went up to God because of their slavery.'"[85]

Next to the saltwater bowls were plates of charoset, a sweet mixture made of fruit and nuts. Amos then passed a container holding slices of bitter horseradish, which he called *maror*. "I want you to dip the maror into the charoset and taste it." The dark appearance reminded them of the color of the mortar.

When all had tasted the dipped maror, he said, "We remember our bitter life in Egypt. We were slaves and made mortar with our hands, placing bricks to build walls and palaces. We eat the maror with the charoset to remind us that the most bitter of circumstances can be sweetened by the hope we have in God.

"The next question asks, 'Why do we eat reclining at this meal?' When we were slaves, the wealthy and the rich reclined while the slaves stood and served the meals. Tonight we are free, and we

---

[85] Exodus 2:23

recline. Our Messiah has said, 'If the Son sets you free, you will be free indeed.' So we are doubly free, first from Egypt and now from sin.[86] When my children were small, in Jerusalem, this was our best moment. Abigail was so delighted to be in our home with our seven children. They held their cup of wine. After I said the name of each of the ten plagues, they dipped their index finger into the cup and splashed a drop of wine onto the empty plate."

He said the words, and they yelled out the plagues, one by one: blood, frogs, lice, insects, sick cattle, sores, hail, locusts, darkness, and, finally, the firstborn! Amos looked around the room. Each plate was speckled with red drops of wine.

It was time for the *Dayenu*. "It would have been enough!" Amos pronounced each word carefully. "If the Lord had merely rescued us but had not judged the Egyptians..."

Those around the table completed the sentence: "...Dayenu! It would have been enough!"

His voice quivered, trying to block out memories from Jerusalem. Amos began, "If he had only destroyed their gods but not parted the Red Sea," and his family completed the statement, "Dayenu! It would have been enough."

Another story of the Exodus came to mind. "If he had only drowned our enemies but had not fed us with manna" was followed by the refrain, "Dayenu!"

He lifted his cup and said, "This is the cup of Deliverance." For a second time, they drank from the cup. It was time for the meal, and Amos lifted a shank bone of a lamb. "This roasted shank bone represents the lamb whose blood marked our houses. This showed we were ready to be obedient.[87] We now have our Lamb of God, who takes away the sin of the world. Our Messiah has become our Lamb. He has paid the ultimate price."[88]

Even though Penelope knew what was coming, she could not hide her joy. *Amos is inviting us to his feast. He has broken down the walls that divided us, and he brought us in! Me with my children, Evander, Rhoda, Hamon, Sandra, and Melody. And Thelma too! He is*

---

[86] John 8:32

[87] Exodus 12:3

[88] John 1:29

saying we are more than welcome at his home. We are in the close circle of his friends! We belong!

The time had come for the meal. Amos spent a silent moment examining the shank bone as though in deep thought. "Some still do not understand it. What happened to the lamb after it was chosen? It was taken to the house of the family. In the case of Yeshua, he went to his Father's house, to the Temple.

"We cleanse this house to remove yeast. That means our homes are to be free from sin. Yeshua, our sacrifice, entered the Temple. He saw yeast at work, the kind of yeast that makes terrible attitudes grow inside us: brawling, greed, malice, jealousy, bitterness, envy, and slander. What did he do? He did the same thing the women in our house did these past few days. He cleansed it. Moneychangers were angry. People who sold animals were furious.

"He was purifying his house and said, 'This house shall be called a house of prayer for all the nations.'[89] So even Yeshua Messiah cleansed his house. And just as the lamb had to be examined, so priests examined the Lamb of God. They looked for blemishes, but there were none to be found."

Many things about the teaching on the Messiah had eluded Penelope when she lived at Olive Grove Farm. But now, during the Passover, she understood more. The meal was rooted in events long ago. *Nikias always spoke of a clean life after he met Anthony and Miriam. I'm beginning to understand more about what he said to me.*

Servants had prepared the meal that the Ben Shelah family preferred: butterfly leg of lamb, broad bean casserole, fruit salad, and Promised Land salad dressing.[90]

After the meal, Amos sent the children to look for the hidden afikomen bread. Sandra found it and brought it back, handing it to Amos. Opening the linen cloth, he explained, "He was hidden from us for three days, and he came back to life. Because of this, we have hope. He lives!" He gave Sandra a silver coin. It was her first, and she said, "Thank you, Uncle Amos."

Tears spilled down Penelope's cheeks. They implied the thrill of hope. She now understood the connection between the Exodus from Egypt and the story about Yeshua, the carpenter from Nazareth.

---

[89] Isaiah 56:7, Mark 11:7

[90] See *Loaves and Fishes: Foods from Bible Times*, pp. 53–56.

That's a word I haven't often heard—hope. Will Thelma tell me why she has been so enthusiastic during the last hour and a half? She needs hope. She doesn't have anything and has no training. But she does know how to clean dirty kitchens, serve bread, and care for children.

With a firm voice, Amos said, "You will notice that the last taste of this meal is one you don't expect. We've just spent a lot of time with this wonderful food. Our servants did a marvelous job with this meal. Thank you to everyone who helped with the cooking! But you will not go away with only the taste of this food. You must remember flat, unleavened bread. You will not forget we were slaves in Egypt."

The time for the third cup had come. "This is the third cup, the cup of Redemption. We were slaves, but we were bought with a price, the price of the Lamb." They reached for the cup again and drank another sip. The mixture of wine and broken matzah bread left a peculiar taste in their mouths.

A few drops remained in the bottom of the first three cups, but they would not drink the fourth and last cup, the cup of Acceptance.

Amos looked around the room, and a slight shudder of joy ran through his body. "By the tradition that we received from our Messiah, we'll not drink the fourth cup now. Instead, when the kingdom is complete and we are in the presence of our Lord for eternity, there will be many drinking it with us."

His words conveyed the hope that each one there would be drinking the fourth cup with the Messiah.

Miriam had been asked to write a song to sing at this time. She stood and looked at her friends around the room. "Philadelphia has *many* gods, and each one has its own name. In school, the boys learn stories of *many* Greek gods. But we believe in only *one* God, and he has *many* names!

"I want to teach you a song. Ruth has been learning to play the harp during this past winter, and I taught Sarah to play the flute. They will help me with this, 'The Name.'"

He comes to us! Shepherd and Sustainer,
Righteous Judge, Creator, Warrior, Most High,
The Portion of Jacob, Holy One, Master,
God of Heaven, King of Glory, now come nigh.
Sovereign Lord, Root of Jesse, our Savior!

He comes! Emmanuel! An angel sings,
"One and Only, Son of God and Son of Man."
Yeshua, Redeemer, our salvation brings.
Holy One of God, a Lion yet a Lamb!
Prince of Peace, the Lord of Lords, and King of Kings!

He comes! The Spirit sent in Yeshua's name.
Come from the Father, now pointing us to Him.
Holy Spirit, bringing fire that inflames,
Convicting us of hate, unrighteousness, and sin.
The Counselor has delivered us from shame.

Miriam sang the song through once and then again, singing each line twice. After she had sung the song, she repeated it.

Thelma did not want the evening to end. "Miriam, please sing the song once more. I like those names. I want to remember them." The request was easy to grant, and Miriam sang it again, looking at Thelma. The evening had come to an end, and the light from the dim lamps shone on Thelma's face.

Miriam reached the last line, "The Counselor has delivered us from shame," and realized her cheeks were also being washed with tears, the tears of Passover.

The guests finally left to return to the city before total darkness fell. Amos felt his heart overflowing with gratitude. He had come through terrible days since the family had escaped-through those city gates. The siege in Jerusalem had brought death to his family. Here, almost twenty-four years later, they still suffered the consequences of that event. Nevertheless, this evening their Passover was turning into a night of hope.

THE REPAIRED WORKSHOPS IN PHILADELPHIA

As she lay on her little pallet on the floor, Thelma felt peaceful. She knew what happened when a body was broken. Thelma had seen that when her husband was crushed to death. His death was an accident in Sasorta, but Yeshua Messiah willingly gave his life for her....

No one understood her in past years, but Amos took time with her. He had shown her who the Messiah really was, and she wanted to belong, to participate.

Thelma had never heard the names Miriam sang about. She had been afraid of goddesses and their rivalries, of gods with their never-ending fights. But this was so different. Miriam's words brought life and healing. Who would ever believe that one God would have so many names?

Seven months ago, Miriam was the only one who listened to my whole story. Now I want to hear all about her life. She taught us a new song tonight. Her family says she sings a lot, and I want to learn all her songs. I could only have sung to the children about giants with disjointed bodies, but that's going to change. Her songs are the ones I want to sing for Penelope's children. I understand so little about the Lamb of God, but I'll ask Miriam to teach me.

Thelma went to sleep quickly, and tonight she did not cry before going to sleep.

AMOS AND ABIGAIL'S HOUSE

At the end of the night, the old man lay in bed beside his wife. "My dear, our home was a light for non-Jews. Abigail, you were wonderfully hospitable. Thank you. I sensed a little of your youthfulness, your openness, and your love of parties."

Abigail was silent as she smiled in the dark. She reviewed the words Amos had spoken, and his words continued to thrill her: "*Yet there will be some survivors; sons and daughters will be brought out of Jerusalem. They will come to you, and when you see their actions, you will be consoled regarding the disaster I have brought upon Jerusalem.*"[91]

Lord, I have been reacting in anger and disappointment for so long. I think you were speaking to me, and I did not want to listen for many years. My life needs cleansing from malice, bitterness, envy, and slander. Perhaps there is healing for my soul and hope for me too.

"Thank you, Amos," she said. "Thank you for your words tonight. They brought healing to me, and maybe others felt healing too."

---

[91] Ezekiel 14:22

Chapter 25
Kitchen Talk

THE INN OF THE OPEN DOOR

Six days had passed since Penelope had enjoyed the Passover meal at the Ben Shelah home. She mixed spices into the food she was preparing, producing tantalizing aromas, which added to her cheerfulness. Small pots with the names of various herbs and spices were neatly stored behind her on a shelf. Heber was on his way up to the office and looked into the kitchen as he passed by.

"Do you have a few moments, Heber?" Penelope asked when she saw him at the door.

"Yes, I do. What's up?

"Lots. I don't think I thanked your Uncle Amos sufficiently for that meal with the story of freedom from slavery."

"I heard you express your appreciation."

"I never saw hospitality like that. Amos and Abigail even enjoyed my children."

"Yes, they talked about how well-behaved they are. How are you managing here?"

"I don't like the talk from some of the soldiers."

"I'm sorry to hear that, but I am afraid things may get worse for a while. Felicior is bringing extra troops from the Meander Valley."

"Is the mayor afraid of further riots?"

"No, two legal issues have arisen. Land titles and contracts could not be honored last year. I'll explain. If a landowner planted grain in the previous year, must he sow the same crop this year, or is he free to go back to other crops? Judges are working on several lawsuits since some want to go back to vineyards again.

"Another problem is that last year peasants cut down vineyards to give the land over to planting grain. That led to many families losing jobs. A few landowners in both Sardis and Philadelphia went back on their previous agreements and rented the land out to others.

Later, when Rome again has enough food, will the original contracts be enforced? Will the previous farmers regain their work, or will the new renters be permitted to continue as if the original contracts never existed? Anyway, it will take a long time to get back to normal as vines take years to produce well."

"Was that what the men were talking about last night at the supper tables?"

"Yes, and I'm afraid soldiers who normally work in the southern cities of our province will stay here for at least three to four months, perhaps longer. Felicior needs them here to help keep order. It pays us well, but they are a bother."

Penelope enjoyed the conversation and wanted to talk more. "Are things getting better for the city? What about the reconstruction?"

"Some construction sites are coming along very well. The old city wall will take a long time to complete. Some more reconstruction is supposed to begin in Sasorta, Castolius, and Clanodda."

She brought the conversation closer to home. "Listen! Cleon is jealous. Heber, he has been complaining that you permitted Evander to ride your horse. He wants one too. He says he isn't paid enough for all the extra work he has been doing."

Laughing, Heber responded, "I'll see what I can do. Cleon keeps guests happy with stories and jokes, and you keep them satisfied with tasty food. People say our inn is the cleanest place along the Southern and Northern Roads. Perhaps I can find the money for a horse. Thank you for letting me know about that. Anything else?"

Penelope bent over the food, stirred the pot, and frowned.

Heber guessed that she had not yet begun to talk about the real issues on her mind. "I'm getting to be quite good friends with your son, Evander," he said. "I'm going to speak to him about the problems you mentioned concerning his behavior."

Watching Heber leave, Penelope tossed back a strand of her long black hair with the back of her hand. It had come loose from her hairband.

I don't know how to tell him my suspicions about Cleon.

AMOS AND ABIGAIL'S HOUSE

Amos went to his library. So much had happened in the last two weeks. His heart ached. He was burdened by the agony of having been rejected by his friends.

On the other hand, he was thrilled with what he had seen during the Seder meal. His awkward thoughts were directed toward the Almighty. "Lord, that Seder in Jerusalem...our last one there. The next day the Romans blocked the gates. Our city was crammed with more than one million people, and people were fighting over food. My oldest boy died because of the war. My daughters starved. Only Obed is alive of the children you gave me, Almighty One. Did this have to be?

"Lord God, by your grace, ten months ago, Arpoxa, Zarrus, and Anthony came to our home. Now Timon, Penelope, and her family know what we believe and who we are. I saw something happening in Thelma's heart. She has never said a word to me about her widowhood, but I have seen the sadness in her eyes. Nothing would indicate that we could be friends in the natural course of events. But we were sharing the wine, eating the same meal, and celebrating your Passover at our table."

DANIEL AND DORCAS'S HOME IN PHILADELPHIA

On the seventh day of the Feast of Unleavened Bread, an argument broke out between Daniel and Mith. Daniel insisted that his son issue a certificate of divorce and leave Sarah.

"No, Father! I have known her for many years!"

"I want you to leave her!"

Dorcas stood up to Daniel. "You expelled Amos and Abigail! Why must you condemn Sarah?"

"She is learning strange ideas."

"My dear! Why banish your own flesh and blood? Just think! Jesse and Ruth," she gasped for breath, "if Ruth has another baby, will you still be so cold-hearted?"

"They chose to walk along Amos's path, not ours. This is their sentence."

"Does God treat us that way? So children must be made to suffer for the sins of the father? Is that how you interpret the Torah?" Her questions had backed him into a corner.

He was uncomfortable, not sure that the elders had thoroughly examined the implications for families and children. "I don't know, Dorcas." He sounded like a schoolboy being scolded.

"What did you say to the elders? Did you agree with them?"

"Yes." He would not back away from decisions laid out by his friends.

"Did you ask them hard questions, the kind I'm asking you?"

"No, I didn't think that my family would be divided."

"Then something is wrong! Think! You're a man! You are supposed to protect us!"

"Yes, I am protecting you from falsehood and wrong ideas."

"No, you are preventing me from seeing my innocent grandson. How can a baby have wrong ideas? Anyway, Anthony was not at the Seder meal, so most of the anger you express is like a puff of air. Now what about Mith?"

Mith jumped in. "Father, I will not put aside my betrothal agreement. Sarah has not done anything wrong! I care for her and love her. What should I do, Mother?"

She answered, "Write a short letter. Say that 'because of circumstances, our marriage has been delayed for a short while.' Don't give reasons."

Daniel realized his wife had a sharp, quick mind, so he said, "Son, you must obey me!" But thinking about the last moments, he realized news about the Seder meal was going around in his house, and he did not know anything about it. "Dorcas, you said that Anthony was not there.... How do you know what is going on in their home?"

She answered, "I saw Isabel and Obed at the marketplace. They told me."

"So my own flesh and blood are against me, no longer going to their home but talking with them in the marketplace! Shelomith," he rarely used his son's full name, "you are my son, so you must listen to what I say! Yes, you were considered married to Sarah after we celebrated the betrothal last May. In our eyes, she is legally married to you. However, you cannot marry into a family expelled by the congregation. It wouldn't be right!"

Mith made a courageous decision. "Father, I don't want to obey you."

"You will not marry her. I simply will not permit you to adopt their beliefs and practices."

Red-faced, he turned to Dorcas. "And you, my wife, I forbid you talking with them!"

THE INN OF THE OPEN DOOR

That evening, Anthony brushed Brutus down after a long ride from the valley's eastern side. He had been away for several days, and he had given his report to Felicior. Penelope had seen him arrive and wandered out to the stable area for a private chat.

"Hello, Penelope," said Anthony. "Are things all right?"

"I'm fine, but the gossip around here isn't good."

"Not good? What's happening here?"

She answered, "Timon came back from the agora. He went to buy fresh vegetables, and he overheard some local gossip about an angry man and his family."

"I guess I shouldn't be asking, but forgive me. I'm curious! What is this about?"

Penelope looked at him. "A Jew is attempting to force his seventeen-year-old son to back out of a marriage. The son wants to marry the young woman, but the father says the family isn't worthy. The young man told a friend about the blowup at the house, and the news is spreading."

"And the son, what does he want?"

"The son told his friend that he doesn't want to obey his father." She refused to name the persons involved. Nevertheless, Anthony fully understood what was happening.

Heber was walking by, and Anthony asked Penelope to repeat the news she had heard. "Heber, I think you should hear this," said Anthony urgently. Both knew a crisis was brewing.

Evander had returned from his studies at the gymnasium. He was seated in the office upstairs, beginning to read Cicero, the great scholar of Roman culture and government. Heber asked the boy to put the book down.

"Take my horse, Evander. Ride as quickly as you can to my house. Ask for Aunt Abigail, Isabel, and Sarah. Tell them that if a letter comes from Daniel Ben Halkai, they must not open it. If Daniel goes in person, they are not to believe him or accept his message. Can you remember that?"

"Yes, I can. When do I leave?"

"You should have left already! Get going!"

Evander ran down the stairs, rushed past Timon, saddled Heber's horse, and rode to the farm as quickly as he could with his message.

Timon walked into the office as Heber sat down, his head in his hands. "Hello, Timon!"

"Why is Evander rushing off so quickly?"

"He's on an errand for me. What can I do for you?"

"I've been here for six months now, and I'm really enjoying my work here at the inn. My father wanted me to be a teacher, like him. But I have other ideas."

"Sit down and tell me your thoughts."

"I like the work and meeting merchants and travelers. Each evening I sit with them, and by listening, I learn what life is like in different cities, both near and far away."

"Well, you are doing well keeping up the accounts and noting the income and expenses. You have improved things. You note the expenses needed to run the inn, and you have separated those from Amos's farm expenses."

Timon said, "Eventually I want to be a merchant, but right now, I would like to work full time for a wage. I want to go beyond being an apprentice."

"I'll have to talk to Uncle Amos about that."

"I also have another reason."

"So you have another reason for wanting a full-time job?"

Timon's eyes sparkled. "It's a secret. If I get a job, then I can tell my father I have a future, and if I have a future, then I can..." he paused for a moment, "well, I can't tell you because it's a secret."

"I'll talk to Uncle Amos tonight. How old are you? I asked you before, but I forgot."

"I've just turned twenty, and I'm ready for, well...that's a secret."

The following day, Heber talked with Amos before he left the farm. "The inn is almost fully occupied each night now that caravan season is underway, with many return customers."

"That's good," replied Amos. "We built our reputation as a clean, safe place, and it's paying off. The letter from Daniel that you warned us about was not received. Everybody here knows not to open it if it does come."

"That's also a good thing," said Heber. "I really thought Daniel would force Mith to write a divorce letter."

Heber walked out through the outer gate. In the winter, sudden gusts of cold wind brought volleys of snow. Later, in the summer, haze sometimes hid the peaks, but now it was spring, Heber's favorite time of the year. An explosion of bright colors greeted these warmer days. He always admired the changing greens and grays on the mountain, but these colors were overwhelming.

The mountain range behind Philadelphia stretched to Sardis and far beyond, almost to Smyrna eighty miles away. Numerous creeks had cut their way through the rock to the valley below, flowing through meadows and gurgling as water trickled over fallen trees and tumbled through the air when rocky cliffs appeared. Erosion in a valley slightly to the north of Amos's farm revealed layers of ancient rock. Heber had climbed up this valley with Evander the previous day, going as far as possible.

A waterfall sloshed over a wall of light brown rock. *This cliff is like our situation with the elders. We're up against a wall, and there does not seem to be a way around it. What will it take for the quarrels to subside?*

Riding to the inn, he dismounted, led his horse at a gentle walk, and prayed silently. He asked for wisdom. He did not want to return to Sardis until Obed could come back to work.

At the inn, Heber walked to the kitchen. "Good morning, Penelope," he called out. "How are you this bright day?"

"I'm fine, thank you. My children are learning Miriam's songs."

He began, "I have many things I want to talk about."

"Start talking. I have lots of time to listen."

"Amos has given permission for Timon to work full-time. He is no longer an apprentice but will manage the accounts. And he's doing better than Obed did on them."

She responded warmly, "Timon will be happy."

"Yes, that's the second thing. Timon is hiding a secret."

"I suspect I know what he is hiding." She hid her smile.

Heber was curious. "You do? Has he told you what it is?"

"No, he hasn't."

"And?"

"It's something that women pick up on more quickly than men."

"Like what?"

She pounced on each word. "Timon has fallen in love with the young woman taking care of my children."

"Really? How can you tell?"

"Don't you see how he brightens up when she is around? She comes here to bring Melody to me. They talk and laugh a lot. Yes, Timon has been smitten by the gods."

"Is that what you believe—that Greek gods make people love each other?"

She laughed. "Not anymore. Nikias taught me a whole new way of living my life, loving, and bringing up children. No, that's just an expression."

Heber persisted in his question, "So Timon didn't tell you?"

"No, he didn't, but she did. Thelma told me she thinks Timon is in love with her. She's changing a lot. After the Feast of Chanukah at Amos's house, Thelma said, 'There's something different about the Ben Shelah family.' She enjoyed the lamps, the meal, and the story behind the celebration; she's a romantic. She is starting to sleep well and has a better disposition."

"So the Seder meal was good for her?"

"Yes, and there's more. It's what happened during the Passover meal. She says she feels clean. Remember when we washed the hands of the person next to us? She told me last night nothing like this ever happened to her before."

"Well, I'm relieved. I suspected Thelma must have had a hard life. I saw it in the lines on her young face. She seemed taut, serious, preoccupied about something."

Penelope wanted to know about Evander. "Have you talked with Evander yet, Heber? You mentioned that you two were going to take a hiking trip."

"Yes. Yesterday I took your son up the mountain as high as we could go. We came up against a cliff and couldn't go any farther. One of the servants at the Ben Shelah home had made lunch for us, and Evander carried water in a skin slung around his shoulders."

"I'm delighted that you took time with him."

He chuckled, an easy laugh. "You know, he is a fine young lad. He has great promise."

"Thank you. His father was very fond of Evander and had hopes for his future."

Heber reminisced, "We talked about many things. Once he started talking, he couldn't stop! He talked all the way! He doesn't like hurling the discus or the javelin, nor does he like the teacher who talks about Greek gods and all of their secret hatreds and hidden madness."

"At home, he tells me the same thing."

"I told him how important it is for him to respect women. Of course, growing up on the farm at Olive Grove, he knows about reproduction. However, I told him about temptations that men face. He said many older boys have already gone to the brothel at least once. One asked Evander to go with him. The older boy told Evander that his mother and father should not learn that he would visit women that way."

"I was afraid that kind of talk was going on."

Heber was happy to be able to tell her the truth. "Evander said that he does not want to disappoint his mother, and he has no intention of doing that."

The expression on her face showed Penelope's spirit was soaring. "I'm happy to know that he had a good time on the hike."

"Oh, yes. A hike brings its own rewards. It was fun, pure fun, and I felt young again. We walked along and watched birds flying and setting up their nests. Wildflowers grew everywhere. I love butterflies, and I watched one with long tails on its wings. We saw two red deer, a doe and her fawn. When the sun was at its highest point, we stopped, sitting down to eat our lunch. I was tired, but he still wanted to climb. Then we came to that cliff. I said we should go back there another time, and he agreed right away. He is a lot stronger than I am, really."

"Well, you are still strong."

"Not like I used to be. In Alexandria, I wanted to sail as far as the Land of Spices!"[92]

"Some time, tell me about growing up in Alexandria."

"I will. After the Festival of Artemis. It starts in two weeks. We have special guests coming in two days. Want to hear the latest gossip? Flavius Zeuxis is going to Rome to sell clothing made by the peasants in Cogamis Valley. He bought lots of merchandise made in

---

[92] Spices and other goods came from India and even farther east. Silks arrived from China.

the homes. His caravan will be staying here on Sunday night. Imagine that! Make your best meals for these merchants, will you, Penelope?"

"I'll do my best!"

At the end of March, Heber had the employees of the inn cleaning rooms and animal stalls. They wanted everything ready before the caravan brought Flavius Zeuxis. Penelope was already preparing a bigger than usual meal for the guards.

Timon spotted the caravan on the Southern Road from one of the upper floor windows late in the afternoon. Flavius Zeuxis was at the head of the camel train riding a beautiful white Arabian stallion and looking very much in charge. He had two of his sales agents, five drivers to control the caravan of thirty-six camels, and five heavily armed guards riding horses.

After they arrived and got settled, Flavius asked if Anthony was available and was disappointed when told that he was on patrol in the far south end of the valley.

The next morning, Flavius and his men gathered for breakfast. Penelope had prepared a hearty meal of flatbread, olives, cheeses, boiled eggs, and sliced fruit. The camels were quickly loaded, and the caravan left, intending to get to Smyrna in three days and spending the first night in Sardis. Flavius would leave Smyrna by ship on his way to Athens and then Rome.

Timon acted as the manager in Heber's place for the early morning caravan's departure and collected the food and lodging fees from Flavius.

Flavius and his two agents would not return from Rome for almost two months. But the empty camel caravan with drivers and three of the five guards would return from Smyrna in seven days for a one-night stay on their way back to Hierapolis.

THE CITY OF PHILADELPHIA

Philadelphia's Festival of Artemis began on Thursday and provided a welcome time of celebration now that planting season was over. From the fifteenth of April until the last day of the month, the festival enthralled both rich and poor. The main provincial celebration was held in Ephesus at the Temple of Artemis, several days' journey away.

On this first morning of the festival in Philadelphia, the deep-blue sky was soft and cloudless. Even the endless smoke over the city had cleared with the breeze the night before.

Observers gathered along the main city avenue, ready to welcome the procession. Mayor Maurelinus Manilius Hermippus sat on a white horse, bragging about the columned street along one side of the marketplace where repairs had been made. As *Asiarch* of Philadelphia, he was proud of controlling the future of the city while preserving its past. Behind him came four deputies, each one carrying a flag. Black matching horses contrasted with the mayor's.

Pairs of horses, each one held in place by a well-dressed servant, waited for the march to begin. Priests and priestesses followed in groups according to protocol created in ages past. Athletes, who came last in the procession, would soon be competing for honor, garlands, and fame. As they shouted, excitement and fanfare filled the air.

Heber stood at a window in his office, watching. Penelope and her children were close to him at the window, commenting as the procession formed. Timon stood to one side. He exchanged glances several times with Thelma, who was holding little Melody in her arms.

"I don't want you to go outside with all those people," Penelope told her children, thankful that they could watch from Heber's office. She had never seen such a large gathering before. The upper floor of the inn provided her family with safety away from the crowds.

"Caesar is lord and god!" shouted the mayor, the signal that the march was beginning. On each side of the square, soldiers raised their trumpets, and the twelve brass horns blasted approval. The procession was underway.

Along the road, crowds roared as the mayor and council members passed by. The Imperial priest was first among the priests, the leader of religious men and women. He wore a toga with a purple stripe down the left side and rejoiced at the city's improved atmosphere.

His helpers led three sacrifices along the Avenue of Philadelphia: an ox, a sheep, and a pig. The ox spoke of the immense power of the empire. The sheep symbolized people in each province, while the pig stood for the land's provision, which produced sufficient food for all.

The city rang with the sounds of cheerful hope. The splendor of spring added vibrant colors as street vendors hawked their dishes. Women walked with wreaths of wildflowers decorating their heads, and happy shouts of satisfied citizens feasting on fresh meat and wares that followed the temple sacrifices. People were filled with the hope of another fruitful harvest in the autumn.

Enjoying its songs and dances, Philadelphia was at its best. For two weeks, people visited one another, dined in the more elegant thermopolia, drank last year's wine, and danced in the streets until midnight.

Chapter 26
Sarah's Special Day

THE INN OF THE OPEN DOOR

Toward the end of the festival, various letters were written in Philadelphia and in Pergamum. The first two had to do with Cleon and Diotrephes and their desire to kidnap Grace.

April 26, in the 14th year of Domitian
From: Cleon in Philadelphia
To: Diotrephes Milon in Sardis

Greetings. If you are well, then I, too, am well.

I have not heard from you for months, making it a challenge to be your eyes and ears. I have a sure bet on two athletes at the Games: one in the javelin, the other in Greco-Roman wrestling. This year I am sure to win.

I want to inform you about the Ben Shelah family. Heber Ben Shelah is more generous than his cousin, Obed, who was managing the inn. Heber sold me a horse at a fair price, a lovely dark brown mare, as proof of my usefulness. Of course, part of my pay will be deducted each month for three years to pay for it.

Previously, Heber fired me from the Ben Shelah store in Sardis, but he tolerates me here. He seems kinder now than a few years ago, and I think he regrets having dealt harshly with me before.

My dear Diotrephes, I count on your understanding and desire to continue this beneficial relationship for both of us.

Diotrephes read the letter three days later, having received it by courier. In the empty space below Cleon's note, he added his own words.

April 29, in the 14th year of Domitian
From: Diotrephes in Sardis
To: Mother and Uncle Zoticos in Pergamum

I include Cleon's last letter for you to read. His habit of gambling will cripple him for life. I will send him a silver coin to keep him happy but will say that I cannot send more. I do not think he is reliable enough to help us get Chrysa back where she belongs.

Yes, I know where Chrysa is being kept, and I will work with my former students to devise a way to snatch her from the Ben Shelah family.

I am almost ready to propose to the mayor's lovely daughter, Cynthia. My relationship with her father has improved. Mayor Tymon Tmolus attended my lectures in March and was impressed with my abilities as an orator. I believe that a marriage between the Tmolus family and the Milon family would heal age-long divisions. It would add credibility to my task of bringing a revival of our Lydian language and culture.

THE HOME OF MARCOS IN PERGAMUM

Marcos, the lawyer for the Ben Shelah estate distribution, was once more on his way to a bank. According to the magistrate's decision, it was again time to disperse the portions of Eliab's will to the Ben Shelah family members. He had written a letter to Miriam this morning encouraging her to be mindful of her family's future needs.

April 30, in the 14th year of Domitian
From: Marcos Aelius Pompeius in Pergamum
To: Miriam Bat Johanan in Philadelphia

Greetings because of the Name. May you all be in peace. If you are well, then I also am well. Funds are again being sent to you and your uncles per the court's stipulations for the distribution.

As you instructed me, I sent most of your share to your Uncle Simon in Sardis. He will be using it for projects undertaken by Kalonice, Jace, and their friends. A minor part of your share is being sent to Jonathan in Thyatira to help children living in the insulae, those who will never learn quickly and naturally.

This leaves only a small portion left over for you.

Miriam, it is undoubtedly none of my business. Still, I am writing as your legal counsel and advisor for financial matters. Please consider where you and Anthony will settle down. You will need a house, a home. If you manage these funds, which are paid every six months, you will be well situated. So I encourage you to plan for your future. I confirm the distribution of your portion of this payment to the Bank of Philadelphia.

A couple days later, in Philadelphia, Miriam read the letter and laughed to herself. She imagined talking to Anthony the next time she saw him.

"Five years ago, I would never have believed that I would be happier when giving to others. Those families can never pay me back. People in Sardis and Thyatira don't know where the money is coming from to help their children.

"Of course, Kalonice and Jace and the young women in Thyatira I worked with know.

"Marcos writes about where we will live. Will you take me to Philippi, far from my family? For the time being, Uncle Amos and Aunt Abigail are happy to have me with them. My dear Aunt Abigail! An old woman who lost her own children is enjoying children again. Maybe we can settle down in Philadelphia."

AMOS AND ABIGAIL'S HOME

The previous year, Sarah and Mith's wedding had been planned for Monday, May 9.

Now, as the date was approaching, the blue sky above was dotted with thin, wispy clouds, and nature seemed peaceful. However, the atmosphere in the Ben Shelah home was tense.

Sarah had been counting the days, and she asked the women, "Why doesn't Mith write to me? Doesn't he know how upset I must be? Our wedding is supposed to take place in four days."

"I know he loves you," said Miriam to her younger cousin. "Once a young man makes a decision like that, he counts down the days until he is married."

"I wanted all the rituals!" Sarah wailed. "A special night just for the women dressing me in my special clothes. Another night to decorate my hands with henna in all sorts of lovely patterns, swirls, twirls, and flowers. I want the customs from Alexandria, but I haven't heard from Mith! He promised to give me a gift four days before our special day. That's one custom he could fulfill, and that's today!"

Miriam's eyes gleamed. "Tomorrow evening, the Sabbath begins. Your special day is next Monday, so this was his day to give you a gift. I have an idea. Let me work on it."

Miriam hurried to the inn and asked Heber to send Evander to the house of the Ben Helkai family. "Have him give this note to Mith," she said. "No one else!"

Evander was only too happy to deliver the sealed note. He rode on horseback to the Jewish quarter and called out at the gate. A servant opened the door.

"A special gift has been sent to Shelomith Ben Daniel from the estate of a wealthy man in Pergamum," read the note that Mith took from the hand of Evander. "It can be picked up from the office of the Inn of the Open Door. Personal acceptance by Shelomith is necessary to complete the transaction."

DANIEL AND DORCAS'S HOME IN PHILADELPHIA

Mith shouted, "Mother! Father! Look! I've been given something from an estate in Pergamum! Isn't this wonderful? It's my first time to be named in an estate!"

"This is suspicious," mumbled Daniel. "Why were you chosen to receive part of an inheritance? You are not an heir! How would anyone in Pergamum even know about you?"

"I don't care! I'm going to get my share of a rich man's inheritance!" he said, slipping into his sandals and disappearing before anyone could call him back.

Cleon met him at the entrance gate of the inn. "You're Mith? I was told to expect you. Go up the stairs."

Miriam was waiting for him upstairs in the office. "I have a special gift for you, Mith."

"I came for my inheritance from the estate," he said, his eyes gleaming.

"And you will have it right away," said Miriam. "It comes from the estate of Eliab Ben Shelah. It will be the first payment for the house you and Sarah will live in one day."

She opened a small leather bag and placed a golden *aureus* on the table. An hour before, it had been in the Bank of Philadelphia. Now Mith was looking at more money than he had ever owned in his life. "This shiny coin is worth twenty-five *denarii*, more than most men take home in one month. It will be yours at the end of our conversation."

"I've never held a coin like this. It's a great treasure!" His eyes shone, but a shadow passed over his face. "A house will be worth nothing to me if I can't be married to Sarah!"

"Believe me, Mith. This is a gift for your wedding."

He sat down with his head in his hands. Miriam heard a slight sob. "Father won't let me be married to her! He demands that I reject Sarah. While Father is saying one thing, Mother and I say another. He demands that I write her a certificate of divorce. I will not do that. I want her as my wife!"

"Perhaps Sarah is waiting for you to tell her what you are going to do."

"Father says he will disinherit me if I try to talk to her."

"What if you told her all you want her to know but don't talk directly to her. Would you be disobeying your father then?"

Mith sat up straight on the chair, dumbfounded. "No, but how could I do that?"

"Mith, I want to tell you something. Can you keep a secret?"

"Yes, I can keep a secret. I promise you."

"I'm married to a legionary, to a Roman soldier. Did you know that?"

"Of course I know it! That's what brought so many troubles on all of us!"

"Well, things are not always easy for us, but we are married and happy. We have a wonderful little girl, Grace, who is the pride of our lives."

"That's your secret?" His expression showed keen disappointment.

"No, everyone knows that. Now listen. Sarah loves you. She will wait for you to marry her, and she will not be married to anyone else."

This was unexpected. "Really? Do you think so? How do you know?"

"She told me an hour ago."

A light dawned in his eyes. "If Sarah talks to you, then I can get her messages."

"Yes, that's right."

The eager expression on his face showed he understood. "And then you would carry messages from me back to Sarah? Would you do that?" She nodded.

"Then tell her that I miss her so much! I wish she were joining us at the congregation. Tell her that we are fighting in our house—no, don't use the word 'fighting.' Say 'discussing.' Tell her that I will not call off our marriage. I made a promise, and I'm standing up to Father. Tell her I will wait."

"I will tell her all that when I return to the farm. How long will you wait?"

"I am eighteen now. After I'm twenty-one, Father can't tell me what to do anymore."

"Let me get this straight. You want me to tell Sarah that you still want to marry her. You are not going to let anyone or anything change your mind. You will wait for her until you are twenty-one, and then you can make up your own mind. You will even go against your father's will, though it will be difficult for you. Is that what you are saying?"

"Yes, tell her that please! But I must give her a present! I had promised to find her a special gift four days before our marriage. It was supposed to be today!"

"What do you have to send to her?"

"I don't have anything! Mother yells and screams. She says she wants to see Asa. I asked Father for a gift, but he sneered and walked away. Miriam, I trust you. I want to send Sarah a lovely present."

He looked at the table, reached out his hand, and examined the coin, turning it one way and then another. On one side was the figure of Agrippina the Elder. It had been minted in Rome fifty-one years before.

"Do you think I could send her this gold coin?"

"Mith, how wonderful! What a loving gesture!"

"Then please do it! And will Sarah send me a message through you?"

"Yes, she can, and she will. And I'll be happy to bring you anything she writes."

"I'll pick up her messages from you here at the inn. Then I'll send her another message."

"Mith, you are one of the finest young men I have ever met. You are clever, generous, imaginative, and loyal to the bride of your youth! I shall be delighted to give her your gold coin as a wedding present. It will be given to her right on time, as you promised a year ago."

He stood up, wanting to shout, but he kept his voice low. "Tell Sarah it's my deposit, my promise, my 'down payment,' the seal of my love. A promise that she is bound to me."

"You are also romantic and imaginative. Now get home before your parents send a servant to get you!"

"I'll tell them the truth but not all the facts. I'll say a coin came from a wealthy man I never met, and it should stay in the family. I'll say that I gave it back. That's the truth, isn't it?"

"It's the truth but not the whole truth. Your father will be puzzled by your decision. Now get going. I'll have a message from her for you later today. I'll meet you here this afternoon just after the sun hides behind the mountain."

AMOS AND ABIGAIL'S HOME

"Sarah, I must talk with you in the library," Miriam said quietly, and then she asked Amos to leave his study. He raised his eyebrows but did not move.

"What are you asking me to do, Miriam?"

"Uncle Amos, today was to be the day your granddaughter received her 'seal,' her promise from Mith. Now would you please leave while I talk with Sarah about Mith?"

Slightly puzzled, Amos went upstairs nap, so Miriam and Sarah went into the library and closed the door. "Sarah, I have some news that will encourage you, but I have other news that may be discouraging. It's about Mith. I want to talk to you about him."

"Oh, Miriam! I'm so concerned! I haven't heard from him!"

"Can you keep a secret?"

"Yes, I can."

"It's the biggest secret of your life."

"I won't say a word. I promise. What is it?"

"I've just spent half an hour talking with Mith."

"What? You met with him?"

"Yes, at the inn. Mith was given a coin…a long story that I won't go into. I asked him about you. He said he can't marry you right now because of pressure from his father."

"I knew Daniel Ben Helkai was going to cut me off from Mith!" Tears were flowing.

"Now listen. I asked Mith if he wants to marry you. I talked with him in a safe place. We were in the office at the inn."

Sarah wiped away her tears. "What did he say?"

"He is going to marry you but not right now."

"Not now? But he wants to marry me?" She was hanging on to every word.

"He loves you, Sarah. He is going to wait, and it will seem like a long time."

"How long do I have to wait?"

"Sarah, do you know our story? I told you about my marriage to Anthony, a legionary, but I didn't tell you about the waiting! I waited until I was twenty-six. Finally, I drifted into love with Anthony, slowly, in an amazing way. I would never have chosen it. It was nothing like I expected, dreamed, or hoped."

"You are telling me that I'm going to wait a long time?"

"Three years is a long time, but you are better off than I was. You are betrothed."

Sarah's tears were flowing freely, and she could not stop. "How can I trust him? How can I believe him? Maybe he'll find someone else."

"No, he will not find someone else, and he doesn't want to. He sent you a gift. Don't ask me how it came to him, but he sent you the first gold coin he's ever had. It's part of a Jewish inheritance and very precious. I'm telling you the truth. It's his down payment, a promise."

Miriam stretched her arm out and took Sarah's hand. She opened the young woman's fingers, carefully placing the gold coin in her palm.

"Listen, he will always be faithful to you."

Miriam folded Sarah's pinky finger over it.

"This treasure is his commitment to marrying you."

She folded the next finger, the ring finger. "Mith's word is more precious than gold."

Folding the next two fingers, she glowed. "This is his seal, the promise that Mith is going to make a home for you." The coin was now hidden in her hand, completely covered and out of sight.

Sarah hugged her older cousin. Instead of tears of sadness, which had flowed at the beginning, she now wept with joy. "He wants me! He has given me a gift on the very day he said he would. He kept his promise! He hasn't rejected me!" She started jumping up and down.

"No, Sarah, he hasn't forgotten you, and he's not going to reject you. He will never forsake you; that is his promise. You are his chosen one. Now listen, anytime you want to send a message to him, just write it on a piece of papyrus and give it to me. He is waiting for a reply from you. He wants your reply before sunset."

"Oh, thank you so much! What can I say?"

"Remember, this is our secret. Now ask your grandfather for a pen and some papyrus. Today is the first time you will be using the writing skills your father taught you. But don't tell Uncle Amos or your father or anyone else about this."

The Ben Shelah family was dumbfounded by the change in Sarah's disposition. Instead of bemoaning her lot, she came out of the library wiping her eyes and humming a tune.

Abigail demanded, "My sweet child, today was supposed to be the day to receive your seal of promise, but Mith's family has abandoned you. Why the singing?"

"I haven't heard anything from either my father-in-law, Daniel, or my mother-in-law, Dorcas." She told the truth, just enough to get by. She didn't say anything about Mith.

Isabel could not understand it. "My daughter, how can you sing when he's disappointed you? The man you are betrothed to made you sad, but you begin to sing?"

Sarah replied, skipping into the kitchen, "God gives us his patience when we trust in him. We have to have hope, good friends, and patience in life,"

Abigail cornered Miriam. "You took her into that library blubbering like a baby. She has been irritated and annoyed, and she came out as if her betrothal doesn't mean a thing. Has she forgotten that Daniel was one of the men who cut us off?"

"No, Aunt Abigail, she couldn't forget her betrothal or her beloved. She waited a whole year for today. This specific day was marked long ago. No, she hasn't forgotten."

"Then what happened?"

"Ask her, Auntie."

"I did, and all she says is 'God has taken care of it all.'"

Miriam smiled, waiting for Abigail to speak. Once again, Abigail sensed that something strange had happened. She frowned, wanting to get at what was bothering her.

"What I can't understand is how you could have been married to a man who is clearly our enemy."

"Auntie, when you spoke to me about him last summer, I said, 'Why don't you get to know Anthony? Then make up your own mind."

"Even looking at him brings back so many bad memories!"

"I'll wait for you to decide. I can't force anyone to like another person."

"Miriam, you've done wonders for one disappointed girl. She's bouncing around as if she is in paradise. But that's impossible! She's so young. Disappointment hurts so much."

"Watch and listen. Sarah is happy today. Why don't you sing along with her?"

Abigail shook her head, not knowing how to respond.

"I have to go now, Auntie. I'm going back to the inn. Heber is there, and I want to take something to the inn's office."

THE INN OF THE OPEN DOOR

For the second time that day, Miriam arrived at the inn, and Mith returned as planned.

"I will take your messages to her, but they have to be only a few words."

"Miriam, my mother says I'm a different person. She threw her hands up in the air and said, 'I don't understand my husband, and now I can't fathom my son. How can he be happy if the marriage is called off by my husband?' She went into the kitchen grumbling."

"I'm sure you are a different person. What did you say to her?"

"I told her that I'm a young man full of hope."

"That was a good answer."

"Father looked at me funny. I think he was disappointed by my joy."

Miriam left the inn immediately, having decided that any meeting with Mith would have to be short. She walked over to the workshops and looked in on Arpoxa.

The lovely Scythian young woman did not see her friend as Miriam stepped into the sewing workshop, which was already illuminated by oil lamps. A dozen curious women from distant villages were captivated by the talented crippled woman whose workmanship was copied as far away as Temenoth.

Zarrus had been given additional space for making pottery. A larger kiln stood next to the one he had been using for months. Workers and students were starting to leave in the dim light of the evening.

Chapter 27
Time for the Truth

A HUT ON MOUNT TMOLUS

Two months later than planned, Craga had finally returned from his trip to see Mithrida. He called his companions together. The four men sat outside a hut near the top of the tree line, high above the city. The tiny hamlet they had designated as their meeting point was usually occupied by shepherds who brought flocks for summer grazing. They had persuaded the shepherds that they were patrols looking out for the welfare of the peasants. In return, they were permitted to share meals with the shepherds, who provided the food.

The shepherds believed Craga and his men looked after them, even though they had never heard of danger so high on the mountain slopes. Shepherds were vulnerable during times of unrest and welcomed men who talked like soldiers.

"We have been blocked at every turn!" said Craga gruffly. He sat on the rough wooden bench outside the door. Below him, pine trees pointed silently to the sky. "Extra troops have been brought to keep the Door open. Our first robbery went well, but we can't attack there any longer. It's too dangerous."

Maza, whose bright disposition and hopeful attitude had helped to attract other rebels, spoke. "Instead of attacking at that curve in the road, our assaults have been made over a larger area. Taba, tell Craga how we carried out our latest robbery."

Taba said, "Two months ago, we returned from the Province of Galatia. We tried to recruit some of that family of robbers you mentioned. They weren't interested in joining us. When we returned here, we joined a small caravan with five men on the way to Attalia. They never knew what hit them! We dumped the bodies in a cave. Luckily, we spent the night near a point where the road begins its descent to the plains and the sea. We sold four camels and the merchandise at the port before they were missed!"

"Brilliant!" blurted Harpa sarcastically. His enthusiasm for the last raid was muted because he didn't want to murder the camel driver and the other four. Increasingly, cruelty left him pessimistic.

This is not what we agreed to do! Craga said we were only supposed to rob people.

"Harpa, you don't sound happy!" teased Craga. "What's up?"

Harpa answered, "I had a challenging winter. I've been sick a lot. Many days we hid in a cave off the road between Colossae and Pisidia Antioch. Frankly, I'm fed up!"

"Why?" asked Craga. "You carry the name of a Persian satrap, Harpagus, one of the greatest governors in this valley!"

Harpa responded angrily, "Craga, you said that you were raising an army! Look at us! I'm consumed by unanswered questions. How did the soldiers find us last year at Prosperity Village? You claimed soldiers couldn't possibly discover our hideout. But what happened? The army recovered every slave sold to the mines and sent them back to Scythia. How many of our tribunes died? Baga, Ota, Arta, Tissa, and Tira—all in the hands of the authorities. All executed."

Harpa's lips formed a downward sneer. "Craga, you promised we would soon become a legion. Now we are reduced to four 'tribunes,' and none of us has armor. Who do we command? Where is our army? We depend on shepherds to provide us with food."

The previous talk of rebellion had centered on Nero, who had been popular in Moesia and Germania. Harpa now knew that the dream of Nero's return had brought them into the dark night of a living nightmare.

Craga realized he had to provide an optimistic vision to get Harpa back in line. "Maza, I'm putting you in charge. Merchants on the road from Laodicea to Iconium will have to 'share' with us.[93] Here's how will do it: A flock of sheep will be driven across the road in front of a caravan. Another flock will be driven behind the last camel. I have it all planned out! There's a stretch of road where I convinced shepherds. They have hundreds of sheep and goats and

[93] Saint Paul preached in Iconium, mentioned in the Book of Acts. Today it is a large city, Konya. The city's population is above one million. The region is known for sheep, and black wool is used for winter coats.

are willing to help us for a reasonable fee. They'll get their fair share. We're going to be rich again."

He repeated his conviction. "We are going to be rich again!"

But Harpa was not smiling.

THE INN OF THE OPEN DOOR

By the end of June, Miriam went back and forth to the inn several times a week. She met Mith and passed his messages to Sarah. One day she took Sarah to the office at the inn. "I have another secret for you and Mith."

"You do?"

"Yes, I do, but you must not tell anyone."

"I won't. Thank you so much for helping us."

"Here at the office, I write a short message for Anthony on a long scroll of papyrus. See this little 'treasure chest'? Later, he opens it, reads what I wrote, and then writes his message to me under my message. If you want to do the same, you two must not come here on the same day. Someday your notes to each other will be a keepsake. Don't be seen together though."

"Miriam, you are so thoughtful! Will you read what I write to Mith?"

"No, that will be your secret. Something else too. Only concise notes, nothing long. Nothing flowery. Never mention these messages to anyone. What you write stays in the treasure chest. I'll show you where I hide the key for our little box."

Walking home, Sarah asked, "Why does Grandma keep Anthony away from you?"

"She is still wondering how to speak to him," said Miriam. "We have to be patient. Besides, I'm getting so busy going back and forth to the inn, talking with Penelope and Thelma, and looking in on Arpoxa and the little group she's training. Sometimes I'm worn out by the end of the day."

Sarah saw a twinkle in Miriam's eyes. She knew that despite her words, Miriam missed her husband as much as she missed Mith.

The next day, students at the gymnasium finished their studies for another year. The longest day of the year had come. Most would be put to work tending vineyards or harvesting fruit, grains, and vegetables.

Damian, Calisto, and others dwelt on Greek drama. Traveling actors arrived, and men switched their attention to theatrical performances.

Calisto was still upset with Timon but accepted his son's new career. Having a good job with a steady wage so early in life was unusual.

Timon sounded jealous when he heard about Evander's hike up the gorge. Timon's friends wanted to climb the mountain, to sleep under the stars. However, Timon could no longer hope for days off. He was working long hours every day.

"Evander," Timon said, "ask Heber to take you on a real adventure! Get a group of your friends together. Maybe he will go on a hike up to the top of the mountain."

Evander's eyes shone. All year long at the gymnasium, he had been called names. The worst one was "mommy's boy."

"I've got a friend who lives right at the base of the mountain. I'm going to ask him to go with us!" said Evander, bragging to his friends.

The following day, Heber looked in at the kitchen. "Penelope, your son is the limit! Some of his friends want me to climb the mountain with them and sleep under the stars."

Penelope was quiet for a moment. Then she replied, "Evander calls you his hero."

"A 'hero.' What do you mean?"

"No other adult takes time with him. You helped him learn Greek words, quizzed him on subjects he had trouble with, and helped him understand Roman government and history."

"I'm not a teacher. I simply ask him questions."

"Well, it's a help...and he likes it," Penelope expressed her appreciation, speaking with a soft voice.

Heber asked, "Is Miriam here?"

"No, Mith came, and then Miriam left. It's extraordinary, you know."

"What's extraordinary?"

"Haven't you noticed? Mith keeps coming one day, and Sarah comes the next. He looks happy, talks cheerfully, and spends time talking with the staff. What's up?"

"Yes, I did notice, and...?" Heber wanted to know her thoughts.

"Miriam is up to something else. I notice Miriam and Sarah laughing and giggling together. Sarah is beaming from ear to ear when she should be sad. She was supposed to be married six weeks ago. Miriam is involved in this."

Heber forgot his resolve to not mention anything about his family's struggles. "Daniel told Mith not to marry Sarah. After that, Dorcas now yells at her husband. Ruth wants Dorcas to come to see Asa, but Daniel insists that his wife obey him. What a commotion! What a family!"

"Not a happy family, is it?" she asked.

"No, and Isabel asks, 'Why did Father cut me off? Doesn't he care about me anymore?' That's what she was asking yesterday."

Heber had not intended to bring up the table talk in their home.

"There must be a huge problem to cause a bust-up like this," Penelope commented. "At the end of the Seder meal, Amos remarked, 'Yeshua Messiah said a son would be against his father, or a daughter will disagree with her mother. It must be that he included in-laws too.'"

Heber nodded. "It's true. Trusting in the Messiah and following his teaching has divided us. You'll have to excuse me now. Sorry. I have said too much to you about our family."

She ignored his last comment. "Are you going to climb the mountain?"

"Yes! I'll probably give in. Evander pressures me, telling me how his friends from the gymnasium want me to go with them. I'll make myself free to climb the mountain."

"He'll be delighted." Penelope held back a smile.

AMOS AND ABIGAIL'S HOME

Tish'a B'Av, the annual day of fasting, humiliation, and sadness, fell on July 8. Recalling the day when Herod's Temple was destroyed brought out the most profound emotions.

Some of the rancor layered in Abigail's words was fading. When her boys were small in Alexandria, she was known for hospitality. Glimpses of that big-heartedness were returning. The previous year, Abigail wanted Anthony to suffer for cruelties committed against Jerusalem. But now she asked her husband if he wanted to open their home to a select few who had joined with them three months earlier at Passover.

Amos agreed that they could meet on the roof, under the shadow of the vines. People could drink water if they wanted to, but no food would be served. He would be dressed in his oldest clothes, reject food and water, and give a brief talk. Their guests could ask questions about his people and Jerusalem's history. After that, people would pass the time in silent reflection.

Heber instructed some of the staff to look after the meals at the inn. Penelope came with her older children while Timon sat close to Thelma. Carpets had been spread over the spacious, flat roof area. Abigail, Isabel, Ruth, and Sarah wore black and covered their heads. Their tongues were dry and stuck to the roof of their mouths.

Amos spoke, saying how much his heart ached for Jerusalem. Penelope asked, "Abigail, who was the first one in your family to believe in the Messiah?"

Abigail had sworn to herself that she would keep quiet today, but she broke her self-imposed silence. "I was the first. It happened when we were given a home after we escaped Jerusalem and lived in the Decapolis city of Philadelphia, about fifty miles east of Jerusalem.

"First it was me and then Amos. Antipas and his wife also became believers. A short time later, we went to Antioch."

Having broken her silence, Abigail spoke of her life after the tragedy in Jerusalem. Memories that had been crowded out for years came pouring out. Amos did not tell her to hush up. Instead, he looked at the love of his life, and tears crept down his cheeks. Abigail was speaking comfortably about her deepest pains with a friendly group of women.

THE SYNAGOGUE OF PHILADELPHIA

Zacharias said little until the fast was over at sundown, when everyone left the synagogue. Later, at home, Zacharias hosted his friends: Michael and Martha and Daniel and Dorcas.

"Unfortunately, instead of stopping Amos in his persistent ways, we seem to have been a catalyst," Zacharias began. "Amos is moving further away from our traditions. You know that he brought people to his house at Passover and again at Pentecost. He held the meal at the wrong time, too early in the evening. I learned that he described it as 'worship in the home.' Yesterday Cleon told one of my servants that Amos has invited pagans to mourn with him at his house."

Zacharias asked a frightening question. "Do you think he's trying to form an alternative congregation? Shame will rest on any family sharing our worship with Gentiles."

Zacharias had other information too. "Let's put aside our fears and anger about Amos Ben Shelah for a moment. I didn't mention this, but we consider Josephus a traitor, right?" [94]

His friends nodded.

"Well, I've just received a copy of his new history book about the Jews. Copies are being made in a *scriptorium* in Rome. Each copy is expensive, but I bought one; it came by courier. Josephus's first book left me with questions. I hope this second book will clear them up."

Daniel's eyes sparkled with joy and yearning. "I heard he had written our history. I wanted a copy but could never afford it. Would you let me read it after you've finished?"

"Thank God for the arrival of this book," Zacharias replied. "Now we can attend to something else instead of constant squabbling over children, grandchildren, and marriages! You would have thought we started a war when we went to that farmhouse. My friends, finally we have something interesting to read and discuss during long summer evenings. Yes, Daniel, let's take turns reading this new book out loud."

---

[94] Josephus's book, *History of the Jews,* appeared around AD 93. It is possible that copies were being made for a year before it was widely circulated.

Chapter 28
Mourning and Ashes

AMOS AND ABIGAIL'S HOME

Anthony had been across the valley again, scouting and trying to find the bandits' lair. With stiff legs from the long ride and a sore backside, he was ready to rest except for an urgent task. "Hail, Penelope!" he said as he dismounted and came into the inn.

"Hail, Anthony!"

"Did Miriam come today?"

"No, she is waiting for you at the farmhouse. This morning Amos and Abigail invited us to the rooftop. We heard about Herod's Temple being burned and left in ashes twenty-five years ago today."

Anthony mounted Brutus and left quickly. He had wanted to come earlier in the morning to share the day's painful remembrances, and now the day was almost over. The sun had set, and darkness was coming on. When he arrived at the Ben Shelah home, Grace ran into his arms before he had a chance to take off his sandals. She met him at the door, and he lifted her high above his head. She yelled, "Mommy, come! Daddy's home!"

Miriam rushed over for a quick hug, and Amos asked where he had been.

"I was across the valley, checking out many places where mutineers might hide. There is more about that, but let me tell you why I raced here from the inn. I wanted to tell you how badly I feel about your city and Herod's Temple being burned." Anthony noted interest on Abigail's face. "I really wanted to be here for your gathering on the rooftop. Penelope told me about it when I rode in.

"I'm certain the gang we're after includes Craga, Taba, Harpa, and Maza. They were the troublemakers when I was at Soma and could be hiding anywhere. My squad found several places they could have been hiding on those far mountains. They look smooth from here, but when you get up close..."

Amos's mouth hung open. "You actually know the names of the mischief-makers?"

"I knew one of them years ago in the army. I know that I can trust you to not talk about it. Craga is one who served in my legion in a different cohort. He was the lead centurion. No one was a more capable soldier."

Abigail nodded and said, "Go on."

"Three officers planned to take revenge for something I did," said Anthony. "I know revenge is a common thought. Everyone feels it at some point, but between soldiers in the army, it's dangerous. Revenge destroys discipline, and on the battlefield, revenge weakens us, leading to defeat...."

Abigail, sitting across the room, burst out, "If that means the defeat of a legion, then it is a good thing!"

He kept on as if he had not heard the comment. "Years ago, my legion had joined forces with another to pacify Upper Germania, but then Domitian decided to separate them. He wanted to do that because tribes in Moesia had not yet been fully pacified, and he needed extra reinforcements there. At this news, two tribunes disagreed with the emperor's instructions. They began to object. I overheard rebellion on their part and reported them to my general.

"When they learned that I knew about their plans, they decided to kill me. They issued a false report of Germania tribesmen threatening our bridge over the Neckar River. The fear they were stirring up was that enemies would try to burn the bridge. So a detachment was formed to find the barbarians, but that was only a ruse to attack me and get rid of me for telling our general that I knew their plans. While on patrol, under the bridge, I was cut up badly and almost died. This scar was the result."

Oil lamps flickered, casting a dull light on his face.

Grace bounced in his arms, twisting her head so she could see the scar on his face. She rubbed her finger along it. "Daddy, you hurt again?"

Miriam corrected her. "No, Grace, say, 'Does it still hurt?'"

With a frown, she looked at her father. "Does it hurt again?"

"I must explain what everyone already knows. The politics of Upper and Lower Germania caused difficulties for Rome. The confusion was the result of an unresolved conflict. After Nero took his life, four generals fought to become the next emperor. The victor was Vespasian. His troops were lined up against Jerusalem, and later they returned to Rome. He had been chosen emperor by the legions in the East when the siege of Jerusalem began."

Amos asked, "What does all this talk about Upper Germania have to do with the rebels you are hunting or with the theft that took place at the Door?"

"Some of the legionaries in my legion deserted. Others joined them and formed a gang, and these are the ones we are hunting. But Uncle Amos and Aunt Abigail, this is your day of mourning and ashes. I came to talk about that, not the army."

He spoke deliberately, slowly, holding his daughter close while stroking her long black hair. "So, yes, right now my work is keeping the Southern Road safe and finding those outlaws. It's my work but not my heart. I didn't come here to talk about revenge or the army. I raced across Cogamis Valley today to say this: I am so sorry that you lost your children in Jerusalem. I don't know why it happened. I don't understand the ways of God. However, I feel deeply saddened. When I see a family like yours, I know the human side of what happened. It was because of the wickedness of men's hearts."

Miriam saw tears appearing in her aunt's eyes. Amos was examining lines on the floor, the intertwined mosaic markings of eternity.

"When I ride miles and miles, day after day, guarding caravans, I hear men swearing and telling vulgar stories. Along the way, I examine trees and rocks, looking for outlaws. As I think about these things, I thank the Almighty for forgiveness and his grace because I learned a different way to think about life.

"Your brother, Antipas Ben Shelah...first I saw him practicing generosity, and then he taught me about the covenant of life and peace. So when I heard that you had gathered, I raced here from the inn to tell you the depth of the feelings in my heart for you. I know about the love and care you give to Obed and Isabel and the love you extend to your grandchildren and to your great-grandson."

Anthony did not know how much more he should say, but he knew he had not quite finished. "I wanted to come on your special day, your day of mourning. I admire your family and the way you stick together. Miriam tells me how kind you are to non-Jews. You are inviting them on special days, helping them to understand the ways of your fathers. I admire that."

He began to lower Grace to the floor, but she would have none of it. She clung to her father's neck and put her face close to his, refusing to let him go.

"I can't stay since I have to give my report at the garrison. Felicior is determined to learn where Craga and his men are hiding out, and he's impatient with me for not having captured them yet, so please excuse this rushed visit."

Amos stretched out a hand. "Please stay, Anthony. You've only been here a few minutes. I would like to hear more from you."

"Thank you, Uncle Amos, but I must get going. I know it is a Roman thing to do, coming quickly and leaving in a hurry." He smiled. "You Jews show hospitality much better than we Romans do. However, I am a man under authority. I am a soldier."

Emotions were close to the surface, and he added something he had not thought of saying. "I was almost killed, but I was remade as I learned about your covenant. Now I have to go."

When he was gone, Grace ran crying to her mother. Saulius ran toward her, but Grace pushed him out of the way. He fell onto the floor, and then both were crying. "Daddy is home! Daddy's gone again!" cried the distraught little girl. Both children needed to be comforted.

Miriam wondered what the family's response would be to the unexpected visit. She looked at her aunt. Abigail was seated, leaning forward with her face between her hands, her elbows resting on her knees.

All day, Abigail's thoughts were elsewhere. *I wanted to hurt that man.... Have I been too hard in my heart toward Anthony? Am I happy or gloomy that he left so quickly?*

The lamp had been extinguished, and Abigail rested her head on her husband's chest. They talked in hushed tones before sleeping. "I could never do what Anthony did, confessing to us."

She readjusted her pillow and then held her breath, letting out a long sigh. "Anthony stands for everything that hurt me. Everything! Yet he is taking us into secret corners in his heart. He even told us shameful things in the army. Somehow, after that, I don't hate him so much."

Both lay silent in the hot night.

It took all her courage to open her heart. If the oil lamp had been glowing or Amos could have seen her face, she might not have said it. "Amos, I can't confess my bitterness, not even to God! How do I hand it over to him without giving up my past? I know that resentment and anger are keeping me away from people. I'm not the happy, outgoing young woman that I was long ago when you told me, 'I want to marry you a year from today.'"

Amos did not know if she expected a reply or not, so he sighed and waited.

After a moment, she added, "How does a man who is my enemy get the strength for a confession like that, to say he is sorry that it happened?"

They went to sleep with her questions unanswered.

The following day, Amos joined his family for breakfast. "I'm beginning to think it would be a good idea to invite people to join us for worship. Shall we think about it?" He knew Abigail was not warm to the idea of visitors in the home too frequently. After a lengthy discussion, she had agreed that worship with others was permissible but should not go beyond their regular feasts: Passover, Pentecost, and Chanukah.

Grace leaned toward her mother and asked loudly, "Mommy, everyone is quiet. Are they sad, Mommy?"

Abigail said a few words to her husband then walked to the stairs and went up to their room. Her eyes were full of tears.

A sudden thought shook her, sucking her breath away. *Something about this soldier, a man who lived for revenge but who is now ready to die to protect merchants and travelers...that is what touched me, Lord. He was driven by hatred but no longer. Is it possible that he really is a true worshiper? And what if I am not the "worthy one" like I always thought? How did he learn about the covenant? Of course, I know that Antipas taught him...but could the one that I have called "enemy" be cleaner in his heart than I am? O God of Israel, I want to be free from twenty-four years of hatred...but I don't know if I can humble myself.*

Three days had passed since Anthony had come to the farm and talked to Amos and Abigail. At breakfast, Abigail tried to open the topic burning in her heart. She tried to toss back her long black hair, but it fell across her face, causing Grace to giggle.

"Can anyone really understand how much Anthony had to humble himself to tell us about his scarred face? Did anyone else notice how much he opened himself to us by what he said?"

Everyone sat silently at the table with a puzzled look. Abigail usually spoke about him with a derogatory tone. She had often talked about him as "my enemy" or "the Gentile," but today she had used his name. "Anthony told us of trouble in his legion. Aren't soldiers supposed to keep all that hidden?"

No one wanted to interrupt.

Inwardly, she was still afraid. *Would my family disapprove of me for humbling myself? Yet I have been wrong. No...I can't go through with it!*

She said, "Don't mind me. I'm thinking about my Amos's ideas of having people come here for worship and learn about Yeshua Messiah. Sometimes I get afraid of having too many people around. At times, I think I'm a bit mixed up, that's all."

She had tried to speak about the secret things of her heart, but the words would not come.

Amos had learned to live with his wife's moodiness, and he whispered to her one night when the hot weather kept them awake. They were on the roof, and thousands of stars dotted the black sky above. "Abigail, I don't like it when people tell me I'm wrong. I think it's because our family line goes back to the potters and linen weavers who worked as servants for King David. Your clan started with singers appointed by the King himself, but on my side, I can see that we pride ourselves on wealth, possessing nice things, and our long history.

"But I've been thinking of what you asked about Anthony. He, too, is a proud man. He traces his family back to the defeat of Gaul on his mother's side. That's when Julius Caesar fought against great odds. His father's family came from Spain, yet despite his family's history and the superiority that Roman soldiers sometimes feel, he did something deeply personal. He opened his heart to us."

For years, Amos had been praying that something would touch her broken spirit. So much resentment lay bound up in the woman he cherished.

Amid these thoughts, Amos had his own struggle. Was it possible that the Spirit of God could speak to them through a Roman soldier?

The next day, he awoke early and walked down the hill to where his servants were milking the cows, and for the next several days, he rose early to walk in the fresh air. Each summer, sunrise quieted his spirit. He was more attentive to Abigail, wondering how he could encourage her without forcing her to do something she was afraid to do.

On Friday, Abigail also woke up early. "I'm coming with you this morning," she murmured. They walked down the hill in the dim light toward the shed where servants were milking the cows. "Amos, I've decided to forgive him. I thought Anthony was our enemy, but I don't think that way now. I want to make peace with him, but I can't do it without your help."

"What do you want me to do?"

"On Sunday, I want Anthony to share the morning meal with us. I'm going to tell him what is on my mind and ask him to forgive me for the bad feelings I've had toward him."

"Do you mean that?"

"Yes, and I want everyone in the family to hear me."

"Let me get this right. You want me to arrange to have Anthony here on Sunday?"

"Yes, I do."

"I'll try, but sometimes he is on patrol."

Amos hitched up both horses and took the wagon to the garrison, asking to see Commander Felicior. "I don't want to impose upon you, sir," he said, "but we want Anthony to come to our home on Sunday morning for the morning meal."

"What's all this about? He and his team are supposed to ride with a caravan on the Southern Road. He's going as a guard."

"It's a special event, planned just for him."

Felicior just looked at Amos for a moment, thinking. "Yes... I'll let him stay for your meal, but he'll have to catch up to the caravan."

Anthony arrived at the farm early in the morning on Sunday. Everyone knew something was going on, but they were too shy to ask. Before they began the meal, Abigail looked at him. She struggled to speak her mind but was gradually overcome by emotions.

"Anthony, I didn't finish telling you my story last year, but I should have done that. I didn't do it because of my bitter heart. I pictured you as…my enemy, and those feelings stopped me. This is hard for me to say openly. I have been…bitter and angry. This influenced my relationship with you. When I saw you, I saw the soldiers who…came against Jerusalem, and…I forgot the promises given to us. One of them is my favorite. 'Once more, a remnant of the house of Judah will take root below and bear fruit above. For out of Jerusalem will come…a remnant, and out of Mount Zion…a band of survivors. The zeal of the Lord Almighty will…accomplish this.'[95]

"I could only think of us as a 'remnant,' not…the promise that went with it. General Titus killed thousands in Jerusalem and then took others as prisoners for sport in Caesarea Philippi before his victory marches to Rome. I have let my mind dwell…on atrocities. I said that I would…never speak to you, but…now I want…to respond with…an open heart. Forgive me if…I cry. I have been…carrying pain and…bitterness for many years, and…I no longer…want that…burden."

She lowered her head and wiped her eyes. She sat up straight, going over the memories once again. "You know that I lost six children. I saw cruelty, but I saw acts of generosity too. General Titus gave us clemency when we left the city wall. A whole group of us…asked for mercy when…we left the city. Titus said, 'Take these starving people in carts to Gophna.'

"Those soldiers didn't take food away from us, as our own people had done. No, they really tried to save my parents. 'Eat slowly,' said the soldiers, 'or you will die. Let your body come back to life slowly.' I remember one soldier. He was carrying a spear in his left hand; I remember his comment. 'Poor Jewish beasts. The whole city must be full of people as…desperate as this. Only fanatics would fight on. They are…dying from starvation.' His words have never left my mind.

"We were overcome with grief but perplexity too. The Romans were our enemies, and now they were giving us food. Father and Mother were so starved they didn't follow the instructions. They

[95] 2 Kings 19:31

stuffed their empty stomachs, but it was too much. Father...died the next week, and...Mother died two days later. There was...no strength left. Soldiers took them away for burial. We were...stricken with grief.

"That's when Amos spoke with an old man in Gophna who remembered a prophecy spoken by Yeshua of Nazareth: 'When you see the city surrounded, flee for the mountains.'[96] It was far too crowded to stay in Gophna, so Amos asked if we could go to Decapolis and Philadelphia, across the Jordan valley and beyond the mountains. We were given permission."

Abigail continued after a long silence, "Then we heard the terrible news. Herod's Temple had been burned...the same day of the year that Babylonians destroyed Solomon's Temple. Now, why am I telling my life story? I am giving...thanks to God for preserving our...lives."

She leaned over, looking directly at Anthony. "And now you have come to our home. I was afraid of you and didn't know anything about you. You represented everything painful in my life—those endless rows of soldiers arrayed against us. In my imagination...it was your face I saw. But you were not there among those tens of thousands of men. I have sinned against you...and I ask for your...forgiveness. I have been...wrong. I will continue to...struggle with my feelings, for as you know, I am a mother...deprived of my children. But I don't want to carry this load anymore."

She hid her face in her hands, tears running between her fingers.

Anthony did not know what to do. "Should I move toward her?" he mouthed.

Miriam shook her head, saying, "No!" silently.

Ruth and Sarah nodded, but they wanted to shout, "Yes!"

He was confused and waited. After a quiet moment, Abigail looked up. Her eyes were red. "Anthony, as Miriam's husband ...you are accepted in...this family. I want a covenant of life and peace between us."

She stopped again but this time looking directly at him. Her voice wavered as she spoke through her tears. "Come and go freely. Be patient...with me when I don't seem...too friendly. It's just that I need to know you better. That might take me a while."

---

[96] Matthew 24:16

He stood up, and Abigail moved toward him. She hugged the big, strong man. The thin, drawn woman who was slightly stooped raised her hand to his face and traced the long red mark on his face with her finger.

"Forgive me too," he said. "I have not been the person I should have been, like when I barged into your house last year. You won't like everything I do because–"

"Hush, I'm glad you did. It made me think long and hard about myself."

Anthony listened intently, thinking about his father. *That means the day they moved to Philadelphia may have been the day that Father went over the wall as a trumpeter! Abigail speaks from the sacrifice of a broken spirit.... This woman has a humbler heart than I have.*

THE POSTAL ROAD AT THE DOOR, NEAR PHILADELPHIA

Anthony climbed on his horse and left an hour later. He rushed at a trot to catch up to the caravan, where merchants were walking beside their camels. When he caught up, Omerod and Bellinus asked why he was late. "I was with my wife for a meal," he said and then added, "with my wife and her family."

Omerod laughed. "I wish I could stay for breakfast with my wife!"

"No! I really was with my wife and her entire family. We really had breakfast together." *Humph! Let them think whatever they want to believe.*

They howled even more. Bellinus said, "Listen to the man! He says he was having breakfast with the family as well! Next we'll be hearing he is friends with his enemies!"

Guarding slow-moving caravans was a monotonous task, and the tedious work brought out strange humor.

A smile filled his face. "Yes, you are right. Someone asked for forgiveness. A woman who was my enemy became my friend! It's called reconciliation."

The soldiers stopped laughing; Anthony's eyes were shining with a strange light. They could not remember hearing the words *forgiveness and reconciliation* ever being expressed by a soldier as something other than a joke.

Those words of peace were not in their working vocabulary.

AMOS AND ABIGAIL'S HOME

Abigail walked back from the kitchen carrying more fruit for breakfast. She walked with an energy she hadn't experienced for a long time. She rubbed her hand, still amazed that she had touched his scar. *I laughed when I woke up today. I was thinking about what I would say to Anthony.*

She chuckled and looked at her daughter-in-law. "Imagine! A wounded man with a scarred face is a follower of the Master—with scarred hands. I welcomed a Roman legionary into our home, a man who should be my enemy!"

Isabel was giggling too. "You scared him, you know."

"What do you mean?" Abigail asked.

"The look on his face. He thought you were going to throw him out or forbid him to come again. His eyes bulged out when you started to talk to him!"

Miriam said, "When you broke the flatbread in half and offered him half and then ate it together... Auntie, that was a sign of peace. Today was like starting to write on a brand-new papyrus scroll."

"Yes, it is like that for me." Abigail drew a deep breath.

Inn of the Open Door

A Chronicle of Philadelphia

Part 3

January AD 94 – May AD 96

Covenant and Community

Chapter 29
Invitation to a Meal

AMOS AND ABIGAIL'S HOME

Abigail hummed all the next day, and the songs she had sung as a child in Alexandria came back to her. She sang the words of songs from long-forgotten events. That night she had a dream. Abigail was acting as a servant, offering Anthony and Miriam a bowl of fruit. She woke up with a start. *Why would I be bringing them the food?*

The following morning, she had a shy smile on her face. "Amos," she said, interrupting him in the library, "I want a special noon meal to be served at the inn."

He stared at her. "When? And who is going to be invited?"

"Three days from now, I'll have our servants help Penelope make a special noon meal and arrange to have enough tables set up in the courtyard of the inn. Anthony can invite his friends from the garrison, and our family will be there too!"

Amos sat back in his chair and looked at the ceiling. A scene from long ago came to mind. He could again smell the scent of the sea and hear the splashing of waves against ships in Alexandria, Egypt. Gulls screeched, flying around the ship's masts then diving into the water and returning to the surface with small fish. The sun sparkled on the water in the port.

He closed his eyes and once again heard the shouts of men on the docks struggling under the weight of enormous burdens. One Egyptian pushed his friend into the water at the end of the day, and men shouted happily at the surprised look on the unfortunate man's face. *Just now, Abigail's voice was like that of the generous, helpful woman to whom I was betrothed. A year later, our marriage in Alexandria was such a memorable day. When she learned she was pregnant with Annias, our firstborn, she decided to give a special meal to thank our dock workers for their work.*

Amos rode on his wagon to the garrison and asked for an audience with Felicior. When the guard took him to the office,

Felicior was not happy to see Amos again. "Not more than one minute. Things are busy around here."

"I have an unusual request, sir," said Amos, aware that he was interrupting.

"I'm too busy for 'unusual requests.'"

"It's about Anthony and the soldiers who guard the Door and the city streets. We plan to thank all the guards for keeping the roads and streets safe. We'll serve a noon meal at the inn on Friday."

"Why?" asked Felicior, anxious to be rid of the old man.

"He and many others are working hard to keep the roads safe. It's a celebration, sir."

"A 'celebration'? Jewish men don't do things like this for soldiers!"

"My wife..."

"Enough about your wife and celebrations! A noon meal, yes! But nothing more!"

THE INN OF THE OPEN DOOR

The inn felt slightly cooler now as the end of August approached. The dining area had been swept clean and washed. Chips of wood from construction sites covered the floor in the stable, absorbing any dampness. Of course, like all inns, the place had the strong smell of animals when the wind came from the wrong direction.

A festive mood filled the inn as Abigail's guests arrived. The servants had helped Penelope and her children prepare a special meal. The event was a surprise to Cleon, for when he arrived at the inn, he exclaimed, "Hey, I never heard of a meal like this today! No one told me." He quickly looked around the room.

"Where is...?"

He stopped before saying too much, but Miriam noted the unfinished question. *So is Cleon after Grace? I think he was starting to ask, "Where is Grace?" but I can't prove it. He is a nasty, wicked man, fast and slippery. Snaring him is like trying to catch a fish with bare hands.*

Abigail was standing beside Miriam and Obed. "I asked you here, Cleon, to thank Anthony and the guards who are keeping our roads safe." When he opened his mouth to say something, she smiled. "Cleon, the guards will be expecting you to be the entertainment with funny stories. Our family will be here, so keep it clean!"

He groaned. "They've heard my stories a dozen times!"

Obed was standing with his head down and his hands behind his back when Miriam observed, "Here they come!"

The sun was at its highest point as Anthony, Omerod, and Bellinus left their gear at the front gate. Decimus, the centurion who coordinated the regiment's movements, sat beside them with half a dozen other soldiers who helped patrol the roads. Abigail had invited her servants and some of their family members. Altogether, the inn was going to serve a meal to thirty-five people.

Before the meal, it was time for introductions. Anthony stood up, looking around at each one. "My name is Anthony Suros. This is my wife, Miriam, and beside her is Abigail, her aunt. These are my military companions, Omerod and Bellinus. Centurion Decimus oversees the 'Keepers of the Door.'"

Decimus introduced the remaining soldiers.

"We've heard about you," said Omerod, nodding to Abigail and Miriam. He did not know how to greet Jewish women. Should he bow slightly, extend his hand, or just smile? In the end, he simply gave a nod of his head. He wondered if his reluctance to show even a smile was related to Anthony's words, "forgiveness and reconciliation." Inside, he was determined to clean up his speech, if only for the afternoon. Today, at this meal, he would not swear.

"And I've heard about all of you," replied Miriam, her eyes bright. These were the men devoted to keeping the roads safe by day and the cities calm at night.

The meal was laid out on tables outside the kitchen. Guests lined up to take their serving and then sat down at three long tables. Penelope's hot dishes were served as well as fruit harvested from the family farm. Peaches, apples, oranges, and figs filled many bowls.

Cleon amused them with stories. He told how one merchant's camel died on a trip before arriving at the destination. They howled with laughter as he recounted the conversation. The merchant tried to figure out what to do with the extra weight of the merchandise. Cleon acted out the efforts of unloading trunks and bags from a dead camel. Its body was too heavy to move, and finally he gave up and fell backward as if exhausted.

Then he imitated men carrying heavy sacks and tripping on uneven roads. People wiped tears from their eyes, laughing until their sides ached. Even the soldiers laughed, though they had heard the story before and knew how it ended.

Amos stood to speak. "I am Abigail's husband. This is a meal in honor of two events. First, you made the highway safe. Second, my wife is feeling better. For many days, she was unable to enjoy good food. She couldn't laugh or sing. Recently, though, she experienced a change, and she wants to say a few words."

Abigail moved from her seat to stand beside her husband. "I've never spoken to a group like this before." She wrung her hands in a nervous movement as Amos sat down. "This meal is a way of saying thank you for the work you do. It's also a special day for me. I am happy to have Anthony Suros as part of our extended family. I didn't think this way until recently. Inside of me, there was a conflict, and it prevented me from getting to know him, so I want to tell you what happened.

"His father was a trumpeter who fought in the siege of Jerusalem. My parents, my husband, and my children were caught in the siege. After that nightmare ended, I held every Roman soldier responsible for the horrors we passed through. I made a mistake though. I saw Anthony Suros as my personal enemy only because he serves in the army. The destruction of our city was only one reason we, as Jews, are not good friends with Romans. There are others too."

Smiles and shaking heads were seen at the soldiers' table.

"We Jews think we are special. It began when the Law of Moses came to us. We have many reasons to keep non-Jews out of our lives, but I won't go into them right now. I will say this: After Jerusalem was destroyed, my family and I went across the Jordan River and found people who took us in. They were kind, and from them, I learned about Yeshua. He showed us a new way to live, and our family became his followers."

This was not a speech soldiers wanted to hear. Abigail noted most men at the soldiers' table preferred to study details like knots and grains on the long wooden planks.

"All my life, I have traveled on Roman roads. First, slaves dig out the loose dirt, and then they smooth it. They lay foundations and finish the road with dressed stone. It all takes so much time. So much work! Yeshua Messiah did something similar. He is the architect of a new path, and he said, 'I am the way, the truth, and the life.' That is all I want to say about my personal thoughts, but..."

Tears were close to the surface, a spring of gratitude. *When I was a young woman, I had an outgoing nature. I haven't been able to express my deepest beliefs like this for years.*

She motioned for Anthony to stand beside her. The gesture was more commanding than words. The thin, slightly bent over elderly woman put her arm around his waist, their heads bent toward each other. The picture made a statement no one would forget.

Abigail finished by saying, "Thank you, Anthony, for introducing me to your fellow soldiers. Now, the last thing is a song from my niece."

The song Miriam sang had been developing in her mind for months. Sometimes songs came quickly, even overnight. She mulled over a theme at other times, getting the melody right and putting her thoughts together in words. Today she felt nervous. She had never sung before such a group of strangers, both soldiers and servants at the inn.

The presence of Anthony's detachment disconcerted her, but she drew a deep breath. "I wrote a song about Abigail. It's really a prayer based on words from Jeremiah, a man who lived long ago. He suffered heartrending experiences during the first destruction of Jerusalem. The approaching army of Babylon was unstoppable, and Jeremiah could see the defeat coming for his people. He was heartbroken, knowing he would lose everything: friends, health, journals, notes, his own safety, and maybe even his life. One day he asked God to be healed from his grief.[97] We feel like that when someone we love—a friend, a neighbor, a mother, or a child—goes through a hard time."

She looked for a moment at Obed. "My song is a prayer called 'Heal Me, and I Shall Be Healed.' It's a song about people around here who have lost their farms and businesses. Decades ago, worse things happened in the Great Earthquake. I'm sure while you are on duty, you come across terrible scenes while keeping the peace along the Southern Road or any other place.

"I watched Zarrus, a lame man you may have seen, teaching some men how to make pottery. One man became frustrated when the pottery wheel would not go around smoothly, and he broke the

---

[97] Jeremiah 17:14

pot after it was fired because it did not look right. Things like that gave me ideas for this song."

She sang her song without accompaniment. Her soprano voice pleasantly filled the large central enclosure at the inn.

Recurring memories and past terrors;
No one knows of my ordeals.
Only I know of my own errors.
And so, with head bowed low, I kneel,
Exposing thoughts, like a scroll unsealed,
I ask, "Will I ever be healed?"

I awoke, frightened by a nightmare.
Knowing I could not conceal
My deepest fears, I whispered a prayer.
Then, with friends at the morning meal,
I hesitated. "Should I now reveal?
Lord, is this the moment to be healed?"

They are my family. Do folk really care?
Can they understand the things I feel?
Thoughts churned inside. I longed to share.
Then came a friendly voice. "Reveal
Memories and pains that you've concealed."
"God, come to me. I want to be healed!"

"Lord, you receive me, for you are my Shelter.
You understand pains and strife.
You're my Refuge and my Helper.
Take control of my troubled life.
Cover and protect me with your shield.
Lord, heal me, and I will be healed."

As they left the inn, ready for the afternoon, each person had a different response.

Abigail felt a sense of joy. Her days as a young bride flashed before her. She relived her betrothal and marriage in Alexandria and then the birth of her firstborn. She recalled the day Amos and she and their seven children moved into their home in Jerusalem. More recently, she had come to their home in Philadelphia for the first time, riding in a wagon. Abigail knew she had done the right thing in inviting all those men to the meal. *Yes, I am being healed! Miriam sang the words that are on my mind. Those soldiers didn't say a thing after the song. What a contrast to the laughter and slapping of thighs after Cleon's stories!*

The soldiers left the city with different impressions. They were on their way to meet another camel caravan. Bellinus scratched his head. "Anthony, did you know that your wife was going to sing that song? A bit too emotional, isn't it? I'm not used to that kind of thing. Do you really believe that people who lost children in Jerusalem can become your friends? Could they be planning something against you? Do you trust them?"

Omerod made another comment. "You're a legionary. Instead of your aunt attacking us and saying, 'I lost my children, and I hate you because of it!' she gives us a feast. She states, 'Thank you for being a soldier, even though you are part of the army that took away my family.' After today, I think nothing makes sense in the world anymore!"

Decimus spoke up, leaning forward in the saddle. "Listen, men," he said above the clip-clop of horses along the road, "what we saw today is unlike anything I've ever seen. How does a spindly, little old woman find the courage to call Anthony a friend? She wasn't trying to fool us. No one jokes about serious matters like that. But I have a question: What gives these people the courage to do that? There's something about what we saw today. More is going on than we can see."

TIMON'S HOME

Once home that night, Timon could not sleep. *Father is never going to believe this. Nothing he taught me comes close. I can't put my finger on it, but this is the fourth time that I saw this family do things differently in six months. Hmm...hospitality, food, and special occasions. Abigail and Amos call us Gentiles, invite us into their home, then invite soldiers for a noon meal that ends with a song. They want strangers to know about their lives. I'm going to ask Father why our leaders don't take us into their homes. ...No, I'm not going to ask Father about it. Instead, I'm going to talk to Anthony.*

PENELOPE'S HOME

After Penelope and Thelma had put the children to bed, an oil lamp glowed in their makeshift home. All evening they had talked with the children about the events of the previous day. Conversations included the soldiers, brightly polished helmets, breastplates, swords, and food. At the end of the day, they were two exhausted, happy women.

Thelma said, "Miriam's song pierced my heart. I'm like an onion with layers of hurt. I never imagined myself as a widow."

Penelope teased her. "Do you need a friend to talk about personal things?"

"What do you mean?" asked Thelma quickly.

"I saw you looking at Timon during the meal," Penelope replied. "You couldn't take your eyes off him. Maybe he would like to hear you take a few layers off the onion."

"Well, that's true. You know, that may be part of the healing."

Thelma smiled in the dark after Penelope blew out the lamp. They whispered in the dark for a few minutes. Hugging herself with a newfound joy, Thelma turned to the wall, comforted.

The song was about me. Heal me, Lord, and I will be healed.

Chapter 30
To the Top!

MOUNT TMOLUS

Toward the end of August, Heber made plans to take Evander and his friends up Mount Tmolus, and the boys could not talk of anything else. "My son will never forget this," Penelope said gratefully.

Heber leaned over so as not to be heard and told her a secret. "He doesn't know it yet, but we are going to celebrate his fifteenth birthday up there—with style! Would you make his favorite food?" She nodded, planning the ingredients she would use.

"There's something else. Obed looks stronger, and I think he'll soon be back to work. When he gets better, I'll be going back to Sardis. My father sent a letter asking when I would be returning. I will leave with a light heart. What did you think about the mealtime event two days ago?"

"Looking around the inn, I found it hard to believe what I was hearing."

"It took a lot of courage for Abigail to express her thoughts." He hung his head. "I wish the same thing would happen between the families in the congregation."

The next day, they spoke again. Penelope asked, "Heber, I meant to talk to you about Cleon. Do you trust him?"

Heber pushed himself back from the table in the office, asking her to sit down. "No, Penelope, not at all. In my opinion, he was the man who helped Diotrephes in his attempt to kidnap Grace, but no one can prove it. Frankly, I was surprised to find him working here. Uncle Amos doesn't believe he's a threat, but Miriam and I do, so I'm keeping my eye on him."

"So am I."

"Is something about him bothering you?"

"He gambled and won at the Games, betting on his favorite athletes. He's bragging about how much richer he will be, but there's something devious about his words. Beneath his bubbly, humorous exterior, I sense hidden motives. No, I don't trust him one bit."

"Nor do I, but we are stuck with him for right now, aren't we?"

"Yes. Take care and have a good time with the boys," she replied, getting up to finish her work.

Heber left to inquire about the best way to avoid the cliffs along the mountain's lower edge. He got directions from a construction worker. "There isn't a road to the top of the mountain, but there's a good trail. The trail starts at the Theater Gate. It angles up on a long curve, winding around the mountain's south flank. It's an easy walk. Attacking the mountain straight on, you run into cliffs, and I wouldn't advise climbing them with a group of boys. Someone might fall and get hurt."

Heber had committed to working at the inn until the end of August, but he asked Obed to take over with the hike coming up. "Somehow, fifteen young boys got it into their heads that I should spend time with them. You know how enthusiastic Evander gets when he's talking with his friends."

"Yes, I think I can manage while you are gone," said Obed with a smile. "Have a good time, perhaps even an adventure, with them!"

Heber arrived at sunrise, thinking he would be early, but loud shouts from fifteen boys standing in front of the inn made him realize how excited they were. *How am I ever going to manage this lot? Five days with them will wear me out!*

They began the hike with gusto. Leaving the city, they pushed each other, boasting about strength and endurance. By midmorning, they had climbed high above the town and were looking over the valley. Farther on, they threw stones over cliffs and back on the trail. Wood carriers with their donkeys met them coming down the mountain. Every day, wood was required for use at the city baths, bakeries, and individual homes.

By noon, shouts had disappeared, and now they were saving energy for the rest of the day because they would continue climbing. One boy asked when they would eat, and Heber, who was wondering if he could keep up, answered, "We'll go a little farther before eating. Our food is being brought from the inn."

Cleon and Timon arrived on horses, leading a donkey packed with food, extra blankets, and some utensils for the hike. They left the donkey to carry the additional items, and the two men returned to the city.

Once refreshed by the meal, the group continued the hike and arrived at a fork in the trail. A smaller path branched off to the left, to the south, and was less traveled because it was only used by shepherds to bring their flocks for summer grazing on the higher slopes.

The trail they stayed on narrowed slightly here, leading higher up the mountain. By evening, all noticed that the trees were more spread out and shorter. Heber found a clearing with a small stream running through it. "Let's camp here. We can drink water from this creek."

Heber froze as four small red deer walked gingerly across the far corner of the clearing. He motioned with his hand, and all the boys squatted down, remaining motionless. The boys held their breath, spellbound. The animals bent down, calmly grazing. One kept her twitching ears forward, ready to sprint away at the slightest noise.

One of the boys could not keep his balance. His thigh was pressing against a sharp stone, and as he tried to balance himself, he fell over. One of the deer was keeping watch, and she turned in a flash, jumped over a small bush, and was instantly lost in the forest. The others also vanished.

That night they made a fire, and sparks exploded, darting up into the starry sky. After their supper, warmed by the fire, they gazed at the Milky Way, unable to count the stars in the galaxy. Heber broke the silence by asking questions. He let them talk freely about their parents, how many children were in their families, and the jobs their fathers did for a living.

Heber said little about himself. This was a welcome evening away from the Ben Shelah home, where he sometimes felt like an intruder. He listened to the boys, trying to understand their comments about teachers. Heber heard a few complaints about the gymnasium.

He noticed how Evander fell silent when they started to talk about their fathers. Neither Evander nor his best friend used foul words. Neither one had anything to say about Calisto, the Greek literature teacher.

The morning broke with a soft light. Dew sparkled on the grass. Gray ashes covered the coals in the firepit, but one of the boys piled on some kindling and blew gently until an orange flame appeared, and everyone cheered. They warmed themselves and ate cheese and bread for their breakfast.

They set out quickly, hoping to reach the top of the mountain. High above, a cloud covered the peak. One ran off shouting, "I'll be the first to the top!" and a chorus followed: "No! Not you. I'll get there first!" They slowed to a walk as the trail grew steeper. Herbs grew waist high in the meadows, and they picked red berries from bushes to nibble as they walked.

"There's been a lot of sheep along here!" said one boy, bending over and examining the droppings on the trail. They were coming around a bend in the path when Heber looked up. He saw a man get up from a simple bench, walk into a dilapidated hut, and close the door.

At this point, close to the hut, the trail ended. Ahead was a wide-open, flat area, the shepherds' pasture. Half a mile ahead, across the meadow and beneath a steep rise, they saw other huts. They walked toward them and saw how an overhanging cliff close by protected them from the northwest winds.

The shepherds' huts were constructed of logs and were close to a slight drop-off. Below was a narrow ledge that ended at a vertical cliff. The rocky precipice fell to the river far below. On the gorge's far side, another stone wall arose, covered with pine trees. The south side of the chasm was almost as high as Mount Tmolus.

At the bottom of Cogamis Canyon, the river flowed smoothly until boulders divided the current. Close to their side of the gorge, the water was white, filled with cascading waves. On the other side, the narrow stream flowed undisturbed down a smooth channel.

They threw stones into the gorge, screaming with excitement. Rocks disappeared into the abyss, and several seconds later, tiny circles appeared in the river. Evander called, "Let's all throw together and watch the splash!" They stood at the edge with their arms thrown back. "One, two, three, throw!" they yelled, and sixteen rocks were flung into space. They watched as many circles spread out on the surface of the river, quickly disappearing beneath the flowing waters.

Late in the morning, Cleon arrived on horseback, bringing stew for their second noontime meal. While Cleon unpacked Penelope's food, the boys called Heber over to another outcropping on the cliff. From there, they were going to roll a larger stone over the edge. They yelled, "One, two, three," and then watched it break into a thousand pieces on a ledge a thousand feet below, shattering and sending tiny fragments bouncing into the valley. Again they laughed and cheered.

Heber returned to talk with Cleon to make sure everything had been unloaded for Evander's birthday, but he was no longer there. Turning around, he saw Cleon walking far across the pasture, leading his horse. He entered the shepherd's hut. A second later, the door closed, hiding him from view.

Heber finished laying out the food but was curious about Cleon. He yelled to the boys to gather for the meal. "Everyone! Come back from the ledge!"

A short time later, the boys had made a quick job of eating everything Cleon had brought. Heber still wanted to talk to Cleon and decided to go over to the hut. "I'll be back soon. Don't go near the ledge. I don't want to drag you out of that river!"

When Heber arrived at the hut, Cleon's horse was gone. He called at the door, and a man opened it a crack, growling, "What do you want?"

"I wanted to talk to Cleon, my servant. Is he here?"

After a slight delay, the answer came back. "Don't know what you are saying. Who are you talking about?"

"I saw him enter this hut, so I know he was here just a few minutes ago."

"Oh, that man! He already left. Was he your servant? He asked a stupid question: 'Where's the shepherd I was supposed to meet?' I told him, 'Only a group of boys over there. Today there are no shepherds here.'"

Heber was curious. "Hey, you aren't the man I saw before. From your tunic, you look to be an auxiliary. What is an auxiliary doing in a lonely hut up on a mountain?"

"Well, son," the man explained, "we are a special detachment assigned to protect the Western Road to Kiraz. From here, you can get around the cliff over there and down to that road far below. If you go a few miles farther on, past the next shepherds' huts, the trail ends at a bridge crossing to the other side of the canyon. You'll find that's where this trail meets the main road. Going down the mountain, the trail takes you to Philadelphia. Up the mountain, going west, the trail leads you through the mountain pass to Kiraz. From there, you can go to Ephesus and Smyrna."

He took Heber to the edge of the cliff and pointed to the opposite side. "Look. You can see the road perfectly down there on the other side of Cogamis Canyon. As you may have heard, there have been robbers about. The garrison demands protection."

"Sorry to interrupt you." Heber excused himself and walked quickly back to the boys, anxious to make sure no one got hurt.

By nightfall, they reached the tree line and walked across a sizable, smooth gray rock. "Tomorrow we will reach the top!" one boy shouted, and their voices reverberated: *"To the top, ...to the top,"* they called again and again. They had never before heard an echo flawlessly repeating their words.

They could not find a creek close by, so they walked back over the gray rock to where a small rivulet provided clean water. Heber had several of the boys gather wood for a fire. By nightfall, a cold wind was blowing along the rock face. They huddled by the fire in close company, shivering in the cold.

A few boys had been as high as the shepherds' hamlet before, but none had made it to this high on the mountain. Gathering shoulder to shoulder around the fire helped them keep warm as they talked about their daily lives. Heber learned that most of the boys had to work doing small jobs. Every family needed each *sestertius* they could earn. A few were already making a quarter of a man's daily wage, and they boasted about their tasks.[98]

He also learned about illnesses in their homes, problems with little sisters, and their grievances toward older, bossy boys at school.

The following day, they were up quickly, ready for the climb, and again they clambered over smooth, gray-white boulders. The

---

[98] A *sestertius* was worth one-quarter of a *denarius*. A working man could earn a *denarius* for a full day's work, probably 10–11 hours of work.

mountain peak looked easy to conquer from down below. But up here, up close, it was hard going. One boy stumbled on a rock, and his big toe started to bleed. Heber found a small cloth, and he attended to the boy's foot. The others were ahead, running to the top.

But when they were assembled on the peak of this crag, thinking they had conquered the mountain, they saw an even higher elevation farther on. Over there, the mountain range stretched far away to the north. They realized that there many miles to go before reaching the highest point. One boy said, "Look how it goes up, always higher, curving around to the west. Maybe this isn't a mountain but a great dragon, like the story that Professor Calisto tells us about in his literature classes."

"Let's go on!" they shouted, excited by the challenge of more distant vistas.

Heber had a difficult time convincing them that the highest peak stood a long way to the north. "It will take more time than what we have to get to the top and back. I promised your parents to have you home after five days."

They complained, but his word was firm. "If I don't have you back at the end of five days, then I won't get permission for you to come up here again." That argument overcame their resistance. Each one wanted another adventure on the mighty Mount Tmolus.

Awestruck by the beauty of landscapes never witnessed before, they caught their breath and looked eastward. The valley nestled up against the mountain, like a toddler leaning against his father at mealtime. Far below, the never-ending, luscious dark green of orchards and grain fields left them silent. They stood in awe of the beauty. Golden harvest days were upon them.

On the other side of Cogamis Canyon, they traced the winding road connecting the villages. The road to Kiraz and Ephesus disappeared to the west, a tiny ribbon winding, descending, rising once again, and then vanishing from sight where it dropped into a remote valley.

"That's the area of a town called Hypaepe," said Heber.

"Where is that?" They were surprised that he knew so much about the world outside of Philadelphia. Heber pointed. "Look over there. After Kiraz, past that hill that's like a wart on someone's thumb, there is a beautiful village of learned men. It's called Pyrgion. The three other small cities in that valley are Palaiapolis, Pentakoma, and Hypaepe. Each is a thriving agriculture center because it is fertile there, like Cogamis Valley near your homes.

"Now turn around. See there, in the east, each mountain is a lighter shade of purple and blue. Persians came from that direction, taking control of this valley about six hundred years ago. Romans control it now, and soldiers keep the roads safe."

"You know so much," said the oldest boy. "You should be our teacher!"

Another said, "When I'm grown up, I want to be a merchant, and then I can discover things like we are doing right now."

"I won't do that," replied another. "My father wants me to work in his bakery. He almost didn't let me come on this hike. He complained that he would have to carry the wood."

Another boy said, "You're lucky. I have to start working right away. My father worked on the restoration project, but he came home with a broken leg. A big stone was being put into place, and it slipped. The healer man says he might not work again for months, so I may not be attending classes in October. When I get back home, I have to go to work to help feed six children younger than me."

In the thrill of the moment, the boys unlocked their hidden thoughts. Each had a dream. However, few could choose to work beyond a limited choice of occupations.

It was noon, and Heber sat them down on some rocks. "I have a surprise. Today is Evander's birthday. We are going to eat our noon meal at the highest point where we climbed." They took the bags from the donkey, opened them, and groaned. "It's cold up here," observed the youngest, "and our food is just as cold."

"I'll remember this day forever!" Evander shouted, and the mountain called back *"...this day forever!"* They listened to the echo. Then he added, "I will remember eating cold food, sitting on a hard rock, and shivering after throwing freezing water on my face this morning."

Feeling a little bit bolder, he remarked, "Heber, you brought me to the coldest, loneliest place I've ever seen. Look! No trees and only rocks for the view. That's the memory I will hold of my fifteenth birthday!"

He could tease Heber, his hero, knowing that his friends were secretly feeling jealous. None had a father who had taken five days off from work to take them on a hike. And all of them knew that Heber was not even related to Evander.

That evening, they went back to where they had slept the night before and crowded around the fire for warmth. A full moon came up over the eastern ridge of mountains, shining with intense yellow light. Huddled around the fire, they watched it in awe, and as it rose higher, the light seemed to turn white.

"Let's sing," suggested Heber. "Who knows a song?" For a while, they sang songs they had learned in class or at the city's festivals.

"Do you know any songs?" asked the oldest boy, and Heber sang several songs he had heard Miriam sing. They listened in silence at first and then joined in. One observed, "These songs leave me feeling good. What is it about your songs, Heber?"

Walking back down the mountain was more manageable, but their muscles were soon sore. They slowly moved toward the city and camped at the same place as the previous day. Several said, "Next year, we'll have to make it to the top. Will you take us all the way up, Heber? Please?"

Heber had calculated that they needed three and a half days to climb but only one and a half to go back down. The boys were off, skipping and jumping and throwing stones into the river. They came to the large meadow, and when Heber went to the cabin where he had seen the men, he knocked and glanced inside. There was no one around.

From there, the boys knew the trail home, and a few sprinted away, racing down the mountain. Others walked with him, happy for his company. They were strung out over a long distance by the time they came in sight of the city.

The group arrived at the inn, bragging to Cleon and Timon about their adventure. "Thank you, Heber, and thank you, guys, for bringing the food. I want to be on the next hike you take," one stated.

Another agreed. "I never dreamed I'd take a hike like this one. I'll remember this all my life!"

The last to leave was the boy whose toe he had bandaged. "Evander was right," he exclaimed. "You are the greatest!"

"Oh, I wouldn't say that!" replied Heber, laughing.

"Well, I would. No one else ever takes time with us. You were right not to let us go on to the other peak, the one far off. We would have run out of food and water. Thanks, Heber."

He limped off, walking to his parents' small apartment, the tiny place he called home.

THE INN OF THE OPEN DOOR

Amos and Abigail had prepared a special meal in honor of Heber's work at the inn, and at the end of the day, they thanked the Lord for the boys' safe return. Obed had been back to the inn for the last five days, and the parents of the lads were still talking about their climbing adventure.

Isabel asked, "How are your muscles after that climb, Heber?"

Heber described his trip up the mountain with Evander and the others. "I thought I wouldn't make it all the way, but somehow I managed. In the end, we had such a good time. We saw many red deer, and the boys threw stones over a cliff. We climbed to the lower peak. For me, the hardest part of the adventure was deciding we didn't have enough time to go to the second peak. The boys were disappointed at the time, but thinking back, it was the best decision."

Ruth's little boy was going to celebrate his first birthday in two days, and he was bouncing up and down on his short, solid legs. She asked, "Maybe Asa can go with you someday. Look! He's trying to get ready for a trek as well. What was the best part of being with the boys?"

"It was developing a friendship with them. Each one has a different personality. None of the lads ever did anything like that before. The best moments were at noon when we had Evander's fifteenth birthday meal. Then we continued the celebration that night around the fire with many of your songs, Miriam."

He laughed at the memories of trying to teach her songs to boys who, in their entire repertoire, did not know a single melody mentioning God Almighty. He added, "How does anyone keep up with an unruly group like these boys?"

Miriam spoke. "I was at the inn this afternoon when you returned and overheard Evander bragging to his mother about the hike. Oh, yes, Cleon said he talked to some men in a shepherd's hut on the mountain who gave him a drink of water. Did you see shepherds there?"

He shook his head. "No shepherds were there, although the pasture was still green."

Jesse asked, "What was the most unusual thing that happened up there?"

Heber leaned his slightly bald head back on the couch. "Unusual...hmm, that would be me seeing an auxiliary in a shepherd's hut, who said he was guarding the road to Kiraz from way up on the mountain. It didn't make sense."

Obed had not said anything at the meal, and he excused himself. "I'm not feeling well. Go on without me. And Heber, I don't think I'm well enough to work at the inn tomorrow. Please, could you stay on for two more days?"

His voice had the same hollow, anxious ring to it that his family had heard before they had to ask Heber to help at the inn.

Chapter 31
Harpa and Maza

AMOS AND ABIGAIL'S HOME

An almost full moon shone as Miriam tossed one way and then another. While she was thrilled with Heber's adventure with the boys, several things bothered her. For one thing, Anthony was far away, across the valley again. She missed his strong arms around her, and he was losing so many precious moments with Grace, who was learning words so quickly.

She turned over again and remembered the look on Cleon's face when he came back from taking the food to the boys. She tossed again. *Obed went back to work full-time too soon. He isn't well. I could hear it in his voice. He left the room without saying a word the whole evening. He shouldn't have taken over for Heber.*

A fitful sleep overtook her, with dreams taking her to places she did not recognize. A stream was flowing down the mountain, and then she was facing a cliff and could not climb it. She saw Anthony riding on Brutus, and he was with many young boys and calling out, "I need more guards!" Looking at the mountain, he said, "Tell the auxiliary to watch the shepherds so they don't cause another riot."

Suddenly she woke up thinking about what Heber had told her. *I must tell Felicior about what Heber described.*

In the early morning, Amos tried to put off Miriam's demands when she requested, "I need a wagon. I must speak with the commander at the garrison!" But he relented when she remarked, "Uncle Amos, I will walk there myself if a servant doesn't hitch up the wagon."

Before leaving to talk with Felicior, she called back to Amos, "Oh, and ask Heber not to leave for Sardis. He's going to be needed at the inn. Obed is not well."

Felicior had been in his office only a few minutes when there was a knock on his door. The sentry informed him that Miriam Suros had requested to see the commander. "She will only speak to you. She refuses to go away, sir. I've told her three times you are busy."

The sentry did not realize that Miriam had followed him into the building and was standing right behind him. At that, she walked around him and faced Felicior. "Sir," she said, "I know this is an unusual request, but it is nothing to do with me." Her calm voice and steady gaze told him she was not going to leave.

"Please go home! We don't accept 'unusual' requests. Whatever your request, the answer is no!"

"I must see Anthony immediately."

"He left the city half an hour ago, gone with two caravans. He won't be back for five or six days."

"If you listen to what I have to say, you won't have to worry about safety for the caravans again. I know where the highwaymen are, but since you won't listen..." She turned around and left the room. After a few moments, she came back to the doorway and smiled. "If you want me, I'll be at the inn."

He cursed the early morning interruption and rubbed his face. The hurried shave this morning had left him with stubble where the razor had not passed over his chin. He muttered, "How could a woman know the hiding place of those mongrels if we haven't been able to sniff them out?"

Then, in a louder voice, "Decimus, take three soldiers with you. Catch up with the caravans going to Laodicea. I want Anthony, Bellinus, and Omerod back here. Leave the three soldiers there to replace them. Be sharp about it. I'll meet you at the inn in an hour. The Jewish woman has information we need to hear."

An hour and a half later, Anthony and his team arrived at the inn with horses breathing hard and nostrils flaring.

"Upstairs." Heber pointed Anthony up the steps. "Miriam and Commander Felicior are in the office. Three other soldiers are waiting there too."

Heber told his story to the legionaries. "A few days ago, I took several boys up the mountain. The plan was to give them a hot lunch. After Cleon delivered our noon meal, he left our group, and I saw him enter a shepherd's hut across the pasture. I went there shortly after that, but the man at the hut said Cleon had gone."

Omerod asked, "Can you describe the man at the hut?"

"Gruff and unkempt. He was wearing a brown tunic, the kind auxiliaries use."

"What else did he say?"

"I asked the man if Cleon was there, but he told me no, that Cleon had left. He also said that Cleon had only asked him about a shepherd he was supposed to meet, which seemed very unusual. The man told me he was part of a detachment assigned to the Western Road, protecting the mountain pass to Kiraz, Ephesus, and Smyrna."

"How will we find the place?"

"After leaving through the Theater Gate, there's a double curve in the trail before you reach the open area where the sheep graze. The hut is to the left as you come out from the trail, and there's a small shed behind it."

Bellinus whistled. "The whole thing is a lie! A bad one too! No auxiliaries are assigned there. We examined that area last year, but at that time, shepherds were watching their sheep. We didn't go there this year."

Felicior exploded, "I want that man for questioning! And any others that may be there. On the double!"

Anthony took charge. "Heber described a perfect hideout. Last year, four got away because we couldn't surprise them. They were at the top of a steep cliff at Prosperity Village. Today they may all be in that hut. Omerod, they have not seen you before, so let's have you pretend to be a recruit coming to join 'The Faithful.' Before we go, change into a plain auxiliary tunic."

Felicior added, "Bellinus, take enough horses—six for your squad and four for the thieves you are going to bring back."

Realizing that there might be a connection between Cleon and the rebels, Anthony instructed, "Heber, keep Cleon busy. Don't let him out of your sight for an instant! Tell him nothing about what's happening. He knows we are talking here, but he has no idea what we are planning."

A HUT ON MOUNT TMOLUS

The legionaries hurried up the trail, passing workers coming down with firewood. Before reaching the double curve leading to the hut, they tethered their horses and walked the rest of the way. Omerod, without his armor and dressed in an auxiliary's tunic, walked ahead of the others. His sword was at the ready. His heart thumped as he came to the edge of the forest. Making this confrontation without armor was dangerous.

A door opened, and a man walked out. Then, after a few minutes, another one came out and looked at the sky. Neither of them noticed Omerod, who stood at the edge of the pasture. Then both entered the hut and closed the door.

Omerod raised his clenched fist twice, the signal they had agreed on. It was a signal for Anthony and Bellinus to circle to the left. He motioned to the other soldiers to swoop in from the right. The detachment was in place, ready for their assault.

Anthony's heart was also throbbing. He breathed, "This is the hideout. Lord, let us arrest them without bloodshed. Destroy the intentions of these evil-minded persons. Give safety to our men and the city."

Omerod walked toward the hut and called out, "Hail! I'm a recruit to 'The Faithful' from the north. I was sent up here from the Southern Road to bring you to where the next action will occur. A long caravan is passing through the Door tomorrow. The time for new profits has arrived!"

The door opened, and Maza walked out, a dagger in his hand. Half-open lips expressed surprise. Bewilderment showed in his eyes. "Who sent you?"

"Who do you think sent me?" answered Omerod obliquely. His sword was sheathed to take the fright out of his arrival.

Harpa appeared. Standing on the narrow porch, he looked to the left and then to the right, looking to see if anyone else was around.

Maza asked Harpa, "Didn't Craga promise to send another tribune? He told us he was going to recruit more men. Good! Another one has come to help us!" He relaxed somewhat, but wide-open eyes suggested he was still hesitant.

"What's your name?" asked Harpa with a harsh tone.

"My name is Omera," said Omerod. He knew the imposters had taken the names of Persian satraps and changed them slightly.

Harpa sneered, his eyes not more than a slit. "No Persian satrap ever had a name like that!"

"It is possible you wouldn't have heard of my family." Omerod smiled. "My ancestors lived in the valley around Hypaepe, over there, past this mountain. Of course, you remember that Persians governed the roads on the other side of the mountain, you know, the Western Road and the four towns there."

The precise details of Omerod's story surprised the two men. The words "Omera" and "Hypaepe, and the mention of those names, confused Harpa and Maza. Neither one knew much about Persian history in this area, even though both had Persian ancestors.

Omerod's trick left them looking at one another with eyebrows raised.

Information gathered during this brief conversation assured Omerod that two of the four men they wanted were elsewhere. He breathed again. The arrest was going to be quick and easy.

Omerod described the hiding place in the rock. "Craga wants you there in that cave for the night. You know the one; it's above the double curve at the Door. I'll stop the next caravan, the way it was done last year. Both of you are to come out and swoop down. You'll be like vultures ready to pick off the best meat. May success be ours!

"We have to be moving quickly to get to our next camp before dark! I wasn't sure I could find you. I have two horses ready to carry us there quicker. They are farther down the trail. Hurry! Grab your gear, and let's get going!"

This was the news that they had been waiting for months to receive. Both were ready to attack a caravan, any caravan, and were prepared for another easy opportunity to become rich.

Precise details dispelled any hesitation. As they walked toward their horses, Anthony and his men moved in, two from one side and three from the other.

"Welcome, criminals! You are arrested in the name of Emperor Domitian! We're taking you to the Philadelphia Garrison. You are accused of many crimes: the murder of Nikias from Olive Grove Farm, the robbery last year at the Door, and illegally bringing in and selling slaves."

Maza and Harpa glanced one way and the other, looking for a way to escape. They could not fathom how easily they had been fooled.

"You have three choices," bellowed Anthony. "Die here offering resistance, come with us and plead to your gods for mercy, or maybe you want to run away. Go ahead. Jump over that cliff! Take the plunge into the river three thousand feet below. Try to survive that splash! The last time you bolted, you escaped over that high cliff behind Prosperity Village. That was a drop-off of only two hundred feet. But here, jagged rocks will break your fall if you don't land in the water."

THE MILITARY GARRISON IN PHILADELPHIA

By the end of the afternoon, the two captives were at the garrison, bound and hobbled.

"Commander," said Anthony, "only two of the four were captured. Unfortunately, Craga and Taba were not there. I assume that our two captives will know where they are. We'll see what information we can squeeze out of them tomorrow. Our team needs to get to the inn for a good meal and a night's sleep first."

Early in the morning, the interrogation started.

"I've already told you!" Harpa screamed. "I don't know where Craga is! Stop whipping me! Ayyyy! You're going to break my arm! He told us that he was leaving for Chalcedon to see if he could recruit more men there."

More whipping by Decimus brought some information. "Please stop! I told you the truth! Craga went to spend the winter in Chalcedon...and yes, he is recruiting for 'The Faithful.'

"Taba went on the road...headed east toward Iconium. He got bored when we were not able to stop another caravan on this stretch of road. He spoke about an old family that lives near Lystra."

Further pain didn't add anything more.

The next day, Decimus turned to question Maza, who kept yelling, "Stop hitting my feet! Stop torturing me! I'll tell you everything! Craga always leaves, and then he comes back!"

Decimus held up a whip with small nails in the tip. "Keep up with the truth, or I'll have to use this on you."

Maza stuttered audibly, unwilling to tell their secrets. "No!"

"Which one was Craga's legion?"

"Craga was a centurion in Legion XXI, the Predators. Yes, he was a deserter."

"Why did he become a traitor?"

"He detested the Flavian family of emperors: Vespasian, Titus, and now Domitian."

Decimus snapped the whip in front of Maza's face. "Is there a leader higher than Craga?"

"Yes, Craga has a leader."

"What is your leader's name?"

"He calls himself Mithrida."

"And where are this leader and his friends?"

"I don't know where they hide. Our leaders told us to say, 'Under the shadow of the fortress Klazomenai Oenaeum,' but I don't know what that phrase means." He sobbed. "They'd kill me for telling you that...and I don't even know what it means!"

"Impossible! It's a lie," Felicior growled, frustrated because Craga and Taba had not been found. "We know that Klazomenai is a small village at the Bay of Smyrna's entrance. Oenaeum is a small village with a Roman fortress east of Sinop on the Black Sea.

"The army controls the entrance to the Bay of Smyrna, and the shores of the Black Sea are no longer dangerous as they were in the day of King Mithradates VI and his family! So I have to believe that you are telling a lie!"

After two days of flogging, Harpa had not revealed anything useful for further investigation. His answers were followed by a pitiful cry. "We were told to say, 'Under the shadow of the fortress Klazomenai Oenaeum.' I swear it on the life of my mother! Oh, don't tell her my life ended with wasteful wishes."

"Forget about your mother! Where did you hide the treasures that you stole from the caravans? We looked all over but couldn't find a thing."

"In the hut," Maza whimpered, but facing further agony, he screamed, "All right! Stop it! Our treasures are hidden in the shed behind the hut...under a pile of flat rocks."

Decimus's face was red from the exertion. Further scourging was useless. "We searched both the hut and the smaller building when we captured these two, but we found nothing But we didn't look under any rocks. We'll have to go back and do some digging!"

When they arrived at the hut, someone had been there first. The shabby furniture was upside down. Plates and pots were scattered on the floor. The door to the shed was open, and inside, they found a small chest. It had been hidden in a hole under some flat rocks, but now it lay empty. Clothing was scattered across the floor. There was nothing of value left in either the hut or the simple shed.

Felicior gathered his soldiers.

"I think they're telling the truth," stated Decimus. "The men will not walk free because execution awaits them. We haven't learned anything new, but everything they said only confirmed our suspicions. We'll take them to Smyrna, where they will be executed."

A prisoner could not be put to death by torture. Capital punishment for criminals had to happen in public, setting an example for all to see.

Anthony rode back down Philadelphia Avenue to the inn. Worry lines on his face were more pronounced. He was tired and discouraged. "Craga and Taba got away again!" was all he would say, and Omerod shook his head in frustration. "Possibly while we were questioning Harpa and Maza, one of the other two returned and cleaned out their treasure chest."

Chapter 32
Drawing Closer

THE INN OF THE OPEN DOOR

News about the arrest spread, moving about like tendrils quickly growing in vineyards. By evening on the third day, the entire city was aware of the report, but then word crept out that only two of the four bandits had been captured.

The next day, Heber called Cleon, Penelope, Timon, and all the staff together for a meeting at the inn. "I'm sorry to tell you that when Obed woke up this morning, he had a bad headache. Speaking honestly, I am worried about my cousin. When we were eating, all he could say was 'Yesterday...yesterday....'

"We thought that Obed could work the next few days, but that won't be possible now. Uncle Amos asked me to put off my return to Sardis. He wants everything to go well for the next two months, until the end of the traveling season.

"However, I want to be home with my family in Sardis for Yom Kippur, so Jesse has agreed to take over for a few days. That's why he is here today. I am training him to take Obed's place at the inn. I think it's time to start training the next generation."

THE SYNAGOGUE OF PHILADELPHIA

The holiest day of the year arrived for those gathered for prayers. Zacharias adjusted his prayer shawl made with blue threads sewn in intricate designs on a white linen sash. In reverence, he covered his head in the presence of Adonai. Yom Kippur, the Day of Atonement, observed on September 6 this year, cleansed one's spirit.

Age-long traditions comforted worshipers wherever the diaspora was found. Men in Philadelphia, Sardis, and Pergamum repeated prayers with renewed determination. They wanted to stop their minds from straying during the long prayers.

"First, our prayer of understanding." The rich voice ringing out belonged to Zacharias. "God favored his people with knowledge, moral understanding, and insight. Let us worship together. Blessed are you, O Lord, the gracious giver of knowledge."

His prayer of repentance was moving. He wanted his flock to follow correct instruction. Each person should worship the Lord Almighty and display the fruits of repentance. Once more, he praised the Holy One. "Blessed are you, O Lord, who delights in repentance."

Zacharias asked for forgiveness on behalf of all present. He knew all had sinned during the year. Their transgressions had displeased the Lord, but the Almighty was ready to forgive. "Blessed are you, O Lord, merciful and always ready to forgive."

They had passed through afflictions in the past year, but the synagogue elder placed his trust in their Redeemer. Adonai would deliver them from worse mishaps in the future.

A forgiven people experienced great healing in their souls. He prayed for the power of God to be experienced in the life of each one. "Blessed are you, O Lord, the healer of the sick of his people Israel."

He ended his prayer with a desire for all the benefits that the Torah could bring. Among these were peace, blessings, grace, and mercy. Most important was the light of the Almighty on each one's pathway. "Blessed are you, O Lord, who blesses his people Israel with peace."[99]

Worshiping God in a foreign land and staying faithful to the covenant delighted these men and women. Not only were they offering prayers, but they also continued customs and beliefs handed down to them from their fathers' generation and those before them.

---

[99] The long prayer brought before the Jewish congregations varies from one place to another but includes these essential elements.

Chapter 33
Concealed Conflicts

THE INN OF THE OPEN DOOR

A year had passed, and during this time, Timon had improved many things around the inn. First, he had separated the accounts dealing with the inn from anything to do with Amos's personal family expenses. Heber was increasingly impressed with the young man's abilities.

Timon climbed the steps to the office two at a time, and Penelope watched him go by as she kept on preparing food. Soft blue skies and the fresh smells of grapes, pomegranates, and figs in September delighted her. Her daughter Rhoda, now thirteen years old, was chatting with her.

At midmorning, Heber stuck his head in. "Good morning!"

"How is Obed?" Penelope was getting another meal ready. Wanting time to speak in private, she asked, "Rhoda, do you want to be helpful? Please go and help Thelma with Melody."

After Rhoda left, Heber shifted on his feet, musing, "I thought Obed was getting better. Remember when I allowed Anthony and his team to meet in the office upstairs? Obed didn't say a word, but later he told me that it really disturbs him and makes him feel hunted by soldiers. Each of the three occasions upset him."

"Why don't you sit down and tell me more?"

Heber pulled a chair close to her worktable. His voice was quiet as he shared his concerns. "He's upset that Abigail has still been occasionally inviting Anthony and the other soldiers to a special meal as thanks for the service they perform. He used to tell his mother that he was improving. Then, when Felicior started putting extra soldiers in the inn, Obed froze. Last month, at home, he said, 'I counted them, Mother! It seems as if all of these soldiers have taken over the inn!' Since then, he hardly says a word."

"What did Abigail say when she heard Obed say that?"

"She quietly explained to him, 'My son, those soldiers haven't come to harm you or anyone else! I invited them to a meal as a way of showing my happiness and gratitude. In Alexandria, after something good happened, I always had a celebration, and..."

Heber stopped. Saying more would be considered gossip.

"And?" Penelope could not stand to hear only part of a story.

Reluctantly, Heber kept on. "Halfway through the meal, Obed leaned down, put his face on his knees, and started rocking back and forth. He groaned, 'Remember what soldiers in Jerusalem did to my brothers? My sisters died because of them! Isn't the same thing happening again, Mother? Soldiers started coming, and now they live at the inn. Death is just around the corner. Soldiers gather in our food area. They come in and out at all times of the day. Mother, I don't want to die!'"

Penelope respected Obed, the man who had given her work at the inn. "Sad, isn't it? I like him. He's kind and gentle, and Isabel must be wondering what to do for her husband."

Heber nodded. "Yes, but Obed seems to believe that everyone is against him. He threw up his hands the other day after Isabel spoke. He complained, 'Michael doesn't let my mother-in-law come to see us! Daniel is breaking my daughter's heart. Sarah was supposed to be married already.'"

Both gave deep sighs for neither had a solution.

Penelope changed the topic. "Do you have any good news? I do if you don't."

"Yes, I have some good news, but let's hear yours first," replied Heber with a smile.

Penelope turned away. She did not want Heber to see the glow on her face and the tears threatening to come. "A few days ago, Timon asked Thelma to marry him. She is so excited she can't sleep at night. Thelma hasn't said yes yet. She doesn't know enough about him. Also, she is worried about his father. He says he's dominating and stubborn! Now, what's your good news?"

"Well, I overheard Isabel talking with Ruth. You know, houses aren't built to keep secrets from each other. Ruth said she is expecting her second baby."

"Oh, what a lovely bit of news! When is the baby due?"

"I don't know. Abigail, Isabel, and Ruth talked for a long time. I heard one of them say April; another one said May."

He thought, *I'm starting to gossip now. It's time to stop.* Reluctantly, he stood up, having enjoyed the conversation.

"I have to go now, Penelope. Take care of those five precious little children of yours! Say, why not bring them to the farm tonight? We are halfway through Sukkot, our Feast of Tabernacles. In fact, let your two boys stay with me at the farmhouse overnight. We're teaching all the farm children about our history. Our ancestors had to live outdoors in the desert when leaving Egypt. We build little shelters on the roof and sleep up there."

He was off quickly, and Penelope watched him leave.

She inhaled, holding her breath as long as she could. Then she exhaled slowly. Tears threatened again as she started to cut off the hard red rind. It was the first freshly picked pomegranate she held in her hands in this harvest season. She reached into the fruit, extracting each tiny, delicious scarlet seed. All were wedged deep inside the white pith.

THE CITY OF PHILADELPHIA

The school year had begun once more for Calisto, and Timon would soon be leaving for work. Before the end of the morning meal, Calisto addressed his son. "Timon, let's talk."

"Father, what is it this time?"

"This is serious."

"You're always serious! You used to have me memorize long passages of ancient authors, trying to convince me to become a teacher. I told you that I am not going to follow in your footsteps. I'm off to work now. Heber gave me special responsibilities at the inn to carry out."

"Sit down, please, my son. I heard a rumor today. Someone told me you are serious about a young widow named Thelma."

Timon dropped back onto the couch. *How does he know that? How did he learn her name?* "What did you hear?"

"So you don't deny it?"

"What did you hear? Who told you?"

"I eat grapes from my own grapevine, but occasionally a friend gives me some too."

"Well, yes, I can't deny it. In fact, I've already asked Thelma to marry me, but she hasn't said yes or no yet."

"How can you think of marriage? Are you earning enough to get married?"

"Father, you married Mother when you were young. How old were you?"

"I was twenty-one years old; your mother was seventeen."

"Yes, and I'm twenty-two years old."

"But, son, this is different!"

"How so? You were the same age then as I am now."

"But this is different. You want to marry a widow. Some things don't change. Remember the story of Oedipus. He also married a widow...and had great troubles!"

Timon understood his father's struggle. He was a widower and grasping at any straw to keep Timon at home. If Timon were to get married, who would look after Calisto later in his old age if he and Thelma found their own place to live?

Father is afraid of being alone! He wants company at meals! No, not just fear...it's also pride! He's too proud to admit it. Perhaps if I bend a bit, he will turn a bit as well.

"Father, if she says yes, I think we would get married next spring. What would you think if we came to live in this house, in our home? I'm sure that if you got to know Thelma a little bit, you would learn to appreciate her, maybe even love her."

Calisto nodded, started to stand up, and then sat down again. "There is something else I must talk to you about, my son. I hear rumors saying that you are spending time with people who worship a different god."

"Yes, two girls from the city have been meeting with Ruth and Sarah out on the Ben Shelah farm. They have a great time together. And Heber Ben Shelah is talking with at least a dozen boys. In the last month, they met twice in his office. They enjoy talking together and plan to meet every Thursday. They ask a lot of questions about Heber's beliefs."

"Are you getting mixed up in those crazy ideas?"

"Yes, I am. Heber's teaching makes good sense to me."

Calisto quoted passages from three plays written by the famous Greek writer Sophocles: *Oedipus the King, Oedipus at Colonus,* and *Antigone.*

"Yes, Father, I remember all that confusion. What a trilogy! Honestly, I find it depressing from beginning to end. Boys end up killing their fathers, their mothers, and then themselves. Each of the three plays is calamitous—terrible events from start to finish. Father, I am going to disappoint you. I hate hearing those things, and I will not use them to model my life on." He turned to go.

"Well, son, I am trying to warn you. Marry a widow, and you never know what trouble you are getting into. What do you really know about her? What do you know about her family?"

Calisto added, "There's one other thing. The grapevine lets me know that you are learning about ancient literature and that Heber is teaching you. Son! I thought you didn't like literature."

"Well, the stories I'm learning from him are far older than Greek plays. Heber is teaching about 'covenant.' Honestly, I like the concept of coming together in peace, not sons killing fathers." He was desperate to put an end to the conversation.

"Covenant'? That will corrupt you, lead you into relationships that you will regret!"

"Not at all. Heber talks about blessing one another and tells stories about being kind to one another. A few days ago, he called it a covenant of life and peace. Father, I must go. This is the day when Heber doesn't come to work. He never comes to the inn on Saturdays. He trusts Cleon and me to run things. In two years, Father, I have found a full-time job. I get paid well, and there is an amazing young woman whom I love. And if she will take me as her husband, I am going to marry her!"

Calisto watched Timon rush out of the house. *Such bad influences on my son...I feel him slipping away. Planning to marry a widow! What does he really know about her?*

THE TEMPLE OF DEMETER

Two weeks of instruction had already been given to schoolboys. A few days later, married women throughout Asia Minor gathered for the Temple of Demeter's annual ceremony. Women had been busy the day before cleaning up the temple for the Festival of Thesmophoria.

The festival began with the sacrifice of food items to Demeter. Crowds of women made silent prayer requests for safety, family peace, and loved ones who were ill. If a woman had a particular need, the priestess assured her that her prayers had been heard.

A long pageant play described the ancient story of the goddess Demeter's daughter, Persephone, being kidnapped and taken to the underworld by the evil god Hades. Prolonged negotiations were carried out for her release. Hades and Zeus, his brother, reached an agreement, allowing Persephone to be freed. Each spring, she was to be released, and the world would revive from the winter.

At night, after the pageant was completed, the women returned home to their husbands.

DANIEL AND DORCAS'S HOME IN PHILADELPHIA

At Daniel's home, a special meal was being served for Zacharias, Michael, and Martha. Mith ate with his head down, trying to ignore the loud voices, fearful of being pulled into the growing conflict.

During the meal, Dorcas said little. But after the main dishes had been taken away and fresh fruit placed on the small table in the center of the three couches, she confronted the men.

"Zacharias, Michael, and Daniel, how long is this exclusion going to last? This has gone on long enough!"

"My dear wife, the Ben Shelah family called a punishment down upon their own heads. This...doesn't...end!" Daniel punctuated each word emphatically.

The nagging in his home was becoming intolerable, and Daniel was being shamed in front of his friends.

However, Dorcas was fuming, in no mood to hide her pent-up feelings. "Zacharias, you read about Job during the worship service. I remember your observations about Job's complaints. You read, 'A despairing man should have the devotion of his friends, even though he forsakes the fear of the Almighty.'[100] Do those words not make you tremble? Don't you feel empathy and kindness toward the Ben Shelah family?"

"Not a bit!" Zacharias answered. He was sitting up, not reclining, a clear sign of agitation.

His answer brought out the color in Dorcas's cheeks, and her eyes narrowed as she addressed each one. "Zacharias, think of Ruth! She has not come to any of our homes! Daniel, will you not have compassion for the grandson you prayed for? Have you seen him or held him?"

Her voice rose as anger boiled to the surface. "Michael, you told me not to go to the Ben Shelah home. I'm looking at three men. Three elders! But all I see are Job's three 'friends'! Where is your compassion? Don't you have any sense of mercy?"

Zacharias responded, his deep voice resonating, "Job was buffeted by Satan, but this is different. Amos has only himself to blame. He continues to entertain uncircumcised non-Jews, even at Passover. My dear Sister Dorcas. Do you not remember the

---

[100] Job 6:14

instructions for Seder? 'An alien living among you who wants to celebrate the Lord's Passover must be circumcised; then he may take part like one born in the land. No uncircumcised male may eat of it.'[101] Why does Amos refuse to obey a clear command?"

Martha spoke sarcastically. "Michael, my husband, I congratulate you for obeying the Law with such zeal. And because of this, we have lost our only daughter, our only child!"

Michael sighed deeply. "Isabel chooses to remain in a home where pagans are welcomed! When she was married, she decided to live with her in-laws, not at home. She disliked the strict interpretation given to all of Moses's instructions. Think of *that*! She rejects our laws. All she needs to do is return to the congregation, repent, explain her actions, and then go through a period of restoration. A year from now, she could be back in fellowship. However, Amos shall not be restored, because he is the cause of this confusion. All the others could be restored if they change their ways."

"So you've cut off Isabel, our daughter!" Martha's voice rose, anger in her tensed jaw. "I thought this would be over by Sukkot! You've cut them all off: Isabel, Ruth, Sarah, and our grandson, Asa. And now you insist on cutting off our next grandchild too!"

As soon as she said it, Martha knew she had said too much.

"What?" shouted Michael. He rose to his feet, looking down at his wife. Fury filled his eyes, and his questions frightened them. "You are in touch with them, aren't you? Who is communicating with them? Is it you, Martha, or you, Dorcas?'"

Mith felt terrified listening to his father. His face went white, his heart beating wildly. After reading Sarah's short note—*You will be an uncle for the second time. Ruth is expecting a baby in May*—he made his mother promise not to tell the secret.

But Dorcas told Martha, and now they were both making clothes for a new grandchild. Neither of the women looked at young Mith. It was enough that he kept bringing bits of welcome information.

Daniel stood up, the master of his own home. "I'm going to talk to our servants! One of them must be talking with someone in that household. Who takes messages back and forth?"

---

[101] Exodus 12:48

His eyes darted back and forth. He saw fear in his son's face and said, "Mith, my son, what's the matter? You look ill!"

"Yes, Father. All this noise, these arguments, and your loud voice, week after week—it's enough to overwhelm anyone!"

Zacharias jumped into the conflict. "Look what you've done, Martha! You bark at your husband, and this has made Mith ill!"

Michael stood, and now the three friends stood in a half-circle, eyeing the two women and Mith.

"How could this have happened?" asked Zacharias. "I am certain none of our family members could be in touch with that household! This evil is the spreading influence of the..." He was so upset he could not say the words in his mind: "the Ben Shelah family."

The next day, the women discussed the clash. "Thank God for gossip," said Dorcas, imagining her future joy of holding her second grandchild. "It is life's strongest chain, and it brings us closer together. We won't break this chain, will we?"

They laughed loud and long. No one would stop passing tidbits back and forth when it came to issues about families. Because they savored every morsel coming to them, no one asked how Mith had come by all these tasty crumbs. The two mothers chewed on the sweet information. "Martha, I think it's going to be another boy!"

"Not me. I'm hoping for a girl."

THE REPAIRED WORKSHOPS IN PHILADELPHIA

The first clouds of the fall season hung low in the sky as Miriam left Abigail's home. Within a month, cold winds would start blowing. Winter was an unwelcome caller in the valley.

It would take five months until dry bushes would become green again, bursting with new life. Miriam breathed deeply, enjoying the final scents of harvest. Brown, dry fields and rough stubble were all she could see. Above, a lonely hawk flew high over the city.

At harvest time, it was easy to be thankful. Amos prayed at the morning meal, praising God for everything: animals, birds, trees, fruit, harvest, friends, and work.

Miriam thought, *Uncle Amos thrives here. He loves the farm, the sheep and chickens, the dogs, and cows but especially the donkeys and horses. This farm would be a fine place for Grace to grow up. Today I only have one assignment: spending several hours with Thelma.*

She had become used to the ebb and flow of life in Philadelphia. Two of the four rebels had been captured, and important confessions were obtained. The other two rebels had not been seen, which gave Felicior ample reason to believe that the threat of more attacks in this area was very remote.

Miriam arranged for a young woman to stay with the children while she spent time with Thelma. The two women borrowed a small wagon and horse from the inn. Their destination was a ridge on the mountain's lower reaches. Miriam spread a rug on the ground, and they sat under olive trees.

Miriam listened while Thelma explained her thoughts. She was opening up about more of her life. "I don't want to lose another husband. I'm so afraid of being widowed again. And Timon says that he must stay close to his father."

"Would you like to live with Timon's father?"

"I don't even know him!" she exploded. "Schoolboys talk about him, you know. Some call him a monster. What if he is a bad man like my uncle was to me? What if I don't like him or respect him? I don't want to argue and fight with Timon."

She looked out over acres of harvested grain fields. "It was such bad luck that my husband went to the protest. I wish he hadn't tried to be so brave, but...I have to get on with my life. Besides, I don't have a place to live, and Timon doesn't have enough money to buy, or even rent, a house."

Hurt and bitterness were passing, and she was weighing her future. After a long conversation, they returned to Penelope's apartment.

Miriam's mind churned with many thoughts as she walked back toward the farm. She considered the lives of the four women she loved so much, and she wanted to express her observations on pain and hurt.

If Anthony were here, she would say, "Each life conceals at least one tragedy. Arpoxa, my friend...there she was...stripped naked to be sold in the marketplace in Pergamum...and then she was freed from slavery. She is almost like a sister. Arpoxa was wounded so profoundly...snatched away from her home in the night and sold to cover her brother's debt. Still, now she can help many women, especially from the towns and villages.

"Penelope lost her husband, as Thelma did. Nikias was a hardworking man. All that the farmworker wanted was to own his own land. He longed for a place where he and Penelope could raise their children. If only Nikias hadn't disobeyed Anthony! If he had taken another person with him when he went to Prosperity Village, maybe he would still be alive.

"Thelma is saddened by her husband's death. She's caught in a struggle. Should she accept Timon's proposal for marriage?

"Aunt Abigail was deeply wounded. A bit freer each day, she's planning an occasion for the people on their farm at Chanukah."

The next day, Miriam wanted to be free to give expression to her thoughts. She sat beside the brook at the lower edge of the farm, where water coming from the mountain, was channeled into ceramic pipes into different parts of the city. No one heard her sing the words that had recently come to her.

Ateas rode his horse to distant lands,
Protecting others, racing on his steed.
Arpoxa, taken from her father's home,
A slave, she wept to see her shores recede.
Wretched men, hungry for dishonest gain,
Ignored their pleas. Who would intercede?
Shown in the market, human flesh on sale.
Her freedom is worth more than gold or deed.
Now they're family! Mercy supersedes.

Nikias couldn't take his eyes off her,
And Penelope loved his daring style.
He dreamed of buying her the best of lands.
Five little mouths to feed made life worthwhile.
Under flickering lamps, copying scrolls at night,
Unaware of rebels' tricks and wiles,
He unwittingly found a bandits' lair.
Through his death, they were caught, brought to trial.
She guides her children, heartened by her smile.

In Thelma, I see a flower blooming.
After her mother's death, her friends agreed:
Her uncle should feed her, but cruelty came.

Her words cover up deep shame. It proceeds
From a home where she lacked both love and care.
For her, past fears and doubts are like a storm.
Her husband died, crushed by a frightened mare.
She knows the words 'Fear not.' She wants to form
A family. Now she follows Yeshua's creed.

Abigail lost the best that she could give.
Six children died. Could she survive that trial?
To her city came legions bent on war.
Twenty thousand soldiers formed in rank and file.
The Lord had mercy on her, showed the way.
He fulfilled his plans to reconcile.
Revenge and hate transformed to life and peace.
I stand in awe! O Lord, how versatile
Your ways! Revenge itself is now on trial.

Miriam stood still. These words would stay close to her heart, a witness to the transformation she was beholding. In Arpoxa, Penelope, Thelma, and Abigail, the four women close to her, she found freedom, love, commitment, and peace. These were growing in different ways within her friends.

With her heart beating quickly, she raised her hands in praise. The stream gurgled steadily, flowing peacefully between its banks.

This is the covenant at work! Lord, I am witnessing its power. I saw it first in Pergamum, then in Sardis and Thyatira. Covenant and community are coming together. The covenant of life and peace...the transformation of hurting, lonely people into a caring community. But how costly! There are wounds to be treated and trust to be created. People can't stop their pain by themselves.

She looked up. The late afternoon sky was majestic, with a soft golden-yellow light glowing above the mountain. She whispered, "Thank you, Adonai. I'm missing Anthony so much, but thank you for Thelma. And thank you for the covenant!"

Chapter 34
Invited to Teach

THE INN OF THE OPEN DOOR

An early, heavy rainstorm in the morning meant that the caravan Anthony was to travel with was delayed. The caravan driver decided to stay in Philadelphia overnight and leave the next day, Friday, on his way to Sardis.

During the rainstorm, it was dangerous for construction workers. They gathered at the only place with a covered area big enough to hold them all, under the entrance to the inn.

Heber was happy for them to come because some men were buying food from the inn's thermopolium run by Penelope. Men noticed Anthony's presence, and they asked Heber to have Anthony answer questions while they waited for the skies to clear.

Anthony agreed to talk to the construction workers. For a while, it remained a simple conversation about how Flavius Zeuxis became interested in buying garments from the Philadelphia area and the new economic improvement.

But then Timon asked a penetrating question. "Anthony, I have heard comments from the Jewish community about you. Can you be a legionary and a follower of Yeshua? They said you are doing that, joining two beliefs."

Anthony laughed, and his easy manner put them at ease. "We all get things mixed in our lives. We were all born in one place or another," Anthony answered.

"I was born in Rome, and I served in the legion with men from many provinces. We are citizens of the greatest empire ever to appear. Our army is the best, composed of men from different languages and backgrounds.

"For example, my father fought against Jerusalem. A few Jews escaped, among them Amos and Abigail. People like them, those who weren't killed and who now live far from Jerusalem, have two names for themselves. One is 'diaspora' because they have been dispersed throughout the world. The other is 'remnant.'

"They have a saying, 'For out of Jerusalem will come a remnant and out of Mount Zion a band of survivors.'[102] They are found in at least fifty cities in Asia, Pontus, Galatia, Cappadocia, and Pamphylia. They no longer have a homeland. Their temple was destroyed, so they can't offer sacrifices. Even with these differences, Abigail and I can talk with one another."

No one noticed that he hadn't answered the initial question.

Eneas, a sculpturer of intricate designs, was one of those who came out of the rain. His specialty was carving leaves and animals on capitals, the carved blocks of stones placed on top of marble columns. He asked, "Are not Jews and Romans natural enemies? You are a Roman, and Abigail is a Jew. We have all heard Jews complain that soldiers destroyed their city and their temple. Then they add that Romans used their treasure to erect the great buildings in Rome!"

Many had similar questions.

Anthony looked around, glad to have so many interested in these topics. "Yes, they do see each other as enemies. But before Jerusalem was destroyed, a rabbi—that means a teacher—walked the narrow paths of that hot province. His name was Yeshua. He came from an insignificant little town called Nazareth. People were amazed by the authority and knowledge with which he spoke and taught about God. Yeshua was a carpenter, and he used everyday stories to describe two kingdoms. One kingdom is here on the earth. It includes rulers, kings, princes, governors, benefactors, tax collectors, centurions, soldiers, and ordinary people."

Ganymede, a carpenter, asked, "What is the other kingdom?"

"That kingdom is spiritual in nature. Yeshua called it the 'Kingdom of God' or the 'Kingdom of Heaven.' Once, when talking with a Jewish lawyer, he explained the two greatest commandments: 'Love the Lord your God with all our heart and soul and mind and love your neighbor as yourself.'[103]

"You see, his commandments don't conflict with the laws of this world. In the Kingdom of Heaven, we learn to love. However, nothing in the Roman Empire tells us to love God or to love our neighbor."

---

[102] 2 Kings 19:31

[103] Deuteronomy 6:5, Leviticus 19:18, Matthew 22:37–39

"Wait a minute!" interjected Ganymede, intrigued. He worked with Eneas and had recently suffered a painful cut to his hand while shaping beams for roof trusses. "Two kingdoms? How can someone fully obey Caesar if he loves that god of yours with all his heart, soul, and mind?"

"Yeshua talked about that," answered Anthony. "He taught, 'The things of this world belong to Caesar. Give Caesar what belongs to him: taxes, honor, and respect. That which belongs to God, you should give to God.'"[104]

"What does that mean?" asked young Timon. "How does anyone keep those things separate?"

"Think of revenge, hard feelings, gossip, bad attitudes, and selfishness. Does the emperor control any of those things? Did Caesar ever tell you not to harbor feelings like hatred? Of course not. Domitian's laws do not command human hearts. No, the emperor's job is to govern, make laws, collect taxes, and make sure public buildings are built and maintained."

There was silence around the courtyard. "So what more does Caesar want?" Anthony continued.

"Taxes, taxes, taxes!" yelled two men who had not spoken previously.

Others added sullenly, "To destroy our vineyards, send less wine, and give him more grain."

"Of course," said Anthony. "You immediately understood the difference. Public servants need houses, food for banquets, and authority to govern. Caesar depends on the army to put down a rebellion. Rome created the best road system ever constructed, and it carries merchants and soldiers for commerce and security. His words instruct citizens from the island called Britannia all the way to Asia Minor. In the East, he is obeyed in Mesopotamia. Taxes pay for roads so that silk and spices can come from far away."

Another man piped up, "I love to hear gossip about their banquets. Why doesn't Caesar invite *me* to such festivities?" Everyone laughed.

"Well, now you understand that there are two kingdoms. I was born as a Roman citizen, the son of a legionary. I had no choice in that. However, when I saw the kingdom of God at work in

---

[104] Matthew 22:21

Pergamum, I recognized that kingdom as a different realm, and I wanted to be a part of it."

Timon was curious. "What do you mean by you 'saw the Kingdom of God at work'?"

"I met an old man who taught me about agape love. That's the kind of love that considers the other person first. It brings patience and kindness. He was the first person I ever heard speak about loving our enemies. Listen! He, a Jew, let me marry his granddaughter!"

The clouds cleared, and the rain stopped. Anthony didn't want to keep the men from work.

"I've got a question," said Eneas. He was passionate about the history of places outside of Philadelphia. "What happened to this Yeshua Messiah? Why are we only hearing about this now?"

Anthony was happy for such questions. "He was crucified by the army on a cross."

"Why would a man who taught good things receive a sentence of death?" several people asked.

"That is a question for another rainy day," said Anthony.

THE MILITARY GARRISON IN PHILADELPHIA

Word reached Felicior two weeks later about Anthony's conversation with the men during the storm. He was called for an explanation. "Something reached my ears, Suros."

Felicior's long face seemed sterner, more severe in the dim light of the two oil lamps. "You talked to several men at a meeting in the inn."

"Yes, twenty-nine men were crammed into the inn's inner courtyard, so in total, we were thirty. We spent part of the afternoon together during a rainstorm. The caravan I was to accompany didn't leave because of that storm, so I was delayed."

"What did you talk about?"

"Some men who are working on the new Lower Baths asked me questions. The next day I went with the caravan to Sardis, and I have also been to Laodicea and back since then."

"What were their questions?"

"Over a year ago, Abigail, the old Jewish woman on the farm, and I made a pact of friendship. They were asking questions about that."

Felicior's eyebrows came together. "Explain to me...what is 'a pact of friendship'? All I remember from the noon meal were her words of reconciliation. Are you dividing your loyalty to Caesar with others?"

"No. We agree to live by the covenant, by what Yeshua Messiah taught about forgiveness. Abigail was greatly saddened by the loss of six children many years ago and blamed Roman soldiers. In short, we agreed to be friends."

"That's not all. Two workmen, Ganymede and Eneas, remarked about a foreign religion. During the rainstorm, you mentioned Yeshua, did you not?"

Anthony nodded.

"Ridiculous! The Roman army crucified him. That man was a criminal."

The two men stood in the small garrison office. One was a seasoned commander; the other was an experienced legionary, now a reservist.

Felicior said, "I am not happy about this, Suros. I warned you against these ideas. They sound dangerous. To me, this teaching contains a seed of rebellion. I could send you to a military tribunal, but I am not going to.

"Instead, you will remain in this city, and I will keep an eye on you. You will not speak that name again in public. This is a temporary demotion. Until the last day of this year, you will do the work of a common sentry. Your pay is reduced. Did I mention that your accommodations are changed? You will stay at the garrison dormitory, where Decimus will be watching you. I'm putting you on the afternoon and evening shifts."

A thought came to Anthony. *Miriam told me not to push away sudden thoughts.*

"So I will not be riding along with caravans again this year?"

"You will not."

"May I make one request, sir?"

"What is it?"

"You buy and sell horses all the time. I've been riding Brutus, the best horse I've ever had. He's intelligent, has good stamina, and shows a great spirit. I want to buy him."

"Why? Anyway, you can't. Brutus isn't old enough to sell off."

"All right, but if you change your mind, I'll pay what you want. Let me know what you think. Am I dismissed, sir?"

Felicior nodded his assent, so Anthony saluted, left the office, and went to the garrison's stable. He felt the remarkable warmth of Brutus's body, patted the horse's long neck, and ran his fingers through the cropped mane.

Good news, Brutus. You are going to have a well-deserved rest! A whole month in Philadelphia! Forget life on the Southern Road. You, like me, are getting a rest! Thank you, Commander Felicior!

AMOS AND ABIGAIL'S HOME

The following day, having talked to Decimus for permission to leave the garrison for an hour, Anthony rode out to the Ben Shelah home. All the fruits were harvested: grapes, apples, figs, and pomegranates. Miriam came running to the door, and Grace jumped into his arms.

"Let's go for a walk and talk a bit," he said. "I have some news to tell you that I don't want the others to hear."

They walked down the farm road. Anthony carried Grace, and Miriam's arm was tucked in his. "I have lots of news," he said, "but I want to hear what is happening with you first."

"Thelma talked to me yesterday. For the first time, she is beginning to understand the covenant. Yesterday she said, 'I learned why Abigail was able to forgive. That means even I can change from deep within.' Then she made me smile, saying, 'There are lots of young men I could probably live with, but Timon is the one I can't live without, even if it means moving in with his father.'"

"I'm happy for this young man. He's fortunate to find someone who loves him enough to risk living under the same roof as Calisto. He has a reputation for being...difficult."

"Yes, and talking about love, I think I am onto something else."

"What is it?" he asked, lifting Grace onto his shoulders.

"Have you been watching Heber and Penelope?"

"Of course. I see them talking together."

"What do you notice?"

"He is relaxed with her, standing there in the kitchen doorway. He keeps his eyes on what's going on around the inn."

"Anthony! Don't you see what's happened? She's fallen head over heels for him...and he's spending as much time there as he can without tongues starting to waggle. Thelma said after getting the children to bed, Penelope has only one topic. It's 'Heber did this,' or 'Heber says that.' Now, my dear, don't say a word to anyone about this, all right?"

"Right, and now for my news. It's both good and bad. First, the bad part: I'm being disciplined for what I said about Yeshua to a group of men. I must sleep at the garrison until the end of the year. That is a seven-week penalty, and my pay is being cut. There is some good news in all of this though. I can meet you at the inn during the mornings before going on watch as a sentry on the afternoon and evening shifts."

He took her hand, and they walked with their fingers intertwined. At first it was Abigail who prevented them from staying together at night. Now it was Commander Felicior.

As the Festival of Saturnalia approached, Amos and Miriam decided to use the days to teach stories to their friends. "Uncle Amos, I will teach them the songs I already have, and I'll compose a new one for the children."

When they explained their idea to Abigail, she agreed. "Yes, invite our friends and people around here. Holding our own little festival during Saturnalia may help some of them skip the debauchery in the city."

For days, the house rang with music as they practiced for their event. Grace and Saulius banged on the tambourines until people got headaches from the noise.

Miriam composed a song to narrate Israel's history. Fear had dominated their lives too many times in her nation's past.

Several invitations went out to the families of shepherds and farmers. The fathers of the boys whom Heber had taken up the mountain dropped by to give their thanks. Some workers who were reconstructing the baths wanted to express their appreciation.

Most of the families were poor and lived in the crowded insulae. All were invited to the "alternate" Saturnalia at the farm.

On the first day of the holiday, with people sitting all around the large room and others standing along the walls, Amos addressed them. "Welcome to our home! We are calling this festival the 'Community of the Covenant.' Like the people in the city, we will dance and eat heartily. Ours is Jewish dancing, and we have our own rhythms."

During the coming days, Miriam would employ her songs to teach stories of their ancestors. Many times in the past, they had to face enemies. She began with an introduction. "This song is called 'I Will Not Fear.' Listen carefully, and you will see how all the stories I am teaching you are mentioned in this song."

Pharaoh speaks! To his laws, all must adhere.
"The Nile is mine! I have enriched myself!"
Were we distressed by his ungodly sneer?
His sentence was the loss of his great wealth.
  Moses's trust in God dispelled his fear.
  Despite Egyptian spears, his Lord came near.

Hiram, King of Tyre, rich beyond his peers:
"Look on me! Be proud, islands of the sea!"
Hiding in his island fortress, his years
Ran out. That tyrant had no place to flee.
  Prophets do not panic nor need fear.
  Facing threats, they carried on, for God came near.

Nebuchadnezzar, Babylon's top premier:
"Look on my mighty image! Now! Fall down!"
They all worshiped the idol's gold veneer,
Proud satraps walked around in ornate gowns.
  Three men standing showed no fear.
  In those burning ovens, their Lord came near.

Haman, the Agagite, demanded all adhere:
"Bow down! I'm the king's most important man!"
His wife, his sons, encouraged with their cheers.
Jews would perish under his evil plan.
  Esther didn't panic, did not fear.
  Despite the ethnic smears, her Lord came near.

Facing conflicts and threats, other people jeer.
"Do you believe the Lord's our guide?"
Loving Yeshua demands a heart sincere.

And like those heroes, we refuse to hide.
Trusting in the risen Lord, shall we fear?
No! Threats mean little when our Lord is near.

THE CITY OF PHILADELPHIA

While the people who gathered at the farm were enjoying dances and food, Saturnalia arrived in the city. On December 17, people sat down to cheap beer, wine, and the loss of good morals. Classes at the gymnasium were out for a week. In the market, hot drinks, sweets, and small gifts were sold. Slaves could gamble for a week.

An oversized couch graced the Temple of Saturn, and the city's plumpest man sat there. He had been elected master of ceremonies for the proceedings. He held a long scepter and bragged about his title, *Saturnalicius princeps*, the "Prince of Saturn."

Cleon acted like a celebrity. He went along the Avenue of Philadelphia, crowing about how he had turned his few silver coins into many more, boasting how the gods had favored him. "Look how Saturn multiplied everything I gambled."

He showed off gems and won the approval of crowds by singing loudly and dancing with musical groups. He loved the irreverence in the bawdy songs telling everyone that he had been favored by the gods.

No caravans passed through the city, so Heber closed the inn during the Roman holiday and kept the inn's front gate closed to prevent troublemakers from entering.

Heber paid attention to Obed and Isabel at home for several days, hoping to help them through their time of loneliness and quiet despair. Isabel especially missed contact with her parents, Michael and Martha.

Chapter 35
Heber's Question

AMOS AND ABIGAIL'S HOME

The old year had gone, replaced by another stormy New Year's Day. Winter gusts blew from the west. Snow, which was already deep high on the mountain, swirled around buildings in the city.

After the storm, the sky turned clear, and cold winds continued. Obed still had not improved. He often lay on his bed without saying much, but at other times, he walked to the city and back. "I'm all alone," he would say, and his mother would hug him. "No, you're not alone, my son. We love you so much."

Instead of improving, he withdrew even more. "My brothers...they all died, didn't they? I can't even remember what they looked like! I had a sister, too, didn't I?"

She answered, "Yes, Obed, you had two sisters."

Amos postponed a Friday gathering until the next afternoon to allow the snow-covered road to the farm to clear. On Saturday, once again, his house was crowded. The floor was cold, but carpets on the marble surface made the place seem warmer, more welcoming. Visitors relished recent memories of December gatherings, the songs, the hot food, and the warmth of a spacious and welcoming home. The room soon warmed up with people sitting close to each other.

"Welcome to the Community of the Covenant! Last year was important for all of us in different ways," he began. "Most of us find God speaks to us in different times and in different ways. For myself, I began last year with some cynicism, some doubts, and family conflicts. I have learned that I can share the pain of others in a new way."

Amos looked at Obed, who had been downcast. The younger man had not participated in the December gatherings when the house shook with noise, laughter, and music. Instead, he stayed alone in his room. Isabel could not bring him into the family circle, and now she, too, had dark circles under her eyes.

"As I was saying," continued Amos, "I have a new confidence. It's not just a romantic kind of optimism, like saying, 'Spring is almost here,' or 'The flowers will be blooming soon.' I know many of you have been hurt by events in your lives, but today is not a time to talk about disappointments. First we are going to sing with Miriam and Sarah. Singing God's praises and worshiping Adonai is the high point of the day. Songs and psalms continue to guide our thoughts long after the singing fades away. Now, the main reason we have come together today is to celebrate young Timon's engagement to Thelma."

Cheers, whistling, and clapping made it impossible for him to add much more.

Heber woke early the next day. He took his morning meal and asked Amos for the best cart and the two healthy horses to take a long trip home. He had only been able to write letters to his mother and father, Simon and Judith, for the fifteen months since Yom Kippur the previous year. Riding against the wind, Heber sped to Sardis.

The sun was about to dip behind the mountain when he arrived at his father's home. For three days, Heber talked with his parents. The time seemed too short to tell them everything of Anthony, Miriam, Ateas, and Arpoxa. He spoke of other matters on his mind also. Slowly, details came out about running the inn and receiving guests, merchants, soldiers, and travelers.

Simon and Judith listened with interest as he described his hike up the mountain with the boys. They glowed with joy learning how the adventure led to the arrest of two outlaws. Heber's parents were thrilled to hear of Timon's engagement to Thelma. Throughout his many stories, he emphasized the importance of the Community of the Covenant.

Judith could not get enough details and asked Heber to describe the inn, but when he spoke about Cleon, the atmosphere changed. "Why does my brother keep that rascal on?" she scowled.

Heber also told of his concerns about Anthony. "I'm worried about his situation. Commander Felicior called him in for an audience. He disapproves of a legionary even talking to common workers about our Messiah!"

Finally, after describing everything else, Heber told his parents about Penelope and her five children. "I want to tell you about our new cook at the inn," he began. He had arrived at the main point of his conversation with his parents.

Three days after Heber left for Sardis, Anthony was called in again. "I have not received further complaints about you from Decimus or any others. I'm putting you back on patrols because smoke was spotted from a cave about twenty-five miles beyond the Door. Strangers are reported living there. Go there with your team to investigate. I decided to restore your normal pay."

"Yes sir. Thank you."

"About your earlier request. Yes, I will permit Brutus to be sold to you now, but it will cost you many months' pay, more than you will want to pay."

"Agreed. I will accept the price, sir."

PLATEAU AND CAVES IN THE LYCUS VALLEY

Entering a forested area at the base of the next set of mountain ranges, the squad moved cautiously. But instead of criminals, they found almost one hundred homeless people huddled in various caves. Women tried to comfort hungry children. All were shivering from the cold. Families seeking shelter were using the caves as a temporary dwelling.

Fathers complained bitterly about decisions made by the judicial courts. Each family had its own story of being forced out of their home. They had lost everything when the vineyards were destroyed.

"For decades, we've had an unwritten contract!" shouted one man, shaking his fist in Anthony's face. He was red-faced with anger. "My ancestors cultivated that vineyard, but when the land was turned over to wheat, we had to leave. Where are we to go with our little ones? There are hundreds of families like ours."

Upon his return to the garrison, Anthony dictated a short report for the records.

January 12, in the 16th year of Domitian[105]
From: Anthony Suros
To: Commander Felicior Priscus

Report on our investigation of the Southern Road:
We undertook a surveillance trip to where the plateau descends into the Lycus Valley. Yesterday we located a group of homeless families, about one hundred persons in all. All are discouraged after their recent loss of jobs and homes. They heard that caves in the area might serve as shelter for the rest of the winter. They are desperate but not dangerous.

However, they could become a problem if their needs are not attended to. They need to be brought back to the valley. I have written a short description of each of the twenty-three families. You might ask the mayor for a temporary provision of food. Housing must be found, especially since many are young children. With attention and care for their families' livelihood, we can prevent these men from becoming thieves and bandits.

THE MILITARY GARRISON IN PHILADELPHIA

Felicior laid down on his bed in the officer's room after returning from an unusual party at the Ben Shelah home. The oil lamp had been blown out, but sleep was far away. His head rested on his hands.

Confusing thoughts tumbled about, and he talked to himself, a habit when he could not sleep.

"I don't know why the Jewish family invited me to that party for Anthony's birthday. What am I to think about the evening? The soldier is forty years old today. He introduced me, and people clapped loudly. The old man, Amos, was limping the whole time. He seemed to be out of breath. The house was full of music and songs I never heard before. Yes, I knew the tunes but not the words.

"After the food was served, they sang a birthday song stating Anthony's age at the end of the second line. It's the song sung at every birthday in this city, with each time through quicker and livelier until, at the end, only the nimblest can articulate the words.

---

[105] January 12, AD 96

Miriam sang a song, and everyone lined up to shake her husband's hand.

"About two and a half years ago, all we had were riots. Loud voices screaming in our ears and an impossible commission from the mayor: Keep the public peace! Suros has done well leading scouts, delegating authority, and forming rotating teams. We learned how to help smaller villages in Cogamis Valley. Suros is at ease with slaves as well as with wealthier families. He and his Jewish relatives get along well.

"After the meal, Suros singled Obed out of the crowd. 'This evening should be about you, not me. I have received more than my share of gifts, but today I want to give you a special gift.'

"When I first heard Suros talk about 'agape love' in Sardis, it meant nothing. But tonight he took me aback. He said, 'Obed, this is my special gift to you!' And then Anthony led Obed into the courtyard. There was Brutus!

"Obed wiped his eyes. He couldn't believe what was happening. A legionary had given him his horse. I felt ashamed to see a grown man cry like that. I didn't know if it was shame or honor that stirred my heart when Anthony talked. 'Obed, I know it's hard for you when soldiers come around. We are known for bringing out the worst in people. But if you knew how hard we are trying to make Philadelphia a safe place, then maybe you could accept us. I hope you find it easier to get back to work. More than that, if you consider how much your family loves you, then maybe you'll feel better.'

"Words like that are impractical. Usually, they would leave me feeling empty. After all, when Suros asked to buy the horse, I thought he wanted the horse for his future farm. But to give such a gift to a man who can't even work a full day? Isn't Obed unfit to work? Perhaps this what Anthony means when he talks about 'agape love.'"

THE INN OF THE OPEN DOOR

Heber returned from Sardis after two weeks away. He intended to stay for only three days, but his conversations with his family made it clear he needed much more time there. He was not required at the inn now since few merchants ventured out in the winter. Besides, all the extra soldiers had gone home for the Saturnalia Festival. If they were needed, they would come back in late March or April.

Arriving at the inn, he felt nervous for the first time in many years. Penelope was at her work in the kitchen when he entered, preparing food for the few soldiers having quarters at the inn.

He stopped, breathing deeply as he took in details that he had seen a hundred times. The long, dark room ended with a smoky wood oven and stove at the far end, where the blackened chimney vented through the wall above the fire. Kitchen utensils hung neatly on the walls, and fresh water for drinking was stored in large brown ceramic pots and food bins. Each container was filled with vegetables and dried fruits.

"I hope you had a good visit with your parents," Penelope said, glancing up briefly.

"Oh, I did. I forgot how much I missed them."

"Well, you've only seen them once in the last year and a half."

"Penelope, are your parents still alive? I never asked about your parents."

"No, they died shortly after Sandra was born."

"I'm sorry about that. I would have loved to have met them." Heber was always a bit timid. He did not know how to get around to telling her why he was talking to her.

"They would have loved to meet you too, Heber. I would have told them a lot about you." Penelope also wanted to speak personally to Heber but did not know how bold to be.

"What would you have said to them about me?" Heber asked timidly.

"I would have told them how my son says you are such a hero. You know, Heber," she said, "I have something I want to talk about."

"Yes," he said, "and I have something I wanted to ask you."

"You go first," she said, laughing. "Men always go first."

His face was slightly red, and he could not bring himself to speak his mind openly. He started with an oblique comment. "Well, in two weeks, on February 2, I turn forty-two."

"I'm catching up to you. On December 1, this year, I'll be forty-one."

"I went to Sardis, and I ended up staying there longer than I intended. I told Father and Mother about you, Penelope."

"Why did it take so long for you to come back, then?"

"I suppose it was because I had so much to tell them about you."

"You're fooling me!"

"Not really, because, you see, I had a tough decision."

A gleam shone in her eye. "What was difficult, your decision or the topic?"

Again he was on the verge of opening his heart to her, but he could not say it. Instead, he told her something about himself.

"I have talked with you many times, but I never told you my full story. I was married and I had the hope of a child. Both my wife and my little son died after she gave birth."

"I'm so sorry to hear that. Actually, Miriam told me about it soon after you arrived."

"She did? I never knew that you knew about my loneliness...I mean, my sorrow."

"She told me that you were going to get married again, much later, to another woman, but her ship went down off the coast of Perga."

"So you know about that pain too," he said, grateful not to have to explain it all.

"Yes, I know a few facts...but I don't know how you handle the ache."

"Well, I know something about your hurt too, Penelope. Anthony told me about the terrible loss of Nikias, your husband. He told me what a dreadful moment it was for you, for your children, and for your husband's brothers too."

"See, I was certain that you knew about me!" Her voice expressed both the delight of discovery and the hope for more. "At first I thought Amos and Abigail were feeling pity for me when they invited me here to the inn. I didn't want to come here. I hated leaving Olive Grove Farm—the quietness there, the orchards, and the smell of fruit. Then I learned Amos and Abigail were concerned for everything, especially for my children, their education, my safety, food, and a place to stay."

"Penelope," he said, having found just the right emotion and the correct expression, "Amos and Abigail can't be concerned about everything. Almost, yes, but not *everything*."

"What do you mean?"

"That's why I had to stay for a while with my father and mother in Sardis. I told them about you. My mother and father listened carefully when I said, 'I want you to understand what I really feel for

Penelope. Father, I need your prayers.' You know it takes me a long time to speak about what is really on my mind."

Penelope placed her knife on the table and tossed her head back at an angle. The sun was shining through the high window in the wall, and rays of light played a magic trick with her hair. Each tiny hair was distinct, swept back from her forehead and hanging down over her back, showing off the slim lines of her neck.

She took a deep breath, almost unable to speak. "So what did you ask for prayer about? Were those prayers answered?"

"Yes, they were answered. I got a double blessing."

"What is a double blessing?"

"It's when a father and a mother in a family agree completely on something."

She could not speak but only swallowed, and her chest heaved with emotion.

He had found both his moment and the words he was looking for. "Penelope, it's fine for me to be a hero for Evander, to take Harmon with me to the agora, and to show Sandra how to write and draw. But that's not all I want. I don't just want to be their hero anymore. I want to be their father, to take them in. More than anything, I want to be beside you every day, to walk with you, to talk together about big things and little things, to share everything together."

Her eyes were shining brightly, her mouth half open in expectancy and joy.

But once he found his words, he would not stop. He took another deep breath. "You are certainly going to ask me how I, a Jew, could marry you, a non-Jew. I know we will face questions every day if you accept what I am asking you. It might even cause problems. But I want to be your husband, I want you to be my wife, and I want us to be a family. I can't ever take the place of Nikias, and I would never try to do that.

"I had to go to Sardis to talk to Father and Mother, not about being a family with you or a husband but about marrying a non-Jew. That was what we talked about for so many days. It was helpful to me. We talked about Eugene and Lyris, an elderly couple who got married there. He is a Gentile too, the grandfather of the two boys Anthony helped in Sardis. Lyris is a Jew, a faithful woman. Lyris and Eugene were drawn together because of Yeshua's message. Then I went to their little house in my father's vineyard, and we talked about Anthony and Miriam. I walked the streets of Sardis and up onto the mountain."

"Then, finally, you got back here!" She had found her voice, joyful and playful.

"Yes, so I have a question for you. Could you ever consider marrying me?"

"Oh, I've considered it many times." The playful part of her personality came out. "You know, you and Nikias are so different!"

"How am I different from Nikias?" His voice had a slightly defensive tone.

"He was so quick! As soon as he got an idea in his head, it was done, good or bad. You are...how shall I put it?"

"I know; I'm slow and deliberate. I make up my mind slowly."

"Nikias was impatient. He didn't get along with Evander. They had lots of quarrels. Evander thinks a lot of you. He says you listen to him. A single comment shapes his thinking."

"So I'm not quick, which is negative, but I'm patient. Is that positive?"

"Nikias was poor. You come from a wealthy family. He wanted to buy land, to start our own farm, but you have land and have never started a family. He was a follower of Greek gods but was learning about Yeshua Messiah. You are a Jew. Aren't you complete opposites?"

Heber had not considered his next step. How did non-Jews accept an offer of marriage? Would they have a Jewish wedding? Would they have a short or a long engagement? How would they deal with all the questions from so many sources?

She had a twinkle in her eye, and he thought she was playing for time. Wondering if she would accept his proposal, he leaned forward, no longer on the defensive but speaking earnestly. "No, I mean it, Penelope. I love you so much. I want to marry you and be a father, as much as I can, for your little ones."

"Yes, I love you too, and if you are going to be a father, you'll soon find out they're not just 'little ones.' Sometimes they have big arguments. You know, they need a father; they really do. Could I ever love two men who are such opposites? Yes, Heber, I think we should be married."

Sandra walked in just then, ready to help her mother in the kitchen, but she had heard the last six words. She clapped her hands. "Oh, Heber, you are going to be our father! Is that right? Is that so, Mommy? Isn't this wonderful, Mommy?"

"So much for keeping anything secret," said Penelope, suddenly awash with tears. She hid her face in Sandra's neck. Heber passed his hand softly over the little girl's head, barely touching Penelope's shoulder.

He felt a thrill hearing her say her words of acceptance of his love.

I'm always too slow. If I had asked Penelope sooner, we could have talked about the way to tell others. What do Gentiles do for an engagement? If they have one and celebrate a Jewish betrothal, how long will we have to wait until we get married? It will be all over the city before the noon meal is served! I'm always too slow, too quiet. Why is that? I've always been that way! I hope Penelope will speed me up a bit; I need her in lots of ways! Thank you, Lord. You heard my prayers.

Heber was right. The news had spread all over before the end of the day. By the time Miriam and Anthony found time to sit with Heber and Penelope to talk with them privately, the last eleven days of January had already sped by.

"We are so happy for you," said Anthony.

Miriam echoed his words. "You will be a wonderful family! I just know it!"

Heber looked bashful and didn't speak, so Anthony asked, "When are you going to get married?"

Faced with a practical, factual question, Heber did not answer right away. "We think the second week of May will be the right time. Chores will be over, the early planting done. Early harvest will be right around the corner, so we can invite my family from Sardis and Penelope's family from Olive Grove."

"A spring wedding in Philadelphia...what could be more beautiful?" Miriam gushed. Plans were being made while some tongues were beginning to wag.

AMOS AND ABIGAIL'S HOME

Many children lived on Amos's farm, and Miriam taught them her favorite parts of their ancient Jewish songs. One was the first

Miriam's mother had taught her, "The Lord is my shepherd; I shall not want."[106] Miriam had heard her mother singing this as a little girl, and Grace picked it up immediately.

During Grace's fifth birthday party, Miriam brought the little children into the center of a circle. Adults sat on the floor or on the couches, and the children danced in the center of the room.

Ruth, who was soon to give birth, helped with the music, as did Sarah. Even Obed clapped, accompanying the words. Being able to hug the horse, comb its mane, talk to it, and be comforted by its warm body during the last month had helped rid Obed of his many fears.

Miriam taught the children a new song. "Come, children, this is the moment to sing 'The Creation of the Animals'!"

God made little butterflies
  flittering about.
Watch those little hummingbirds
  flapping tiny wings.
Storks fly with long, strong beaks
  and sharp eyes like a scout.
Bees fly. Don't bother them.
  Careful of their painful stings!

God made little fishes
  swimming in the waters.
Starfish and octopus,
  look for a slimy arm!
Big blackfish, small white fish,
  many sons and daughters.
Bass and trout are great to catch,
  But not one swims at this farm.

Giant animals in forests,
  hunting for their brunch.
Lions roar, vultures soar,
  cheetahs run really fast.
Cats' tails wag, eyes alert.

[106] Psalm 23:1

That one found its lunch.
Calves start life standing wobbly,
Walk before a day has passed.

Donkeys let the whole world know
God gave them no song.
Cows moo loud then munch.
Cats stretch their backs and purr.
Horses proudly stretch their necks,
marching through the throng.
Dogs and cats are best of all.
Come to stroke their silky fur.

The children had never seen most of the animals. Still, they enjoyed the actions and moving about, and everyone laughed, joining in with the children. Part of the fun was learning to make animal sounds, and when Miriam asked her daughter how old she was, she held up five fingers, saying, "I'm five years old."

Chapter 36
Amos

AMOS AND ABIGAIL'S HOME

Winter ended in Philadelphia with early warm spring breezes. Oleander bushes burst open earlier than people could remember. Their red, pink, and white blossoms added to the fragrance of other flowering bushes. Varieties of wildflowers with dark red and light pink petals kissed the warm air blowing softly from the south. Snow on the mountain had reached its lowest points in the winter and was now receding quickly.

Like young dancing calves and colts, boys flocked to the sports arena. The training was in full swing for the Games to be held in May. The thrill of physical activities beckoned stronger than mathematics, government, philosophy, and literature.

Discontent in Martha's home turned into a steady drip, something like Michael's leaky roof during the winter. "You are keeping me away from my own flesh and blood!" she complained. Michael forced himself not to shout at his wife. He had formed a new habit; he closed his eyes when she started ranting this way.

"Michael, do you remember our ancestor, Jacob? He had twelve sons and a daughter, and you won't even acknowledge one great-grandson!" But nothing she said would change his mind.

Dorcas kept getting tidbits of news, including the words of the song Miriam had sung to the children the day before. A generation younger than Martha, she was proud that her son, Mith, had found a way to keep them up on the news. Asa was now walking. She told Martha, "At Grace's birthday party, Asa laughed hard. People imitated the sounds of animals, and he lost his balance, suddenly falling on his bottom. He didn't know whether to laugh or cry. You know, it's strange, but I've noticed it's after Mith comes back from the inn that he tells me about the Ben Shelah family."

The three elders found themselves forming a stronger friendship. They regularly confirmed the correctness of their decision. "Have you heard the latest?" Daniel asked. "Simon Ben Shelah encouraged Heber, his son, to marry a non-Jew. Yes, she's a widow with five children. The entire Ben Shelah family has now been corrupted!"

Zacharias threw up his hands as this new bit of news took his breath away. "So we did the right thing! Antipas permitted his granddaughter to marry a legionary; that was the first mistake. Next, Simon encourages his son, a widower, to marry a non-Jew. But their brother, Amos, is worse than both Antipas and Simon. He has everyone—Greeks, Romans, and Scythians—to his house. Someone said he calls the pagans his 'brothers and sisters.' Worst of all, he's calling his gatherings the 'Community of the Covenant'!"

Amos felt tired as he woke up late on the day of Purim. He wanted to imitate Esther and all her friends long ago who participated in a great feast. This feast was one of his favorites. Amos eagerly awaited the funny comments that would be made about ancient enemies after the supper hour.

I must continue to depend on Heber to manage the inn. Even if he is slower in speech, he is truthful and honest. I hear that my old friends at the synagogue are distraught. How do the women in my house know what's going on with those families? I've never figured that out.

However, he simply rolled over in bed, collecting his thoughts. Instead of motivating his family and friends with a rousing talk after the supper feast, he decided to honor Abigail. She had more energy these days and a willingness to speak with old and young alike.

Amos rested in bed all day, and he knew exactly what he wanted to say to his family and their guests. By evening, he felt a little stronger. Once again, the great room was packed. Food poured out of the kitchen while the people ate and chatted until the last platter and bowl were collected for cleaning.

Amos stood in the middle of the room, delighted at such an attentive gathering. "Our people were persecuted in the time of ancient Queen Esther. This evening we are going to tell this story from our scriptures and say some funny things. This is because intense emotions arise when someone wants to do us harm. For example, an evil man in the story, Haman, fostered feelings of hate. He asked the king for a special day to kill all the Jews in the Persian Empire.

"Unless something stops those emotions, jealousy and anger will grow unseen, underground like the roots of a tree. Eventually harmful fruit appears on the branches, bad for everyone. Anger is the bud that blossoms into revenge; retaliation is the fully formed fruit.

"Forgiveness and reconciliation were never part of Haman's life. This evening I want to speak about jealousy. It's something we don't like to admit as being in our own lives.

"Distrust causes us to think of ways to hurt others. We can cut off joy in another person. We may try to seize a person's riches or damage his reputation. In the worst situations, children are left fatherless. Haman conceived an evil plan and directed it against Jews in the entire realm. Resentment leads to terrible words being spoken. Do you know of people who find themselves rejected or bullied? Harsh words said today are remembered decades later.

"Is there any way to remove those toxic emotions? Yes, there is. When Yeshua hung upon a tree, he prayed for his enemies. The Tree of Death was supposed to do away with him, but it became something different. It is a Tree of Life bringing forgiveness. Not only the thirst for revenge but every other sin is also taken away. I saw this happen to my precious wife. She is being restored, returning to the beautiful woman I married almost fifty-four years ago.

"This is what I mean when I call our gathering the Community of the Covenant. We are people who want to be rid of all bitterness, rage, anger, brawling, and slander, along with every form of malice. We seek to be kind and compassionate to one another, forgiving each other, just as in Christ, God forgave us. That is how I want us to live."[107]

Thelma was so excited about her upcoming wedding that she could hardly concentrate on what Amos was saying. She imagined her plans coming to life, the flower arrangements, and the way she would comb her hair. She wanted Penelope's girls to be part of the little procession.

Miriam saw Thelma and Timon holding hands, trying not to let others see their physical attraction. Miriam knew they were secretly communicating about the wedding.

---

[107] From Ephesians 4:31–32

Her attention was far removed from the talk being given by Amos. *Thelma and Timon will soon be married, Lord, and they will have children. Why have you not yet given me my own?*

She caught herself drifting into self-pity, and recognizing the sign of jealousy, she forced herself to listen to what Amos was saying. Still, it took effort, minute by minute.

Two weeks had passed, and Amos looked tired and gray. Abigail wrapped her arm around his shoulders. "Amos, my dear, let younger men do some of the things!"

"No, I'm fine," he said, casting aside her suggestion. "I've just been working too hard around the farm. Ever since Sarah began bringing friends to our home, I've been tired. Young women...so much noise, squealing, and laughter. I'll lie down and rest until everyone is here. Call me to come downstairs. This is a special day, the Sabbath before Passover. I must help them all prepare for this holy time. For that to happen, I must be prepared."

Abigail walked down the steps carefully. She felt her age.

Amos lay on the bed, once again remembering his father's blessing. Although he was ready for the Sabbath meditation, he returned to that day seven years ago. It was as if he were back in Pergamum with his father, Eliab.

"Amos, my third child, and my first son. Your sisters were burned by the flames, young lives whose loss still leaves me distressed. You will always feel that grief because you loved each of them. But Amos, my son, you will be healed too, and you will bring healing to others. You will rise above the level of our enemies. Your weapons will be words of peace, piercing deeper into men's hearts than a double-edged sword. You will avenge your enemies because your door is open. Hospitality will make you an overcomer."

Father gave me his blessing. It's strange because even though he spoke so softly, those words still echo loudly in my heart. In a few moments, I will lead our Community of the Covenant. I will remind them, "Hear, O Israel! The Lord our God, the Lord is one. You shall love the Lord your God with all your heart, with all your soul, and with all your strength."[108]

---

[108] Deuteronomy 6:4–5

Amos sat up, ready to go downstairs, but felt a painful constriction in his chest. "Abigail!" He called her again and lay back on the bed. Abigail came, touched his forehead, and held his hand. "I'll bring some water, shall I?"

"Yes, please, some water. I'm thirsty."

Amos felt better after stressing, "Abigail, you speak better than I do. I can't explain my emotions to others. You used to do it, and now you've started again. Your amazing openness to others has blessed me ever since we were married, years ago today, remember? It's been since we went to Jerusalem that things changed."

In their memories, they went back to Alexandria, and then she talked about the upcoming wedding. "Ruth is due to deliver her baby. How I love seeing Heber and Penelope; they have a new glow on their faces. Timon and Thelma are planning their wedding. So many good things are happening."

Amos reached for Abigail's hand, and suddenly he felt an intense, streaking pain down his left arm. He gripped Abigail's hand with his right hand and tried to sit up, but the pain in his chest intensified. Abigail watched him as his eyes widened.

"Here! Take another drink of water." An urgent tone flowed through her words.

Trying to sit up, Amos dropped back, his head sinking into the pillow. It took her a few moments to realize his breathing was strained, irregular, and fading.

She cried out, "Come! Everyone!"

One by one, the family members came to the room, running.

A thin pillow supported him. Amos wanted to speak, but he had no breath left. *I didn't have time to bless you, my family. Sorry...I'm so sorry! I should have had a blessing for each of you like my father did for me. I'm so sorry. Obed! I wanted to bless you with words like my father did for me before he passed away. I had those words ready to give to each of you, but I can't...now. I wanted to comfort you with my last breath. I'm so...sorry.*

His hands grew limp, and the crying began.

Abigail gave a dull moan, held both hands to her chest, then took the limp hands of her husband and wailed. Her repeated cry was a loud, long "Oh" starting high and falling slowly. Abigail's hands covered her eyes. She had no words for her ultimate loss. For her children, she had grief, but for a long life shared with Amos, there were no words.

Isabel came to one side, holding Abigail, and Miriam, on the other, comforted the old woman.

Wailing filled the house. "Today of all days...the Lord took him on our fifty-fourth anniversary! Amos didn't know how special this evening was going to be. I planned the biggest party since we arrived here. It was a surprise for him!"

Her grief grew as her cries became louder. "And now grief instead of a party! Ohhh!"

Heber called the servants and told them that their master was dead. All the people coming for the event arrived, and most stayed all night, sharing the pain of the widow who refused comfort.

After his death, the eyes and mouth were closed with special care. By the light of the oil lamps, his most trusted servant carried out the hair and beard ritual shaving as it was done in Alexandria. His body was washed, covered with herbs, and wrapped in a white linen shroud.

Timon went to the garrison to tell Anthony, but he was away.

Another servant went to the pigeon pens, attached the first tiny parchment message to a homing pigeon's leg, and then tossed it in the air. The bird circled and then headed for its own distant city. Heber waved to the bird as it flew around the farm. He whispered, "I hope this reaches Marcos and Marcella in Pergamum. Our lawyer needs to know right away."

He repeated the action four more times. Similar letters went to Jonathan in Thyatira, Simon in Sardis, Daniel in Laodicea, and Joshua in Smyrna.

In Pergamum, early the following morning, Marcos was having breakfast when his steward excitedly rushed in from the back garden. "Master Marcos, this message just arrived by pigeon from Philadelphia."

Marcos wrote a letter expressing his sorrow to the family. He recommended that they immediately contact their local family lawyer to handle any legal considerations.

Heber took a horse and rode to the homes of the Jewish families. "Amos Ben Shelah died last night in bed at home," he said at the doors of several families. "The funeral will take place at high noon. Please come if you want to extend your sympathies to the family."

Of the men, only Mith came. The others kept away. As far as they were concerned, Amos had died the previous year. But Dorcas and Martha brought food, saying they were going to remain all day. It was their first visit to the Ben Shelah home in a long time.

Heber took one of the farm wagons and hurried to the inn. He told Cleon that the inn would accept guests, but regular meals would not be served that day. Guests would have to go to the local thermopolia for their meals. He ran across to Penelope's home, the makeshift place where she was living with Thelma. Then he went to Ateas and Arpoxa's room. By late morning, they were all back at the farmhouse and found it full of mourners.

One of the servants went outside with Heber. In the morning, they dug a deep trench near an apple tree. It was Amos's special place of prayer, overlooking the valley.

Amos preferred this spot to all others. It was where he often spent the early morning hours. Bright petals on its branches promised abundant fruit at harvest.

They cried for him, sobbing as the men carried Amos's body out of the house. The sun had just passed its highest point in the sky. Mith, Jesse, Obed, and Heber recited Psalm 91 together, and then Heber led the prayers.

Afterward, he said, "I wish Zacharias were here to say the prayers for burial. Forgive me if I don't do it just the way it should be done, but I loved my uncle, and I know he won't mind if I don't say things perfectly at this moment." He wiped the tears from his eyes as he told everyone gathered in the circle how much Amos meant to him.

Obed and Abigail held onto each other. Isabel stood with Sarah on one side, the daughter's head resting on her mother's shoulder.

Ruth stood on the other side, weighed down by the child about to be born. Mith came to stand beside his promised bride, and Dorcas nodded at Martha, who had her arm around Ruth's waist.

It was a moment for silence. For thankfulness of a life well lived. For reflection on untold pain and grief. For success, love, and a man who knew how to draw others into his community.

Amos was placed into the grave in a linen shroud. By tradition, the burial place would remain uncovered for three days in case Amos should wake up.

The Ben Shelah home was transformed into a house of mourning, and grief was expressed in many ways. Abigail cried, lamenting. Miriam offered consolation and put her arms around her aunt.

Obed wrapped his arms around his chest and leaned forward and then backward, repeating words of affection for his father.

Penelope and her children watched the family, sharing in the grief but still observers, not yet fully part of the family. She watched Heber sit down. He brought her children close to him, the five he was about to adopt, and he included Grace and Saulius and then the farm children. He explained to them, slowly and carefully, what had happened to Amos, how he died, and why everyone was crying.

"No, we are not going to see him again, not here, but we will see him in heaven one day," he said. "This is a moment of mystery. Because Yeshua rose from the grave, we, too, are going to rise after we die."

In the evening, Timon and Thelma knelt beside the bereft widow. "Aunt Abigail," said Timon, "we are going to postpone our wedding. We want to be with you. We will be married later, but we don't have a date right now. First we will grieve with you."

Ruth sat down with Jesse on Monday morning, the day after Passover ended. "This was supposed to be Thelma and Timon's wedding day," Ruth said, squeezing his hand. Then she squeezed his hand again, harder this time. She clenched her teeth as a second contraction came. "Oh! I think today you are going to be a father for the second time." She smiled then winced again. He hugged her, putting his face beside her neck and stroking her hair.

"I'll go and call Mother," Jesse said, rushing out to hitch a horse to the wagon. He had not been in his father's house for more than eighteen months. He knocked on the door and announced the need for a midwife. Dorcas began to ready herself when Daniel objected. "My wife, two weeks ago you spent the whole day there! Do not go to their house again!"

She exploded, "I'm a midwife, and I'm not going to let my daughter-in-law bring a child into the world without help! No matter how much you order me around, you will not interfere in this!"

"You disobey me!" Daniel yelled. "There are consequences for women who disobey their husbands!"

His voice was threatening, but she knew it was only his way of objecting, so she remarked, "You are so obstinate! Why yield to those whose minds have made you stray from Adonai? He gave us the gift of children and grandchildren."

She could argue the traditions, beliefs, and obedience as intelligently as, or better than, her husband. "Should I neglect my own flesh and blood?"

"But they've been excluded!" Daniel yelped like a tiny dog being backed into a corner.

"And you have forgotten the first commandment of the Torah!" Dorcas retorted. "It says that man and wife were to leave their parents and cling to each other—not to their parents!"

Dorcas took Jesse's arm in her own. The young man looked around his old home and left with his mother. "Now get this cart up to the Ben Shelah house as fast as you can," she demanded, sitting beside her son. He looked older, and she had been missing him so much.

Dorcas looked around the family circle when she arrived and said, "Rejoice in the life that God gives us. Be grateful for those who are faithful until death, and welcome those who begin their lives. Amos was a faithful man, and I considered him my friend."

She hugged Isabel and looked her in the eye. "You and I are almost the same age, but we are in such different surroundings. I'm sorry about the confusion between our families." She quickly left the great room and went upstairs to where Ruth was about to deliver her child.

In the late afternoon, the healthy crying of a new little voice sounded from upstairs. The squeals were those of a healthy baby boy. Ruth and Jesse held their second son, Hakkatan Ben Jesse, just two minutes old.

Dorcas said, "I knew it was going to be a boy! I'll have to tell Martha she may have to wait another year until the great-granddaughter she wanted is born. Jesse, go and fetch her and tell her that her second great-grandson is healthy and wants her to kiss him."

Miriam could not contain her smile. Others thought she was pleased with the arrival of the baby. Instead, she was thinking, *Yesterday was my thirty-first birthday. Five years ago today, Anthony and I adopted our little girl.*

Chapter 37
The Inn of the Open Door

THE INN OF THE OPEN DOOR

Later, looking back over the events, Miriam had trouble remembering how the date was picked for Penelope's wedding. She could not remember if it happened because Heber said, "Out of respect for the life of my Uncle Amos, I think we should wait forty days."

Or perhaps it was Penelope who said, "My husband breathed his last on May 9, and I can't be married until two years have gone by. It wouldn't be right for my memory of him. Also, we need at least forty days as we accompany Abigail's grief. So why don't we wait until the end of May?"

Thelma had wanted to be married sooner, but Timon urged a delay. "I think my father is willing to come after classes are over. If we could wait just a little longer...."

In the end, it was Heber's suggestion that immediately gained acceptance. "Why don't we have a double wedding?"

The date and the place were settled by Abigail. She said, "I know my husband would approve if he were alive. A special event like a double wedding calls for the largest celebration ever! Our house is too small, so let's have it at the inn on May 27!

"Heber, you can set tables in the center of the inner courtyard with the wedding party inside. The main entrance doors will be open so our friends, Zarrus, Arpoxa, and others, can watch. We'll offer the guests sitting outside something sweet and tasty. Meanwhile, the wedding guests inside will receive a wonderful meal."

Penelope beamed. "You know what Sandra says every night? Before she goes to sleep, she beams and tells me, 'Mommy, we are all getting married!' I try to tell her, 'No, darling, I'm getting married, and you're going to have a new daddy,' but she won't hear of it! She says, 'We're going to get married is absolutely clear, Mommy.' She doesn't understand it all yet."

They laughed at her childish interpretation, wiping tears from their eyes and struck by the innocence of an eight-year-old and how Sandra often expressed herself in fascinating ways.

Heber smiled. "I don't mind Sandra expressing it that way. Let her keep on saying it."

Around them, the events of the Festival of Artemis swirled for two weeks. The flower festival and hymn-singing groups progressed along the avenues. Priests and priestesses dressed in their brightest colors escorted each procession up and down Philadelphia's streets.

This was April. The world had come fully alive, promising harvest and prosperity.

May 1, in the 16th year of Domitian
From: Cleon in Philadelphia
To: Diotrephes Milon in Sardis

If you are well, then I am well. Burn this letter after reading it. The time has arrived to take your uncle's daughter to her rightful home. When you lure her away, you must call her by the name Grace. That's the name Miriam uses.

A double wedding is planned for Friday, May 27. Here are the plans: The wedding party will take place in the open space inside the Inn of the Open Door. Their friends will be seated on carpets outside, looking in. When you come, bring four or five men as helpers. Sit outside to the left as you face the main doors of the inn. Four tables, each with nine persons, will be set inside for the marriage supper. Large torches will light up the room.

Following the meal, I am going to tell stories, and then Miriam will sing a song. Everyone will clap after she stops, which will be your signal. Be ready. A stable boy will knock a torch over. Flames will engulf a pile of straw that has just been "accidentally" dropped on the ground.

Anthony will be at the table on the right as you look in from the entrance. For an instant, he'll take his eyes off his "daughter" when the fire starts. Any guards they may assign will be startled when I yell, "Fire!" Everybody will be jumping out of their chairs. Soldiers will rush to put out the flames. When you see them no longer guarding the door, at that moment, you and your men should run in, saying you want to help put out the fire. Increase the confusion by yelling loudly as soon as you see the flames.

The stable boy will be watching me. At the end of Miriam's song, I will drop my arm as a signal to him. Don't come to the center of the courtyard. Go to your right because the child will be at that table. You will have enough light to see the child while everyone is screaming. Seize the child, and leave the city immediately. Go to Sardis and then to Pergamum.

Remember, the child is five years old. Tell her, "Don't make any noise. We are taking you where you will be safe. We have to get you away from the fire!" This will keep her quiet...and afraid.

The Games begin in a few days, and I know I will win once more. I trust that you see the value of this information, both for you and for me.

After reading the letter, Diotrephes burned it. The thin roll of papyrus went up in smoke, leaving tiny filaments of black ash that curled and then fell limply. The smell of ashes was sweet to his nostrils. Cleon's secret was secure.

He told his new wife, Cynthia, about business in Philadelphia at the end of the month. "I will be away for three days, and then I will be going with friends to see my mother and uncle in Pergamum. I should be back home in nine days."

THE MILITARY GARRISON IN PHILADELPHIA

Felicior had already read the letter from the governor's office in Ephesus. Since he did not expect this kind of reassignment, he rolled it up and set it on the table. Then, opening the small scroll once more, he reread it as he paced across his small office.

May 6, in the 16th year of Domitian
From: Marcus Atillius Postumus Bradua, Propraetor
To: Felicior Priscus, Commander, Philadelphia Garrison

The time for new appointments has arrived. The commander of the Miletus Garrison is being transferred to another port city, Chalcedon. Winds can sometimes be contrary to ships passing through the Dardanelles. I want him to leave Miletus in mid-June and spend a week here in Ephesus giving me a report and speaking with the port authorities about the continuing problem of the silting in the Miletus harbor. His new duties will begin in the Garrison of Chalcedon on July 1.

Your actions of dismantling the bandits' gang on the Postal Road three years ago and more recently on the Southern Road speak well of your leadership. The social order has largely been restored around Philadelphia, so I have lifted the state of emergency. I noted your part in these accomplishments.

Commander Servius Callistratus, previously the commander in Soma and presently in Sardis, will replace you at the Garrison of Philadelphia. I am promoting him, so he will command both garrisons, those in Sardis and Philadelphia. Callistratus will reside in Sardis, traveling to Philadelphia as needed. His assignment begins on the last day of May.

Centurion Decimus, whose service has been notable during the time of social unrest, remains in Philadelphia. He will answer to Commander Servius. This is also a promotion for Decimus.

I am assigning you to a more responsible position, Commander of the Garrison in Miletus. You are to leave your post on June 1 and be in Miletus before June 6. That will give you a week with the present commander to familiarize yourself with the garrison.

Felicior paced the floor once more. He took a key from around his neck and opened a small wooden trunk. He removed a leather pouch holding two scrolls, which were among his most important documents.

The first was the original directive from Governor Marcus Atillius Postumus Bradua commissioning him to keep the public peace in Philadelphia. It read, "Remain in Philadelphia until the threat to commerce on the Southern Road has been removed."

The other document was from Commander Servius Callistratus, written three years before. It accused Anthony Suros of violating the Law of Majestas, the "Law of Offenses Against the Empire."

As dawn broke, Felicior stood at the open window for several minutes before sending a guard to the inn. "I want Suros here immediately," he said.

Soon Anthony stood before the commander. "I have been transferred, Suros," remarked Felicior. "My new assignment is Commander of the Miletus Garrison, on the coast. It is a challenging task. Security there involves not only port activities but travel for pilgrims coming to Didyma at the Temple of Apollo, the oracle of the gods in Asia Minor."[109]

"Congratulations, sir," replied Anthony. "This is a significant appointment."

"Propraetor Marcus Atillius Postumus Bradua, our chief magistrate in Ephesus, has ended the state of emergency. Soldiers called to quell the riots are being sent back to their respective garrisons. After the capture of two rebels, I am disbanding the squad. This meeting affects you."

"Why is that, sir?"

"This garrison will soon be under the command of Sardis."

"Which means?"

"Commander Servius Callistratus will now be your commanding officer."

"I see, sir." Anthony's heart started racing. During his duties on the Southern Road, Servius's finger-pointing had been forgotten, but it was coming back again.

Felicior took one of the scrolls from the leather bag. "This is his first denunciation. It reads, 'Anthony Suros consistently refuses to declare the Solemn Oath.' That is his first accusation.

---

[109] The massive Temple of Apollo in Didyma, modern-day Didim in Turkey, was known throughout the Greco-Roman world for "oracles," or prophecies and warnings about the future. The Sacred Way, a 10.7-mile (17 km) processional route, connected the port of Miletus to the Temple of Apollo. Based on markings made centuries ago, estimates suggest 20,000 man-days were needed to complete each enormous column. Thus, twenty men would take almost three years to complete just one of the scores of columns.

"Also, Suros, let me remind you that Servius has six more complaints. They were only made verbally. As of now, they have not been written, but they may haunt you in the future. I must tell you what else Commander Servius charges.

"Second, he believes you lied to receive land in Philippi. He says you exaggerated your wound. It would violate army regulations.

"Thirdly, having 'miraculously recovered,' he charges you with receiving rent from the farm, also against our regulations.

"Fourth, you were not present at the Declaration of the Solemn Oath in Pergamum in the tenth year of Domitian. Instead, you chose to train young boys for the Games.

"Fifth, Servius states you gave inadequate training to scouts serving in Legion XXI, the Predators. As a result, your legion was wiped out in May and June in the eleventh year of Domitian.

"Sixth, he believes you were incompetent. He says you should have captured the rebel leaders at Port Daskyleion. To complete that ineptness, you permitted their slave ship to escape.

"And lastly, he complains about the four gang members who escaped at Prosperity Village. Suros, I must warn you. Half-truths or not, Servius is working to prosecute you in a military court."

"Yes, Commander Servius has spoken to me about each of these concerns, sir."

"It is a little more complex than that, Suros. You signed up for five years as a reservist. You've completed three years, so you have two more. You will serve them here in Philadelphia. Servius may bring all these charges against you when you are directly under his command. Understood?"

"Yes sir."

Felicior disagreed with me about my belief in the Messiah when I began serving under him in Sardis, but he has never objected to my conduct as a soldier. Felicior is taking me into his confidence. Why? He didn't need to tell me about the personal correspondence he had with Servius. If Felicior disagrees with my beliefs, why hasn't he acted on these charges?

Just as he had done when he asked about Brutus, Anthony heard a voice inside prodding him to do something unexpected. "Sir, I have three requests."

"You aren't going to ask for another horse, are you?"

"No, but I want you to come to a double wedding as the guest of the Ben Shelah family. Secondly, I want you to post two soldiers at the door of the inn during the wedding."

"Two easy requests. What's the third?"

"The third is this: I want Omerod and Bellinus with me at the wedding. It will be a farewell gesture. They will return to Sardis, and I would like to publicly thank them for their help in keeping the peace."

"Easy requests, as I said. Why didn't you ask something difficult?"

THE INN OF THE OPEN DOOR

All day, the women at the farm laughed and talked. Heber, Obed, and Jesse had been ordered out of the house, and no men were allowed in. Penelope's hair had to be suitable for her wedding. One of the servants combed it three different ways before everyone liked it. Penelope wore a tiny crown made of gold on the top of her head. Her hair hung down to the middle of her back. Starting at her temples, two strands met at the nape of her neck, keeping her freshly washed and scented hair in place. A filament of gold was laced through flowers. These were woven through strands of hair and hung down her back.

Her oval face was shaded with rouge, darkening was around her eyes, and a hint of blue shone from her eyelids. Her nose ring came with matching earrings. The red ointment for her lips came at considerable cost from the lands beyond the East.

The white linen *peplos* she wore reached to her ankles. It had short sleeves, and a sheer scarf made of the thinnest cotton covered her head. The cotton was embellished with long threads of deep blue. It would be her "covering of humility" when they declared their covenant of marriage. The scarf was a symbol of God's presence over her head, over her life, and over her home.

Obed and Isabel had given Penelope a gift of an expensive necklace made of silver. It held five red gems, one for each of her children.

Penelope's children had never seen her dressed like this. They were playing in the large central room of the house when she came down the stairs. "Mommy, you are sooo beautiful!" breathed Sandra.

Rhoda, now thirteen years old and already considered a young woman, hugged her mother. "I'm so very happy for you, Mommy."

Thelma was radiant as well. Her light blue *peplos* had been embroidered by Arpoxa as a gift from her and Ateas. Over her heart, two eagles soared, their wings extended. The wings just touched each other, a symbol of their coming together as husband and wife. Thelma's black hair reached below her waist. She wanted her hair done in several thin braids; it was a fashion common among young women in the city.

The same color of blue used by Penelope was lightly painted on her eyelids. She wore a simple silver nose ring and matching earrings, gifts from Miriam. As she emerged from Miriam's room, where she was being readied, the household burst out, "You are beautiful! What a wonderful wedding day!" White lace around her waist accentuated her lovely figure. She was given flowers to hold: red, pink, and white oleander sprays.

The horses and carriages arrived at the farmhouse as the sun began to dip behind the mountain. The drivers drove down the hill, through the Northern Gate, and on to the Avenue of the Temples. People along the way saw them coming. Shouts were heard, and by the time the wagons drove past, people were on the edge of the streets, waving, exclaiming, and caught up in the event. "Look, everyone! A double wedding!"

About six in the evening, they arrived at the inn. The men were waiting inside. Penelope gracefully lowered herself and passed her daughter, Melody, to Miriam. Grace walked beside her mother, holding onto her mother's tunic.

Thelma looked around and exclaimed, "Look, it's as if all the workers repairing the baths have decided to come and see what's happening. There must be hundreds gathered outside the inn on those carpets! And there's Timon! My husband! He's so handsome! I think I am going to cry!"

"Come this way," said Obed. He had been made the new leader of the family in his father's place. He seemed calmer now, and with hardly any soldiers in the inn during the past month, he was better able to control his feelings.

Abigail got down from the wagon. She was wearing black, out of respect for the recent death of her beloved husband. She said she would wear black for one year. "I'm the one who lost my husband. You are both gaining yours! I'll wear black even while I enjoy looking at your bright colors." She had laughed saying that but knew a wide variety of memories would shake her emotions all evening.

Inside the inn, the canopy had been set on four posts. Blue cloth matched the color of the sky during the day. "It's where you say your vows," Miriam whispered to Penelope.

Heber's family had arrived from Sardis, including Simon and Judith, his parents; Ezar, his brother, and Chenya, his sister-in-law; and their three children: Elaine, Tamir, and Amath.[110] They were waiting in the courtyard.

Felicior, talking with Omerod and Bellinus, stood to one side. Overlooking the pavement in front of the inn, they remained in position, watching over the entire courtyard. Three other soldiers stood at the entrance, slightly inside the building.

Obed and his family had invited Mayor Aurelius Manilius Hermippus and his wife. Five others joined them: Damian, the gymnasium director, and his wife; Giles and his wife; and Calisto, Timon's father. Felicior and these important guests wore the same wedding garments as the others. All were gifts from Arpoxa's workshop.

Two tall torches were lit, and stable boys poured oil on long rags, which were bunched up and tied to look like a cauliflower. Two more torches were placed at the front, on either side of the door, and were occasionally replenished with oil.

The blue canopy fluttered as a light breeze passed through the courtyard. Heber and Penelope stood under it, smiling.

Obed read the words of their faith and proclaimed, "God, the Lord of Israel is One." Heber promised to love and cherish Penelope. Sandra moved to the canopy and stood holding one of its four legs. Penelope took her necklace and wound it around Heber's neck, forming the symbol of eternity.

Jesse gave them a cup of wine to drink, and each one sipped a little, alternating until the cup was empty. Then Heber reached outside the shelter of the canopy and dropped the ceramic cup on

---

[110] The stories of these persons are found in *Never Enough Gold: A Chronicle of Sardis.*

the stone floor. It shattered into hundreds of tiny pieces. Their old lives had ended, and a new life was beginning.

The sun was setting behind Mount Tmolus when Timon and Thelma took their turn, making the same promises. Timon looked at his father, and a look of restrained pride covered Calisto's face. The wedding ceremony was performed, and a second cup was dropped outside of the canopy's protection.

Isabel was standing beside the respected guests from the acropolis. Miriam saw her explaining the symbols of the wedding ceremony. Suddenly, she saw Calisto smile. Then he bowed his head and covered his face with his hands. He seemed to have understood the profound symbols of the strange wedding his son had just completed.

Slightly deaf, Calisto leaned over to his friend Damian and whispered, except his voice was loud enough for everyone to hear. "It's like Greek theater! Look at these Jews! Symbols of eternity, wine, and broken cups! Why it's better than Greek plays because their faces aren't hidden by a mask. Look, here come the torches lighting up the night as love lights up their lives! My son has become so cultured! I must ask him how he thought up all these nice touches for the ceremony."

As the wedding vows were made, people seated outside the inn were told several times to be quiet. Abigail had not counted on so much noise.

Obed invited the guests to recline at their respective tables. Heber and Penelope reclined on the central couch. To their right, in order of age, were Evander, Rhoda, Harmon, Sandra, and Melody. On the couch to the left, Thelma reclined against Timon's chest. Melody kept climbing down to the stone pavement and climbing back up. People outside chuckled at this and nodded understandingly.

The table to the right, the one Diotrephes was watching, also had nine people around it: Anthony, Miriam, and Grace; Obed and Isabel; and Jesse, Ruth, Asa, and Sarah.

The new little boy, Hakkatan Ben Jesse, was sleeping in a crib in a room next to the kitchen. Zarrus and Arpoxa had agreed to look after the little ones there if they cried or needed attention. From that position, generally used as a storage room, they could see the entire wedding party. No one could see them in the dark interior.

Heber's family reclined around the third table, the one to the left of the wedding party: Simon and Judith, Ezar and Chenya, and their three children: Elaine, Tamir, and Amath. Lyris and Eugene had also come from Sardis, special guests Miriam wanted to be present.

Finally, close to the kitchen, which was on the left side of the courtyard, the dignitaries of the city of Philadelphia were present: Mayor Aurelius and his wife; a council member, Damian, and his wife; Giles and his wife; Felicior; and Calisto.

The evening was slightly marred by the absence of Penelope's family. Her four brothers-in-law had been saddened by the death of Nikias. Three brothers wanted to be present, but the youngest brother and all four wives were adamantly against attending. They might individually see Penelope in the future. However, they could not support her marriage to a man who, like Nikias, followed Yeshua as the Messiah. They were offended by Penelope leaving the worship of their Greek gods.

Mealtime had arrived. Servants kept filling plates on the small, square tables. Lamb, cut into cubes, was served in heated ceramic bowls. Chickpeas with sesame sauce, uncooked nut crescents, turnip baskets with pine nuts, cabbage salad, and flatbread were served with wine. The meal was finished with fruit and raisins.

During the meal, Anthony brushed Miriam's hair. She was leaning against his chest, and he said in a hushed voice, "If you look carefully out the door, you will see an old friend."

"Who is it?" she asked.

"Would you believe it? Diotrephes!"

The smile froze on her face. "Tell me again!"

"Diotrephes is outside, watching the wedding supper. There's a crowd now, and he's standing among the spectators."

"How would he know about this event?"

"There's only one way."

"Which is?"

"Three years ago, Cleon helped Diotrephes get into Simon and Judith's house."

"Yes, and that's when Ravid caught him."

"Did Cleon have the details of this wedding supper?"

"Aunt Abigail and Obed explained every detail. Cleon is not only present! He's in charge of all the arrangements!"

The crowd watching outside had grown, and some were clamoring to get a better look inside.

"Well, Diotrephes can't come in since two armed soldiers are guarding the entrance. Ah, wait, have I just caught a glimpse of four muscular men standing behind Diotrephes? No…well, maybe there is another one. I can't tell if he is with Diotrephes or… Yes, four, maybe five, strong men are with him. It's a very suspicious situation."

At that moment, having finished the meal, Obed asked for silence. "Distinguished Mayor, members of city hall, honored guests, ladies and gentlemen: My father blessed me every day of his life with his wise words, hard work, and kind hospitality. Unfortunately, he passed away recently. We all miss him. He would have loved to have been here.

"Tonight, five children will be blessed because a groom is adopting them as his own children. Friends, this wedding supper is not only a double wedding. We are honored to have Mayor Aurelius Manilius Hermippus dine with us tonight. Only he can authorize adoptions, so you are going to see five children being given new names. You are all witnesses to this."

Clapping and whistles sounded as each of Penelope's children came forward. Heber stood on one side and Penelope on the other. All seven held hands, forming a line. For them, the wedding supper also meant getting a new name. Today, on May 27, each child knew the name given by their father. Now they had Heber's name as well, the man who had come into their lives so unexpectedly.

The mayor stood to his full height, his dignity on display to hundreds of people in a happy moment. "You have a new name, my boy, Evander Longinus Ben Shelah."

People clapped and cheered. The same family name was given to Rhoda, Harmon, Sandra, and Melody.

When it was Sandra's turn, she looked up at the mayor and said in a loud, piercing voice, "See, Mommy! I told everyone we were *all* being married tonight!" Most people watching had never heard this interpretation of adoption. They cheered loudly, clapped, and whistled after her unexpected remark.

Heber explained what adoption meant. He spoke loudly so the people in the inn could hear as well as those gathered outside.

Anthony hardly paid attention to the short speech. He was too busy looking at and thinking about the heavy-set men outside. Still, he heard a few words of Heber's talk: "unity, lowliness, meekness, patience, forbearance, kindness, tenderheartedness, love, and forgiveness."

Anthony whispered again. "On the other side of the door, can you see anyone?"

"No, I can't. Who did you see?" Miriam asked, speaking in a whisper.

"Dorcas is sitting close to the entrance, watching all this, together with her son, Mith."

"Sparks will fly in that home, Anthony! No wonder you were good as a scout. How did you spot them?"

Cleon emerged from the stable area. He was going to tell some of his famous jokes.

"Anthony, look at Cleon. What is that?" Miriam said under her breath. "I've seen him dressed up many times, but never like this! What he is wearing must have cost a fortune!"

"What do you mean?" asked Anthony, and then he saw it.

He heard nothing during the jokes and stories for which Cleon was famous. His eyes were fixed on the gold armband Cleon was wearing on his left arm. It was wide with tiny red stones around the edges that sparkled in the light of the torches,

"Titus Flavius Zeuxis!" said Anthony under his breath.

"What did you say?" Miriam asked. She felt Anthony get up, and she turned to look at Cleon again. People were roaring with laughter as he described the antics and various personalities of the merchants who had spent time in the inn. He added, "... and I never expected to have the mayor here in our humble surroundings." People cheered again.

Miriam looked around to speak to Anthony, but he was gone. She looked for Grace. She had been climbing onto the couch, getting down and climbing back up again, and she had also disappeared.

In a moment of panic, Miriam prayed. *Dear God, don't let anything happen to her! How am I ever going to sing the wedding song? Those children just got a daddy.... Have I just lost my baby?*

Anthony had taken Grace, and he walked, crouched over, close to the ground. He went around the back, close to the area where the animals were kept.

"Take my hand and walk with me to the very back, where the animals stay. See, you can smell the place where the camels and horses sleep. Let's pretend no one can see us. Isn't it fun to play hide and seek at a wedding?"

"Yes, Daddy! This is fun! Let's play hide and seek!"

They walked behind the wedding party, where it was dark. Anthony bent down to be out of sight. As he walked around the far end of the inn, he escaped the light from the torches.

"Look, darling, would you like to see Ateas and Arpoxa? Ateas is called Zarrus now. I'll tell you why later. They are in that room over there, and I want you to stay with them. Can you be quiet? The new little baby is in there. They need your help to keep the baby sleeping. Can you help?"

"Yes, Daddy!" she said.

Her sweet little voice was drowned out by a loud guffaw as people laughed. Cleon had described a caravan that left without one of its slaves. He conveyed the panic of an indolent slave, who woke up to find he had been left behind. The angry slaveowner tried to sell the slave, but no one wanted this lackluster man.

Anthony came to the room where Ateas and Arpoxa were sitting, and he whispered, "Keep Grace quiet. She must not go out of this room until I come for her! It is dangerous for her out there."

He approached the steps to the office where Omerod stood watch on the first step.

"Up to the office, Omerod. I need to talk to you! Quick!"

They climbed the stone staircase up to the office. "The stolen armband! Cleon is wearing it. Remember our trip to Hierapolis? Flavius only cares for one thing, and I've seen it."

"Ah...so he's the one! Cleon is like a cat that hunts at night, turning up to show off its prize...in this case, a gold armband instead of a dead mouse!" breathed Omerod.

"Bring Bellinus up to the office. Miriam is going to sing a song after Cleon finishes his entertainment. The instant she starts to speak, go to him and say, 'Cleon, you will receive a reward for what you did tonight. Such a great performance! Quick, this will only take a minute. Come up to the office. It's about gold.' Say it, and he'll fall for it. He'll come running up the steps to the office of his own accord."

Below, in the large open area at the center of the inn, Miriam was speaking to introduce her song.

"My song is 'The Wedding Supper,' and it commemorates everything happening here tonight. This song is for young and old, for rich and poor. It's a song that tells both Penelope and Heber as well as Thelma and Timon how much we love them.

"I chose words especially intended for children because there are so many in here and outside. I put in words that the little ones will remember because this is their evening too...and for them to leave here knowing what marriage is about. It should be easy to learn the words.... The tune is often used...in wedding dances."

She realized she was hyperventilating and tried to stop her heart from beating so quickly. *Where is Grace?*

Anthony had disappeared, and she did not know where Grace was. Miriam was standing on a small, raised platform. Everyone at the wedding party could see her. Outside, she could see the light flickering on many faces. She decided to keep speaking until she could see Grace or until Anthony returned.

Miriam spoke about her friendship with Penelope and her joy at seeing Thelma find happiness in her relationship with Timon. "My song is for both couples."

Looking at the crowd, she saw Diotrephes's face outside. A gust of wind blew the flame on the torch, increasing the light. When she looked again, she saw his back but not his face.

She nodded to her young friends, and Penelope's children took their instruments. All the folk outside had stopped talking. Miriam's clear voice rang out with the accompaniment of flute, tambourine, harp, and drum. Children's voices added to her words. They sang as a chorus, repeating each verse twice.

The lamb is cooked, the plates are served,
And flames burn bright.
A guest's delight!
Come! Here's your seat, your place reserved.

The meal is spread as guests recline.

Each little bite,
Passions excite,
While nimble servants pour the wine.

The host has ordered just the best,
No hint of slight,
On such a night.
No cost was spared for any guest.

The bride shines bright; this is her day!
Spotless, she gleams
Beneath the creams.
Her face! Her smile! Her best array!

The groom's arrived, her love comes near.
His smile, it seems,
Brings hopes and dreams.
Live together, laugh and cheer.

Thus, the kingdom "Wedding Supper" comes.
A kingdom bright,
The king's delight.
Listen! Trumpets, harps, flutes, and drums:
The bride is us: kids, dads, and mums.
The bride is us: kids, dads, and mums.

The big crowd loved the performance and wanted her to sing again. Even Calisto enjoyed it. He said, "I liked this just as much or more than the last Greek drama I saw."

While Cleon was coming up the steps, Anthony whispered to his friends, "Cleon is proud of his treasure. We'll play him like an animal about to be caught in a trap. Let me do the talking."

Grinning from ear to ear, Cleon climbed the steps as fast as he could, following Omerod and delighted to have been singled out to receive a gift of gold. He longed for even greater treasures and was convinced that he had made an excellent name for himself.

The mayor was watching me perform! I'll be famous and will receive a reward!

Omerod blocked his view until he was entirely inside the room, and then Cleon abruptly stopped. Anthony and Bellinus were standing beside the table.

"Come, pull up a chair and sit down. I want to ask you some questions. Congratulations on a fine performance," Anthony began.

"Thank you. It was good, even if I do say so myself." Cleon breathed easily, anticipating warm words of support and trying to imagine the result of such talent.

"We want to talk with you about gold, about rewards and just payments."

"I'm delighted to cooperate. Be quick though! I'm not finished with my responsibilities. I have one more thing to do tonight."

"We admired your jokes, but most of all, we admire your armband! What a fine piece of work!"

"Yes, it's beautiful, isn't it?" Cleon held his arm out for the three soldiers to examine. The gold shone brightly under the steady flame of an oil lamp.

"I know a rich man in Hierapolis who would love to own something so exquisite! Where could I find something like that?"

"Well, you know, I'm a genius at many things, not the least of which is gambling. In the last year, I've won every single gamble, especially in the Games two weeks ago."

"Such good luck! Congratulations. Tell us more!"

"Yes, I gambled many times over the past couple of years, and each time I won—when boys threw the discus or when they wrestled or participated in the long jump and the running. By the end of the week, I had a huge amount of money! I even exchanged that money for gems and still kept on winning."

Cleon continued to boast. He realized his clenched left fist gave away the pulsing tension inside, so he placed his open hands on the table. The grin was gone. *I do not want questions about the gems that I found together with the armband behind the hut.* He knew that too much detail could lead to his having to make up more lies.

"So you bought this old piece of...what is it? Lydian or Persian jewelry? And you used your money?"

A tremor of excitement in Anthony's voice sent a shudder down Cleon's back. "Yes, I don't know how old the armband is, but it's old, isn't it? That would make it a lot more valuable, right? Do you think it is...what, three hundred or four hundred, maybe even five hundred years old? From the time of the Persians? The man who sold it didn't say."

"Oh, yes, I know it is old. I can put an age on it. It has exactly three hundred ten years of history, so it is invaluable to at least one family. Congratulations on the prize. So you bought this treasure using winnings from your gambling, correct?"

"Yes, I got lots of money from them and traded it for this."

"Can I ask you who sold it to you?"

Cleon was unprepared for Anthony's question. He stuttered and lost his way for a moment, looking from one to the other.

"A traveling merchant came through the inn. He wanted some quick money." He banked on the possibility that a traveling merchant might never be traced. "Yes, it was a merchant!" He gave a false surname, merging names from various caravan owners.

Anthony smiled broadly. "I'll tell you where to get such a precious piece...shall I?"

Fear showed in quick eye movements as Cleon looked from one soldier to the other. He realized that he might have misjudged the generous nature of these men at the beginning. His breathing was shallow. Veins in his neck started to throb.

"I think you could find something like that high up on Mount Tmolus. If I'm not mistaken, it takes a man about an hour to ride on a horse up to the snow line, knock on the door of a little hut, and then obtain such a gem. What a treasure and what great cost!"

"Well, yes, that's about right. It was last fall when they sold it to me. Oh, I just remembered! What I bought from the traveling merchant was another gem. I've been trading in lots of gems recently. The god of fortune and future looked on me with a smiling face. Artemis...I made a sacrifice to her, and she has blessed me with...this!"

His face lit up with a huge grin. He counted on his magnetic personality to get him through the next difficult moments.

"Did you pay a lot for it? Perhaps you intended to pay the money in several installments."

Once again, Cleon had no idea of what to say. He decided to go along with Anthony's question, agreeing slightly. "Yes, that's right. I didn't have all the money I needed at the time."

"Cleon, you just contradicted yourself! You said you got this treasure with the money from the Games two weeks ago. Then you agreed with me when I said you got it last fall. Now you agree that you didn't have all the money. Which story is true?"

Blinking half a dozen times after these boldfaced lies, he said, "Well, all are true."

"I would say you bought it from a few evil men. Those men on the mountain were the bandits we've been looking for. Surely you haven't been dealing with imposters, have you?"

"Oh no, I had no idea! I had no idea at all those men acted in cunning ways when I bought it from them!"

Cleon gasped. Without meaning to say anything, he had given away the whole story to someone he considered his enemy. He looked at the closed door. *I've got to make this quick and then get down to the wedding party and have the hay set on fire. How did I ever get into this mess here in this office?*

"Yes, and further, they didn't sell it to you. You stole it from the men who lived in the cabin. They were clear when we tortured them. All the gems were safe in Craga's wooden chest, hidden under some rocks in the little shed. You stole the treasure that the robbers had stolen from others, isn't that true?"

Cleon licked his lips, which had suddenly become dry. He wanted to breathe, but his heart was pounding. At the word "torture," his future caved in on him like the well that collapsed on Ateas, who escaped with only a broken leg. But Cleon could not escape. Hope was a tide beginning to ebb. *What if they cut me to pieces? What did they mean by talking about "torture"?*

"So, Cleon, here's what happened. You have been dealing with army deserters, haven't you? These men rebelled against Rome, and we've learned all about them."

"No! I would never do something criminal!"

"Yes, you did something unlawful! You found out what was happening on the Southern Road by going around the tables here in the inn and heard soldiers talking. We had no idea you were working against us! And then you went to that hut after you learned we had captured Maza and Harpa. You broke in, didn't you? You found their gems and simply took them. Since then, you've been showing off your stolen loot!"

At first, Cleon refused to speak. He did not know what the next accusation would be. Then he changed his mind. Nothing had been proven yet. He might still get away and remain free.

"I will tell you the truth. You don't have to torture me! Yes, after I heard that the crooks had been apprehended, I went up there to see what they had left behind. I met those men last year when Heber went on an outing with the young boys. I didn't carry out any business with them, but after I heard you captured them as criminals, I went to the shed and took everything in it. That's the truth!"

He had found a way out of the ambush facing him. "Actually, I was going to return all the gems and this armband to the rightful owner. I was only going to use this armband tonight."

Anthony would not let him speak anymore. "Everything you said about winning at gambling is a lie! You became so bold you decided to become 'famous' tonight. Mayor Asiarch Aurelius is present, and you wanted to be known, not only as a storyteller and entertainer but also for your wealth!"

Each accusation was now met with silence. The questioning had revealed what was in the recesses of the dark mind of the man who sat shaking before them.

Stay silent. I cannot make things worse.

"You learned about the caravans. Who was traveling with each caravan? How many soldiers were assigned as guards? You may even have told them the value of goods in the caravan."

How could Anthony know all about this?

"You worked for those thieves, didn't you? Oh, yes, you certainly are a spy. By the way, we know about Diotrephes. Do you know what happens to spies?"

The man was utterly broken. He let out an unconscious gasp, an uncontrollable admission of guilt. The trap held him tightly. He had been caught, and there was no escape.

"How were you going to tell Diotrephes tonight when to steal my little girl? You know, he is going to be disappointed, Cleon! Diotrephes is here with four strong men from Sardis. Or is it five? What is the signal you were going to give him? If he came here only to be disappointed again, I wouldn't want to be walking in your sandals."

Cleon began to whimper. He could not explain himself, for he was too ashamed to say anything, and he had no honor left. There was no room for repentance. For the first time ever, he forced himself to say nothing more.

"Now, who would you prefer to face? Do you want Diotrephes and his strong men to punish you, or would you rather face Roman justice?"

Torture and possible death had never crossed Cleon's mind. He hadn't considered the potential consequences. All he had wanted was to get rich quickly. He feared revenge from Diotrephes and did not know what was worse. He had become addicted to the few coins Diotrephes tossed his way, and this was his end.

"Cleon, here is what is going to happen. You are going to stay here, in this office. Our two friends, Omerod and Bellinus, will keep their swords aimed at your throat. If you so much as make a squeak, you will be dead. Instantly. Now, take off the golden arm bracelet. It belongs to Titus Flavius Zeuxis.

"We will keep you quiet for the rest of the evening until you are taken to the garrison jail. I will tell Zeuxis, the best-known man in Hierapolis, that Cleon, his friendly host at the inn, found it. Perhaps he will be grateful to you and make you rich somehow. What do you think he will give you as a reward for finding it for him?"

Anthony's questions; the zigzagging between accusations and questions, ideas, stories, and threats; and, finally, a prospect of an actual reward were too much. The possibility that Zeuxis, who had been a guest at the inn many times, would give him a gift pacified Cleon enough to provide him with a sliver of hope.

The clever little man did not want to suffer. Cleon was good at exaggerated stories and making people imagine events. However, Anthony made him see hidden details of his life pass before his eyes.

Miriam's song had come to an end.

Obed was speaking, thanking everyone for coming to participate in the wedding supper. "You know, normally such a supper would last until the early hours of the morning!" he stated in a happy tone. "But this is not a typical wedding. I mean, these were not normal weddings! Little ones need to sleep, and the inn will be receiving guests tomorrow morning."

Downstairs, Obed looked around and saw straw spread over the polished marble at the back of the courtyard, away from the light. "Quick, get that straw out of the way!" he ordered. "It's a fire hazard! We never allow straw near flaming torches!"

His voice carried the sharp tone of authority, and he ordered the stable boy who had surreptitiously placed it on the floor to clean it up.

"Not quick enough!" commanded Obed. "All of you, get the straw away from the torches, now!" Heber and Timon were on their feet, as were Calisto and Giles. Distinguished guests bent over, scooping up the straw. Men in clean wedding garments found themselves protecting the inn from a fire hazard.

"Before we can leave the inn," said the mayor, "I want the pavement area outside the inn cleared. All of you have watched a pleasant night's entertainment at no expense, and everyone received sweet, tasty things to eat. This was unusual. If this wedding had been at the acropolis, none of you could have come this close, but Abigail and her family have strange ways. I have never seen so many people invited to a wedding supper. You have seen two weddings, a banquet served, and five children adopted, but it is now time to go to your homes. Only after the path is clear will we come out."

The crowd dispersed. Those who were learning skills from Zarrus and Arpoxa went home full of stories. The workers and families on the Ben Shelah farm climbed into wagons. Those who worked all day rebuilding public buildings drifted off to tiny, dingy apartments in the insulae.

Diotrephes, burning with wrath, was one of the last to leave. Ever since Miriam had begun singing, he had lost sight of Cleon.

Reluctantly, he climbed onto the wagon on which there were many heavy blankets piled to keep a little girl's voice from being heard if she cried out.

What went wrong? What a little weasel! Imagine Cleon doing this to me! I sent him two fine gold coins. I trusted him. I came all this way and...a complete disappointment! There was Anthony. I saw Miriam sitting with little Chrysa, my niece! After Anthony disappeared, I never saw him or the child again. Cleon has played a trick on me—deliberately—to keep getting money from me. He mocked me, bringing me here to see the child to make sure I knew where she was. I know what happened! Cleon must have told Anthony about me. This is the second time Cleon spoiled the plans of the Naq family. I'll have Mother put a powerful curse on him. He will pay for this!

Once again, Diotrephes gnashed his teeth, planning revenge. Deep disappointment boiled within his spirit. He wondered why his frustration tonight at the wedding supper hurt more than his twisted shoulder three years before.

Chapter 38
Servius's Accusations

THE MILITARY GARRISON IN PHILADELPHIA

"Commander Felicior, I have a request."

"Not again!" Felicior exclaimed as Anthony appeared at the office. "Requests! That's all I hear these days." His mood was buoyant, even if his words were tinged with sarcasm.

"Yes sir," replied Anthony, not sure how he should proceed.

Felicior felt generous this morning. "The Ben Shelah family's double wedding yesterday was memorable. You should be proud of your wife's singing, especially teaching children how to play instruments and perform in public. Thank you for inviting me."

"I am proud of her, sir. Cleon is in chains. I'm not sure we can charge him with being a thief. Most of Flavius Zeuxis's personal treasures, the gems, were hidden in his room at the inn. None of the stolen clothing was found. Ever the liar, he tried to bribe us! Cleon said he would go to Hierapolis to return the armband, and if he could do that, he would give us much information in return."

"How hard were you on him?"

Anthony said, "I was hard on him last night, mentally but not physically. This kind of petty criminal is easily scared and will squeal freely to avoid physical pain. I kept him in the office at the inn so he couldn't help the man trying to kidnap our daughter."

"What man?" Felicior asked, surprised at this news.

"Sir, our daughter was an orphan, abandoned. My wife and I took her in. She was the child you saw with me last night. For three years, Diotrephes Milon has been attempting to abduct her. In the first two attempts, he almost succeeded. Last night, that troublemaker came again, waiting outside the inn. I believe he came with at least four strong-arm thugs to kidnap her. Diotrephes is a teacher in Sardis."

Felicior realized what the danger had been. "Ah-ha, he's the one who wrote a letter of accusation against you. Now, did his being here have anything to do with the hay spread over the floor?"

"Cleon intended to have a fire! That's the kind of man we are dealing with." Anthony's anger spilled over. His fist rested on the table. "I can't prove a motivation, but he's a dangerous man."

"Enough of this weasel! I will have Cleon kept in irons for a week and then send him away from this city. Now, what is your request?"

"Two requests actually, sir, about the gold armband."

"What about it?"

"I want to return it to its owner."

"Titus Flavius Zeuxis lives in Hierapolis."

"Yes, in Hierapolis. He is waiting for the gods to return it."

"Suros, do I perceive that you don't want to serve under Servius? Of course, the army must return stolen property to its owner. Is this your way of asking me to reassign you? If so, you are very clever."

"The depth of your understanding is why you were appointed to the Garrison of Miletus, sir."

"Spell out your request so that I understand clearly."

"Sir, I officially request a new assignment. I wish to continue as a reservist based in the Lycus Valley. Initially, the commission would be to take the armband to Titus Flavius Zeuxis. You could write a transfer order assigning me to the Garrison of Hierapolis.

"This transfer would be based on information received from the bandits we apprehended. Two dangerous members of 'The Faithful' must still be captured. I want to pursue Craga and Taba. Could Omerod and Bellinus accompany me to see Zeuxis? I would also request to take my family and Miriam's belongings."

"Under torture, Harpa and Maza both said Craga and Taba had been east, as far as Iconium. So technically, I could assign you to the garrison in Hierapolis."

Felicior looked out of the window for a minute and made a quick decision. "Yes, I will reassign you. Now, as for Omerod and Bellinus, they cannot go with you to speak with Zeuxis. They are returning to Sardis." Felicior used his fingers to count the days forward into the following week.

"Today is the twenty-eighth of May. Tomorrow will be my last day in the office. I will start to pack my belongings. Servius arrives in Sardis on Monday, the thirtieth, and then, on the last day of the month, I will turn over my command to him. The next day, on Tuesday, I leave for Miletus."

He pursed his lips. "Yes, I will write your transfer, but remember, this does not mean you will be free from Commander Servius's accusations. You must leave tomorrow, on Sunday, the twenty-ninth. I am granting your request, and I will write up the transfer orders for you and your salary today. Pick it up from my assistant tomorrow morning. By the way, tell me how you paid for Brutus so quickly."

"I had my wages saved up for my retirement, sir."

"Anthony," Felicior intentionally used the legionary's first name, "you are your own worst enemy. You have abilities beyond that of any scout I ever met. You braved barbarians in Upper Germania. Under my command, you captured thieves in Sardis. For two years, you followed men who despise the law, first along the Northern Road and now you have eliminated the dangers on the Southern Road. If it were not for your personal misguided beliefs, you would be awarded honor. Why do you persist in your beliefs?"

Anthony stood firm, persevering in the face of adversity. "I believe in the power of changed lives. You witnessed it last evening. A Jewish man married a non-Jewish woman. A wealthy man adopted five fatherless children and gave them his name. That is what the kingdom of love looks like."

"Be careful, Suros. Servius will search for ways to bring you before a Roman court. He is young and determined, and I suspect he wants a major triumph. Discovering religious rebellion in the ranks would get him promoted to Rome. He yearns for that."

"Thank you, sir." Anthony saluted and turned to leave.

Just before he opened the door, Felicior said, "Suros, you provided security across this district. You will not get honors, but you have the gratitude of the people of Philadelphia. Remember, you will leave the city tomorrow. That gives you three days to get to Hierapolis before June 1."

After Anthony left, Felicior called his assistant and described the instructions for the transfer. "Write this: 'As of May 31, Anthony Suros is reassigned from the province of Asia to the province of Phrygia."

Once the simple document was complete, Felicior sat still, scowling.

So Suros will be gone before Servius is responsible for this garrison. Someday Servius is going to bring Suros to a court-martial. Nothing will stop the young, ambitious commander. He is hungry for power and prestige, and a successful accusation against Suros will be another plume in his helmet. I hope Suros understands this.

AMOS AND ABIGAIL'S HOME

Anthony sped to Abigail's house, half relieved and somewhat apprehensive. He dismounted quickly and handed the reins to a servant. Miriam and Grace met him at the door, and he laughed. "My little girl. You almost knocked me over!"

"Why are you here?" Abigail asked. "Has the garrison given you the day off?"

"Soldiers have to be ready for change," he answered. "For example, I've just come from Felicior's office. And..." he paused, knowing every member of the family gathered close by was waiting for the next word, "I'm assigned a new task. Tomorrow I will be leaving Philadelphia. I am reassigned to Hierapolis. Miriam and Grace will be coming with me. I begin my new duties there on June 1."

As Miriam thought about it later, the rest of the day was like walking about in a dream. Saying goodbyes at the farm, going to the inn, visiting the women in Arpoxa's workshop, and then explaining to Ateas that she was leaving took most of the day. Miriam wiped away the tears as she told her friends how much she was going to miss them.

It was late when they got to bed, and they slept for only a few hours. They woke up long before the sun's first dim glow in the east.

Ruth could not find the right words to express her thanks to Miriam. Sarah clung to her older cousin. "Miriam, what would we have done if you hadn't been here? How would I have ever found a way to send the news to Mith? After the special evening with two weddings, he told me the next one to take place would be ours! But that means waiting some more!"

Miriam laughed, but tears were not far away. "If I hadn't been here, then Anthony wouldn't have been here either. If we had not been here, you would be married by now, Sarah. Our being here in this house brought confusion and delayed your marriage."

Anthony also struggled with his feelings. No one in the family among the servants, the staff at the inn, or his other friends knew about Servius's written accusation against him. He frowned, wondering if other denunciations might be forthcoming.

He saddled a horse and rode to the garrison to pick up the transfer papers Felicior had prepared. He checked them to make sure all were in order and then rode to the inn to pick up the few personal items left there.

Amos's wagons now belonged to Obed, and he had instructed a servant to drive Anthony and his family to Hierapolis. The trip would take three days, almost twice as long as Anthony's first visit to see Flavius Zeuxis.

The last one to talk to them was Abigail. She held Anthony's arm tightly and said, "If I hadn't been so obstinate, you would have slept in my house before now. Still, you did get to stay here for one night. I know Adonai is changing me. I can see it happening, even in an old woman like me."

Anthony took her words as an apology and answered, "Aunt Abigail, your kindness and generous hospitality flow out to others. That is bringing about a transformation in the lives of many people. Thank you for welcoming me."

He bent over and kissed her on both cheeks.

Kisses and hugs were shared all around, and many tears flowed as the little family climbed onto the wagon. Anthony took his place beside Miriam and Grace. The orders explaining his transfer lay securely in his soldier's leather pouch.

Abigail's last words stuck with them. She told them as they sat down on the wagon, "Anthony, you stood for many ideas completely different than mine, but I'm glad I got to know you. Take care of Miriam and Grace. I wish you were staying here longer. My home will always be open to you."

"Thank you, Aunt Abigail. Thank you for everything."

Anthony called Obed to the wagon and spoke softly. "Don't go back to work full-time. Why not work only one or two days a week? Be careful of the strength you have, and get lots of rest. Let Heber help you. He is the best friend you'll ever have!"

Then he called, "Aunt Abigail and Isabel, we'll be sending for Antipas's scrolls as soon as we have a safe place for them."

Anthony and Miriam found it hard to say goodbye. No one wanted to see them go. They waved to their new friends who stood beside the refurbished workshops.

Approaching the Valley Gate, Anthony commented, "Heber is welcome in Philadelphia. The mayor told me Heber deserves to have a good space for these five children. I'm happy for him."

Miriam replied, "For now, they have a good temporary place close to the inn…but Anthony, we don't have our own home. Where do you think we'll live when we settle down?"

"All I know is that we have a tiring, three-day trip before us through beautiful places. I will show you spots where I've been working for the last two years. Then I'll begin to think of where we will live after I'm finished in the army."

Anthony got down to say his goodbyes to the guards at the Valley Gate. He had spent two years with them. In a few moments, they were on the Southern Road, going to Hierapolis. There were few caravans or travelers on the road so early in the morning.

Anthony, Miriam, and Grace sat on the backbench. They did not want their comments concerning the family to be heard by the servant who was driving. Two hours later, they reached the Door. The horses slowed down, their neck muscles straining as they pulled the wagon up the steep hill. They rounded a sharp bend a quarter of a mile ahead.

"This was the place," said Anthony. "Here is where it all happened."

"What? Here? Is this place dangerous?" Miriam asked.

"Yes, bandits stopped caravans here. The first time, they gathered the camel drivers down there, at the lowest part. That left the last camels in the caravan unguarded, up there, around that bend. They made off with four bags of merchandise. That's what started this whole situation. It led to our being here."

"And you learned about their secrets?"

"Yes, and after the second robbery, we found the criminals' escape route. It was a small, natural break in the rock that let them get close without anyone seeing them. We filled up the cave with rocks, so they won't be using it again. You should have seen the soldiers' faces when they realized they were destroying an escape route. Grown men acted like boys, whooping, hollering, and stacking rocks in the cave! Even their horses seemed happy to not have to climb the hill all the way that day!"

"Speaking of horses," said Miriam, "why did you give your horse to Obed?"

"He needed it."

"I thought *you* would need it! Look at the work you do!"

"Obed needed someone to talk to."

"What? You gave him your horse so he could *talk* to it?"

"Haven't you watched Obed stroking Brutus's neck? He goes out in the evening and is with his horse for hours. I've seen him start to cry standing next to it and caressing its mane. He found a way to talk about himself without having anyone answer back to him. Too many people at home, I guess. I think he is almost back to his normal relationship with Isabel. She's had a lot to cope with during his illness."

News of Miriam leaving Philadelphia spread as soon as Mith came back from the inn. Dorcas called on Martha, and the two women talked in Michael's home. Curious about why Dorcas had arrived so early, Michael asked, "What brings you two together at this time of the morning?"

Michael was on his way to work and didn't want any more disturbances in his home.

Dorcas answered, "Anthony was transferred to the Garrison of Hierapolis. Miriam left with him this morning."

Michael glared at two giggling women, turned around, and opened the door. "Don't talk about that family again."

"My dear husband," said Martha, "if I go to see my great-grandsons, I will not be talking with Amos. He was excluded from fellowship, but he is gone. Is there a non-Jew living in the house? No. Penelope and her children and the two cripples and their children live near the Valley Gate."

"Do not disobey me!" he said sternly. "Abigail is worse than her husband! Look at her! She is fomenting a spirit of disobedience. She's friendly with outsiders in her home, at the inn, and who knows where else."

With that, he stomped through the doorway and left, a dark look covering his face.

Later, as Dorcas brought the food to the table for the noon meal, Mith rubbed his hands together. "Mother," he said, "I've decided to open up to Father. I'm not going to hide things from him anymore."

Dorcas looked at her son and smiled. *May you be blessed by Adonai, my son! This will be difficult, but it will show you are now a man.*

"If you feel that way, then I think you should talk with him today," she said. "It's the best thing to speak up right away."

Miriam watched the Cogamis Valley grow smaller as they rose above the green vineyards and grain fields. Individual fields appeared as a patchwork quilt. The valley stretched away almost forty miles to the north and twenty miles to the east. Anthony pointed to towns where he and the other soldiers had kept the population under control during the unrest: Castolius, Malonia, Silandus, Temenoth, and Clanodda. However, she could only distinguish the closest town, Castolius. The others were lost in a haze hanging over the valley.

They were halfway up the hill. "Silandus and Malonia, where Thelma comes from, are located on those distant hills."

Miriam observed, "I can't imagine anyone riding over all those roads and the dangers. But about your horse, couldn't you have given Obed another one? Why did it have to be yours?"

"I watched Obed for a long time. For months, I thought Abigail was the one most wounded. Yes, she was wounded, but so was Obed. He lost four brothers and two sisters. Everyone always comforted Abigail, but who paid attention to him? One day it came to me. Obed needs to know that the army is not acting against him personally. The only way to make him understand that, especially after I seldom appeared at his house and only slept at the inn, was for him to know that I cared."

She looked away, taking in the mountain range to the south and hiding threatening tears.

He asked, "Now let me ask you, Miriam—why do you give your inheritance money away?"

"The same reason you did. You sacrificed for Obed. I love those people in Sardis, those boys and their fathers, and people like Melpone in Thyatira and her little son."

Exposing their inner motivations was like walking out into the summer sun after an afternoon rest in a darkened room. Bright sunlight made a person hesitate for a moment so they could see the way ahead. Spontaneous acts of generosity came from seeing other's needs as more significant than their own personal desires. Both Miriam and Anthony realized that they had learned something precious about one another. For many minutes, the only sound was that of the horses' hooves, a squeaky axle, and Grace singing the wedding song.

The horses strained up the steep slope. Nearing the top, Miriam added a thought. "Of course, now that Penelope is married to Heber, she doesn't need money. The children will be well cared for."

"Which brings up the topic of inheritances."

"Yes, I've been thinking about that. Amos had only one heir, and Obed will look after his mother well. He told me that he intends to keep the home open for Isabel and their daughters. I suppose Jesse and Ruth and Sarah and Mith will inherit the house, the farm, and the Inn of the Open Door when Obed passes on. But, of course, Sarah and Mith have to be married first!"

Anthony chuckled. "You were quick-witted when you had to find a way for Sarah and Mith to 'talk' to each other. But they are waiting until he is twenty-one years old, right?" She nodded.

He turned to Miriam. "What about Ateas and Arpoxa? He is being called Ateas and not Zarrus since there is no worry about Cleon anymore."

"The mayor has granted them space at the top end of the workshops area, close to the Valley Gate. They can stay as long as they wish. If they leave, the large room where they stayed will be used by artisans for weaving and making clothes. The pottery area Ateas worked in will continue as a place to teach others."

Miriam recalled her last seven weeks. "I was surprised to learn that Thelma and Timon wanted to be married according to Jewish customs. When Thelma thought about her former life, she told me, 'I want to do everything like Heber and Penelope. My mother was so young when she died. I didn't learn important things from her. I want my wedding to be just like Penelope's.' Of course, her wedding dress was her own design. Wasn't she beautiful?"

"What did Calisto think of the weddings?" asked Anthony. "What a strange man!"

"Isabel told me that she talked to Calisto and Mayor Maurelinus and his wife. The three were standing together when Calisto asked, 'What I didn't understand was why, after they drank the wine, each couple threw their cup on the floor, breaking it.'"

"So what did Isabel say to Calisto?"

Miriam put her right hand over the little gold ring on her finger. "Isabel explained, 'The cup is broken to remember Jerusalem was broken. Our greatest joys can also become our greatest pains. Our city is no more. For each of the couples, the old life has passed away. From then on, they will drink wine from a new cup. One day we will have a new cup in a new Jerusalem."

Anthony stopped for a noon meal at one of the army's checkpoints. Usually, merchants walking with camels would stay the night there.

By the second evening, they had arrived at the small city of Tripolis. "We have crossed the border from the province of Asia Minor into Phrygia," said Anthony. "I'll be safe serving in the Hierapolis Garrison."

"Why say, 'I'll be safe'? You aren't afraid of men hiding behind trees, are you?"

"I'll tell you tomorrow," he said. "We'll stay at the Tripolis garrison's equivalent of an inn tonight. It's not fancy but much cleaner than the other places there."

DANIEL AND DORCAS'S HOME IN PHILADELPHIA

In Philadelphia, the evening meal was served at Dorcas's table, and Mith's palms were sweaty. Telling his mother during the afternoon what he would say was much more comfortable than finding the right words now.

"Father," he began, "I need to tell you something."

"Please do, my son. What do you want to tell me?"

"Father, I will not hide things from you. First, I am going to marry Sarah. I am not going to put her away."

Daniel sat up straight, not used to direct statements from his son.

"I have been talking with her for a year. She leaves notes for me at the inn one day, and I pick them up the next. That's how I knew–"

"So that's how Dorcas and Martha knew Jesse and Ruth were expecting their baby."

Mith interrupted, unwilling to have his father stop him. "Yes, and I will go to the Ben Shelah house to visit the one I want to marry. I will go often and will always have a chaperone, our normal custom before a marriage. I plan to marry Sarah after I turn twenty-one."

Daniel drew back, his face dark and his eyes livid. "Are you telling me that you are deliberately going to betray the confidence I placed in you?"

"Father, I want your blessing. When we were betrothed, you were so happy about it. I want to see the same signs of pleasure in your face again."

Dorcas added her voice to Mith's. "The elders determined a punishment against Amos Ben Shelah. They disciplined him, not Abigail. Their penalty no longer affects the others. As for me, I will visit my grandsons when I want to and as often as I desire. This afternoon, Martha made the same decision. Right now, she is telling Michael that she will visit her great-grandsons too. My husband, why should you be so hard and stiff-necked?"

Daniel stood up and then sat down. He got up again, left the table, and started to pace across the room. Suddenly, he opened the front door, his jaw clenched tight.

"I'm going to talk with Zacharias and Michael. What has happened to my family?"

ON THE POSTAL ROAD FROM TRIPOLIS TO HIERAPOLIS

On the third day, Anthony and Miriam left the army's inn to finish the journey to Hierapolis. She picked up their conversation from the previous evening. "What is going to happen to Cleon?"

"Such a sneaky creature! He got off too easily. He spent a week in jail and was given five lashes for not reporting the robbers' location and then going to the robbers' hut and stealing the treasures. He also didn't hand stolen items over to the garrison. The rascal is being sent away, and I heard him say that he intends to go east to the province of Galatia. One of the merchants he knows was passing through and heard Cleon say, 'I think it's time for a move.' I could not prove that he had helped with Diotrephes's plan to abduct our little one. Both men escaped punishment for what they did."

"Let's come back to yesterday. What did you mean when you said, 'I will be safe'?"

"So many questions, my dear!" he said, smiling. Grace was tucked between them, singing her favorite songs. "I requested this transfer from Philadelphia to Hierapolis."

"Good! Then we are going to make our home there!"

"The reason I requested the move was that Commander Felicior was being transferred to Miletus. He stood up for me these last years."

"Stood up for you? What do you mean?"

"Commander Servius is the new commanding officer for Sardis and Philadelphia. That will take effect tomorrow. He doesn't like it when I leave off the word 'god' in the Solemn Oath. And we must repeat it so often, almost daily! He wrote an indictment against me because I refuse to call Domitian 'god.'"

She shivered. Even though the sun's rays were already warm in the late days of May, she felt a chill. They were passing large wheat fields. Cows grazed in an open pasture in the distance. Higher up, small hills were crowned with pine trees continuing up the mountains on both sides of the valley. The fresh scents of the forest blew softly over them.

He pointed at a stone set into the ground beside the paved road. "There is another marker. It tells me that we are crossing into the province of Phrygia. We are leaving the district of Tripolis and entering the district of Laodicea. I hope to be a reservist in another district, Hierapolis. We'll settle down and have more children."

"Mommy's going to have a baby?"

Miriam stroked Grace's hair and shoulders. "No, dear, not now but later. Daddy is talking about our future."

THE HOME OF ZACHARIAS IN PHILADELPHIA

In an unusual gesture, Zacharias closed his gold shop early. Michael and Martha arrived at the elder's house, leaving the pottery workshop in Michael's manager's hands.

Daniel, Dorcas, and their son Mith also came for this encounter.

After the prayer, "King of the universe, blessed be your name for the bread that comes from the earth," a servant brought hot flatbread to the table but left slowly. He was anxious to listen in to his master's words.

Zacharias began, "Martha and Dorcas, I speak with a heavy heart. Yes, Amos was disciplined after being given a chance to repent of his ways. And, yes, indeed, he was cut off. Furthermore, I cannot punish both of you women and you, Mith, if you go to that house.

"So much ungodliness occurred there. Now you must not be there when non-Jews are present. Abigail, Isabel, Ruth, and Sarah are all Jews. Ruth and Jesse's two sons were circumcised. Each one has a certificate of circumcision, so they are a Jewish family in these respects.

"However, if you attend any of the celebrations that Abigail offers to families on the farm and workers from the insulae, then the elders will revisit what I say to you now. I know that Abigail intends to keep on with her gatherings. She calls it the Community of the Covenant, something we will not accept."

Mith looked at his mother and smiled, and Zacharias added, "Young man, we recognize the duplicity you have been involved in. You are betrothed to a Jewish woman, and Miriam, who helped you communicate with Sarah, is a Jew. However, you have shown a rebellious side to your father. Such deceit is a sin."

Daniel felt humiliated by his son's actions. He rose from the table. "I'm sorry, Zacharias. My wife and my son have been hiding their actions from me for many months."

Glaring first at Dorcas, Daniel turned to address Mith. "My son, I expect you to obey me in the future!"

He arose to leave for his carpentry shop, and then he looked at Dorcas. "All this is because you were trained as a midwife. You are far too generous...too compassionate."

He went to the door and left Zacharias's home.

Dorcas squeezed her son's hand, and looking up, she closed her eyes. *We will continue to see our daughters-in-law and my grandsons. Mith will be married to his beloved. Thank you, Lord.*

ON THE POSTAL ROAD FROM PHILADELPHIA TO HIERAPOLIS

The sun was hot as Anthony and Miriam followed the river along Lycus Valley. Humming a tune, she composed another verse of a song she treasured. She did not know when she might sing it to Anthony. The quiet of the mountain pass, the sound of the wheels and the axle, horses' hooves, and the nearby creek flowing down to the Lycus River Valley—all these gave birth to words to her new song.

Peasants marched, and families lost their land,
In Philadelphia's valley, a quiet, fertile plain.
"Guard merchants and caravans!" came precise commands.
Divided, hungry families endured strife and pain.

Our daughter's life was threatened, almost lost.
That wedding day, I watched Heber give his hand.
Our nemesis was undone by a treasured boast.
In every crisis, God showed what he had planned.

Forgiveness, reconciliation, and hearts set free.
"A transforming hallelujah!" I sing with glee.
Lives changed forever. I gladly bow my knee.
I will trust you for your hand is guiding me.

Anthony looked at Grace, who was curled up asleep, and Miriam put her arm through his. "I'm so glad for the double wedding. The most powerful and wealthiest guests learned about the covenant. The poor and the lame were there. Ateas and Arpoxa, who rarely have two copper coins to rub together, helped us. There we were, Jew and Gentile, rich and poor, old and young, former slaves, masters and servants, men and women, boys and girls."

Anthony chuckled. "Yes, lots of opposites came together!"

"I'm not finished yet," laughed Miriam, pinching his ribs. "We were family: widows and fatherless. Because of Heber's earnest, steadfast love, five fatherless children received a new name."

"You enjoy Thelma, don't you?"

"At the beginning, she was reluctant to talk to me, not knowing if she could trust me or not. I gave her time to see if she really wanted to talk. Then, yes, once she started talking, she was so expressive. She has unique talents and abilities she never knew about. She was badly hurt. Thelma was lost and now is found. She was unloved and abused, but now she has a fine young husband."

Anthony pointed to white marks on a hill. "The city above those white cliffs—that's Hierapolis. It's where we are going to stay tonight. Another hour and we'll be there, meeting the guards at the garrison."

"Well, tonight you will have to guard yourself against me!" said Miriam, pinching his ribs again. "I was at home almost all the time, and you've been away too long, too many days."

"Tomorrow I will give Flavius Zeuxis his treasure. We'll visit your Uncle Daniel in Laodicea too. I'm sure he will be delighted to see you."

She touched Grace's hand to wake her up. "Come on, Grace. Wake up! If you sleep now, you won't get any sleep tonight." Grace sat up, comforted by her father's arms and the warmth of her mother.

She looked up into Miriam's face. "Will we go back, Mommy? See Aunt Abigail, see all your friends? Will Saulius and Melody and Asa and the new baby be here tomorrow?"

Miriam realized that Grace would feel the dislocation of moving. They had left places suddenly before, first from Pergamum when Antipas was killed then when they had to leave Sardis on Anthony's assignment to capture the insurgents. Afterward, they were transferred from Thyatira to Philadelphia, and now they were going to another strange city.

"Anthony, this is the fourth time we've left a city!" She added quickly, "It's not going to happen again, is it? We can find a place to settle down, can't we?"

"We can't know the future, my love. But tomorrow a wealthy man is going to have the most important thing in his life back in his hands."

"I'm glad that we have friends in different cities, and I will always love and cherish them because friends stay in our hearts forever. But I want our own home and more children."

Anthony put his arm around her shoulder and drew her toward him gently. "We are rich when we have friends. And if we go back to any of those cities, we will take time to see them all."

The horses kept their regular clip-clop. As the shadows began to lengthen, they passed through the outer gate on the long entrance into Hierapolis. She was holding Grace, and he pulled them both close, whispering in her ear, "Miriam, you helped make friends for us in each city, and you've always found a way to enrich others. You helped bring about so much change. Healing, forgiveness, restoration, and reconciliation—that's what I observed in

Philadelphia. It's more than I could have imagined when we first came there, and I'm going to miss our friends."

She replied, "Yes, love made us truly rich. And remember the last thing we heard from everyone who said goodbye to us? They waved and called out, 'Come back!' We will always be welcome at the Inn of the Open Door."

MAKING SENSE OF THE NOVEL AND THINKING ABOUT *INN OF THE OPEN DOOR: A CHRONICLE OF PHILADELPHIA*

The following questions will help the reader consider how each character in the novel fits within the overall story. Some characters will continue throughout the set of seven books. It is helpful to consider the motives and experiences that drive them and reflect on our own experiences.

1. One of the main themes in the novel is facing ongoing difficulties between family members. Yet amid the conflicts, flow healing, forgiveness, restoration, and reconciliation.

   Describe the journey to reconciliation for Abigail and Anthony.
   How does she relate to Ruth and Jesse, Sarah and Mith?
   What part do meals and conversations take in bringing about harmony?
   How do you relate to persons younger than yourself, those who need your wisdom, care, compassion, and patience?

2. Miriam has many complex relationships in Philadelphia. Her relationships involve both older as well as younger family members.

   How does she relate to Amos? To Abigail? To Obed?
   What can we learn about the ministry of reconciliation from how Miriam acts in many awkward situations?
   Are you going through a situation needing reconciliation and forgiveness?

3. Anthony is one of the two principal persons in this novel. The other person is Miriam, and most of the time, they are kept apart.

   What qualities enable him to live an upright life in the military?
   How does Anthony relate to fellow soldiers?
   Think about how he gradually won Abigail over and brought about a reconciliation. What can we learn from his humility?
   Anthony gave a horse to Obed. Why did he do this?
   Think about your life and various tense relationships. What do you do to bring about reconciliation and harmony?

4. Another theme deals with emotional stability following intense periods of stress.

Review the life story of Abigail and Amos in Alexandria and Jerusalem. What experiences brought about emotional stress?
What does the stress do to Abigail's long-term mental health?
Abigail's mental and emotional health improves. What brings this about?
Obed's mental and emotional health, instead of improving, become worse. What does the family do to help him back to health?
Do you know of anyone who needs your love and care?

5. Generosity brings about positive changes. Miriam learned to be generous through Antipas's life, and he affected Anthony too.

Think of moments in your life when generosity helped to break down barriers.
What is the relationship between generosity, worship, and love?

6. Many types of conflict pepper the pages of this book. Think of the conflicts in these relationships:

The military and the thieves in "The Faithful" gang
The elders of the synagogue and Amos's family
The farmers and the city's authorities
What conflicts do you see around you, and how do you relate to the various persons you meet from time to time?

7. Love, marriage, and growing relationships bring an appreciation of younger and older people falling for each other. Heber forms a relationship with Penelope, Timon with Thelma.

What observations can you make about these personalities?
What do you think of a man marrying a woman with several children and adopting them as his own?

8. Throughout the story, a power stronger than normal human strength brings about spiritual transformation.

What changes came about because of the Passover meal?
How does Commander Felicior come to appreciate "agape love"?
What difference does the message of Yeshua Messiah, Jesus Christ, make to each person in the novel?

If you enjoyed this book,
please consider rating it on Amazon or another book site
and posting a brief review.
You can also mention it on social media.
Please contact the author at:

Century One Chronicles,
PO Box 25013
255 Morningside Avenue
Toronto, ON M1E 0A7 Canada

If you would like a Zoom visit to your book club
or an interview for your blog:

centuryonechronicles@gmail.com

Website:

https://sites.google.com/thechroniclesofcourage.com/chroniclesofcourage/home

PHILADELPHIA IN THE BIBLE

Revelation 3:7–13

To the Angel of the **church in Philadelphia** write:

These are the words of him who is holy and true, who holds the key of David. What he opens no one can shut, and what he shuts no one can open. I know your deeds. See, I have placed before you an open door that no one can shut. I know that you have little strength, yet you have kept my word and have not denied my name. I will make those who claim to be Jews though they are not but are liars—I will make them come and fall down at your feet and acknowledge that I have loved you. Since you have kept my command to endure patiently, I will also keep you from the hour of trial that is going to come upon the whole world to test those who live on the earth.

I am coming soon. Hold on to what you have, so that no one will take your crown. Him who overcomes I will make a pillar in the temple of my God. Never again will he leave it. I will write on him the name of my God and the name of the city of my God, the new Jerusalem, which is coming down out of heaven from my God; and I will also write on him my new name. He who has an ear, let him hear what the Spirit says to the churches.

DIOTREPHES, GAIUS, AND DEMETRIUS IN THE BIBLE

3 John 1–13

The elder, to my dear friend, **Gaius,** whom I love in the truth:

Dear friend, I pray that you may enjoy good health and that all may go well with you, even as your soul is getting along well. It gave me great joy to have some brothers come and tell me about your faithfulness to the truth and how you continue to walk in the truth. I have no greater joy than to hear that my children are walking in the truth.

Dear friend, you are faithful in what you are doing for the brothers, even though they are strangers to you. They have told the church about your love. You will do well to send them on their way in a manner worthy of God. It was for the sake of the Name that they went out, receiving no help from the pagans. We ought therefore to show hospitality to such men so that we may work together for the truth.

I wrote to the church, but **Diotrephes**, who loves to be first, will have nothing to do with us. So if I come, I will call attention to what he is doing, gossiping maliciously about us. Not satisfied with that, he refuses to welcome the brothers. He also stops those who want to do so, and puts them out of the church.

Dear friend, do not imitate what is evil but what is good. Anyone who does what is good is from God. Anyone who does what is evil has not seen God. **Demetrius** is well spoken of by everyone—and even by the truth itself. We also speak well of him, and you know that our testimony is true.

I have much to write to you, but I do not want to do so with pen and ink. I hope to see you soon, and we will talk face to face.

Peace to you. The friends here send their greetings. Greet the friends there by name. (Emphasis added)

Rich Me!

A Chronicle of Laodicea

Part 1
June AD 96

Fame and Fortune

Chapter 1
The Return of an Heirloom

HOME OF FLAVIUS ZEUXIS, IN HIERAPOLIS

"I'm too busy to see visitors!" Flavius Zeuxis, the wealthiest merchant in Hierapolis, was bellowing to his head servant. For the fifth time, he ran his hand over his thick, wavy hair and shouted, "These figures don't add up. The number of tapestries I'm taking to Rome doesn't match this list ... my purchases from weavers!"[111]

Rising quickly, swear words poured out. "I told you not to interrupt me! I don't care that there is a soldier is at the gate!"

The slave, Ciryas, whose ancestors had lived in Carthage,[112] bowed and said politely, "Master, the soldier said ..."

"Only official business! He'll have to wait until I return. Why am I so far behind?" Zeuxis compared the two lists in his hands, and lines of worry crossed his forehead.

---

[111] Titus Flavius Zeuxis was one of the wealthiest merchants in Hierapolis. His funerary building is a well-preserved chapel close to the Northern Triple Gate. It is made with a rectangular plan, a gabled roof, and surrounded by a bench. An inscription states that Flavius went to Rome 72 times. The decorative frieze of *metopes* or decorations on the outside of the chapel is evidence of his wealth. A sarcophagus in the Hierapolis Museum bears the name of "Maximillia," believed to be his daughter. The tomb hints at the wealth and influence of this *ergastes*, or merchant. Italian archaeologists determined that the funerary building was constructed at the end of the First Century. There is a strong possibility that Zeuxis was a descendent of Satrap Zeuxis. He was the Persian prince who governed Sardis and its surrounding region about 220 BC. The story of Flavius Zeuxis in this novel is fictitious. So are the details about his house, the highway robbery, the loss of his armband, and his business dealings. However, the physical description of an armband from the period described is accurate. The armband is based on examples of that time.

[112] Carthage, known today as Tunis, the capital of Tunisia, had been conquered by Rome in 146 BC at the end of the Third Punic War.

"Master, the soldier standing at the gate is with his wife and a small child. He said, 'Please, tell your master I am here to keep my promise ...'"

"Send him away! People flock to my door before a voyage. They want messages taken to some person or a family in Rome. You would think I was a common courier ..."

Ciryas understood his master's frustration. It was like this before every trip. It had happened dozens of times before they traveled to the coast and sailed across the Aegean Sea. He added in a soft voice, "The soldier returned to make your trip safe and your next entry into Rome unforgettable. He has a long red scar down the right side of his face."

At these words, Zeuxis sat straight up. He placed both papyrus sheets on his desk and wiped his mouth. His eyes opened wide. With his breath coming in small spurts, he whispered, "Oooh! Is his name Anthony Suros? He is the only one with permission to bother me today. Call him in!"

Standing outside on the avenue above the city and facing the intricately carved double doors forming the entrance to the Zeuxis residence, Anthony stood beside his wife, Miriam. Three years had passed since he was invited to enter this gate and vivid memories flashed through his mind. Before leaving, he had promised it would be to bring back a stolen heirloom if he ever returned.

A short double-edged sword hung across Anthony's left hip, and a soft brown soft leather pouch hung from his neck. His helmet and breastplate lay on the wagon's floor. The horses brought Anthony and his family from Philadelphia. For three years, they had lived in the chief city to the west.

"Miriam, this is the place I told you about. Look at the carvings on the oak wood."

Grace, their five-year-old daughter, was running her fingers over carved images. "Daddy, why is this gate so big?" Her fingers traced a bear standing on its hind legs. "Doggies?" she asked.

"No, Grace," said her mother, "not doggies. That is a bear, and up here, it's a wolf. This family needs a strong gate to keep robbers out!"

Ciryas reappeared. "Welcome! My master will see you in a few minutes. He is busy, so don't expect him to give you a lot of attention. In four days, he's going to Rome."

Once inside the gate, they stood in a spacious courtyard. Several slaves attended a well-cared-for garden with flowering shrubs. Miriam and Anthony took off their sandals before stepping into the house, and another slave bent down to wash their feet. They were given soft sandals to wear inside the home.

"So, you kept your promise!" Zeuxis beamed. "I didn't think you would return! Have you fulfilled your promise?" He turned his attention to Miriam and Grace. "And who are these fine people?"

"Sir, this is my wife, Miriam. Grace is my daughter, five-and-a-half years old. Miriam, this is Titus Flavius Zeuxis, about whom I've told you so much. Grace, please say 'Hello, sir.'"

Gone were Zeuxis's anxiety and earlier disquiet. "Come in, come in!" gushed the merchant. He led them into the exquisitely furnished great room. Miriam took in the details.

From head to foot, Flavius's appearance conveyed pulsating energy. She remembered Anthony's description almost three years before.

His hair is a wavy salt and pepper, and it fascinates me. Why does *it remind me of the waves of the sea? They are always restless. He has endless vitality... it flows through everything he says and does. You never know if he is talking about past trips to Rome or the upcoming ones. Just when you are overcome by his details about senators, he mesmerizes you with particulars about his Persian ancestors.*

Flavius's voice was pleasant but loud enough to be heard throughout the house. "You've arrived just as I am preparing to leave on another trip!"

"Yes, sir. Commander Felicior Priscus at the Philadelphia Garrison instructed me to return your treasure. Here it is. I'm glad we arrived before you left."

Anthony removed the leather cord from his neck and handed the bag to him.

Zeuxis's hand was shaking as he pulled the drawstrings, opening the bag. Reaching inside, he pulled out a precious golden armband. It had been stolen three years earlier on the road to Philadelphia.

His lower lip was trembling as Zeuxis opened the hinge and placed it on his arm. He gazed silently at his left upper arm. Red rubies decorated the top and bottom edges. It opened on the long hinge, and several other gems were lodged: jasper, topaz, beryl, and a large jacinth. Roman senators had run their fingers over the jewels in adoration before buying his delicately made garments.

"Suros, only four bundles were stolen by the bandits, but they ran away with my greatest treasure! And here it is, back on my arm. Thank you for bringing it back!"[113]

He bent his left arm one way and then the other. The gold armband had been worn by his ancestor, the Persian governor who ruled this area hundreds of years earlier.

"With my dignity now restored, displaying my connection to the satrap of Sardis, I can again boast about my family's ancestry! It makes me feel uncontaminated by Rome's riff-raff."

He saw the puzzled expression on Miriam's face and addressed her. "My ancestor, Zeuxis, governed this province!"

"What a happy afternoon! These guests are going to freshen up while I plan a celebration. An omen of success!" Flavius called a slave. "Bring in the best wine for these guests!" His attitude had changed more rapidly than the weather in Hierapolis in early April.

He called another slave, "Call Modesto Aelianus and both his sons, Donatus and Galeo. They must join us. This is a real celebration!"

Looking around, he saw a female slave who was expecting a baby. He spoke in a quiet voice, "Tell Maximillia that I want her here, too!" He softened his voice and said slowly, as if the slave woman could not understand more than one word at a time. "Go! Tell your mistress that her prayers to Artemis have been answered. The link with my Persian forefathers has been restored."

Zeuxis turned to Anthony and Miriam. "Where are you staying?"

Anthony answered, "I was going to speak to Commander Claudius Boa, but he went up the Lycus Valley today, sir. He'll be back tomorrow morning, and I must report to him. Commander Felicior in Philadelphia gave me a new assignment. So, I will be staying at the garrison while I am in Hierapolis."

"No, not at all! You will all stay here. In fact, I'll put you in Maximillia's bedroom! My daughter is married now, and she lives with her husband."

---

[113] The theft of Titus Flavius Zeuxis's heirloom is told in *Inn of the Open Door: A Chronicle of Philadelphia.*

Flavius Zeuxis asked Anthony, "Will your assignment keep you here for long?"

"We want to find and arrest two bandits. Four robbed your caravan. Two were apprehended, and we are searching for the others."

AFTERWORD

How did a tiny group of followers of Yeshua Messiah not only survive persecution in the Roman Empire but continue to grow in number despite pain and suffering? How did their faith in a Jewish Messiah spread, reaching both rich and poor, men and women, Jews and non-Jews, slaves and free?

Such thoughts intrigued me while living in Turkey, with its 5,600 archaeological sites. My teenage interest in the Roman Empire as a boy in Kenya, Africa, returned. Later I was blessed with other teachers who made history come alive.

Turkey's unique geographical features are enhanced with the unending beauty of changing seasons. The visual attractiveness of the land is deeply satisfying. The country is famously known for millions of tourists who arrive each year. Seeing this opportunity, I joined others in promoting faith tourism, which is important to the country. Tourist groups I hosted wanted to spend time at the sites of seven ancient cities.

At the end of each day, we relaxed and often engaged in questions and discussions. Having explored Troy one time as a tour group, we sat down for a fish dinner. We searched our imaginations to describe people who might have lived there three thousand years ago. What were their professions? What happened at the port every day? Who built the buildings?

Out of those conversations came a solid impulse to go beyond the stones strewn over the ground and to imagine an ancient city throbbing with all sorts of people. From this came the idea of Antipas being the central character of a novel.

I wanted readers to travel in their imaginations, walk up and down steep streets, learn to shop in crowded markets, and receive invitations to come for a tasty meal in ancient homes. It was essential to meet living, breathing people. What were their hopes and fears, their politics, and religious beliefs? I wanted to understand their conflicts and difficulties, their victories and defeats.

At first, I thought a single book would do. It would include seven sections, one for each ancient city. But as I thought further about each town, it became clear that a single novel would not do justice to the geography, history, civic functions, Roman government, and Greek culture in each case.

Three years passed before the story spanning seven novels had jelled in my mind. The seven novels would weave elements of the seven letters of the Revelation into the cultural background. Unlike the order of the seven churches as they appear in the first chapters of the Book of Revelation, this saga begins in Pergamum and ends in Ephesus.

At the conclusion of the story, many characters from the earlier novels are brought face to face for a climactic ending.

If you have enjoyed this book, I hope you will take the time to post your thoughts in a customer review on Amazon.com and mention it on social media. Along with telling your friends about it, this is an effective way to spread the word about a book you enjoyed.

ACKNOWLEDGEMENTS

For years my wife, Cathie, and I were privileged to live in Turkey, where we learned to appreciate the commitment of present-day believers in Jesus Christ. We have friends who live in the same region as these seven novels. Our Turkish friends encouraged me in ways they will never know.

During those years in Turkey, many Turkish citizens offered us friendship and hospitality. They not only helped me to enjoy their country but they made us feel safe. My thanks to them for helping us learn about their way of life and the history of their land. Archaeologists continue to excavate numerous ancient cities in Turkey. Findings by these researchers supplied dates, names, and details for cities and towns mentioned in these seven novels.

Museum staff members were delighted to have interested visitors examine their displays. They passed on a lot of helpful information. I am grateful to the countless scores of people who enriched my life in the locations mentioned in these novels. Without their help, none of this would have been written.

During my high school years, I was blessed by capable history teachers at Rift Valley Academy in Kenya. Dr. Ian Rennie at Regent College, University of British Columbia, guided me in historical research at a critical time in my life. He demanded accuracy, which was character forming.

Several friends provided the impetus for the effort needed to create the story line and bring it to a conclusion. Blair Clark worked with me for several years, especially in coordinating faith tourism. Raye Han, a Turkish tour guide of boundless enthusiasm, taught us about her country, giving endless details and sharing a spiritual passion. Visitors to Turkey were amazed at her professionalism as well as that of other tour guides.

Friends at the City of David Messianic Synagogue in Toronto, Canada, contributed much to the Jewish aspect of the novels. I am thankful to each one in this Messianic congregation. Through them,

I became aware of various aspects of Jewish life and thought, and they helped to build me up in my faith.

Without the help of Jerry Whittaker as an editor, these volumes would not have made it to the press. No one could wish for a more capable and discerning friend. His creative suggestions and analysis improved the story line and character development at each stage.

Friends and family members enriched the story through their comments. Robert, Elizabeth, Samuel, and Aimee Lumkes offered unique intergenerational feedback. Pearl Thomas, Anne Clark, Magdalena Smith, John Forrester, Susan and Max Debeeson, George Bristow, Noreen Wilson, Frank Martin, Ken Wakefield, Lou Mulligan, George Jakeway, and Michael Thoss provided helpful opinions as early readers.

Other support came from friends and churches; their names are found in the Book of Life, and my appreciation extends to each one. Daphne Parsekian graciously became my final editor, and I am grateful for her careful reading and her willing spirit in going through the final steps before sending this manuscript to the printers. She helped me immensely.

My wife, Cathie, has been patient with me through the many ups and downs while working on these manuscripts. No words can express my appreciation for her unending encouragement.

APPENDIX

Philadelphia: After the Letter in the Revelation

Historically, Philadelphia was a Greek cultural center. About AD 160 it became a Christian center. As followers of the Messiah became increasingly separated from Jewish believers, many looked to Philadelphia for answers about the form of church government and which books would be included in the New Testament canon. A religious movement defined Philadelphia as the "New Jerusalem." Several women led this movement involving ecstatic emotions and a longing for the return of Christ. This church helped in the formation of Christianity.

After the Great Earthquake of AD 17, Philadelphia was rebuilt with secure walls. This protection enabled it to be one of the last cities in Asia Minor to withstand the Selcuk Turks. The city capitulated in 1390. The city was subsequently defeated by Tamerlane, or "Timur the Lame," who is said to have built a wall in 1402 with the corpses of his victims. The city finally submitted to the Byzantine Empire.

Richard Chandler, in about 1750, noted the presence of three hundred Greek Orthodox families. Today few, if any, Christians live in Philadelphia. The city still holds the title of "Metropolis of Lydia" under the Greek Orthodox Church.

The city is known as Alasehir, or "Red City," possibly because of the color of the soil, the local plants, or red fruits. Philadelphia is sixty-five miles (105 km) from Izmir (ancient Smyrna). The city government values its links with other Turkic countries, principally those of the Central Asian republics.

The remains of a fifth century basilica have been uncovered at the center of the city, but the building is not, as some locals say, one of the original buildings of the Seven Churches of Asia. No remains of the original church in Philadelphia have been found. The modern city is built on top of ancient ruins. However, remains of the Byzantine walls in the lower city still stand, and a few traces of the Acropolis, the stadium, and the theater are on display.

Made in the USA
Las Vegas, NV
25 April 2024